# Samantha Watkins

# AURÉLIE VENEM
# Samantha Watkins

TRANSLATED BY S.E. BATTIS

CHRONICLES OF AN EXTRAORDINARY ORDINARY LIFE
BOOK 1: NO CHOICE

amazon crossing

Text copyright © 2014 Aurélie Venem

Translation copyright © 2016 S. E. Battis

Previously published as *Samantha Watkins ou Les Chroniques d'un Quotidien Extraordinaire: Tome 1: Pas le Choix* by Amazon Direct Publishing in 2014 in France. Translated from French by S. E. Battis. First published in English by AmazonCrossing in 2016.

Published by AmazonCrossing, Seattle

www.apub.com

Amazon, the Amazon logo, and AmazonCrossing are trademarks of Amazon.com, Inc., or its affiliates.

ISBN-13: 9781503952997

ISBN-10: 1503952991

Cover design by Kerrie Robertson Illustration Inc.

Printed in the United States of America

# PROLOGUE

Many people say that facing Death, like when you get in an accident, changes your life forever. For me, that's exactly what happened.

Except, that night, I found myself not facing Death itself, but rather the dead . . . who were, in fact, still quite alive . . .

# CHAPTER ONE

## *Kingdom: Banality*

But I'm getting ahead of myself. To understand the complete mess that the unexpected encounter with the dead brought to my life, I should start by describing the monotony that distinguished it before.

By the way, my name is Samantha Watkins. My friends called me Sam. Except I didn't have any friends. Pathetic, I know.

I always saw myself as a painfully unremarkable person. Physically, I wasn't much to look at, but I liked to go unnoticed. I exuded ordinariness with my medium height (five and a half feet), my silhouette (neither too thick nor too thin), and my chestnut hair (always up in a ponytail so it wouldn't fall in my face). I took particular satisfaction in the color of my eyes, which were black, so black that my mother and father, who had green and blue eyes, respectively, felt like they were being hypnotized and sucked into my gaze. My parents never could tell me where in our family my black eyes came from. I liked that my eyes gave my appearance a bit of exoticism despite my white skin and otherwise ordinary features.

My parents had been in finance: my mother as a bank teller and my father as the director of the same bank. We had nothing to complain about. We had a nice house with a pool and a small backyard, an old car that my father loved to fix up in the garage, and a dog, Wally, who was supposed to be my consolation prize for never getting a little brother or sister to look after. In short, ours was a family typical of our dear little town of Kentwood, Virginia.

With its ten thousand inhabitants, Kentwood was a peaceful haven for people who could no longer stand the turbulence and fumes of the neighboring metropolis of Kerington, which was inhabited by around 190,000 people. As a quickly growing business center, Kerington, was attracting more and more young wolves eager to make money, by legal means or no. Consequently, despite its great wealth, Kerington had carved out a cutthroat reputation for itself, and quite a few inhabitants had vacated its neighborhoods in favor of the suburbs, which were more suitable for raising children.

Indeed Kentwood met all the conditions for attracting happy families: brand-new schools, gyms, a movie theater. It was a town of happiness for some, of utter ennui for others. Anyway, I had felt at home there, despite certain unpleasant memories.

For me, school had been a success results-wise (and my parents were very proud), but when it came to my social life, it was a total disaster. As in any school, there were the popular ones and everyone else. I didn't even figure into that second category. The only times anyone had ever noticed me were when a teacher remembered my existence and asked me a question, to which I invariably gave the right answer. I came across as a bit of a nerd and therefore suffered the pitiless social destiny of those who cultivate themselves more than others their age. Meaning . . . I looked like a complete dork not worthy of friendship, let alone romantic relationships.

At sixteen, I stupidly had become infatuated with Scott Reinfeld, *the* hot boy at school. My admiring glances in his direction were detected by Ursula (yes, like the undersea sorceress) Caulm, *the* bitch of the school and incidentally Scott's girlfriend.

One day, she asked if she could talk to me in private. I followed her naively, too surprised at having been finally noticed by someone to be suspicious. We went into an empty classroom, and there she let me know what she really thought of me.

"I've seen how you look at Scott, so I'm going to explain something to you. And you should remember every word because I'm *not* going to repeat myself. He *doesn't* want you for the simple reason that you don't exist to him. Do you understand? Do you honestly think he could be interested in a *nobody* like you? You are a *nonentity*, so forget him. I'm saying this to you *nicely* because I don't want you to be upset and make a fool of yourself."

I wasn't an idiot. Her seemingly sympathetic smile was anything but. This was pure and simple cruelty and a thinly veiled threat; she could make my life miserable if I even dared look at her man—her possession—again. Satisfied to see that I'd understood the lesson, she gave me one last disdainful look and left, after taking great care to check that there wasn't anyone in the hallway who could have witnessed her speaking to me.

Shortly after that conversation, I had crossed paths with the two lovebirds and their friends in front of their lockers. As I walked past, I was trailed by stifled laughs (including Scott's), which fully inoculated me against love. From that moment, I swore I wouldn't let my heart beat like a drum for someone who was too different from me . . . and I found myself once again ignored by everyone.

It didn't bring me down as much as you might think. I actually liked solitude, and I still preferred the company of a good book over that of a group of muscled idiots surrounded by their fangirl admirers, all of whom had been rendered stupid by an overdose of adolescent hormones.

In retrospect, however, I have to admit that I had envied them—more than once.

Anyway, eventually we all went our separate ways. I studied literature because I dreamed of becoming a writer, but at the age of twenty-eight, I was back where I started: I'd returned to the very site of my social ostracism to work as a librarian at my old high school.

My parents had died a few years earlier in a car accident, and I'd kept their house. I was used to my routine, and I looked forward to the day when I would find a man to have a family with and continue the banality that I had always known with him by my side.

Obviously, nothing happened the way I expected . . .

\*\*\*

Friday is a hallowed day for all self-respecting workers because it ushers in the weekend, and this is even truer during the first week back at work after the holidays. People generally are still tired even a few days after ringing in the New Year, but my New Year's Eve—which involved a frozen dinner and a DVD marathon—had been anything but extraordinary. So I wasn't the least bit tired when I returned to my post at Griffith High School after the holidays, and that Friday wasn't anything special.

As usual, I made bets on how many students would appear in my library. And as usual, I wasn't surprised by their absence.

At the end of the day, two serious students showed up to do research for their presentation on Martin Luther King Jr. They were followed by two clearly stoned idiots looking in the botany section for books about growing marijuana.

With infinite patience, I explained that the illicit substances that were influencing their behavior at the moment would, in the long run, make them run the risk of ending up as limp, slimy, and intelligent as mollusks.

From the looks on their faces, I knew right away that I had found the right words to get through to them. When they left, completely alarmed, I couldn't help but laugh, but I froze a moment later when Christine Angermann, the German teacher, whom everyone at school—students and adults alike—called Cruella de Vil, walked in. Her voice, allure, and likely her physique would have made the most war-hardened generals of the 1930s Wehrmacht shake in their boots. I was quite sure that I was about to be raked over the coals.

Nostrils flaring, she launched in with what little respect she could muster. "Watkins, where are the new dictionaries that I asked you to order?"

"Hello, Ms. Angermann, Happy New Year. I'm pleased to see you on this beautiful winter day," I said, my smile wide and innocent. "The last time we had this conversation, I told you that all big orders must have the principal's approval. Nothing's changed, you see. Mr. Plummer thinks that we have enough dictionaries now for—"

"Don't be deliberately obtuse, Watkins. I asked for new dictionaries to replace those old relics you keep here and—"

"Ones you personally selected two years ago."

I was proud I had found the courage to confront that shrew, even as I understood—as I watched her turn purple with rage—that I'd committed a fatal error.

"Those are not the ones I ordered! How do you expect my students to pass their exams if they don't have the right tools to study with? But I don't see why I should wear myself out talking to someone as hopelessly unprofessional as you. I'm going to go tell the principal about your incompetence! Has anyone ever seen such a ridiculous librarian? It's not surprising that your life is so devoid of meaning—your life is as empty as your skull!"

I'd expected a storm, but not this hurricane of maliciousness based on a heap of lies, albeit with a touch of truth about my empty life thrown in. Stunned, I hardly heard myself say the words that signaled the end of the conversation.

"Get out of here."

Pitiful. I know.

"Oh, believe me, I'm doing just that. I should have realized a long time ago that it's pointless dealing with the *staff*," she said in a tone as icy as an Antarctic breeze. Then she turned and left with her nose in the air and a smirk on her face, clearly savoring her superb comeback.

I was short of breath, and my cheeks were hot and, undoubtedly, red; my dignity had hit rock bottom, because of her words, yes, but also because of my inability to bite back.

It was getting late. The students were leaving, and night was falling. What to do? Go home and play back that scene in a continuous loop in order to figure how I should have reacted? No. I had to clear my mind. I picked up the phone and called Hank, the old and kindly custodian that I'd known since childhood.

"Hank, it's Samantha."

"Who's that now?"

Humph. I needed to stay calm.

"You know. Samantha Watkins, the librarian. I'm going to do some cleaning, so I'll be leaving late. I have my key. I'll lock up."

"Very well. Have a good evening."

He hung up before I could wish him the same.

For several hours, I sorted books in the back rooms and organized the shelves. Despite the distraction, my mind was busy, contradicting Angermann's allegations that my skull was empty. In fact, the retorts began to come to me hard and fast.

"It's not surprising that your students don't pass their exams with a fat, emasculating cow like you as a teacher. And one who's incapable of ordering the right books or ever taking responsibility for her own mistakes! Get out of here, you ill-tempered hag!"

It didn't matter that I wasn't saying these things to her face; there was still comfort in imagining them.

Around ten o'clock, I decided it was time to go home.

***

Since I didn't live very far from the high school, a car wouldn't have been a useful investment. So I always walked to work. I also thought that in this small way, I was helping preserve the planet. That evening, I took the usual way home. It was cold, and though I wore a wool hat and gloves, I warmed myself up even more by rubbing my hands against each other and blowing on them. I was used to walking, no matter the weather. It had become such a routine that my body guided me while I let my mind wander. I had always arrived safe and sound.

I hadn't considered the effect of Cruella's words, but suddenly I realized that I'd made a wrong turn. I was among the warehouses and the dark and uninviting alleys that ran behind the main avenue.

Kentwood wasn't known for crime, but it also wasn't an idyllic utopia where everyone loved their neighbors. I had no desire to find myself among the crime statistics. There was no one else around, and I started to get really scared.

Nevertheless, nothing—not even my nightmares—could have prepared me for what happened.

# CHAPTER TWO
## *Dreams of Ordinariness*

For some time now, the news had been reporting mysterious disappearances. Allegedly there had been several kidnappings in nearby Kerington. People were saying that two young women from Kentwood who had been missing for ten days, and who lived just a few blocks from the high school, had also been kidnapped. The police advised against going out alone late at night, and some third-rate newspapers reported that there might be a serial killer or black market organ traffickers on the loose, further scaring an already frightened population. I remembered all this now as I realized that I was in a fairly precarious situation myself.

I turned around to go back to the main street and my usual route, but I hadn't even taken ten steps when I heard a horrendous noise in the alley ahead of me. My brain stopped working just when I needed it most. The only thing I was able to do was grip my handbag tighter to my chest.

Just as my feet registered that running would be beneficial, the noise intensified, as if someone were throwing enormous objects against the sheet-metal walls of the warehouses. I didn't want to get any closer, but I had to pass the warehouses to get back to the route I knew. I started running, and then I was in front of the alley . . .

When I opened my eyes after falling hard to the ground, I was stretched out on the concrete, a few feet from the entry to a dead end. I ached all over, and breathing was difficult. Something hot and sticky trickled down my forehead, and I knew I was bleeding.

I told myself that I must have been hit by a truck . . . except that I hadn't heard any engines. I was trying to gather my thoughts when a dark mass landed right next to me. I cried out in surprise. The dark mass turned out to be a man, tall and blond, and I realized that it was he—and not a truck—who had rammed into me. Just as I was processing that thought, a second human cannonball flattened the first one, who had been getting to his feet.

Then I did what any reasonable person would have done.

"Aaaaaaaaaaaaaaaaaaaaaaaaaaaaah!"

I immediately regretted the piercing scream I'd let out. Two pairs of eyes stared at me, then lit up brightly. It looked like the two men wanted to devour me. I swallowed back a second scream, and a lump of pure terror wedged in my throat.

Then I heard another voice.

"Gentlemen, it is truly unfortunate that in the middle of a fight, you are so easily distracted by the prospect of a good meal. And it is rather impolite as well. You both need a lesson in common courtesy."

In the dark I couldn't see this person clearly, but the tone of his voice—oddly velvety and smooth despite the threat—chilled my blood, especially as I realized that the good meal he had referred to was *me*.

"Don't worry. We'll take care of her once we're finished with you," the second man said. He had brown hair, and though he wasn't very tall, he was unbelievably brawny.

Intuiting that these two raging crazy men were going to go for each other's throats again, I tried to flee to avoid being collateral damage. But

I'd overestimated my strength. After taking barely two steps, I started to feel dizzy. I couldn't stay there, particularly because behind me the fight had started up again. And to think I'd never taken the time to go buy myself a cell phone! I could have at least called the police. I turned around to make sure that I'd put some distance between me and my assailants, and what I saw made me open my eyes wide with horror.

The head of the brown-haired brawny guy had just been torn right from his body, with a horrible sound of bones cracking, by his velvet-voiced adversary. The very next second, the headless corpse transformed into a fine dust that blew away in the wind.

Stunned, I tried to run again, but in the space of a breath, I felt someone grabbing me by the arm, the one that by some miracle was still clutching my bag. Suddenly I was lifted up from the ground and projected right toward Velvet Voice. I'd become a human cannonball too, and the impact drove us both to the ground.

While I was sinking into the void of unconsciousness, I heard something that reassured me that my insipid life was definitely over and that I was going to see my parents again.

"Watch your back, Phoenix. In the meantime, don't forget—no witnesses."

***

*I am dead.*

*Is this heaven? Or maybe this is hell . . . there's only darkness around me. That's it, I'm dead. So why does it feel like I'm in a bed? Is this the kind of torture inflicted on sinners in the underworld?*

Honestly, sometimes before waking up, I got some really weird ideas. I was unconscious, but it took me a little time to understand that. Eventually a light shone.

Sheets, a pillow, a soft mattress. Eyes still closed, I let myself smile blissfully. It had all just been a nightmare.

A horrible nightmare, but one that was thankfully over. I really should stop falling asleep while watching science fiction shows. Whatever. As if a superhuman existed who could hurl two big, luminescent-eyed men into the air!

Reassured, I snuggled deeper into my pillow. However, I was surprised how much this simple movement made my body ache. Good grief. I must have really been on edge during the night, especially when Velvet Voice uttered his threats. I hoped to never hear him again . . .

"So, our Sleeping Beauty finally decides to wake up. I was starting to lose my patience."

That voice straight out of my nightmare put me on the brink of cardiac arrest. I'd once learned from a news report that in a state of panic, people will do just about anything because their neurons are shot through with a surge of adrenaline. That was happening to me too.

I tried to scramble out of the bed, but I ended up tangled in the sheets, crashing pathetically to the floor and knocking over all the things that had had the misfortune of being on the nightstand.

In a thrash of ridiculous movements of legs and arms, I managed to extract myself from the prison of fabric that covered me only to find myself face-to-face with Velvet Voice himself, who was seated in an armchair. My heart was beating out of my chest, and I felt blood rushing back to my face. I could do nothing more than stare at the man in front of me. His eyes, a shade of light blue I'd never seen before, were enough to make me tremble with fear that eclipsed everything else.

That is, until I noticed his little smirk, which was soon explained by the fact that I was only wearing underwear and a bra. Immediately, my cheeks flushed again, and I'm sure I turned redder than a tomato. Modesty outranked safety in my line of immediate priorities, and I grabbed the sheet and covered myself with it frantically. Good grief. Having no sexual experience whatsoever, I'd never needed to buy lingerie. This was the first time I found myself seminude in front of a man, and I was wearing a pitifully plain white bra and white cotton panties with *flowers* on them. My cheeks got even hotter—no doubt they were scarlet by now.

Through all of this, Velvet Voice didn't make the slightest movement, contenting himself with watching me from his armchair. To defend myself, I decided to go on the offense.

"Where have you brought me? Who are you? What do you want from me? I warn you, if you try to touch me, I will destroy you—I took karate and I am a black belt." False and very false, but he didn't have to know that. "And give me back my clothes, you dirty pervert!"

I said all that, or rather shouted it, with eyes closed, not pausing to take a breath.

When I finally dared to make eye contact with Velvet Voice, I had trouble swallowing. The smirk was now gone, replaced with a glacial stare that made me step back against the wall, which I hoped I could melt into, thereby becoming invisible. The encounter with Cruella should have served as a lesson: truly, I impressed no one.

He, however, hadn't budged. I looked at him then, avoiding his eyes.

He was a tall man with brown hair, lightly layered to his neck. A few rebellious locks fell softly on his smooth forehead and brushed against his perfectly arched eyebrows. He wore a well-cut suit that accentuated his athletic build. He looked about thirty years old, but his piercing eyes hinted that he was older. I would have been attracted to him if all my internal alarms, which had never sounded before, were not screaming mortal peril. It wasn't just his voice that radiated an intimidating power; it was his very person. A truly formidable presence. What was troubling was the absence of the slightest wound on his body. No trace of injury. But the fight in the alley hadn't been fake. He didn't even flinch during my evaluation of him, which led to me to suppose that he'd done the same of me but in the space of an instant. He broke the silence, thinking it had gone on long enough.

"A 'thank you for saving my life' would have been more appropriate than that ridiculous tirade. Kentwood has charm, perhaps, but no etiquette," he said sharply as he stared at me even more intensely.

He got up and headed to the door.

"There are clothes for you to change into. Yours were . . . unsalvageable. I expect you for dinner. In twenty minutes."

Then, without even a backward glance, he left.

***

For a few minutes afterward, I stared at the door Velvet Voice had walked through. I had to get myself together—at least enough to find a way out of this mess.

I started by inspecting the room he'd put me in, looking for an exit. It was more than a bedroom. It was a suite, soberly but sophisticatedly decorated. The walls were painted a pale blue that gave the room a peaceful aspect; there were, of course, the bed and the armchair, as well as a black leather sofa that matched the chair and an armoire. The shutters were closed and latched. The soft light in the room was provided by a few lamps, minus the one on the nightstand that I'd sent crashing to the floor. No way of escaping. I was definitely a prisoner.

I checked my body. I ached all over, with bruises on my arms, especially the arm the big blond had grabbed, and there were grazes on my legs and knees. My ribs hurt, and I remembered that I'd been struck twice by projectiles. Well, the second time, I *was* the projectile. Then I remembered the blood on my face, and I touched my head, but there was no trace of the wound. Impossible.

In order to avoid the headache that loomed at the memory of recent events and at the whirlwind of questions that they inspired, I chased the thought away and resumed my inspection of the room.

There was a dressing table against the wall, with clothes laid out on it. I headed toward it, and my jaw dropped as I lifted up a magnificent evening gown that Velvet Voice had provided for me. Again, I wondered what his intentions were. If he'd wanted to rape me, he could have done it while I was unconscious, though certain freaks like to see the fear in their victims' eyes . . . Why had I watched two episodes of *Criminal Minds* the night before? The show scared me every time and gave me nightmares. Was that about to become my reality? I shivered . . . then I remembered he'd mentioned dinner.

Perhaps he wanted to kill me after giving me something to eat, all while dressed as a movie star. What time was it anyway? When I left work, it was ten o'clock, definitely not dinnertime . . . How long had I been unconscious?

These were all questions to which I had no answers. The one thing I knew for sure was that I had to leave that room.

There was another door, but it led to a bathroom—spacious and gorgeous, with marble nearly everywhere. Perfect. I'd come across a psychopath with expensive tastes and a full wallet. But I was rather fortunate in my misfortune, seeing as how I really needed a shower. Velvet Voice had provided toiletries, and it was a great relief to be able to soap up and take advantage of the hot water after all I'd just been through. Hair washed and left down to dry, I returned to the table to get dressed. I noticed there was a bottle of Chanel No. 5 as well. Well, better take advantage of that.

I pulled on the black velvet dress with fine lace and a slightly low neckline. It was down to my ankles and fit me like a glove. When I caught my reflection in the mirror, my unfamiliar elegance made me uneasy, and I was even more uncomfortable when I saw the stilettos that went with the dress. I've never had much success walking in high heels. I started to get irritated. What exactly did Velvet Voice want? To ridicule me before doing me in?

My anger gave me a newfound confidence, and I found the courage to exit the room.

\*\*\*

I didn't really know where to go, because a series of corridors led to numerous finely sculpted wooden doors, which were locked. I must have been in a manor. I finally reached a staircase that led downstairs, and once I'd gone down, I stared, dumbstruck, at the stately entry hall, which was more than twice the size of my living room at home.

I noticed light coming from one of the rooms. I took a deep breath and pushed back my hair as I entered.

It was the dining room, and what a dining room indeed. Enormous, with crystal chandeliers, wall hangings depicting Renaissance battles, large oil paintings that looked valuable. In the middle of the room, a large, glossy wooden table took center stage, surrounded by twelve chairs, all with high backs that were carved into a curve.

My attention was quickly diverted to a case displaying a collection of weapons. There was a sixteenth-century French sword, a seventeenth-century musket, and even a Prussian bayonet from the end of the nineteenth century. I gasped in admiration. I loved old weapons, but I didn't have the means to collect any.

"I see you have an interest in antiques."

I hadn't heard my kidnapper approach, and I jumped at the sound of his voice, staring at him without daring to speak.

"I hope that gown is to your liking. I live alone, and I am not in the habit of keeping women's clothing here. One of my acquaintances forgot to take that with her."

What? Who would leave such an expensive thing behind? He likely killed her, buried her somewhere, and kept her belongings as a trophy.

I must have gone pale. Given the mocking smile that took shape on his face, it seemed clear he'd caught on to my train of thought.

"My acquaintance is a woman who attaches no importance to material things, given the size of her bank account. When she left, she forgot to gather her things from the evening before, and she has not reclaimed them since. The latest news on her is that she is as well as ever."

Reassured by the health of dress's owner, I remained no less furious at being the prisoner of a pervert.

"So you made me put on the dress that your ex-lover was wearing during your last night of debauchery?" I hissed.

Gross. I hoped he had at least washed it.

"Perhaps you would have preferred to keep me company in your undergarments? That is rather fashion-forward of you."

Pig. He'd said that with such irony that I wanted to slap him. I burned with shame and anger, but mostly shame.

"I didn't give you permission to undress me! Who do you think you are? You kidnap me, you hold me prisoner, you terrify me, and then you find it amusing to ridicule me before killing me? And I should accept all that? What is your problem?"

When he answered me, he lowered his voice to a threatening whisper.

"Has no one ever told you that it is better to avoid angering the person who is going to kill you? That is, if you do not want him or her to torture you first in order to teach you some decorum?"

Frightened, I responded with a pitifully high squeaky voice. "And to top it all off, you lecture me as if I were at fault when all that I did was be at the wrong place at the wrong time! I have the right to be afraid and to scream when the person in front of me is a pervert capable of ripping someone's head off without any effort at all and who forces me to wear castoffs from a lewd soiree before murdering me!"

Success. I'd made him angry.

He stepped closer, grabbed my arm in his steel grip, and marched me toward one of the chairs in the parlor that adjoined the dining room—all before I'd even had the time to say a single word. He pushed me down unceremoniously, and I found myself seated, shocked and terrified by his eyes staring daggers at me from above.

"If I had wanted to kill you, you would have died yesterday in that alley, and no one would have ever found your body. And yet, you are still here, and you are alive. That is, unless you decide to make me lose my temper by calling me a pervert. So I suggest staying silent unless you are answering my questions. Have I made myself clear?"

I nodded my head to indicate my acquiescence. He couldn't have been clearer. Having a good sense for witty comebacks is all well and good, but in some circumstances, it's better to shut up if you want to live.

"Let us start from the beginning. Who are you?"

"My ID is in my bag—you didn't look?" Gulp. "OK, OK, sorry. My name is Samantha . . . Watkins . . . I'm a librarian at Griffith High School."

"What were you doing near that alley?"

"I had a long day, I let my mind wander instead of paying attention to my feet, and I found myself there. I wanted to turn around and get back to the main road, but I ran into you and those two other guys."

"What do you remember exactly?"

"I passed in front of the alley, and when I came to, I'd been hurt because a man landed on me, who knows how. The second man arrived just after and . . . good God, it wasn't a dream, their eyes glowed and they wanted to eat me! You said so yourself. Then you killed the muscled one, and the other one confused me for a cannonball. I think I'm going crazy. All that was just a nightmare, and I *am* going to wake up."

Reliving that horrible episode brought tears to my eyes.

"It's the truth."

He said that with something akin to sympathy, but I wasn't about to let my guard down.

"Even if you say otherwise, I know you're going to kill me."

"You are either more stubborn than a mule or else you understand absolutely nothing," he said.

Nope. He was not going to start that again.

"'Watch your back, Phoenix, and don't forget—no witnesses.' Don't take me for an idiot. That's the truth. I know what I heard. You're under orders to kill anyone who gets in the way, most likely to conceal your identity. You think I'm stupid? A human is incapable of tearing someone's head off with bare hands. Who are you, dammit?"

There, again, I'd raised my voice, but the panic that was taking over wouldn't let me stop. Velvet Voice stood up to his full height and looked at me with absolute scorn. The silence seemed to last an eternity, but I was waiting for an explanation.

When he answered me, I knew that my ordinary life was over and everything had changed.

Forever.

# CHAPTER THREE

## *Second Life*

"I am a vampire."

I should have laughed, but I didn't. In my head, a voice, a voice of terror, was shouting at me that vampires didn't exist; they were only figures from legend that emerged from the deepest of our societies' fears. Another voice, this one belonging to reason, was whispering to me that recent events obliged me to believe his declaration.

Appalled, I looked at Velvet Voice, and in the space of a single moment, I believed I detected a flash of pain on his face before he recovered his indifference.

"I believe you," I said calmly. "What now?"

He was no longer looking at me with disdain. He just seemed weary.

"Let us begin by introducing ourselves. My name is Phoenix. I have been a vampire since the age of thirty."

Phoenix. Good vampire name. A dead man who returns to life.

"How long ago was that?"

Aurélie Venem

"Five hundred years, give or take. I became a vampire around 1510. At that time, no one kept good birth records."

I must have looked ridiculous, with my mouth hanging wide open and my eyes bulging. But the man in front of me had experienced centuries of human life. Suddenly the Renaissance touches in the decor made sense. The librarian in me, passionate about history, wasn't able to set things straight in her head; tons of questions jostled about for attention. The me who was also a prisoner was trying to silence those questions so as not to offend this monstrous drinker of blood.

"Hm. That's a very long life."

He sat down on the chair facing me.

"Yes. And it is the secrecy of it that allows my race to survive," he said, studying my reaction.

"People have always been afraid of vampires. You would've been exterminated if people had known that you weren't just characters created by Bram Stoker. So you prevent humans who discover your true nature from divulging it to others. I suppose you kill them," I said. "Which leads me to ask, why am I here discussing this with you?"

He had listened to me very attentively, his inquisitive eyes aimed right at me.

"After five hundred years, I have seen enough carnage. Killing innocents disgusts me."

Then I had a chance.

"Are you really obligated to kill them? I mean . . . don't vampires have powers of suggestion to erase compromising memories?"

"That is only in films. In becoming a vampire, we acquire a strength that increases with time, but no power of suggestion."

"But then . . . why are you sparing me?"

"Contrary to what you may think, murder is not the only option. Vampires appreciate forms of manipulation, like blackmail, quite a bit. When we are discovered, we can allow some human witnesses to live, as well as their families, in exchange for some services and great discretion. You could be useful to me."

"Me? I don't see how."

"I am a practical man, and I abhor paperwork, but my employers, to my sorrow, like detailed reports. I need an assistant."

If I hadn't already been seated, I believe I would have needed a chair.

\*\*\*

"You're joking."

He didn't answer me, and he really had no need to. It was not a joke.

"No way," I said. "I have a life, and I want to get back to it."

"Your former life just ended. Turning back now is impossible, unless you wish to die."

His monotone, detached voice unhinged me completely. Rising from the chair, I exploded. "So that's it! You spare me just so I can become your slave! You made me come here, you dressed me up as a starlet just so I would be just dazed enough to give up my freedom. Well, you're mistaken. I don't want this life, or rather this death. Because that's what you are, right, a walking corpse? Kill me! Because I won't be a monster's plaything!"

I couldn't stop the tears from streaming down my cheeks while I was saying all that. My life may not have been exciting, but all that I wanted at that moment was to get back to it and forget that vampires existed at all.

He stood up too. The silence that surrounded us oppressed me more than if he had put his hands around my throat to strangle me. I couldn't look at him, but I felt him watching me.

"I beg you, let me go home," I ended up saying, pathetically.

I expected to be attacked for my outburst; instead, he answered me calmly.

"I told you, you cannot go back. You no longer have a home. You have to stay with me if you want to live."

His tone gave me no choice but to look up at him. Again, I thought I saw pain in his eyes.

"I don't understand."

"Why do you think I interrogated you about your identity rather than searching through your bag?"

I frowned and thought. The last time that I had my bag . . . good grief, it was when the big blond vampire had thrown me at Velvet Voice.

I looked at him again in horror.

"I see that you understand now," he said to me. "You were unconscious all night and all day. He had time to go to your house with some of his men to learn more about you. They'll want to know what you were doing in that alley, and if you have anything to do with me and my business there. If you go back to your house and they are still there, they will torture you for more information, and before they finally finish you off, they'll make you regret you were ever born."

My legs were trembling so badly that soon they wouldn't be able to support my weight. I could barely breathe.

"But . . . I was only there by accident."

"No matter. If they cannot find out anything, they will at least have you to feast on if you go home." He sighed. "You can refuse to work for a monster, but you really have no choice."

I suddenly felt very sick. With great effort, I said, "Bath . . . room."

"On your left as you leave the room, third door."

I ran out of the room and made it to the bathroom just in time. I vomited everything that I could into the toilet bowl, all while still crying at the thought of what was waiting for me if I returned home, or if I accepted Velvet Voice's offer. When I was finished, I somehow managed to freshen myself up.

But that was the most I could do. My mind no longer had the capacity to absorb all this, so it decided to take a break, and I fainted.

***

The bathroom floor was not as hard and cold as I was expecting when I woke up. In fact, it was rather comfortable down there. But when I opened my eyes, I saw that I was in the parlor again, stretched out on a long sofa slipcovered in a soft beige cloth.

"Where are you?" I croaked.

"I am here."

He walked across the room, from the fireplace to the armchair that was facing me, and sat down. There was a glass of water on the small table between us. I sat up with difficulty and took a swig. I laughed nervously as I set the glass back down.

"Please enlighten me as to what you find so funny," he said.

"I was just telling myself that I am so pitiful and useless that you must already regret not putting me out of my misery. Sorry, but I think that you've picked the wrong person."

"I do not think so."

His mysterious tone made me wonder what he was implying. But I didn't need the headache that thought would give me. On that note . . .

"By the way, what did you do to me? I was hit on the head, back in the alley. I remember the blood on my face. When I woke up, I checked for damage, but there was nothing there."

"I healed you with my blood."

"Your blood?"

"Vampire blood has curative properties. It is very powerful when swallowed, but we can also apply it to small wounds to make them disappear."

I gagged. "You made me drink your blood?"

"That was not necessary. Your head wound was only superficial, even though it was bleeding profusely."

I sighed with relief, but I couldn't stop myself from asking, "Would I have become a vampire if you had?"

His face showed irritation, and there was a far-off look in his eyes, as if he were recalling bad memories.

"No. I must first empty you of your blood. And it is a, *ahem*, very particular step."

Judging it safer not push him, I turned the conversation in another direction.

"Are you sure I can't go home? If those men really searched my house, then they realized I have nothing to do with your business, whatever that is, so maybe they left."

"That is not guaranteed. Moreover, try not to see your family and friends anymore either. These men might get the idea to keep on an eye on them too."

Turning my face away, I whispered, "I don't have family or friends."

I thought that he was going to change the subject so I wouldn't be embarrassed, but he seemed content to keep staring at me.

His steel-blue eyes made me uneasy, and I started to blush again.

"Stop doing that," I cried out.

"Doing what?"

"Looking at me with that X-ray stare of yours, like I'm a freak-show monster."

"I thought I was the monster here," he said, arching an eyebrow.

I glanced at him, hardly amiably, disliking his banter even though I was convinced he wasn't really joking.

"Listen, as you must have noticed, I'm not really good at talking to people. I'm usually alone. All the time, in fact."

"That is of no importance to me. Incidentally, I have lived alone for an eternity, and I do not feel bad about it, so there is no shame in it. I am not sparing you for your conversation but to have you as an employee. Are you competent?"

"I think I really don't have a choice," I sighed. "At least I'll be paid."

***

He rolled his eyes before rising, offering me his hand.

"What?"

I had accepted the deal, but I was still afraid of him. I didn't dare touch him.

"I believe I mentioned dinner. A self-respecting host keeps his promises."

His hand still outstretched, he signaled to me to look at the dining room. Indeed, the table had been set for one. I ended up letting him assist me in getting up (seeing as I still had jelly legs, this was not a bad idea) and guiding me toward my seat.

There were a number of dishes that I hadn't seen arrive in the room. I should also say that, given the size of the table, I hadn't paid any attention to details, so when I saw the pinkish slices of roast beef, the vegetables, the cheese, and the strawberry tart, my stomach produced a growl hardly suited to the refinement that surrounded me. I blushed yet again, likely turning a shade of pink similar to the meat.

"Sorry," I apologized miserably.

"I have never met a human who blushes as much as you. We shall have to work on your confidence, among other things."

"What do you mean?"

With a wave of his hand, he brushed aside my question.

"Later. This evening, you will rest, and then you will be more solid on your feet again. We shall go over the practical questions tomorrow. Now, eat."

"But what about you? You don't eat anything?"

I wanted to be polite, but honestly, I had no desire whatsoever to see him sucking the blood out of someone right in front of me.

"Your concern is touching, but I have already eaten. Once again, eat."

I grabbed a slice of roast beef and some vegetables, but at the mention of his dinner, a knot of fear had caught in my stomach.

"Um, have you, um, killed someone?" I asked, trying to be as calm as possible while pointing a piece of roast beef skewered on my fork at him.

For the second time, he rolled his eyes.

"Certainly not. I have reserves in a cold room, and I have a contact at the blood bank."

"OK, I don't understand any of that."

"The vampire community has evolved quite a bit. We are no longer psychopathic monsters obsessed with murder via exsanguination, as humanity's collective imagination depicts us. Eat."

"You say you're no longer a monster. That means that you were once."

"Yes."

I suppressed the desire to ask him if he'd also had psychopathic tendencies; the thought was already making me tremble.

Velvet Voice spoke again. "But we had to revise our method of consuming when the secret of our existence was threatened by our greatest enemy."

What enemy could be so powerful that it could frighten a group of immortals with special powers?

"What enemy?" I managed to ask while swallowing the bite of roast beef that I had been brandishing on my fork.

"Forensic science."

Of course. The police benefited now from advanced tools to conduct their investigations. Moreover, the pooling of resources and information via computer technology allowed them to make progress more quickly and to connect cases that had happened in different places and at different times. Leave several bloodless cadavers behind around the country, and you'll find yourself with a pack of detectives on red alert, ready for a fight. I understood why this secret was indeed in danger.

I then imagined Horatio Caine of *CSI: Miami*, his famous sunglasses and his drawling voice. He would've quickly destroyed the myth of the stolid detective when he figured out what kind of murderer he was dealing with. I was sure that he would have taken off yelling, his mop of red hair in the wind. I laughed at the picture of the scene.

"You are truly strange," said Velvet Voice. "You are ready to jump down my throat when I take care of you, and you laugh when I mention murders perpetrated by my species."

"Huh?"

"That's precisely what I was saying."

"Forgive me. So you're saying that you changed your diet?"

"You could say that. We still feed on blood, but we no longer get it directly from the source. We get our supplies from blood banks and other places where such things can be procured."

"That's a bit hard to imagine . . . vampires with shopping carts in aisles filled with plastic pouches . . ."

"Technically, it happens differently. But certain vampires in our community thought as you do, and they refuse to be compared to humans shopping at a supermarket."

"The transition must have been difficult for them."

"Indeed. There are vampires who are still in an uncivilized state. They see themselves as hunters, and nothing pleases them more than a victim that they hunt down themselves. But the punishment is horrible for those who put our Secret in danger by killing to feed."

"So there's vampire legislation that regulates their activities? But who enforces it?"

"Do you always ask so many questions?"

"I just discovered a supernatural, unknown world. It's normal that I would want to know more."

"You know enough for this evening. And I'm tired of repeatedly asking you to eat . . ."

His tone dissuaded me from making more comments. Besides, I was starving. I abandoned my reserve and began eating in earnest.

Everything was delicious. The meat melted in my mouth, the vegetables were perfectly seasoned, the bread was crusty, the cheese soft, and the tart . . . to die for. I was so absorbed by my meal that I didn't realize until my second slice of strawberry tart that Velvet Voice was staring at me.

I felt embarrassed, and I found it useful to tell him so. "Whydyou hafta lookit me like tha?"

Raising an eyebrow, Velvet Voice looked at me with scorn. "Pardon?"

I swallowed, aware that I was behaving like a cavewoman.

"You're analyzing me again. It's very irritating."

"I have been studying the rules of proper table etiquette of the twenty-first-century woman. Very instructive . . ."

I blushed. Again.

"You're not being fair! It's been a day since I last ate. You should know that I've received a very good education and I know how to behave when the circumstances require it and . . ."

Once again, he rolled his eyes at me.

"I feel like we have a lot of work to do. Finish your dinner, and then go rest. I will see you tomorrow at sunset. Do not leave the outer wall of the property during the day. It is too early for that. I have a library upstairs, filled with books I've collected over the years. You are free to go there. You will be in your element. We begin your training tomorrow evening," he said as he got up from his chair.

"But . . . you're leaving me . . . you haven't even answered all my questions. And . . . I have nothing. All of my things are at my house."

"All that can wait until tomorrow."

Without another word, he left, leaving me alone in front of the remains of my feast.

What an idiot. I hadn't even been able to make him tell me where we were. He had led me where he wanted all through the conversation. It would be an understatement to say I wasn't gifted at this sort of thing. What to do now? Escaping the manor and going home wasn't an option unless I wanted to find a tall blond vampire sitting on my sofa, waiting to devour me. So I exhaled and started to clear the table.

I was astonished by the kitchen when I finally found it: it was spacious, sparkling, and cutting-edge. It was two times as big as my bedroom. Velvet Voice truly spared no expense.

I inspected the fixtures, starting with the refrigerator. I admit that I was curious about its contents, so I opened it and was bewildered by the abundance of human food: fruit, vegetables, fresh products, soda . . . It wasn't logical. I should have found blood in there. Maybe vampires hid their personal reserves away from prying eyes, like bottles of great wine.

Then I opened the cabinets and found boxes of cookies and crackers. If he wanted to have a party with humans, then he was well supplied, but surely a bunch of humans would jeopardize the preservation of the vampires' great Secret.

At least I wouldn't go hungry. Having finished my exploration, I made several trips between the kitchen and the dining room to finish clearing my dishes and the leftovers from the gargantuan meal, all while taking note of the elegant decoration of the corridors. The white tiles were tempered by the warm tones of the light-brown paint of the walls, which were ornamented with mirrors; under each mirror were small, Japanese-style wooden tables, both Zen and practical for tidying up.

On my last trip, the strawberry tart fought me. I couldn't get it in the fridge. While I tried to make space for it, I must have triggered some mechanism, and previously hidden shelves slid on a track toward me.

"Ew," I said aloud, cringing when I saw the packets of blood stored on the shelves.

This was Velvet Voice's secret pantry. Quite an ingenious system, in truth. If the police had to search this place one day, they certainly wouldn't think of hidden shelves in the fridge as a place to look for compromising evidence.

Conquering my revulsion, I picked up one of the pouches. A+. My blood type. I picked up another one. Also A+. All the pouches were the same. Apparently vampires had preferences, a bit like humans with orange or grapefruit juice.

I really had some luck. I'd been hired by a bloodsucker, a consumer of A+ blood, and as it happens, I was a big old walking bag of A+ blood! Even if I wasn't particularly a believer, I muttered a little prayer that Velvet Voice wouldn't ever be really hungry if I was close by.

I put everything back in place so that he wouldn't notice that I had discovered his hidden stash. I preferred not to imagine his reaction, or his glacial stare. I shivered at the thought, and I wondered if he'd had that sword-like stare as a human or if his eyes had changed after his transformation.

Under normal circumstances, I hate doing the dishes, but I went to the sink and washed my silverware by way of distraction. In any case, I didn't like disorder, and something told me that Velvet Voice didn't either. At least we had that in common.

By the time I put everything away, I was starting to feel exhausted again. Since escaping wasn't an option and I had no idea what training my host had planned for me, a good night's sleep seemed the best choice.

I headed back to my new bedroom. Before undressing, I collected and threw away the pieces of the broken lamp and remade the bed. Even if I'd slept close to twenty-four hours, I was worn out. I needed sleep, especially so I could digest everything I had heard that evening. I threw myself on the immense bed, rolled myself up in the covers, and closed my eyes, avoiding thinking about what would await me the next day and the day after that . . .

***

When I woke up, the room was pitch-black, and I had trouble getting my bearings. I got up anyway and moved around blindly, reaching for a lamp. When I managed to find one and turn it on, I was surprised to find a bunch of clothes neatly folded where I had left the evening gown the night before.

On top, there was a note: "The rest is in the armoire." No signature. Not that I really needed one.

I glanced quickly at the clothes: a white shirt, a pair of black pants, and some gym clothes. I opened the armoire and was dumbstruck.

The armoire had been completely empty the night before, but now it was filled with clothes, all of good quality. Velvet Voice had given me an entire wardrobe.

Even if he were a dangerous and terrifying vampire, and even if he had my life in his hands, I was touched by his gesture . . . at least until I opened the underwear drawer . . .

*Good grief.* What on earth was he thinking? I bristled, holding up a lacy pair of underwear that would reveal much more than it hid. At least he hadn't bought any thongs. I hated them.

He must have really been looking at me from every angle in order to know my sizes. Oh boy. I preferred to not imagine how he did it.

The bras were just as lacy as the underwear, though there were also some sports bras that went with the gym outfits. Everything looked quite expensive.

In the shower, I wondered how he could have procured that entire wardrobe in so little time. Maybe he stole everything from a store using his superpowers, or maybe there was a special vampire store that was only open at night. I couldn't believe I slept right through him coming into the room to drop off the clothes. I hoped I hadn't been snoring.

After my shower, I put on the white shirt and the black pants. I opted for the ballerina flats, the only shoes without heels. Lastly, I gathered my hair into my usual ponytail. What I saw in the mirror wasn't bad. I really looked like an assistant . . . at a law firm. That was a big change from the high school librarian in jeans and sneakers.

After one last look at my reflection, I left my room and headed to the kitchen—curious to find out what time it was and to eat some breakfast.

The room was bathed in soft winter sunlight, and the windows looked out onto a magnificent garden that I hadn't been able to see the night before. A large, perfectly manicured lawn extended out to the high walls around the property; at the foot of the walls, rosebushes and little thickets livened up the garden, even though it was winter. A solitary weeping willow gave the whole scene a nostalgic touch. It protected the intimacy of a little wooden bench that was likely a lovely place to read when the weather was warmer.

My stomach growled rather ungraciously, reminding me that I needed to eat. The clock on the oven read 1:15 p.m. Although the breakfast hour was long past, I took advantage of the kitchen equipped entirely for human use to make myself coffee and something to eat.

When I was done, I decided I wasn't risking anything by taking a few steps into the garden for some fresh air. I'd spotted a large closet by the entryway, and I hoped I'd find a coat there since Velvet Voice hadn't put one in the armoire. Sure enough I opened the door to find a very chic long black coat with a fake-fur collar, a matching hat, a white scarf, and leather gloves. My host had thought of everything.

I walked out onto the front steps, taking in my surroundings. On the left were huge metal gates that opened and closed over a gravel path; the height of the gates, combined with that of the outer walls, undoubtedly deterred the curious. The garage was actually a kind of brick double-entry storehouse with modern electric rolling doors, which hid the cars from view. What exactly would a five-hundred-year-old vampire drive? Given how modern the kitchen was, I imagined he might have abandoned the idea of a horse and cart; in any case, I hadn't seen any stables. Maybe he drove an Aston Martin like James Bond or a Dodge Charger like the brothers in *The Dukes of Hazzard* or maybe even one of those small European cars like the Smart car or the Renault Twingo? No, I didn't know the proprietor of this place very well, but I was sure he wasn't the type to drive around in an old jalopy.

I went down the steps and began my stroll in the garden. The walk itself was restorative and invigorating, but I had to wonder who looked after it all. Velvet Voice didn't have the look of a landscaper . . . perhaps he had another enslaved helper as a gardener?

Sitting on the bench under the willow tree, I realized I hadn't been mistaken about "my" new residence: it was indeed a manor. Not enormous, but still impressive, with a brick facade typical of the eighteenth century and a blue slate roof. The number of windows (their shutters carefully closed on the upper level) made me wonder how long my exploration would take.

Chilled to the bone, I took a deep breath and looked once more at the gardens before I went back inside, where it was considerably warmer. I wandered around for the purpose of discovering my new residence and workplace. On the ground floor, there was the kitchen, the dining room, and the parlor, as well as a series of smaller rooms, all just as refined in their decor. I didn't stop at the bathroom (I knew it well already), but I did step into a small study, which was furnished with a bookcase, a desk with a state-of-the-art computer atop it, a chair, and a black leather sofa. I inspected the books and found several law books, foreign language dictionaries, and some philosophical works. This selection reminded me of the big library my host had mentioned.

A number of doors on the upstairs level were locked, but when I finally found the library, I was astonished. The room was bigger than my bedroom suite, and it was filled with carved bookshelves packed with books that were organized by subject: philosophy, history, geography, literature. The leather sofas, identical to the one in the study, created an inviting, relaxing setting for reading. Velvet Voice was right when he said I would be in my element in this room.

An illuminated glass case on the far side of the room caught my eye. The object on display took my breath away: it was an incunabulum, a book printed sometime between 1450 and 1501.

I couldn't get over it. My new employer, despite his deadly tendencies, at least cared about cultivating himself. He said he'd collected books over the years, but that was quite a modest description. This made my opinion of him rise a little.

After I completed a full tour of the room, I picked out a few books and got so immersed in the story of a knight who had lived during the Hundred Years' War that I jumped when I heard a voice.

"I knew I would find you here."

Velvet Voice stood in the doorway. Every part of him exuded power and danger, though he didn't have a menacing attitude (fortunately, or else I would've wanted to make like an ostrich and dig a hole to hide my head in while waiting to get eaten). I was impressed by his presence and charisma.

"I've never seen a place like this . . . it's marvelous," I said, smiling sincerely.

His perpetual sardonic smile, which exasperated me so much, began to materialize again on his face.

"Curious how all it took was a few books to put you in a better disposition toward me."

"You call this a few books? It's more than I could ever accumulate in my lifetime!"

"You forget that I have had several lifetimes to put this collection together."

"Well, at least you're educated. Someone who likes to enrich the mind couldn't be completely evil."

"Your logic is quite strange. Do not forget that I am a vampire, and consequently, evil is part of me."

"Believe me, if there is one thing I won't forget, it's definitely that."

"So much the better. Trusting a vampire is the worst error you can make. Since our nature has changed, our conscience does not torment us if we betray someone. That will be the first, and most important, lesson of your training."

"Don't ever trust a vampire," I repeated.

He nodded earnestly. If I'd been an elementary school student, I think I would have gotten a gold star.

"Hm, and all the more so when the vampire is your boss?" I added.

He turned away, but I was able to see his smirk. Obviously, I had a comedic soul . . .

*Ridiculous* would be a more appropriate adjective. I knew I wouldn't get an answer from him.

"Come, we will discuss all that in my office," he said as he exited the library.

I followed him without saying a word, wondering what the nature of my job as his assistant would be. If it was only filling out paperwork for his mysterious employers, I considered myself rather fortunate in my misfortune. But a feeling of foreboding nagged at me, leaving me to think that my life may have been spared, but I certainly wouldn't gain anything from it.

# CHAPTER FOUR

## *Training*

"Please, have a seat."

He sat down behind his desk and indicated the chair facing him. My fate was in Velvet Voice's hands, and his civilized tone gave me the impression of being interviewed by the director of human resources. I couldn't wait anymore to know what fate had in store for me.

"Tell me what you expect from me."

He leaned forward and folded his hands together. He looked like a politician about to announce to the nation his important plan for economic austerity. I felt like I was about to be made indignant by his words (as *indignant* as the Spanish anti-austerity Indignados).

"As I said, I am a practical man, and I hate the administrative side of my work. My employers, I do not know why, like very detailed reports, and writing them up is true torture for me."

"Why not ask another vampire to help you?"

"Have you already forgotten your first lesson? The missions that I am charged to carry out are secret and must remain so. Particularly for those of my kind."

I snickered. "Let's not forget that it's much simpler to put pressure on a human woman who doesn't have immortality. What do you do exactly? Are you a secret agent for Her Vampire Majesty?"

"The less you know about our hierarchical organization, the better off you will be. But that is roughly it."

Imagining Daniel Craig as a sexy vampire James Bond was completely effortless, but the image was superimposed by that of Queen Elizabeth II, with her mop of gray hair in the wind, baring her fangs. I shivered. God save the Queen indeed.

He continued, "Do you know how to use a computer?"

"Of course."

I could at least be proud of my abilities in that regard. I was good with computers, especially since, with no friends, I had plenty of time to devote to them.

"You don't?"

"I never had the time to learn," he said.

Surprised, I pointed at the computer on his desk.

"Then what's that for? Decoration?"

"I bought it not long ago. I looked among the vampires I know for someone who could help me get familiar with this machine. Computers aren't widely used by us. Some vampires are so bound to tradition that they do not even want to hear about it and swear by paper alone."

As he spoke, he rolled his eyes to make sure I knew what he really thought of that. Before stopping to measure what I was about to say, I blurted out, "I could teach you."

He stared at me so intensely that I had to lower my eyes.

"I mean, if you wanted," I finished.

That was just like me. Samantha the Good Samaritan. I should've held my tongue. If he had hired me, it was also so he wouldn't have to spend his time on the computer. As if at twenty-eight I could teach a five-hundred-year-old historical figure a thing or two. Moreover, he had kidnapped me, so what possessed me to offer to help him? It was stupid of me, really.

However, his response was the opposite of what I feared.

"Yes, I would like that."

"Really?"

"I should really make an effort, at least know the basics, should you die while carrying out your duties."

At that I was speechless. I tried to spot the joke . . . but I'd forgotten. Velvet Voice, what a prankster! Not really the type to make little jokes. Good grief.

"Wh-what? I thought I only had to take care of the paperwork. Like a secretary."

"You are my assistant, not my secretary. Consequently, you will go on missions with me."

"But . . . but . . ."

"Rest assured, I shall not put you in any danger. All that I ask of you is to take notes."

"So I run no risk?"

"Well, I did not say that. My duties give me a certain status in vampire society, but they also mean I make enemies. Someone could attack you just to get to me."

My mouth became as dry as the Sahara. I felt my heart beating more than necessary, too much more. He must have heard the hubbub in my rib cage because he continued, "But I do not think that will happen. You will learn that our kind, we have very high opinions of ourselves, and we do not demean ourselves with practices contrary to our dignity. If we wanted to make you disappear, we would pay human assassins to do the dirty work. That reduces the danger."

"That's supposed to be reassuring? I certainly feel better now!" I said with irony.

"Do not be mistaken. Your work, in every case, will be dangerous. Nevertheless, I shall give you the means to defend yourself. I shall teach you to fight."

"Fight? Have you taken a good look at me? I'm as squishy as a marshmallow and as quick as a snail! I have no chance whatsoever against a vampire."

"There is always a chance, if you know how to take advantage of it. Against a human, you will be fully capable of getting by, and you will do me honor as your instructor."

I frowned at his last remark.

"So, to be clear, I should avoid dying stupidly if it means preserving *your* honor and *your* reputation."

I tried to overcome the rage that had been tormenting me since he'd announced the nature of my work and the risks he was making me take. I was certain that this was all going to backfire and I would pay the price. That awful foreboding feeling that was plaguing me materialized, and I almost started to regret being alive. Why on earth did I have to pass by that alley? The rage got bigger than me, and I exploded.

"You sure have some nerve! You turn me into a night owl, like you, to risk my life, not like you, and what's more, if I die, I have to do it with the panache of Cyrano de Bergerac so that you can show yourself among your bloodsucker friends while boasting about having toyed around with a human woman, teaching her some wrestling holds! You know what, you are a sick man!"

I got up, flush with anger, and tried to leave the room. Velvet Voice didn't give me enough time.

I saw nothing coming. In a fraction of a second, he was in my way, blocking my exit. Crouching in an attack position, his eyes had become luminescent, but not yellow like the eyes of the other two, the ones who wanted to annihilate me. His eyes were somewhere between blue and white. The icy shiver that went down my spine became a pure trembling of terror when from his throat rose up a kind of animal growl.

"Bu . . . but wha . . . what ar-are you d-doing?" I yelped, trying to take a step backward.

Fatal error! He came a step closer, and his eyes became even more luminous, as if the thought of my escape galvanized him. I was reminded of those animal documentaries that say that the instinct of predators is to pursue prey when it runs. I tried to stand still, but when another growl sounded and his lips curled, revealing his all-too-bright and sharp fangs, my legs decided to run, no matter the direction.

I let out a cry when I felt something strike me and throw me to the ground. When Velvet Voice turned me around and straddled me, I couldn't do anything except scream and struggle. I tried to claw at him, but he was pressing my arms to the floor with such force that I thought he had crushed them.

"Let me go! Let me go, you . . ."

I had begun to utter the first syllable of the worst profanity that I could think of when I suddenly stopped myself, at the feeling of contact between two canines and the hollow of my neck.

"Aaaahhh!" I screamed, expecting to feel, in the space of a breath, those fangs sinking into my carotid artery.

I stopped shouting when his mouth let go of its hold and moved toward my ear. If I had ever dreamed of a man lying on top of me and murmuring things in my ear, it was surely never this.

"This is what you risk happening if you do not have the least knowledge of self-defense. And this is what you really risk happening if you continue to be disrespectful toward me. I know I stole your life from you and that I am asking you to put that life in jeopardy by working for me. I am well aware of that. But do not forget that I also saved you back in that damn alley, and it would be better to be in *this* moment with me than with the big blond who found you so mouthwatering, in every sense of the word . . ."

His voice was velvety but also as sharp as a razor. I couldn't stop trembling, tears streaming of their own accord down my cheeks, and

I tried hard to suppress the enormous sobs of terror that threatened to escape if I opened my mouth.

"Have I made myself clear?" he said, still at my ear.

I yielded, quickly nodding my head. He got up and held out his hand for me.

"Now get up."

I took the hand he offered and let him help me to my feet. I was still trying to hold back sobs, and the result was that I was sniffling loudly and shaking all over. He handed me a handkerchief (of course he had a handkerchief . . . just like any gentleman), and I wiped my face before blowing my nose.

"I'm so-sorry for be-being rude. After all, you did save my life, and God knows what the blond vampire and his pack will do if they find me in Kentwood."

I had figured out at least that we weren't in Kentwood, because there were certainly no manors there. I inhaled deeply, and then said, "I accept your conditions."

What other choice did I have?

\*\*\*

I was treated to another X-ray observation (luckily his eyes had returned to their normal color, though that was hardly reassuring). I didn't shrink away from his stare, though. I wanted to get my dignity back.

"First of all, you will call me by my name, Phoenix. I shall give you a cell phone that you will have on you at all times so I can reach you when I need to. At night, you will come with me. During the day, you will write reports for my employers."

I wondered when I would get to sleep in the midst of that schedule.

"But we shall get to the reports when the time is right. For now, you are going to change into something suitable for combat training."

"What, now?"

"Your training is going to take me some time, and it will slow down my work, so it is best to start as quickly as possible. There is a door on the ground floor near the staircase, on the right. It leads to the basement. I expect you there in fifteen minutes."

With that, he left me alone. Bursting into tears seemed like an appropriate response, but it wouldn't get me anywhere, so I shook myself. After all, I had asked for it. I didn't know what my problem was. This was the first time that I was reacting this way. Normally, I let everyone walk all over me without saying a word, but for some reason, I had verbally assaulted, several times over now, a person who was capable of dismembering me in an instant if he was ever inclined. Besides, he had certainly thought about it. I was convinced that I would have nightmares about it as soon as I fell asleep.

It had taken me five minutes to regain my composure. Better to not lose any more time, so I went to change my clothes.

Once I got back to my room, I quickly changed into the gym clothes he had left on the table, and I took the opportunity to splash my face with water to erase the last traces of tears. I glanced in the mirror: I looked like death warmed up, and my fight with Phoenix (I was going to have to call him by his name) had gotten the better of my ponytail. I fixed it before heading for the staircase.

I found the promised door and descended the flight of stairs that led down to the basement. And wow, it was enormous. It must have extended below the entire area of the manor.

Where most people might store old furniture, boxes, or bottles of wine, here there was a series of rooms reserved for the art of combat, including a firing range.

In the biggest of these rooms, mats covered the floor, and weapons of all kinds and from different origins hung on the walls. There was even a punching bag, though I wondered how, with all the strength he had, my boss managed to not destroy it with a single punch.

Speaking of my boss, I didn't see him anywhere. I stepped into the room and stopped, eyes wide. Phoenix was in the back, pulling on a shirt. The muscles of his back followed the movements of his arms and allowed me to see a long scar that ran from his right shoulder to his left hip. I shivered, thinking that he must have gotten it when he was still human or else it would have healed. Next to that my head wound was only a small cut, nothing at all. I was still thinking about it when he spoke.

"Are you going to join me, or are you going to stand there all night?"

He still had his back to me.

"How'd you know I was here?"

"Your heart was beating as fast as racehorse's hoofbeats. I could hear it."

Hm. Not sure if I appreciated the comparison. It wasn't my fault I had a heart.

"OK, I'm ready."

"Lie down on your back," he said, advancing toward me.

He was dressed like the kung fu masters you would see in Bruce Lee films: a loose white shirt and a pair of black pants. His feet were bare, of course.

"You're not going to bite me again! I understood that lesson."

"Stop spouting nonsense and do as I say."

I yielded, huffing, and then he knelt at my feet and placed on his hands on them. Oh, his hands were *cold*.

"Let's begin with a set of two hundred."

"Two hundred what?"

"Sit-ups. Go on. I'll keep count."

I must have been gawking like an idiot, because he felt obliged to tell me two more times before I grudgingly complied.

After thirty, I felt like someone was sitting on my stomach. I was sweating buckets, and I had trouble lifting my back from the ground.

Phoenix continued to count and urged me to push past my limits. Yeah, sure, I had passed them after just ten sit-ups. But I would have preferred to burn in hell than admit that to him.

At the hundredth, I was on the brink of a stroke. At two hundred, exhausted and close to cardiac arrest, I shifted to my side to catch my breath and also to check that instead of doing sit-ups, I hadn't just created a giant hole in my stomach.

"Good. Now we will do some stretches before moving on to more serious things," my trainer said, stretching out his arms even though he had, strictly speaking, done nothing at all.

I stared at him wide-eyed. Serious things? He wanted me to die during my first lesson? If that was the case, he should've drained me of my blood in his office.

He sneered.

"You didn't really think that some sit-ups would be the only thing on the agenda. That was just a warm-up."

"Uh, but *I'm* not a vampire," I protested, painfully getting up.

"That may be, but you must know how to defend yourself, and we do not have much time. Which is to say that your training will be . . . intensive. You will see, over several days it will be less hard."

"Easy for you to say. With your invincible vampire superpowers, this is a piece of cake!"

"Don't be so sure. It took me years and a number of teachers to master the use of the weapons you see in this room. What's more, I am not invincible . . . I can be hurt, feel pain, even be killed."

"How can a vampire be killed? Other than decapitation of course. Is it like in the books?"

"We will get to that during another session if you would like. As for now, follow my instructions."

Humph.

His stretches made me work muscles that I didn't even know I had.

"Now, go to the punching bag. Hit gently at first, then harder. I want to see what you are capable of. Do not hold back—use your fists and your legs."

He was surely going to die of boredom (I know, I know, he was already dead) watching me trying desperately, punching like a little girl. Nevertheless, I did what he said and positioned myself in front of my "adversary."

"Empty your mind, then use that anger you have in you. It does not control you. It is your ally. Now, strike!"

Fire up my temper again? Sure, that was easy. I closed my eyes and concentrated.

When I opened my eyes, I started to hit, gently at first, then with more force. I thought about my failed life, from start to finish, how it was uncontrollably getting worse, and how at some point I was not going to get out of this unscathed, like that moment in Phoenix's study, or this crazy training . . .

I hadn't even realized that I'd let myself go under completely. The rage was coming out of my body through the strikes I was delivering, and I was even forgetting my pain from earlier. A red veil had fallen over my eyes, and I no longer felt anything apart from my breathing and the impact of my punches.

Suddenly I felt strong hands clasp my shoulders and pull me away from the punching bag.

"That's enough for now. Stop. *Stop!*" he said firmly.

Phoenix had pivoted me around to face him and, still holding my shoulders, stared at me intensely. I returned his gaze, out of breath. The veil had vanished.

"That felt good," I murmured.

He raised his eyebrows skeptically. However, I was being sincere, for I had found an outlet for my anger over losing my tranquil life. This sudden change must have appeared on my face, because Phoenix was staring at me, perplexed.

"You are truly a strange young woman."

"You have no idea," I answered, catching my breath.

"You were engulfed in your anger. You couldn't hear me anymore. You were too busy getting even with that punching bag."

"I did what you told me to do."

I knew that wasn't the whole truth, because he had told me to use my emotions, not be controlled by them.

"You lost control. We shall have to work on controlling your emotions. In a fight, you need to know how to keep your cool."

"I know, but I let off some steam. It did me a world of good."

"Well, at least now I know what you are capable of."

There was something like an air of satisfaction in the way he said that to me, but his face was as indecipherable as ever. In any case, it was a sure way to a headache to try to figure out what was on his mind.

"OK, and now?"

I had a hard time believing it, but my temporary madness had refreshed me. I was ready to destroy a brick wall with my bare hands. Of course, I couldn't really do that, but that was how I felt.

Phoenix must not have expected that. He raised his eyebrows again. He obviously had the same limited range of facial expressions as Teal'c, a character from *Stargate SG-1*, my favorite series, who could only show his emotions that way.

"I think you deserve a break."

He went to the back of the room and took a small bottle of water from a mini fridge. There must have been more than just water in there. But so what? With my discovery in the kitchen the night before, I no longer had any desire to take a look. He threw the bottle at me.

"Drink," he ordered when I caught the bottle.

*Eat. Rest. Drink.* He was certainly not going to dictate every move that I made. But sure, he was right, it was better that I quench my thirst than end up with cramps.

That fresh water was more than welcome, and I drank it all in one gulp. When I'd finished, I realized that Phoenix had been watching my movements . . . and I hadn't even done anything this time. Better get used to it: everyone has their quirks after all. Maybe he liked to watch humans drink and eat because he could no longer do the same.

It was already eleven at night, and I wondered how much more time this session was going to last. In any case, I didn't really feel like going to sleep.

"Are you ready to continue?"

"Yes."

"Good, let's move on to the basics of karate."

"Do you honestly think that you're going to make a karateka out of me in just a few weeks? I'm having trouble believing it myself."

"I seem to remember hearing you say that you were already a black belt," he said with irony.

It was my turn to roll my eyes.

"Oh, please, have you taken a good look at me? I said that because when I'm terrified, I say everything and anything that passes through my head. You never believed me."

For the first time, he gave a hint of a real smile.

"Certainly, but I like hearing you say it."

I had to hand it to him, he had a sense of humor. Besides, who liked to work for a boss she despised?

For three hours (oh yes, and I put my heart and soul into it), I studied the basic movements of karate. It was really difficult, especially knowing that I had been born awkward and clumsy. I don't even know how many times I fell to the ground, but I was surprised that I liked the exercise.

Finally, I begged for mercy. I had fallen to my knees. I didn't think my legs could support me any longer.

Phoenix knelt down beside me.

"Congratulations. I am pleasantly surprised. I honestly did not think you would last this long."

I lifted my head to look at him, trying to catch my breath.

"You mean, you expected that I would ask you to stop?"

"Exactly. It was good to test your limits. And I must say that this is rather encouraging."

I glowered at him. I felt like I had climbed and descended Mount Everest, and for him, this was just "encouraging." I was going to have to teach him a lesson too: tact!

"Thrilled that I didn't bore you," I grumbled. "If that's the only compliment you have for me, at least help me get up again, or else I'll just spend the night here."

And he did. That was becoming a habit. I would have to strengthen my leg muscles so he wouldn't take me for a whiner who falls to the ground as soon as something doesn't go right. But I wouldn't have asked him to leave me there. His support was essential to my balance, since I felt like I'd gone through a meat grinder. After drying myself off with the towels he provided for me, we climbed back upstairs, and he helped me sit on the sofa in the parlor. You could have compared the scene with the care of little grandmothers in a nursing home; the only thing missing was a walker. Completely ridiculous.

"Whew, thanks," I said, wedging a cushion behind my back.

He then left me for a few minutes, returning with two glasses. One was filled with lemonade and the other with a thick red liquid that I immediately identified as blood.

He handed me my lemonade, then took his place on the armchair facing me, his glass in his hand. The silence that settled between us seemed to drag on and made me ill at ease. I needed to break it, to try to satisfy my curiosity.

"I thought that vampires needed to drain a human of blood to sate their appetite. Is that enough for you?"

He didn't respond right away, lost in thought, gazing at his liquid nourishment. I thought he wouldn't even bother answering, but then he said, "You seem to have read quite a bit about vampires."

"I studied literature, and I'm a . . . or rather, I was a librarian, and I have no social life. So I read everything that comes into my hands. And I might as well tell you, I like the world of the fantastic, so I obviously have read some books about vampires."

"I see. And what have you read?"

"Well, *Dracula*, but it didn't really grip me. Um, the Twilight saga too, but everyone read those books, I think, and then some others."

I wasn't sure if Phoenix was the type to read about the romantic trials and tribulations of a group of big-hearted vegetarian vampires, shining like diamonds in the sunlight. Personally, like millions of readers in the world, I'd been engrossed by them.

"Oh yes, some of us read those out of curiosity. It appears that they are outrageously funny. But I'm not the type to read about the romantic trials and tribulations of a group of big-hearted vegetarian vampires, shining like diamonds in the sunlight. That does not resemble us at all." He broke off suddenly with a disgusted look.

Oh! Had he read my thoughts? Or had I read his?

"What, vampires don't feel love?"

"Our kind guards its independence fiercely. To love is to depend on another person, and dependence is an open door to weakness. So we avoid it if we can."

I stared at him, surprised and floored by that collective, negative vision of such a beautiful sentiment. He noticed my look and gave a mirthless laugh.

"We are far from being Edward and Bella," he said, as if he were announcing a verdict.

"Then it never happens? That a vampire falls in love?" I pursued, too astounded to conceive the idea.

After all, vampires had been humans before their transformation, and humans felt emotions.

"Yes, but it is rare. Vampires think of themselves first and foremost. Never forget your first lesson. Worrying about someone else means abandoning that conviction, and those of my kind have difficulty imagining that."

It seemed that for him, love between two people was an indecipherable riddle. Strange . . .

"You vampires really have a strange mentality. But then, what holds your community together if you have no feelings?"

"We have feelings. The first and most important is the loyalty we feel toward those we recognize as our leaders. We form friendships too, sometimes deep ones. But it stops there."

That was something at least. In a sense, I was feeling compassion for the vampire species. I wasn't a great romantic, but I'd always thought that to love someone and be loved in return was a way to move forward in life and definitely not the opposite. The vampiric vision of things was less shocking than it was sad. I decided to return to the topic of exsanguination.

"By the way, you never answered my question earlier, about how much blood you need to drink."

"Ah, yes. Your books are not completely wrong. In the old days, humans were drained of their blood because of the frenzy of the hunt and of biting. Killing a human that way allowed a vampire to go without eating for several weeks, except for those who really had a taste for blood. But that all changed."

"How so?"

My curiosity was truly piqued now.

"Well, not every vampire is a bloodthirsty monster, and some tried to not kill their victims, only taking small amounts of blood. But the victims had to be killed in order to keep the Secret, so it amounted to the same thing. Then we realized we did not need to completely drain a human to survive. The truth is that small but regular amounts are plenty to keep us alive and healthy. The Great Change was decided in part thanks to that realization. What's more, we discovered that the aggression connected to our predatory nature was significantly reduced because of the new way of consuming blood, and relationships between vampires became less violent, more diplomatic."

"That's not always the case, according to what I saw in the alley."

"Indeed."

It looked like I wouldn't be learning anything more about what he had been up to with those two awful men. Fine.

"Do your eyes always shine when you're in, um, attack mode?"

"As I have been telling you, we are predators. A taste for hunting is part of our nature. Luminescent eyes are a manifestation of excitement at the prospect of a hunt."

"Not very discreet, if you want my opinion." Then, without thinking, I blurted out, "Additionally, you look like the Goa'uld in *Stargate*."

"Pardon?"

"Oh, nothing. I watch too much television. But why weren't your eyes shining like the other two vampires, the ones you were fighting?"

I shivered at the memory of Phoenix's metallic stare before he had jumped at my throat.

"I do not really know. I have often been asked that question, but I do not have an answer."

"When I saw their eyes, I already thought I was lost in a straight-up nightmare, but I can tell you that your eyes are even more terrifying."

There again, he disappeared into a contemplation of his glass of blood, silence settling in once more. It was at this very moment that my stomach decided to chime in, as an odious rumbling coming from my gut made itself noisily heard, putting an end to my employer's reflection. He lifted his head to stare at me, tightening his lips.

"Good grief," I yelped, giving myself a punch to the zone in question, as if by this simple gesture I could recover my lost dignity.

I squirmed in my seat, getting the impression that my cheeks were ablaze like a forest of pine trees in full drought. Despite his five hundred years of vampire existence and all the time he had had to acquire an exemplary sense of self-control, Phoenix had to surrender. I then understood why he was tightening his lips so hard.

He burst into laughter, a booming laugh that convinced me at last that if someone could die of shame, I would have dropped dead on the spot.

"Oh, good grief."

I hid my face in my hands, for I would have preferred to be struck by the lightning of his glare than see him convulse like that, overcome by amusement.

He was still laughing when he said, "Truly, Miss Watkins, you are a very *interesting* human. I don't think I've laughed like this for at least fifty years."

"Happy to put a little joy in your life," I thundered, aiming less at him than at my stupid stomach.

Even if I suspected that my new boss didn't laugh often, it reassured me to know that he was at least capable of it. It humanized him in a way, and made him a little less terrifying.

"I think that you shouldn't have hired me as your assistant. Maybe your personal entertainment. I could certainly do that better," I pointed out to him, smiling.

"Maybe I should revisit the clauses of your contract," he answered, returning my smile.

"While you reconsider the nature of my position here, if it doesn't bother you, I'm going to regain my honor in the kitchen and eat a good meal. Then I am going to sleep, and I will pray that I will be able to get out of bed tomorrow without feeling like my body is about to come apart with every movement."

I rose from my seat slowly. "Good night, or in your case, good day. Well, it doesn't matter." Without a look back, I headed for the kitchen.

It was past two thirty in the morning. I was so tired that I didn't concern myself at all with my new boss's activities. Indeed, I made myself a sandwich and drank some water before going up the stairs that led to my room. I wasted no time, undressing quickly, then getting into bed. A shower could wait until the next day. I didn't have the energy. With my eyes barely closed, I sank into a deep sleep, and to my great relief, I didn't dream at all.

***

"Ow. Ow. Ow, ow. Oh, ow. Ow, ow, ow," were the only syllables I was capable of uttering when I tried to get out of bed the next day.

I felt like every joint in my body had been hit with a hammer. I headed toward the bathroom and only reached it after ten minutes of inching step by step forward, duck-footed. Good grief.

Taking a shower was true torture. As soon as I lifted my arms, I felt like someone had spent the whole night trying to draw and quarter me without being very successful at it. It was even worse when I had to get dressed: pulling my clothes on became an epic battle, but in order to preserve my already quite bruised dignity, I won't speak about that ordeal any further.

When I was ready, I went to get my breakfast (at two o'clock in the afternoon), despairing that with so little strength, I wouldn't be able to swallow a hot chocolate while chewing two melba toasts like a little granny without her dentures. I spent the rest of the day in Phoenix's study, familiarizing myself with his computer, and in the library, because I didn't feel fit enough to take a stroll outside; this was particularly important, I figured, if I had to train again at sunset.

When my new employer joined me, I was in the middle of washing up after dinner. No way was I going to exercise without having eaten first, and I wasn't going to go to bed again with a full stomach either.

"The smell in here is very tantalizing. It almost makes me hungry," he said to me by way of hello.

"Thanks, but avoid telling me that, or else I will end up afraid of becoming your dessert."

"Rest assured, I will not eat you."

Nice try, but I had already discovered that his preferred blood type was *my* blood type. So that didn't reassure me at all.

"Delighted to know that. But tell me, how do you manage to get all these fresh products here?"

"I have a supplier."

"I see. It's another one of your enslaved humans?"

Judging by his face, he didn't appreciate my tone. But even if he wanted to keep certain secrets, he was going to have to tell me some of them so I could live here and do my job correctly, right?

"Listen, I'm not asking you to tell me the identity of your employers or the precise location of where you hide to sleep. I just want to know where all this food comes from, food that you, incidentally, do not eat."

"In my situation, you have to be prepared for any and all contingencies. I always have human food here for appearance's sake. I have an agreement with the manager at the shopping center. I give him a list of what I need, and it is delivered to me once a month."

"You're not afraid of someone discovering who you are?"

"They do not know who I am. They put everything in the delivery, and I take care of the rest. Actually, they only know me by my checks. Given the sum they receive in return, the arrangement suits them perfectly well."

"No one knows you in the vicinity? And by the way, where are we? There aren't any manors like this in Kentwood, or near it."

"We are near Scarborough, north of Kerington. We're lucky—even if it is a small town, the people here are not very curious. Of course when the manor was newly inhabited, everyone wondered who the new proprietor was, but I managed to make everyone believe that I am a sickly and grumpy old man who does not want to see anyone. It worked, and they leave me alone."

"And the other vampires, do they know where you live?"

"Only my employers and a few friends."

"And do you have a lot . . . of friends?" I ventured, not very comforted at the thought of seeing a bunch of the living dead show up for a reunion dinner during which I could be featured on the menu.

"It would seem that we have something in common, Miss Watkins. I am a solitary person, and I can count the number of my friends on one hand."

"At least you can count them. By the way, if I have to call you by your name, you could do the same with me."

He stared at me, then simply nodded his head to express his agreement. I had held my breath while he decided, before trying to push my advantage a bit further.

"Um, since we're far from Kentwood, one could suppose that the threats to my life are not so great here. If I don't put your cover in danger, could I leave the manor and go to Scarborough? Just to . . . um, well . . ."

His stare became unbearable, and my determination melted like snow in the hot sun. I started to stammer when Phoenix finished for me: "Just to spend some time with the living for a change."

"Well, I do want to work for you, but I refuse to cut myself off from the world and the sun of the living."

I didn't dare look at him anymore, preferring to admire the kitchen tiles.

There was a silence, then he said, "You are not my prisoner, and I am not asking you to renounce your humanity. If your work is efficient, I don't see why I should refuse to let you go into town. However, it is an absolute necessity that you be prudent and use a cover for yourself.

We will say that you are the proprietor's granddaughter and that you have come to help him. It will placate the skeptics about my identity."

"So you agree?" I asked enthusiastically.

I resisted the urge to jump up and down and clap my hands.

"Yes, but you will have to wait a while yet."

That was a real cold shower of disappointment.

"Why?"

"It's better to let things sink in first. You can hold out for a few weeks. If we create a new identity for you, it will take some preparation to get the details straight."

"Oh. OK."

I was miffed . . . but then . . . I had an idea.

"Um, you know, thank you so much for all the clothes that you got for me. But I don't have any personal things anymore, and I'd like to take advantage of my free time to, say, set up my room to suit me better. Since for the moment I can't go into town, I could do as you do and have everything delivered."

He raised an eyebrow.

"And how will you pay for this?"

Ouch. There was the flaw in my plan: I had no means to pay for anything.

"Maybe you could give me an advance on my salary . . ."

He burst out laughing. "You really have some nerve."

"Does that mean no?"

"That means that I prefer you like this rather than as a tearful, depressed person. Make your list. I certainly owe you enough to pay the bill myself. In exchange, I hope that your motivation for this work will be more *visible*."

Whew. Well, there was no doubt that he should expect a hefty bill. After all, this was fair payback. As for motivation, he shouldn't exaggerate. Whatever he thought, I was well and truly a prisoner. I was somewhat free in my movements, but I was not free to choose my life: it was either him or the crazy blond in Kentwood. Yeah, sure, what a choice.

"You won't be disappointed. I guarantee it!" I lied.

"I truly hope so."

"And how much will I be paid?"

"Oh my God," he said, turning and walking away.

I couldn't stop laughing as he left the room, thrilled at having gotten on his nerves and forgetting that vampires had superpowers, like a very sharp sense of hearing. Predictably enough, I was called to order by a distant voice.

"Don't celebrate too quickly. I'm expecting you downstairs in fifteen minutes."

If there was a trace of smile left on my face, it vanished immediately. I wondered how I was going to be able to train with all these aches. I finished clearing up in the kitchen before going to change.

When I arrived in the basement, Phoenix was waiting for me. Without a word, he pointed at the rug; without a word, I lay down, demoralized in advance by the tortures I was going to suffer through. And I was not disappointed.

The program was demanding, and like the night before, at the end of training, I finished on my knees. My breathing must have sounded like a bull that was made to pull the plow for too long, but between two gasps for air, I was able to say, "I'll never make it."

"Don't be defeatist. It is only your second session."

"But I'm hopeless! Don't tell me I'm not!"

"I am not the kind to lie to someone to protect her ego. If I am not telling you that you are hopeless, it is simply because you are not."

"That's too kind. But that's really not the impression that I'm getting."

"I do not mean to offend you, but you know nothing. So let me be the judge in this case."

Well, on that score, he was very good: he successfully and simultaneously complimented and belittled me. I didn't know if I should be annoyed or flattered, so I said nothing.

"I am starting to think that you are a combative and determined young woman. Don't tell me I am wrong."

"Frankly, I'm wondering what made you think such a thing. People have always walked all over me without me ever saying a word. I was always one of the weak ones, never the strong. It's simple, they stomp on me because I am unremarkable and useless."

I'd spit out those words with all the bitterness I'd stored up since childhood. For some unknown reason, that bitterness had chosen that moment to release itself into the world.

"And now? That part of your life is over," he said scornfully as he towered above me.

I snickered sarcastically.

"Believe me, I tried to change. I really tried. I have as much charisma as a mussel on a rock, waiting for the tide to come in."

"That might be because you have never really been motivated."

"Thanks for the analysis Dr. Freud, but you're wrong. I did what I could. I'm a hopeless case. It's a pity you had such bad luck in the draw."

I was looking at the rug again when I heard a growl rise up from Phoenix's throat. I raised my head and froze when I saw that he was staring at me, and little by little, his eyes were taking on that horrific metallic tint. With another growl, I could see his fangs.

"I think you are right. I was mistaken—you are indeed useless. What could I possibly do with an assistant who spends her days whining and wallowing in her own mediocrity?"

I didn't dare move. His words cut right through me as surely as if he had sunk his fangs into my throat. I had an inkling of how the rest of this discussion would play out, and that seemed to lead right to my execution. I was certain of it when he continued, "Samantha Watkins, I was wrong to let you live. It would have been a service to you to leave you in that alley. You know too much now, and now you are a threat to the Secret . . . a threat that must be eliminated. Besides, the world will get on fine without you since you offer the world nothing and you refuse the opportunities it offers you."

He was getting dangerously close to me, but I didn't make even a hint of a movement to flee, I was so immersed in what he was saying. His words poured over me like a river of molten lava that burned me from the inside. They echoed what I had always thought about my life: that I'd been left on this planet by accident and that I was so unremarkable that there was no place for me. Phoenix was putting words to my thoughts and my most profound fears, and he was stabbing me with them.

"I think I will cut your suffering short and make you quit this world in which you are only dead weight. I'll find someone else without any difficulty and forget you immediately."

Since I hadn't reacted, he leaned forward slowly, making me realize that he was going to carry out his claims in the following seconds. Like a film in slow motion, it was during his approach, and the prospect of my imminent death, that I fully understood the extent to which I still clung to life. Deep down, I was sure that I had more to offer the world than what I had given before. I knew that Phoenix had given me a chance to realize all this, to finally become someone else, the person I should really be. At first, I had accepted this job just to stay alive; I hadn't estimated how much importance it would take on for me. In accepting new employment, my insipid ordinary life would end, and despite the risks, it would allow me to have new experiences all while protecting my own kind . . .

I became aware of the fact that all the weight of my former existence was disintegrating, and that this time, I was truly ready for a fresh start. I felt like I had a new lease on life, even though a vampire was on the verge of murdering me. I clenched my left fist . . .

And sent it, with all the strength I could put into it, right into the jaw of my angel of death.

\*\*\*

Surprised, he backed away, without a single trace of injury or sign of pain. As for me, I was going to have to plunge my fist into a bucket of ice. It didn't matter. I was trembling, but not out of fear. I rose and pointed in his direction while he was still seated on the floor.

"I warn you that if you start trying to bite me again, I will drive a stake through your heart without the slightest hesitation. I don't give a damn what you think of me. I know I can do better than what you've seen. Exit the librarian who is afraid of everything, stage left. You'll see, in a few weeks it'll be *me* beating *you*, and it'll be you begging for mercy! I am Samantha Watkins, human to be sure, but not weak or hopeless! And I don't give a damn about your vampire superpowers! Good night!"

I turned around to go to bed, my heart lighter than it had ever been before, keyed up with a newfound determination—that of a second life. I was so happy that I didn't care what effect my speech had had on my patron. I was thinking—no, I was hoping—that he wouldn't kill me, just give me a good dressing-down the next day. That wasn't the case.

I couldn't know this at the time—indeed, I didn't learn about it until much later—but when I left after empting my mind of all its darkest thoughts, it wasn't fury on my boss's face . . . but rather a sincere smile of satisfaction at having reached the goal he had set for himself when he decided to back me into a corner.

We didn't speak again of what happened that night. It was like a new beginning.

Fortified by this feeling of rebirth, I became an attentive and determined student during the training sessions, to the point where my progress seemed lightning quick. I was always asking to do more, and Phoenix kept raising the level of difficulty. He began by teaching me weaponry, and I became even more voracious in wanting to acquire complete mastery of them. Even during my free time, I trained by myself an hour per day, going over what I already knew perfectly.

I also made it a point of honor to keep in touch with reality. I enthusiastically ordered everything I wanted to transform my new room to my liking. I redecorated (I was great at do-it-yourself projects), and I built a nest for myself. I repainted my room from a cold blue to a warmer tone of lilac, and I often gathered fresh flowers to put in the vase that I had moved from the manor entryway. And what happiness I felt when my television was delivered and I could once again follow my favorite shows!

Phoenix had given me permission to go through some of his reports so I could understand what he expected of me. Reading them was often a hair-raising experience, especially when they described giving a solid lesson to some vampire who had been careless about their laws, but they gave me an understanding of the duties of my employer, who finally ended up answering the questions I had asked about them. After all, an assistant should know the content of her boss's work, or else what use would she be?

That was how I learned that Phoenix was what was called, in the vampire community, an angel (yes, a very paradoxical name for monsters who fed on human blood), meaning the right hand of the vampire leaders. He was charged with completing the most secret and dangerous missions, notably eliminating "purist" vampires who continued to massacre humans shamelessly without any regard to the Great Change and the Secret of their race's existence. But that wasn't his only occupation.

I thought that vampires lived their lives hidden away from the human world, but I discovered with amazement that even if they don't put their secret out in the light of day (a truly bad play on words, knowing that Phoenix had confirmed to me that the sun was fatal to vampires), it wasn't exactly the case that they were detached from the world. This was a species that liked power and money. Thus my boss's bosses, and Phoenix refused to tell me anything about them, were in real estate, and evidently, the transactions didn't just concern small houses. This assured them substantial revenue, allowing them to live in the shadows as it suited them. Phoenix traveled all over the country to see these transactions through when his bosses were too busy to handle them alone. This happened all the time, in fact, and I was expected to follow him on his travels.

One evening, when he had joined me in the kitchen during my dinner, I questioned him.

"The humans that you encounter for your business, they never ask questions about why you only deal with them at night?"

"Materialistic people have other things on their minds than questions about the existence of vampires. What interests them is the profit they will make from dealing with them. And rich people are often . . . eccentric. Thus far I have not had any difficulty."

"How long have you been working for your bosses?"

"Hm . . . I have known them for two hundred years, but they did not trust me until a hundred years ago, and I became their angel fifty years ago."

"Is that why you stopped laughing?"

I remembered his burst of laughter and the number of years between then and the last time he had laughed like that. At the time, I hadn't paid attention to it, but with hindsight I found it rather sad.

"My work takes up a great deal of my time. I really do not have the opportunity to amuse myself."

As usual, I tried to figure out his emotions. I had challenged myself to this task a while ago, and thus far it had come to nothing. This time, as always, his indecipherable expression remained an enigma. I sighed.

"It would do you some good. Believe me."

"Are you insinuating that I am depressed?" he said, raising an eyebrow.

By now I was used to this mannerism of his, but it drove me crazy. I always felt like he took me for an imbecile in those moments. I'm not even going to tell you about his sardonic smile.

"Of course not! *You* are the life of the party," I said sarcastically. "Come on, you only think about work. Try to relax from time to time."

"And what do you do to relax?"

"Well, thanks to your generosity, and until I can go to town, I like to relax by reading a good book with some light music in the background or by stuffing my face with popcorn while watching a DVD marathon on my new television."

"A DVD marathon?"

"Well, yes, you watch episodes of your favorite television show until you think you have better things to do."

He seemed confused.

"Don't tell me that you never watch TV."

"You must be well aware that I do not have one here. I get my updates from print media."

"Who said anything about news? I'm talking about films or series to empty your head when you have a bad day. A bad night, I guess, in your case."

"I do not have time for that."

"For what, then? You criticize your colleagues for not wanting to hear about computers, but you're just as old-fashioned as they are. We need to get you up to date. There's more to life than work. Between real estate transactions and the pursuit of the other living dead, you need to take it easy, or else you'll end up a grouchy old vampire hermit. Even your kind will find you depressing."

There was a silence, and then he answered, "Well, well, who would have known you would worry about my well-being?"

His sardonic smile materialized on his face. Grrrr.

"Your well-being is all the same to me, to be honest. But I think that you would be more pleasant on a daily basis if you exuded some joie de vivre. But you know what? You've lived alone for a very long time."

I had hit the nail on the head. His expression was irritated.

"Curious to hear that from someone who never had a social life herself."

Touché. He was getting on my nerves.

"I may not have had a social life, but at least I know how to appreciate life. You, you just suck its blood, bloodsucker!"

We stared daggers at each other. With my new resolutions, it was out of the question that I lower my eyes first.

"There will be no training tonight. I will let you appreciate life as you like. As for me, sucking someone's blood would not be a bad idea . . . It will help me unwind and keep me from wanting to suck yours! Have a good evening," he said, his tone glacial, before turning his heels.

At least he hadn't jumped on me, which was what had happened every other time I had shown him disrespect. That must have meant that our relationship was getting better. He was infuriated, but I was persuaded that he knew deep down that I was right. He may have been a vampire, but he had to accept criticism when it was well-founded, even if it came from a human woman five hundred years younger than him.

In any case, I didn't feel any remorse, and I was even happy for the time off, for I was going to be able to go to bed early for once. I thus took advantage of my free evening to have a well-earned DVD marathon. I was in my pajamas on my new loveseat (the suite was so big that I could have fit three in there) facing my flat screen, when I heard knocks on my door.

"Come in."

I thanked heaven that I had picked the comfort of good flannel pajamas, purchased via the mall, instead of the alluring camisoles that my employer had provided at my arrival. As beautiful as those garments were, I had no interest for performing in burlesque shows.

Phoenix entered. He seemed ill at ease, which was strange coming from him.

"Listen . . ."

Silence. I truly wanted to listen, but he had to at least open his mouth!

"I'm listening."

"I thought about what you said, and I think I owe you an apology."

I should have had a recorder so I could play his words over and over in a continuous loop. I couldn't believe my ears.

"What you said to me earlier, well . . . you were right. I have lived alone for so long that I do not know how to be social anymore. My employers are the only ones I have to answer to, and they don't meddle in my private life. I am not used to being criticized so openly. I should not have spoken to you about your solitude. Please forgive me."

I was looking at him, wide-eyed, mouth hanging open. He rolled his eyes to the ceiling.

"Please, this is costing me a great deal to say this to you, so stop looking so stunned and say something," he grumbled.

Boom! He really had a way of making me tumble back to earth.

"Uh . . . I forgive you. Anyway, I shouldn't have called you a bloodsucker. It was rude. So I also ask you to forgive me."

"Consider the matter forgotten."

We exchanged a brief smile. Phoenix then transferred his attention to the television.

"Is this one of your famous marathons?"

"Yes. Since I'm unable to recover my own things, I bought the first season of my favorite series again. I'm at the pilot episode."

"Hm."

I took a deep breath, and then, with an encouraging smile, I asked, "Can I tempt you?"

He was silent a moment, and then he said, "Let's have a relaxing evening, then, shall we?"

And he settled onto the sofa.

He said nothing as we watched. I wondered if he liked it or if he was bored stiff. When he left so I could sleep, I was still asking myself that question.

I had my answer the following morning, when I saw an open space in the parlor where a new piece of furniture took center stage: on it was an enormous flat screen and a DVD player. On top, there was a note: "Wait for me to watch the rest."

I couldn't stop myself from laughing.

# CHAPTER FIVE
## *Trial Period*

It was the beginning of March, and as spring approached, I was all the more aware that I had been living as a recluse at the Scarborough manor for eight weeks. During that time, I'd turned twenty-nine, on January 15; to tell the truth, this was a birthday that left me completely indifferent, and I hadn't even informed my host about it. My daily life was patterned by training, walks in the gardens, reading, and restorative sleep. I wasn't complaining, but I was starting to find time lagging. I needed to get off the property.

Though I can't say that Phoenix and I had really gotten to know each other, we had come to understand each other better. He wasn't very warm, but he tried to be more sociable. He encouraged me during training—pushing me for more sometimes, and other times slowing me down when I was trying to do too much and risked hurting myself. He had asked a lot of questions about my life from before, and even if the discussion hadn't gone on all that long, since I didn't have much to say about it, he had listened attentively. He seemed especially curious about the color of my eyes; according to him, they were very distinctive. But there again, I didn't have much to say.

As for me, I tried to decipher his emotions, but I always failed. That man was truly a walking question mark. He always answered my questions, though, whether they were about combat or vampires. Well, up to a certain point.

I learned that there weren't many vampires. This was fortunate, or else they wouldn't have been able to reroute donor blood from blood banks or hospitals. Because of internal wars over the control of territories densely populated by humans, their numbers kept decreasing, to the point of reaching an alarming low point before the Great Change. Then, at the beginning of the twentieth century, the number stabilized as violence between vampires was reduced, thanks to the installation of their new method of consumption. This world, so strange and frightening, was no less fascinating, and I couldn't stop myself from trying to satisfy my curiosity.

"You said that vampires cannot procreate and that the only way they can increase their numbers is to transform humans. But if you multiply too much, won't it be hard to be discreet about the supply you take from blood banks? What will you do in that situation?"

"Before, a vampire would transform a human without anyone asking any questions. That time is over. There are also rules for that, in order to prevent overpopulation. Additionally, it doesn't always work. Most of the time, the person dies . . . definitively. As I already told you, the process is very dangerous . . . and very painful for those who go through it."

And to think that some humans dreamed of becoming just like them! They must really have a screw loose, seeing what it entailed.

I was beginning to understand my boss's world a bit more, which allowed me to better understand him also. I knew that it was pointless to ask questions about his own bosses or his species' hierarchical organization, for he remained consistently mute on those subjects. I also learned, the day when I wanted to know a bit more about his life as a human, that there was a boundary to never overstep. He became abruptly withdrawn, then left the room without a word. I didn't see him again until the following evening, when he acted as if nothing had happened. The message was clear: his life as a human was a taboo subject.

That didn't prevent us from having completely normal conversations about current events, literature, and, of course, my favorite show, *Stargate SG-1*. Surprisingly he had become even more addicted than I was. But he had an awful flaw: he had to analyze everything.

"This is crazy! The scriptwriters are so good they have managed to make us believe that on *all* the planets visited by the team, the people they meet speak English!"

I sometimes wanted to tell him to keep quiet, let me watch in peace, but mostly I found these moments with him rather nice. They certainly gave our pattern of work and training some variety.

However, there came a time when I couldn't stand being confined anymore. I had noticed that the moment when he was the most relaxed was when he kept me company in the kitchen while I prepared my dinner. We didn't always chat; sometimes he would just sit at the table and read the paper. I know what you're thinking: what a nice little couple. Rest assured that that was only the appearance of it. His presence, so charismatic, was so imposing and frightening that even the most romantic of young girls would have thought twice before falling in love with a man such as him. But this wasn't a man, and I wasn't a romantic. The only sentimental thing I felt when looking at him was an irrepressible fear when he moved into attack position, his fangs all out, to train me to face a vampire. Even if it was only practice, my knees still knocked together a bit before defending myself.

Thus I had no desire to disturb his reading. Nevertheless, it was the time I chose to address the subject of the end of my captivity, with a nice plate of spaghetti Bolognese to give me courage.

"Phoenix, I've been wondering . . . how much more time do you think you'll keep me locked up here?"

Gulp. At the look he gave as he raised his eyes from his newspaper, I knew that I had to quickly rephrase my request.

"Uh, I mean . . . I've been here for eight weeks now. The big blond and his henchmen surely think I'm dead. So I was wondering if . . . maybe . . . you could keep your promise and let me go out in Scarborough as I please."

His piercing gaze was unbearable, just like the silence that he let settle in between us (deliberately, I'm sure), knowing perfectly well that it would make me uneasy enough to feel sick. Turning his attention back to his paper, he finally gave in.

"As it happens, I was going to talk to you about that. Your intensive training phase is over, and it is high time that you started working. I have set aside my own work for too long. Consider your trial period begun, starting now."

"My trial period? And if I don't fit the bill, what will you do?"

"Oh, the question does not even deserve to be asked since we both know that you will do efficient work that will satisfy me."

In other words, it would be best if I keep my commitments.

"Good, and we start tonight?"

"Tomorrow night. You will accompany me to Drake Hill. I have someone to see."

"I'm going to need to know a bit more than that."

"Soon we will focus on what you must bring with you. I will brief you on the mission while en route tomorrow."

"I see. Serious things are starting now."

"This has always been serious."

And while I finished my spaghetti, thinking about what was waiting for me the following evening, he returned to his reading.

***

We were in the basement. Identification and credit cards as well as a gun and a cell phone were piled on a table.

"Good. Let us begin with your identity. You understand that it is advantageous for no one to know you by your real name. For the people of Scarborough, you will be my granddaughter. Here, everyone knows me by the name Peter Stratford, so I created a new identity for you under the name Samantha Stratford. You were living on the other side of the country, in Seattle, and after the death of your parents, you decided to come here to care for your sick British grandfather. You two are the only family you each have left."

"Super, but everyone will assume that I'm only playing nurse so I'll be named in some old eccentric's will."

"It is up to you to make sure that no one thinks that. Let us move on. You also understand that in the context of my job and to keep my home in Scarborough secret, I do not introduce myself under the Stratford name. I am Peter Livingstone, and you are Samantha Jones."

"Samantha Jones? Like from *Sex and the City*? Is that a joke?"

"What is *Sex and the City*?"

I looked at Phoenix to try and figure out if he was making fun of me. That didn't seem to be the case. He really had no idea who Samantha Jones was, or what she did in her free time. Maybe it was better that way.

"Forget it. I'm Samantha Jones for business purposes, and your granddaughter, Samantha Stratford, in and around Scarborough. Got it."

He shrugged his shoulders. "Here is a notepad and your cell phone. It should always be on. And your gun. Always check that it is loaded."

"A gun? What if I get stopped by the police? I don't have a permit."

"Samantha Watkins does not have a permit. Samantha Jones and Samantha Stratford both do."

"Do you think that this is necessary?"

"Yes. Even facing a vampire, weapons are useful. Only decapitation or piercing the heart will kill us. Remember, silver is a veritable poison for our species. Right in the heart, it is fatal, but a simple wound is enough to weaken us to the point of rendering us as harmless as a human. That would give you time to flee if need be."

"Great. I can't wait," I said sarcastically.

"Remember your lessons, and everything will be fine."

"And if it's a human who causes a problem?"

"Well, he or she will have the pleasure of being maimed by a very expensive bullet."

"Maimed?"

"Yes. Aim for the legs."

"But what if I aim badly, and instead of shooting at the leg, I hit the head?" I exclaimed, horrified at the idea.

"Accept the fact that it is possible that you may have to kill to defend yourself. But I would not worry too much about aiming poorly. For someone who has never touched a firearm before, you have shown an impressive proficiency in training, whether on a still target or a moving one. You have a knack for it."

"Hm . . ."

I found it strange to have never had a particular talent and then at twenty-nine to discover one in the use of firearms. I would've preferred knowing how to sing, but just between us, it wouldn't have been useful for this line of work.

"Ah, I forgot something. Your assistant gear. You will use a smartphone and a notepad. I think that is everything."

"You've forgotten to tell me how much I'll be paid to do all this, because you always dodge the question when I ask. I should have already gotten my first paycheck."

"Your new identities were not yet entirely official. Your new bank accounts either. And given the bill you presented me for your 'moving in and adjustment' expenses, I do not think you have suffered at all from not getting paid this month."

How on earth was I to answer that?

"So does this mean that now Samantha Watkins doesn't exist anymore?"

"Yes. Except between us."

"And in Kentwood? Someone must have noticed my disappearance."

"That would surprise me. If the man who attacked you is not an amateur and he does not want to attract the attention of the police, which would also risk getting *my* attention, he would have made sure that everyone believed you left town the very night we met."

I thought I was feeling some sense of loss, but I realized that wasn't the case. Even if leaving the house I had grown up in, where I had such good memories of my parents, caused some heartache, I knew that I wasn't missing anything in Kentwood and that no one there would miss me.

I shrugged.

"The important thing is that I know who I am. The rest is only incidental."

"That is good reasoning."

"What are we doing next? It's not late."

"I thought that you would take advantage of your new freedom by going to Scarborough."

"Now? No. I'd prefer to explore the town when I can also enjoy some sunlight."

"As you wish. I was going to give you the evening off so you will be rested for tomorrow."

"If you don't mind, I'd rather we do some training. I don't know how ready I feel for tomorrow. Training will reassure me. And it'll spare me from thinking too much about what's ahead."

"Very well. Join me downstairs when you are ready."

With that, he stood up and left the kitchen.

I didn't hurry. For once, he hadn't given me an exact time to heed, so I could keep him waiting for a bit. I took the time to watch the evening news while thinking about what Phoenix had said about my disappearance. Up to that point, I had the vain hope that someone had been looking for me. It wasn't as if I wanted to leave my new employment—I'd already settled that issue—but I wanted to know if anyone had noticed my absence. I routinely watched the local news, wondering if I would hear my name or if someone was hoping for my return, but there was nothing.

Even if all signs of an attack hadn't been covered up, it still might have been the case that no one was looking for me or wondering about my fate. Well, no, I forgot: the IRS would have sought me out. Small consolation.

For a moment, I felt depressed. But that feeling dissipated when I thought about the second chance that I'd been given. After all, Phoenix had given me more attention in eight short weeks than Mr. Plummer, the principal of Griffith High School, had over the course of six years.

Once again on the sunnier side of things, I got ready and then went to join vampire Bruce Lee, who was waiting for me below.

"You kept me waiting . . . if I did not know you, I would say that you did not do it on purpose," he said with his back turned to me.

He was starting to figure me out. I gave him a big, innocent smile. "You didn't tell me to hurry."

"Get into position," he sighed.

For two hours, I practiced shooting. The basement was so immense that there was a room just for target practice. I often thought that Phoenix had built secret rooms in this manor. Sometimes, when I had nothing to do, I meandered up and down the hallways, searching the walls for a mechanism or secret lever that would open a hidden room, like the Room of Requirement in Hogwarts. It was a pathetic pastime, but it helped me get to know the place.

I was treated to some shooting practice, with both stationary and moving targets, and I also had to move around to simulate a chase. I don't know how I managed it, but I hit the bull's-eye every time. I had to admit that when it came to marksmanship, I was quite ready for the next day.

Exhausted, I raised my arms in surrender. "I think that's enough. I'm going to bed now." Just as I was about to leave the room, I reconsidered. "Phoenix, what do you do the rest of the night after I go to sleep?"

"Good night, Samantha," he said, turning away to clean the firearms.

"Good night," I sighed.

When I got back to my room and settled into bed, I told myself that all the training Phoenix had put me through was nothing compared to the real work he'd chosen me to do. And all that would start the next day . . .

Before that, though, I was treated to my very first sleepless night.

*** 

"Good evening. Are you ready?"

It was seven o'clock. He was wearing a custom-made dark-gray suit, a white shirt, and a black tie. Very elegant. His hair, lightly layered and neck-length, gave him a soft, friendly look that was immediately contradicted by the hardness in his eyes. He certainly wasn't going to kill the man he had to see, or else he would've put on something he could get dirty (you never know with blood), so I didn't regret my own outfit. I'd picked out a red blouse, a tailored dark-gray skirt (pure coincidence), and red heels. For some time, I'd been training myself during the day to walk in high heels. The skirt had a slight slit on the side, which would facilitate my movements as needed, and my black opaque tights would keep me warm.

I clenched my teeth as Phoenix scrutinized me from head to toe, but after a nod of approval, he led the march toward the door. Silently, I sighed in relief. I grabbed my coat, inside of which was the complete arsenal of a perfect assassin, as well as my handbag, inside of which was the complete arsenal of a perfect assistant.

Phoenix and I got into a powerful black Audi R8 with heated seats and tinted windows. I preferred this car a million times over the Camaro in the garage, whose vivid red would have turned the heads of everyone we drove by, human and zombie alike. No way was I getting in that car.

As we headed out, I was able to catch a glimpse of Scarborough, which I had put off visiting until the next day. It seemed rather elegant to me.

We pulled onto the road leading to Drake Hill, a medium-sized city northeast of Kerington, about an hour away. I wondered how we were going to pass the time. When my parents had taken me to the Williamsburg amusement park, about an hour's drive from Kentwood, we sang songs or my mother would arbitrate a competition on general knowledge between my father and me. If I won, my parents bought me an ice cream; if I lost, they bought me one anyway. I adored them. Suffice it to say that this ride with Phoenix would not offer the same comfort.

Twenty minutes had passed since we'd left, and we hadn't exchanged a single word. He needed to brief me on the mission, so what was he waiting for?

Luckily, I didn't have to wait for long.

"The man that we are meeting is named Kiro. He is an herbalist."

"Human or vampire?"

"He is human. But I have known him for thirty years."

I immediately raised an eyebrow.

"So he knows your secret too."

"Yes, and he understands the stakes very well. He always has his eyes and ears open, so he has become my informant. Now he has information that will likely help with a matter I am working on."

"What type of matter?"

"Disappearances in and around Kerington."

"They've been talking about that on the news for months now. Are vampires involved?"

"I do not yet know. I am in charge of finding out."

"Does it have anything to do with the disappearances in Kentwood a couple of months ago? Two people vanished just about ten days before we met."

"I cannot confirm that. Many vampires have small side deals here and there, and they do not like people, let alone the angels, interfering in their business. I came across two such vampires while investigating one of these disappearances when we first met. Their reaction toward me proved that they were hiding something, but not that they were involved. When new vampires enter our territory, they have to make themselves known to my employers and myself. I did not know the ones in the alley, but they certainly knew me, so that is another mystery for me to solve."

"Is that what you do when I go to bed?"

"I slowed down my investigations to train you, but I did not stop everything."

"All in all, you never stop."

"Well, thanks to you, I learned to relax with a DVD marathon. And I sleep during the day."

"If I ask you where, am I going to hit another brick wall?"

"I have a secret room that I use."

"Why don't you use the ones downstairs? You've sealed off all the windows."

"Vampires are distrustful by nature. We are at our most vulnerable when we sleep, so we are not foolish enough to sleep in full view of everyone."

"But what if I need to contact you in an emergency? How do I find you?"

"I keep my cell phone on me. The ring will wake me. In any case, in full daylight, I will not be of much use to you. Unless what you need is a torch."

"Am I dreaming, or did you just make a joke?"

"How was it?"

"Pathetic. But don't get discouraged," I answered, smiling.

He groaned.

"OK, what do you want me to do when we're at Kiro's place?"

"Take note of all that he says. Do not disregard anything. Even the tiniest details can prove to be important."

"Very well. Actually, that's comforting. It doesn't seem to be a very difficult mission."

His silence should have given me pause.

***

We arrived at Drake Hill shortly after eight o'clock. It was cold, and so I appreciated my big hooded coat and my tights all the more. We weren't in a great neighborhood, judging from the little alleyways and the street lights that could have used some repair. The facade of the herbalist's shop was impeccable, however, and the front window displayed dozens of different small bottles. Phoenix held the door open for me, and as he did, a bell rang, announcing our arrival.

Kiro walked through a beaded curtain that separated the shop from a private room in back. I evaluated him from head to toe as he approached my patron, all smiles and wide-open arms. He was an old Japanese man, about seventy-five years old, short, thin, and bald.

"Phoenix, it's been so long!" Kiro exclaimed, giving Phoenix an embrace that, surprisingly, my boss returned.

"Hello, Kiro. How are you? Your family?"

"Oh, everyone is doing well. Same for me, except for my damn rheumatism. I'm not as spry as you. But you can ask Aoki, who's in the back room—I'm still a lion."

He elbowed my boss, putting some force into it, a signal of a knowing, masculine complicity. I must have been hallucinating. Where I was only ever treated to a cold indifference, Phoenix was joking around with this old eccentric, who finally got interested in me.

"But who is this beauty? Another of your conquests?"

Kiro ogled me without restraint, even having the audacity to linger over my breasts.

I felt my cheeks turn hot, and I knew I had instantly turned beet red. I opened my mouth to give the lecherous old fool a piece of my mind, but I was interrupted by Phoenix.

"You are mistaken," he said. "This is my assistant."

The old man finally deigned to move from my chest to my face, then redirected his attention to my boss.

"As long as I've known you, I've only seen you working solo. Since when do you trust humans?"

I was waiting for the moment when Phoenix would put Kiro back in his place for talking in such a familiar tone.

"Times change. As for trust, you know well what that means."

"How is she?"

I'd had enough of his little game.

"Hello? I'm right here. Stop talking about me as if I'm not in the room with you. And mind your own business."

There was silence and a severe look from Phoenix. Kiro observed me more attentively before exclaiming, "Beautiful and temperamental. Those are the most attractive women, and the hardest to handle."

"You do not even know," my boss said, rolling his eyes.

Then I treated Phoenix to a murderous look, which make the old man guffaw loudly.

"You've chosen well. She's a rare pearl," Kiro said.

Then he finally addressed me directly.

"Shall we make our exchange official, Miss . . . ?"

"Wa—Jones. Samantha Jones."

Nice job. I'd almost slipped up.

"Miss Jones, please be assured that it's better to be under Phoenix's thumb than that of any other of his kind. I'm quite content that he let me live in exchange for the services I render him from time to time."

"How did you discover his secret?"

"He must've told you that I was his informant. I've always had a tendency to listen at doors, and I know plenty of people who do the same. They say that curiosity is a nasty flaw, and I paid for it the night I approached Phoenix too closely. The alternative he proposed to me couldn't be refused, but you know that. And you, how did you find yourself in this situation?"

"Let's just say that I also got too close to him, but not on purpose."

I thought about our first encounter, when the big blond had thrown me at him.

Kiro came closer, and I couldn't help taking a step back, fearing that the old man wanted to touch me.

"You must be very special for him to choose you to go on missions with him. Do you have a particular talent?" he whispered.

They say that wisdom comes with age. I didn't know how to answer, so Phoenix did it for me.

"She has a gift for asking indiscreet questions, a bit like you, Kiro."

This idiot had forgotten about the supersensitive hearing of vampires. He looked sheepish, like a little kid caught doing something stupid.

"We have work to do," Phoenix said, cutting off our host's curiosity.

Kiro invited us to follow him into the back room, and we sat down around a small table.

"Can I offer you something to drink, Miss Jones?" he asked me politely.

"No, thank you," I replied as I took out my notepad.

He sat down with a serious expression on his face and said, "The disappearances in the news are only the tip of the iceberg."

"Meaning?" asked Phoenix grimly.

"People have only been talking about the missing persons with families, because the families are informing the police about the disappearances. There have also been abductions of homeless people, prostitutes, and junkies, but the journalists aren't covering them. In Drake Hill alone, there are at least twenty people who haven't been heard from. So imagine how many there are in Kerington and the neighboring cities."

Kerington was the biggest city in the county, and despite the millions of dollars handled by a small untouchable elite, Kerington County was poor, and it figured high on the list of national statistics concerning income inequality and meth addiction. Consequently, because the people being kidnapped were those who wouldn't be brought to the police's attention, the crime numbers were inaccurate. I shivered.

"It is even more serious than I thought," said Phoenix. "Do you have anything else for me?"

"Some strange things are happening in Kerington's industrial zone. An acquaintance of mine warned me that funny things are going on in certain warehouses, but he didn't know what precisely. In fact, a man in an advanced stage of decomposition was found by the police in an old barrel used for storing chemicals. The man must have wanted to get a closer look. I don't know anything more."

"How often are the warehouses used?"

"No one really knows. It's never the same ones, and the frequency is impossible to determine. All that anyone knows is that the next day, the warehouses are empty and clean. Not a trace of what happened there." Kiro shook his head before continuing. "Phoenix, I don't know what's going on or if it has anything to do with vampires, but no one feels safe anymore. Aoki refuses to take a single step outside after sunset. She's beside herself with worry and warns the children so often they are worried. As for me, I admit that I stay cooped up too, but I have a business to run. This must stop."

Phoenix turned to me.

"Samantha, we have finished here for this evening. I need some things from the minimarket two streets back. Here is the list."

He placed the list on the table in front of me as I tried to quickly scribble down everything Kiro had said about the warehouses.

"Go on. I will catch up," Phoenix said.

I stood up, nodded at Kiro, who was eying my cleavage again, and walked to the door. Before I walked outside, I heard Phoenix's advice to Kiro.

"I am going to figure all this out. In the meantime, you and your family should keep a low profile. No need to attract the attention of the abductors."

When I got outside, I found the streets deserted and dark. I didn't see any sign of a minimarket. The only explanation was that there was no minimarket. If it had been a long time since Phoenix had last come to this neighborhood, maybe he didn't know it had closed. I wanted to turn around and go back to Kiro's shop.

The wind picked up. The light of one of the streetlamps crackled, giving the street a murky look. I tightened my coat around me and kept going.

Down the street, there were two men heading in my direction. My danger alarm signaled that I was about to run into trouble. I hoped it was only two drunkards too tipsy to be a real threat, but their balanced gait dashed that glimmer of hope. Because of that, I crossed my fingers and hoped that they weren't vampires.

When we passed each other, I heard whistling behind my back.

"Oh, Jack, get a look at the li'l' lady. She's lost, right?"

"I don't know, Tony. Maybe we should ask her if she wants us to bring her home and comfort her."

Their salacious laughter echoed behind me. I had no illusion about how they thought events would play out when their footsteps became louder as they approached me. Being raped was out of the question. In my previous life, the only thing I would have done was run in the hopes of being faster than my attackers, but so many assaulted women try that option without success.

Then I remembered this wasn't my previous life. I was not without defense, and I spun around. Surprised, they slowed the pace of their advance toward me.

"Tony, looks like the li'l' lady is waiting for us. She wants to have a good time too!"

"She'll see what studs we are, that's for sure."

They finally arrived in front of me, and I could see their faces clearly. One was bald and puffy, likely due to the alcohol that he reeked of; the other, skinnier, had pockmarks all over his face. Both had insipid smiles that filled me with disgust, as much for their lewd expressions as for their rotten teeth. Before making a move, I composed my face into an inscrutable mask so they wouldn't sense my fear.

"Is this how you treat women, gentlemen? Do you have no pride, taking pleasure only by forcing yourselves on women when you could try to seduce them instead?"

Puffy and Pox looked at me, wide-eyed.

"What? What're you talking about?" said Puffy Tony.

"Have you seen our faces, you bitch? Little ladies like you give us the cold shoulder because they think we're gross, but we get them back for being . . . what's the word for it? Yeah, for being hot tea."

Jack really had a refined vocabulary.

"I think the word you're looking for is *haughty*. *H-a-u-g-h-t-y*," I spelled out.

That was a mistake, because they went ballistic. Both of them let out a drunken growl . . . "Oooowwweeerrrooooo!"

Pox spit on the ground during the *r* part.

"The li'l' lady sure is being high and mighty. You'll see. We'll make you choke on your education! And when we've both been on top of you, you'll scream like a dirty whore!"

Pox's jeering had stopped, replaced by a cruel predatory glare that seemed like a precursor to action.

During my training sessions, I had been facing Phoenix, and I knew he wouldn't hurt me, so I always wondered, in case of real danger, if I would be able to apply his lessons or if I would be paralyzed with fear. I had my answer in that moment.

A great calm engulfed me, and discreetly, I tensed my muscles to prepare for an attack.

I looked at Pox and said, "Appearances can be deceiving. I'll give you a chance to leave and change the way you treat women. If you don't take it, I'll see to it that you never have any children." I said this in a tone as cutting as a razorblade (I'd modeled it on my boss's).

Puffy laughed like an idiot. Pox said nothing, happy to just keep staring at me. And then everything happened fast.

As if it were a well-choreographed ballet, Puffy made the first move: he hurled himself at me, trying to push me on my back. I was surprised by the force with which he struck me, and I toppled over with him. Puffy's steps were to hold me down while his accomplice did what he wanted with me, waiting for his own turn.

But Phoenix's lessons were solidly engrained. I bit Puffy's arm, drawing blood. He let go, and I punched him in the mouth, smashing the few teeth he had left. Pox decided to intervene and tried to throw himself on top of me too. I rolled onto my side to avoid him, and while he crashed to the ground, I got to my feet.

My two attackers scrambled up, angry and wielding knives. That complicated things, but in theory I knew what to do, so I gathered my strength.

When they both came at me, I managed to pivot and elude Puffy's knife while elbowing him in the face, breaking his nose, and sending him to the ground. Then I disarmed Pox with a kick to the wrist. Pox looked at me uncertainly.

Writhing on the ground, mouth and face covered in blood, Puffy shouted at Jack, "Fuck, just kill that fucking whore!"

As if he had rediscovered all his courage from this speech worthy of a king inspiring his troops before battle, Pox attacked me again.

I dealt him a punch to the face that sent him to the ground too. I thought about the women they had said they'd already attacked, and the red veil fell over my eyes as it had when I was going at the punching bag. I lowered my gaze to Pox's crotch and lifted my foot. He screamed bloody murder when I used all my force to land my heel directly on his man parts.

Puffy cried out, "No!" while holding his own reproductive apparatus, then screamed like a warrior on the attack when he got up to charge at me. I hit him a third time and ended up smashing his jaw along with any desire to return to the fray. He finally approached his unconscious accomplice and tried to lift him while glancing fearfully in my direction. He limped away, but I refused to let my guard down, especially since the red veil hadn't left yet. Still in a trance, I pulled the gun from my coat.

I was in luck, for the one called Jack, supposedly unconscious, managed to lean on his friend and then turn and point an object in my direction. He didn't have time to aim.

My weapon was smoking after the shot that sent Pox's gun flying. Judging from the bestial howls coming from him, I must have shot off some of his fingers too.

They were almost at the street corner when I aimed at them again.

\*\*\*

A gust of wind flitted through my hair, which had mostly come undone from its ponytail. A hand removed the gun from my hand, while another forced me to turn around.

It was Phoenix.

"It is not necessary to kill them. I doubt they will risk trying to hurt a woman again. And like you said to that filthy brute, he will never be able to reproduce again."

I stared at him, scared of understanding what he was saying.

"You mean you were there? And you didn't do anything to help me?" I said slowly to make him absorb the idea as well as make him guess just how much I wanted to hit him, disregarding the pain I was feeling.

Might as well hit a rock.

"You coped well enough on your own. I did not think it of any use to intervene."

I was shocked. "You're a monster."

"This just in!" he said, rolling his eyes. "Tell me something I do not already know."

"What if it had turned out badly?"

"You were never in any danger. I followed you from the moment you left Kiro's shop. I orchestrated the whole thing."

*"Excuse me?"* I screamed.

"I told you that you are in a trial period. I wanted to see what you were capable of doing on your own if you were in real danger. So when you left to look for that imaginary minimarket, I ferreted out those two, whom I had noticed hanging around when we arrived, and I told them that I was looking for a beautiful young woman who was supposed to meet me and who was probably lost. Those imbeciles wanted to mug me. I pretended to flee, and they left in search of you. You applied the lessons I gave you well. Congratulations, your trial period is over."

I had listened without interrupting, stunned by the ruse he had dared put in place to know if I was going to chicken out when faced with a real threat. For a resourceful being, that was quite efficient. I should have been proud of myself. Clearly he was.

But I felt stupid at being manipulated and terribly angry with Phoenix, who was smiling as if it were all a game. However, the women that those men claimed to have attacked, they really existed, and I knew it. Those two wanted to do the same to me because my boss had sent them out to find me.

I moved away from him, feeling nauseous.

"Those men weren't just simple thieves. They were rapists! And you sent them after *me*."

Disgust supplanted my anger.

"I questioned Kiro about them when you left. Those men tried to assault his granddaughter a few weeks ago, but no one took care of it. I killed two birds with one stone. Those bastards deserved even more than what you inflicted on them. But you are not a murderer. I had to stop you from killing them."

His sincerity made my anger evaporate. Those men had learned their lesson. Maybe they deserved to die, but it wasn't up to me to send them to the grave. Phoenix was right: I wasn't a murderer.

Phoenix held out his hand.

"Let us go back."

I stared at him, and then took his hand. All I wanted was to take a shower, go to bed, and forget this evening and my trial period.

# CHAPTER SIX

## *Investigation*

We made the return trip in complete silence. Phoenix likely thought that I was still angry with him. I knew that as a vampire, the rules of morality were more relaxed for him, so he probably didn't feel at all guilty for throwing me into the path of two barbarians. I was sure that he thought he'd done me a service. In a sense that was true: I learned I was capable of defending myself in real danger.

In fact, I didn't feel any animosity toward him. I just didn't feel like talking. I wanted to use the time in the car to take stock of recent events.

I, a pathetic librarian without any particular aptitude, *I* had maimed two oafs who had wanted to do me harm. It had all been in legitimate self-defense, but I could have spared Pox his near castration. I had let the disgust inspired by those two men take me over completely. But I'd never feel guilty about it. By the time we arrived back at the manor in Scarborough, I decided that I had done what was necessary. Anyway, Phoenix had warned me that I would have to hurt and kill to defend my own life. That experience would certainly not be the last. With a calm conscience but incredible fatigue, I got out of the car and walked up the front steps. Then from behind me I heard Phoenix.

"It's strange. Since we left I have been expecting an explosion of fury and accusations against me, but you say nothing. I think I would prefer shouting to this overwhelming silence. Are you going to say anything?"

He seemed exasperated. He couldn't see the smile that appeared on my face while listening to him, and I decided to needle him further. Turning around, I arranged my face into an inscrutable mask.

"I seem to remember hearing you say that you aren't paying me for my conversation."

He rolled his eyes.

"Kiro is right. You can really be insufferable."

"And you can be quite tactless."

We went into the manor.

"You want me to say something to you? I'm going to need new heels. Good night!"

With that, I left him standing there in the hall.

***

When I opened the blinds (my employer had given me permission to leave them open during the day), the sun was already high in the sky.

I was in a great mood. I had slept like a baby. The events of the evening before were nothing more than a distant memory to which I was completely indifferent. I was also planning my trip to discover the charming town of Scarborough and its two thousand inhabitants. At this point, past midday, the best way to do it was to try out the local restaurants. I decided to dress casually since I wasn't on duty: T-shirt, sweater, jeans, loafers, ponytail.

It was early March, and it was still cold outside. I was very happy to have my long coat, which kept me warm and provided ample concealment for my firearm. The coat hadn't suffered at all from the scuffle with the two brutes the night before, so everything was perfect . . .

At least it was until I realized that Phoenix had said the manor was far from the center of town and I would have to drive. I had a choice between two cars: the powerful sport Audi R8 or the red Camaro with black stripes. For a discreet visit downtown, neither was ideal. These vampires and their taste for showing off!

I decided immediately to set money aside to buy a car as soon as possible, one that would belong to me and would be much less conspicuous.

In the interim, I sighed and grabbed the keys to the Audi. To avoid destroying the car, which would have earned me the telling-off of the century from my boss, I did a few maneuvers in the driveway. Once I felt comfortable, I activated the remote that opened the outer wall gates and left.

\*\*\*

As I feared, parking such a car in the middle of a small town got me some looks from a good number of my fellow citizens. I took it upon myself to look relaxed and smile, but I still hurried to put some distance between the car and myself.

I was on Main Street, whose historical buildings resembled the private mansions of the well-off quarters of nineteenth-century New York. There were lots of little shops and some restaurants. The bright blue facade of one, Danny's Good Eats, caught my eye, and I walked over to it. When I pushed open the door, heads turned in my direction, and instead of returning to their meals, the patrons continued to stare at me.

"Good afternoon," I said with a nervous smile.

There was an open seat at the counter, and I headed there, happy to turn my back on all those curious eyes. Good grief. There was a mirror on the wall so I could see they were still wondering who I could be. I also had a good view of the decoration. I thought I'd been sent back to the 1950s: there was a huge poster of Elvis that presided over one of the sky-blue walls of the restaurant and old leather booths.

A man who looked about sixty years old and wore an apron came over and handed me a menu.

"Good afternoon, little lady. I'm Danny Robertson, the owner of this restaurant. Pick what you want, and I'll make it for you in a minute."

I immediately thought he was nice. He had grizzled hair, a bit thinning on top, a solid paunch, and an infectious smile that I returned as I took the menu from his hand.

The menu items were simple but appetizing. I picked the roast chicken and fries.

"And for my last customer," he said as he brought me my plate a bit later.

It was true that I'd been the last to order. He looked at me as I attacked the plate and ate my first mouthfuls . . .

"Yum . . . this is the best chicken I've ever eaten," I said with my mouth still full, which made my host burst out laughing.

"So, what brings you to Scarborough, little lady? Are you lost?"

I suspected that people were going to ask me questions, and Phoenix had prepared me for that scenario. I absolutely had to keep my story straight.

"No, I'm not lost . . . I'm Samantha. I'm from Seattle."

"That's all the way on the other coast!" Danny reacted, whistling. "What brings you here?"

"Well . . . my parents died a while ago, in a car accident. I don't have any other family left there, so my grandfather asked if I wanted to come live with him. Since he's old and he can't really get around on his own, I'm sort of his live-in nurse now."

Danny stared at me with round eyes. He had taken the bait.

"So your grandfather, is he the mysterious Peter Stratford?"

"Mysterious?" I repeated, feigning surprise.

"Well, it's been a few years now since your grandfather moved into the manor, but no one's seen him. All that we know is that he gets everything he needs delivered by the stores at the Pembroke Mall. The manager there likes to give the impression that he knows your grandfather, but everyone knows even he hasn't met the man. It's good that you're here, because some weirdos are starting to think that the manor is housing an undercover drug lord! Haaaa-ha-ha-ha-ha!"

I forced myself to roar with laughter like he was, confirming that the idea was clearly foolish. If only he knew!

"You can tell them that my grandfather truly exists. I can attest to it. He stays cooped up at home, though, and not just because he has trouble getting around. He also suffers from some social anxiety."

"I don't need to say this, but everyone is listening to you. By tonight, all of Scarborough will know."

"I see. Advantages of living in a small town, I guess," I said ironically.

Danny burst out laughing.

"Go on, eat up. Two or three months from now, people will stop thinking of you as the new local attraction."

He laughed even more seeing my miffed expression.

"I'm not looking for notoriety. I just want to blend in."

"You're in the right place. The people here are the most welcoming that I've ever met."

"You're not originally from Scarborough?"

"No, I'm from a small town in New Mexico called Crownpoint. Leaving that place was the best decision I could have made. I went here and there, and then I ended up in this town and I met the people. That was thirty years ago. Scarborough, little lady, when you come here, you stay. This place is a true gem."

His story was touching, and Danny was truly friendly.

"I haven't had much time to visit, but the little I've seen, I've found charming."

"Go to the candy store. All the kids in town rush there after school. A friend of mine, Ginger Wood, she's the owner. Tell her I sent you and she'll spoil you!"

He leaned in closer, gave me a knowing wink, and whispered, "She's crazy about me."

I loved sweets, just as much as I thought I would come to adore Danny, his chicken, and his good ideas. Before leaving town, I would make an obligatory detour to that shop.

"I've deduced that you're not married, Danny."

"A heartbreaker like me? No!"

As we got to know each other over the course of an hour, the restaurant emptied out and I didn't even notice. That's how captivated I was by the story of my host's life.

His hometown offered no future to a young man with a curious and adventurous mind. At sixteen, not having any family, Danny decided to leave his hometown and travel across the country, working various small jobs. Kerington interested him, and so he headed there. After several years, he discovered Scarborough while following one of his lady friends who wanted to visit it. She left the town, but he didn't. The people had been seduced by his personality and they welcomed him with open arms. With their help, he started his business, which did so well that it had become a source of local pride, and Danny a local celebrity.

No one had ever opened themselves up to me like this before. Even if I suspected that Danny was thrilled at any opportunity to recount his adventures to any and all of his patrons, it gave me the impression of being his confidante, which I had never been for anyone.

I didn't even notice when someone had entered the restaurant.

"Dad, stop taking the tourists hostage and making them listen to your life story in detail, or else they won't come back!"

The sudden interruption made me jump, and I looked around for its source. A man about my age was standing at the door and taking off his coat. He was a bit shorter than Phoenix. He had short black hair and hazel eyes, and he was wearing a heavy wool sweater and jeans.

"Sorry to scare you, Miss, um . . . ," he said, offering me his hand.

"Stratford. Samantha Stratford," I answered, vigorously shaking his hand.

"Stratford? Like the mysterious Peter?"

"Well, for me, he's not a mystery. He's my grandfather."

"Oh."

I couldn't help smiling at his embarrassment.

"Pardon my indiscretion. I haven't even introduced myself. Matthew Robertson. As you may have guessed, the chatty chef who runs this place is my father."

I looked at Danny. "I thought you'd never married?"

I must have missed an episode of his life story.

"It's the truth, though I've known a number of women, believe me!" Another wink. "But none of them made me want to tie the knot. Twenty-nine years ago, I went to see an acquaintance in Kerington. Passing by an alley, I heard a baby crying, and when I looked around, I found a little guy near a heap of garbage cans. He was cold and hungry. I wasn't going to leave him there. We really tried, but we never were able to figure out who his parents were. So I kept him with me."

I didn't know what to say. To reveal all that to a perfect stranger must have been rather uncomfortable. I looked at Matthew out of the corner of my eye.

"It's OK, I've accepted it and the fact that Danny is a complete chatterbox. Anyway, the whole town knows the story. I'm sure all the people in Kerington do too," Matthew said.

I'd hardly set foot in Scarborough, and the first two people I started conversations with were astoundingly down-to-earth and kind.

In Kentwood, the people weren't disagreeable, but they weren't warm toward strangers either.

It was nice to chat, the three of us. Matthew told me that he had completed his entire education in Scarborough, and after earning his diploma, with honors, he launched himself into management studies. There again, he was the top of his class, but instead of pursuing an ambitious career by accepting prestigious job offers, he preferred to live his dream of working with his father to run the restaurant, and he would take his place when the time came.

Our conversation drifted toward our respective interests, but when father and son began to squabble over which soccer team was the best in the county, I knew it was time to leave.

Besides I wanted to continue my exploration of the town while I still had a bit of time. It was about three in the afternoon when I left Danny's Good Eats—though not before accepting Danny's warm invitation to return anytime—and I strolled around the neighborhood. The houses were colorful and welcoming; the shops were numerous and varied. There was a small square with a fountain and benches, where a bunch of elderly women gathered. They chatted as they knitted, and somehow seemed not to suffer at all from the cold.

I walked up the street to a bookstore and went inside. The aisles were narrow and dusty, and they overflowed with all kinds of books. An incredibly beautiful blond woman with azure-blue eyes came out of the back room and welcomed me with a toothy smile and an enthusiastic hello.

"I'm Angela Schumaker. This is my shop. How may I help you?"

In general, old-fashioned bookstores were run by people who were also . . . old, but Angela looked about twenty-five years old and had incredible style. She should have been a cover model for magazines, not a bookstore owner. I was sure that her usual patrons didn't come merely for the pleasure of reading.

"Hello, I just arrived here and—"

"Samantha Stratford. News travels fast."

Actually, word of mouth worked with such speed here that it put the fastest Internet connections to shame.

"Indeed. I don't know Scarborough and the region well. Do you have a book about the town's attractions, and maybe good local walks?"

"Of course, wait just a minute."

She headed for one of the shelves and without hesitating climbed up a ladder to grab a book. Her graceful gait and delicate frame made me think she must have taken ballet for years; her tight-fitting clothes and her high heels gave her a sex appeal that she didn't even seem aware of.

"Here you go," she said, handing me the book in question. "*Scarborough and Its Surroundings*, by Ellen McCoy. It was published three years ago. She was a food critic who was passing through here. She had only scheduled a quick stop to try out Danny's restaurant, but he and the town made such a strong impression on her that she stayed a year and immortalized us in this book."

"I suppose the part concerning Danny must be glowing."

She laughed. "That's for sure! But she didn't exaggerate. You can go for miles and miles, and you won't find a better chef than Danny. His roast chicken is famous."

"I know, I ate some this afternoon, and it was delicious. So how much for *Scarborough and Its Surroundings*?"

"Seeing as you just arrived, let's say that it's your welcome gift."

"That's completely unexpected and very nice, really! I can't wait to read it. I'm going to continue my visit of your town. I'm delighted to have met you."

"Me too. See you soon, Miss Stratford."

She gave me another toothy smile. The Claudia Schiffers and Gisele Bündchens of the world could go put their clothes back on: men must be jostling at this woman's door. In comparison, I looked like a badly groomed cavewoman.

"See you soon."

In a great mood, I left to look for the candy shop that Danny had told me about. I hoped that the owner would be as kind as the others I had encountered.

I didn't need anyone to give me directions. Even from a few blocks away, I could clearly see the red-and-white rock candy sign. I walked in to a profusion of colors: there were sweets displayed everywhere—on stands and shelves, hanging from hooks on the walls. The store was divided in two. On one side were chocolates, on the other were candies, and, in the middle, a cashier's station. I rang the small bell next to the register, but no one came right away.

Supposing that I could help myself freely while waiting for the cashier, I grabbed a small plastic bag and gave free rein to my self-indulgence. I usually didn't buy any of this stuff to avoid fattening up or getting cavities. It wasn't that I worried much about the scale, but I wanted to fit comfortably in my pants. I was grabbing some strawberry lollipops when a high, squeaky voice made me jump and drop my bag of candy.

"Samantha Stratford!"

A woman had cried out as if she knew me. "Oh, I'm so sorry I scared you! I'm Ginger Wood. Danny told you about me, and he told me about you. I just came from his place. He lives below his restaurant."

During this whirl of words, she grabbed my hand, and by way of introduction, she shook it so hard my teeth rattled.

"Um, yeah, he told me about you. That's why I'm here."

Her energy and vigorous handshake contrasted with her physical appearance. With her short permed white hair, her round glasses, and her checkered skirt, she looked like an older woman. It was hard to figure out how old she was. Fifty? Sixty?

"What a charming man, that Danny! And his son, Matthew, is so handsome in addition to being so nice and smart. You saw him—what did you think? And what's your impression of our little town? And your grandfather, does he like it here? Because we've never had the pleasure of meeting him."

While she talked, I noticed a sign hanging on the wall that Ginger had won a prize for best chocolate maker, and more than once. She could have held the title for Miss Gossip too. I thought it would be prudent to watch what I said; I was quite sure she would go repeat everything to her friends as soon as I left her shop.

"Danny and his son gave me a very warm welcome, as did your bookseller, Angela Schumaker, which makes me think that as well as being beautiful, your town is very friendly."

"Oh, you went to Angela's? She's magnificent, isn't she? All the single men here and for miles around dream of marrying her. She's had a few proposals, but she declined them all. She only cares about books. As if that's how you have children. Bah!"

I had already planned on doing so, but that last bit of information made up my mind to go back to Angela's bookstore. We shared a passion for books, and I found her very pleasant, so maybe I could at last make a friend. Ginger was talking so fast I had to stop thinking about the bookstore and a new friend so I could focus on what she was saying.

". . . the people of Scarborough are all speculating about her future husband. Everyone thinks that she and Matthew will end up together. I say that neither one of them will take the plunge. They've always been friends, but for that to evolve into something more, one of them has to decide to do something about it, and they're both *equally* foolish."

I wondered if Ginger would finish her monologue at some point. I'd just arrived, and I was curious to get to know the town, not the love stories of its inhabitants. It was time to change the subject.

"I've never been in a shop like yours. Your sweets are all so original! As soon as I walked in, I wanted to eat everything."

The diversion had worked. Ginger smiled with delight.

"I've never imagined doing anything else. What I like best is when the children come here after school. They pick their favorite candies with hungry eyes and leave beaming with happiness."

"Where did you learn how to make candy and chocolate?"

"I took some classes in Paris with leading chocolatiers. But my mother and my grandmother taught me particular techniques and original recipes. They are family secrets handed down from generation to generation. My daughter, Valerie, will take my place when I'm no longer here."

"That's very touching."

"I'm very proud of what we've accomplished. I like to please people with sweets. So, tell me, what will you have?"

"I was thinking of adding some chocolates to all this."

She recommended some to add to my bag and even had me try a few right there in the shop.

"Thank you, Mrs. Wood."

"Come on, none of that. Here, everyone calls me Ginger."

"Thanks, Ginger. I think I have everything I could need. How much do I owe you?"

"Darling, you just got here, and what's more, it was my dear Danny who sent you. The least I can do is offer you some sweets."

"Oh, no, I couldn't—"

"I insist. Anyway, I still come out on top because when you've eaten all this, you'll come back right quick to buy more from me!"

"Well, when you put it that way, I accept. I've got to get back, so until next time. And thank you."

Ginger waved one last time as I closed the door behind me. It was time to return to the manor. I still had to write up the report on the events of the previous night, and I needed to do that before Phoenix got up at sunset, in an hour or so.

On the ride back, I turned on the radio and sang along, happy that my first exploration of Scarborough had been so satisfying.

\*\*\*

I made hot chocolate and selected a few lollipops to fuel my work. I had already familiarized myself with my boss's handwritten examples, so I knew how to present the reports and what to say, but I would be taking advantage of the computer to do it more quickly. I got down to it, printed everything when I was done, and left the dossier on the desk so that Phoenix could read it and then approve it (or not).

There was only a little time before sunset, so I used it to surf the web. I wanted to know more about these disappearances in Kerington County, particularly its biggest city. I'd unearthed a map of the area, and I was marking an *X* on all the places where the disappeared had last been seen or heard from. There were more in Kerington, which was logical because it had around 190,000 people, but the entire county had been affected. The majority of those reported had been young men and women in good health, both mentally and financially stable. The most horrible thing, besides the fact that some of these missing people were parents, was that the victim count was less than it should have been because not everyone who had been abducted was reported missing. As I searched the Internet and went through press clippings, I discovered that the rate of disappearances had started to increase four months earlier, peaking over the past two months. The detectives didn't understand the motive behind these abductions: there were no demands, no ransom requests. Nothing but unanswered questions.

I really hoped that Phoenix would catch whoever was involved in this, but that wouldn't be easy seeing how well planned and discreet the abductions appeared to be.

"For once I find you with your nose not stuck in a book. What are you doing?"

Phoenix's arrival out of nowhere made me jump. I inhaled the piece of lollipop that I had in my mouth and almost choked. While I was coughing and tearing up, Phoenix settled comfortably in the chair across from me.

My voice hoarse, I said, "You could make a little noise to warn me that you're there. You scare me every time. And I could've choked just then!"

"I did not put that lollipop in your mouth. From what I can see, you made the most of your outing to Scarborough."

He was dressed more casually than usual. In fact, he had unbuttoned the top of his shirt and swapped his suit pants for a pair of black jeans. I think he could have dressed in garbage bags and he would have still been elegant. In comparison, I looked rumpled and badly dressed. He really could make a girl jealous.

"I had a lovely afternoon if you must know. I visited the town and I met some people. And I didn't slip up once," I announced proudly.

"Our alibi worked with your new acquaintances?"

"Yes, and you were right, they're wondering what you look like. They call you the mysterious Peter. I told them you have trouble getting around, and I added that you have terrible social anxiety, and that convinced them. I wasn't lying, really."

"Elaborate on that, please."

His honeyed tone set off alarms, but I continued.

"You said that you have friends, but I've never seen you visit them or them visit you, and you're so addicted to work that it's hard for you to relax. Lastly, I'm right here and you never talk about yourself."

"Are you about to propose becoming my confidante?"

For a change, he raised his eyebrows, and for a change, that made my hackles rise.

"Listen, it's been eight weeks since I got here. We're going to spend a lot of time together in the future, unless I get myself stupidly killed, so maybe it would do you some good to talk to someone from time to time. Someone who knows your secret and who is not a vampire."

He said nothing, content to just stare.

"Oh, forget it."

A change of subject was necessary. "I was in the middle of mapping out the disappearances in the county. With Kiro's information, there's quite a bit to worry about. The whole region is affected, small towns and big cities alike."

"Show me."

He rose, came around the desk, and positioned himself behind me to look at my work. I didn't know why, but that proximity made me uneasy. Phoenix didn't breathe, but I thought I felt his breath on my neck. Before my heart started racing with discomfort, I decided it was time to retreat.

"Take my place. It'll be easier. After all, it's your desk," I declared as I got up.

He did. He was silent for several minutes as he studied the map. "For now, I see no place that could serve as a base. This is a real conundrum." Another silence, then he looked up at me. "This is good work. I appreciate your initiative. I suppose that your knowledge of computers helped, and not just to finalize the report I see there."

"Tell me what you think. If you've been doing everything by hand for years, I can see why you loathe paperwork so much. I tried to be as precise as possible even though I doubt that the episode with Puffy and Pox will interest them."

"I am satisfied to see that you are not mad at me."

He had understood well what I was alluding to.

"Why would it interest them? So what do we have scheduled for this evening?"

"We are going to visit an old acquaintance."

"Is this one of your friends you spoke of?"

I admit that I was curious to meet his friends.

"On the contrary, this vampire hates me, and if he could kill me, he would not hesitate for a single second."

I felt a metaphoric ice cube slide down my spine. I was going to meet another vampire, and it happened to be one of the ones who, unable to lash out at Phoenix directly, would cut me into pieces while imagining I was my boss. Gulp. I had to make an effort to swallow.

"Why does he hate you?"

I was afraid to know the answer.

"For the simple reason that if he allowed himself to drink blood from the source, as he likes, I would flay him alive without the slightest hesitation."

What was more shocking, imagining this vampire killing someone or hearing my boss calmly announce that he would rip the skin off him, quite literally?

"I see. I'll have to check that I have everything I need to settle a score with an angry vampire."

"I do not want to kill him, just ask him some questions."

"Do you think he knows something?"

"That is what we are going to find out. Go get ready."

***

We had to go to the suburbs east of Kerington to find this man. The route was going to be long: likely there was an hour and a half of silence on my horizon. I'd brought my antivampire defense gear, and I'd decided to appear strong and useful and not show my fear.

"What can you tell me about this vampire apart from the fact he likes to drink from the source?" I asked.

"His name is Bill Miller. At one time, they called him Thirsty Bill. I do not think I have to explain why."

I nodded to show I'd understood.

"He owns a strip club and has some ties with the local mafia. He is thirty years old. He has gathered together a small group of vampires who rejected the Great Change. They tried to create mayhem within the fragile equilibrium that was established in our community since we agreed to stop killing each other for humans. When his cohorts rebelled, and I tracked them down and eliminated them, he turned and ran. He let his men be killed in his place. That man is a coward as well as greedy and stupid."

Clearly Phoenix hated this Thirsty Bill.

"Why do you say he's stupid?"

"Instead of leaving the country and escaping the rules of the Great Change, he prefers to stay and dwell on his frustration."

I must have missed something.

"Leave the country? I thought the Great Change applied everywhere."

He waited a bit before answering.

"Only in sufficiently organized countries that could jeopardize the Secret."

"*What?* And you're only telling me this now?"

I was furious. It was completely ridiculous to have kept this crucial information from me. In eight weeks, he hadn't thought to brief me on this? He must have already realized his error, for he seemed embarrassed.

"Why didn't you tell me this earlier?" I asked.

"Learning about our method of consuming put you in a better disposition toward your work. I did not want to spoil that by telling you that the Great Change only applies in . . ."

He was looking for the right words. I facilitated the effort.

"In *rich* countries! But that's outrageous!"

He went ballistic.

"You see everything in black and white! It is not that simple! You will not find blood banks and hospitals on every street corner in the world! Why do you think that our laws are so strict about transforming humans? We must control our number. Furthermore, to impose the Great Change suddenly in every country in the world would mean war, guaranteed! The choice is simple. If a vampire does not want to obey the laws, he simply does not go to the countries where it applies."

Phoenix's logic was firm and unavoidable, but I wasn't satisfied yet.

"So what is this Thirsty Bill still doing here?"

"I told you that vampires like power and money. Some sacrifice their taste for murder to enjoy a life of luxury in a country that has the means. Others cannot manage that, and they exile themselves, generally to a war-torn country. Unfortunately, in the world right now, those are not too difficult to find."

"Humph. A strip club. You call that living in luxury?"

"I told you Bill is stupid . . . Unfortunately he is an idiot who has connections, and he is a bit of a pig too."

I didn't respond. And to think that a few weeks ago my biggest preoccupation was to keep myself as far as possible from Cruella Angermann, and now I was sitting in the passenger seat of a race car, talking to a five-hundred-year-old vampire about the way he and his fellow creatures preferred to drink human blood. I liked science fiction well enough, but I'd never dreamed that my life would resemble the films or books I bought. I turned my head to the passenger-side window and watched the landscape fly by, lost in my head.

"Samantha, what are you thinking about?"

"I was wondering if one day you'll trust me," I sighed.

He looked at me briefly, then turned his attention back to the road . . . without a word.

I chuckled a bit. "You see, I'm starting to know you. I'm not stupid enough to ask what you're thinking about right now."

I turned my attention again to the world outside.

\*\*\*

"Wake up, Samantha!"

I felt a hand press my shoulder gently. I opened my eyes. We were arriving in Kerington.

"You nodded off."

In fact, I was having trouble waking up even though I hadn't felt tired before. All it took was a bit of warmth and music to put me to sleep. Except that it didn't agree with me at all.

"Uh, I don't feel well."

I thought I might throw up.

"You're joking!" This was the first time I'd ever seen him worried. "I forbid you from vomiting in my car."

OK, he wasn't worried about me. I shot a dark look at him and then said, "Your concern is touching. Don't worry, I'll grit my teeth so as not to stain your pretty seats."

"Vulgarity does not suit you. Open the window and take a deep breath. It will clear your head."

He had barely finished his sentence when he opened my window for me. The cold wind rushed into the passenger side. It was a real boon. Forgetting all sense of elegance, I did what dogs do, putting my head out the window and enjoying the fresh air (fortunately, I didn't start barking). The nausea subsided and I sat back in my seat, facing a very grouchy Phoenix.

"You look like a ghost now. Why did you do that?" he reproached me.

Oh, he really could be a killjoy. He needed to relax. I made a face at him.

"What . . . what are you doing?" he said, startled, looking at me.

Instead of answering, I made things worse. I managed to touch the tip of my nose with my tongue, something only a few people could do (I was proud of that), and as a bonus, I ran my fingers through my hair to highlight the effect.

"Booooo!"

It worked. Phoenix looked at me like I'd lost my mind, and he must have been wondering if he would have to leave me at the closest psychiatric facility. I put an end to his torture, resuming a normal manner to explain my behavior.

"I'm showing you what being a ghost is like! You need to relax."

I knew after my third funny face that I had won, because he ended up setting free the laugh that he was trying to keep in. I'd finally succeeding in loosening him up, and this time on purpose. I'd have to mark this event on a calendar to remember it.

"You see how it can be good from time to time to not take yourself so seriously?"

He was still smiling when he announced that we'd arrived.

I turned my attention to our surroundings.

We were in lower Kerington. The eastern suburbs were known for bar brawls, illegal drugs, and confrontations with the police. There were prostitutes on every street corner, some negotiating their prices with potential clients. I pitied these women, pushed into that trade by life's vicissitudes.

My chauffeur turned a corner and parked in front of a strip club called Sexy Thong Show. A bit farther down the street, a group of young people with leather jackets and gleaming motorcycles were having a discussion so heated that it convinced passersby to hastily cross to the other side. We got out of the car.

"You don't think coming here in a luxury car is going to cause problems?" I said to Phoenix, indicating the aspiring bikers with my chin.

"On the contrary. In this neighborhood, those who get around in cars like this are usually big shots in the mafia. Minor bosses of this type are not senseless enough to try and steal from them. I will go around the back to enter discreetly. Wait here. When I call you, come in through the front and join me."

I nodded. I was ready.

"And them? What do I do if they come over to bug me?"

I'd already messed up two creeps, but I didn't see how I could manage against fifteen thugs.

Phoenix smiled. "Surprise me," he said, and then left.

I crossed my fingers that everything would be fine and got back into the car. After all, he hadn't told me to freeze outside while waiting for his call. A few minutes passed, and I wondered if my boss had gotten his hands on Thirsty Bill.

Then the thing I was dreading happened. One of the bikers turned and must have seen the car, and maybe even me in it. The others wasted no time doing the same, and together they moved in my direction in a concert of whistles and "Damn, look at those wheels!"

When they circled round the car to inspect it from every angle, I felt my legs begin to tremble. But panic was out of the question. I had a mission to complete, and in order to get those guys to leave me alone and to believe that I was truly working for a big mafia boss, I had to make an impression. I plucked up my courage and opened the car door.

When I stepped out, in elegant clothes and looking like the assistant to a rich dealer, the whistling increased.

I took on the haughtiest attitude I could muster and stared at each man, trying to see which one was the leader. I didn't need to look for long: he came forward on his own. With an attitude of infinite superiority, he ran his hand through his blond, curly hair and crossed his arms across his chest. He didn't look older than twenty-five.

"Hey, honey, your john shouldn't have left you here all alone. Want some company?"

Men obviously only have the one thing to say when they see a woman by herself. It was in these moments that jokes about where men's brains are located start to make sense.

"It seems my boss has overestimated you. He said even the simplest street thugs know the fate in store for them if they touch or scrape his car. But if you all want to find yourselves buried in the concrete foundation of the next building under construction in Kerington, you're welcome to continue enjoying yourselves."

I moved aside, indicating the car.

My little tirade seemed to perturb them. Without a doubt, they knew that the mafiosi use rather sophisticated, and slow, killing techniques. But the leader pulled himself together.

"Don't you worry, we're not gonna touch the car. But you, how about you come have a dance with me? I'm sure your boss won't see anything wrong with that."

He looked to his friends for masculine support.

"Ha!"

"Yeah, show her!"

I sighed with exasperation, which surprised the leader.

"Listen, I'm working right now, and I don't have time to play around with you. Now, I see that you're not going to leave me alone until you've gotten your daily dose of adrenaline, so I have a deal to propose."

"And what do you propose, doll face?"

"The first to make the other bite the dust wins. You win, you get a dance. I win, you leave me alone and you go back over to your corner and you keep an eye on the car in case another pack of imbeciles decides to come close. Oh, and I forgot—if I win, your friends will also honor our deal and you will use more polite language when addressing me."

He stared at me, mouth hanging open. He must not have expected that a well-dressed woman would propose a fistfight.

"This is the first time a girl has ever *asked* me to knock her around. If you want a spanking, I'm your man. And after, I'll make you dance like never before," he said, laughing, sure of his victory.

"We'll see about that. Ready?"

"Oh yeah! Come closer!"

I approached, closing the distance between us. Phoenix had taught me that it was best to be quick to prevent your opponent from anticipating and dodging your attack.

So without giving him any time to prepare, I grabbed his wrist and pulled. Surprised, he lost his balance, and I took advantage of it by twisting his arm against his back while making him pivot around. One kick behind the knees and he collapsed facedown on the ground.

Before he could get up, I drew my silver knife from my coat. I placed my knee against his back to keep him from moving, pulled his head back by his hair with one hand, and pressed my knife against his throat with the other.

The others looked like they were going to come help their leader, but I pressed the knife even harder against his skin while looking at the men surrounding me. I shouted, "A deal is a deal! Your gang doesn't have any honor?"

They didn't move away. That was complicating things, but then he said, "Get back! A deal is a deal."

He said that with difficulty, given his precarious position, but with enough force and authority to have an effect.

I waited for his goons to back off, then I slowly withdrew my knife and stood up, letting my opponent do the same.

When he was upright, he massaged his throat, staring all the while. I held his gaze, hoping he would keep his word.

"*Daaamn*, I did *not* see that coming."

"That was the point," I responded. "And now?"

He said nothing, but then offered me a sincere smile.

"Now we go and we leave you alone. We can be rather indelicate, miss, but our gang knows what honor is."

The others made noises of approval, nodding and saying, "Yeah, that's true."

He held out a hand.

"Don't worry about your car. We'll look after it. And if you and your boss ever need help in your work, keep Bobby the Eel and his Dark Angels in mind. We're always around."

"I'll think about it."

We shook hands, and he rejoined his group. I finally allowed myself to breathe. During that entire exchange, I had kept my legs from turning to jelly and my bladder from relieving itself in fear. What a relief that it was over.

Then my phone rang. I picked up, and without preamble, Phoenix said, "I'm waiting for you."

"I'm coming."

Better not make Phoenix wait. There had been muffled noises in the background. Thirsty Bill must not have been very cooperative.

I hurried to the club door, where the bouncer wanted to stop me. I must not look like the regular clientele. But I didn't have time to chat.

When the bouncer found himself on the ground after getting a well-placed kick to the knee, I heard admiring whistles from the sidewalk across the street where I had left my hoodlums. He must have refused entry to them as well, so this was a kind of revenge for them. For their further viewing pleasure, I turned back to my fans and made a deep bow before entering the establishment, escorted inside by their hollering.

Once inside, I stopped to get my bearings. The light was dim; the tables were close to each other; the stage where the girls danced was forlornly empty, and there wasn't a single patron. I saw a staircase at the back of the room. I headed that way.

As I walked up the steps, I took out my gun, which was loaded with silver bullets, and slid it into my pocket so I could reach it easily. I figured I was going in the right direction when a dancer ran down the stairs, afraid and bare breasted. There were sounds of a fight coming from above, and I sped up.

As soon as I arrived, I saw Phoenix being thrown to the other side of the room by a fat, bald, tattooed brute who came at me, but taking me for a simple human, he didn't hurry. I didn't wait for Thirsty Bill: I took out my gun and aimed.

"These are silver bullets, and even with your super speed, you can't dodge them. So I advise you to stay where you are."

Surprised, he stared at me like a predator, his eyes becoming luminescent; he revealed his two canines, as sharp as surgical scalpels.

"Miserable human! You don't know who you're dealing with. You can do nothing against me!"

"Me, no. But him, yes!" I said, jerking my head at my boss, who was coming up behind him.

Bill tried to defend himself, but it was already too late. Phoenix grabbed him and flattened him against the wall, twisting both his arms. A resounding crack reverberated, and Bill cried out in rage.

"You angel bastard! You broke my arm!"

Phoenix, despite the fight he'd just had, talked as if it were nothing. If it weren't for the gash on his arm, I wouldn't have known anything had happened. "Be quiet! It won't even show tomorrow. Stop fighting me and answer my questions, or I will have to cut your immortal existence quite short."

His voice had taken on that harsh and threatening timbre wrapped in velvet that terrified me. I could tell from Bill's face that I wasn't alone. He acquiesced, and Phoenix sat him down unceremoniously on one of the few chairs that hadn't been reduced to splinters. Then he signaled me with a nod. There was no need for explanation: I got out my notepad and sat on another chair, ready to transcribe everything.

Bill's hatred toward my boss was visible on his face. I wondered if he really was going to answer Phoenix's questions. At the same time, he didn't really have a choice.

"Good, let us begin. Why did you attack me when you saw me?"

"I thought they'd sent you to dispose of me. I'm quite attached to my skin."

"Interesting. Do you have something to hide, something to make you think that they took me away from my urgent business to come take care of you?"

"What do I know? Every chance they get, Talanus and Ysis think I'm getting in the way of their business, and they take advantage of their status to send their *lapdog* to settle the score under the cover of the law."

Yikes. I didn't know who Talanus and Ysis were, but I'd definitely understood that the lapdog was Phoenix. Bill should have thought twice before opening his mouth. We didn't have to wait long for Phoenix's reaction.

In the blink of an eye, my boss grabbed Bill's head and smashed it against the table. He pressed it down firmly as he said, "You are forgetting who you're talking to, Thirsty. I do not tolerate that kind of language and insinuation against me. Start that again and I shall rip your fangs out, is that clear?"

He let go of Bill and sat next to him. Bill had clearly lost his arrogance; if he could have, I was sure he would have begun sweating profusely. In an attempt to regain his composure, he fixed me with a look.

"And her, who's she?"

"My assistant. But that is not the point of our meeting. Do you know anything about all the disappearances in this county?"

The other man contented himself with looking scornfully at Phoenix.

"Your assistant? A human? You're getting weak, Phoenix! Worse, you're becoming *human!*" he sneered.

With that, my boss's eyes became luminescent, turning that particular color between blue and white, and his fangs came out, threatening.

"Do you want to see just how weak I am? Just give me a reason to rip you into pieces," he snarled.

Bill waited a beat, and then finally decided to cooperate.

"I've heard rumors about these disappearances, like everyone else. My dancers are afraid. But I have nothing to do with it."

"Are you sure, Bill? At one point, you would not have opposed a small massacre of humans. So what's a few kidnappings?"

"Don't worry, you've made your message clear," Bill spit out with hate. "I'm clean," he finished.

"Let's assume that you've done nothing. What do you know?"

"I don't know anything, I told you! I've come around. I'm clean. When are you and your bosses going to forget about me and leave me alone?"

"As long as you are in their territory, that will never happen. I have my eye on you. And if I ever hear that it is not just a rumor that you are mixed up in this, I shall come back. And when I do, I will be far less amiable than I am this evening. Am I understood?"

His glacial tone dissuaded any further comment. Even though that speech hadn't been addressed to me, Phoenix had still made my hair stand on end.

Phoenix stood up and motioned for me to pass in front of him before turning back to Bill.

"One last thing. If you decide to take this out on my assistant, directly or indirectly, I swear you will suffer so much and so long that you will beg me to kill you."

Despite the atrocities that that threat implied, it was very nice of Phoenix. Especially since, seeing the look on Bill's face, Bill clearly would have loved to settle the score with me as a consolation prize.

We headed for the exit, passing the bouncer who had come inside and who took care to clear out of our way. When we stepped outside, the gang was around the car, and they were clapping for us.

I felt Phoenix stiffen next to me, ready to attack. To stop a massacre, I put a hand on his arm to reassure him.

"Come on, there's no danger."

He glanced at me discreetly.

"That is the group of bikers from earlier," he said, as though I'd lost my mind.

"What? You told me to surprise you, didn't you? Come on."

I crossed the street, with Phoenix a step behind me.

The younger gang members scattered to let us through, and Bobby the Eel came over.

"Oh, miss, you've fulfilled a great dream of ours! That damn bouncer has deserved a swift knee to the ba . . . I mean, to his *parts*, for a long time."

His reconsideration of his language, a clause of our contract, made me smile. Bobby turned to my boss.

"Bobby the Eel, sir. Me and the guys from Dark Angels, we took care of your car. If one day you need an extra hand, think of us."

Phoenix sized him up, raising an eyebrow.

"We shall give you a call if there is ever need. Now, if you don't mind, excuse us . . ."

When we left, I saw in the rearview mirror that Bobby the Eel, proud as a peacock, was strutting about for his admiring fans.

In theory we were safe, but my boss waited until we'd left the red-light district to initiate conversation.

"You were more than useful tonight. I must admit that you even helped me."

"Are you talking about the moment where I found myself facing down Bill with my gun? I really thought I was going to die of fear!"

"You were perfect. I am proud of you."

In truth, I was also proud of myself. I'd made a group of biker thugs believe that I was a mafia goddess adept at kung fu, and I'd stopped a bloodthirsty vampire from fleeing and from tearing my head off at the same time. I was in an excellent mood!

"What if we were to celebrate this?" I proposed.

"Pardon?"

"You may have forgotten what it's like to feel hungry for food, but I haven't. At this hour, we should be able to find a restaurant that's open. We can discuss our new information and our impressions in some tranquil setting. What do you say?"

"Hm . . . Why not? You certainly deserve it."

Comfortably settled into my heated seat, I let Phoenix choose the radio station. We left the eastern neighborhoods behind, looking for a place to eat.

# CHAPTER SEVEN

## *Trust*

We ended up at a small pizzeria run by eager Italians. There were only a few other people there, and the waitress offered us a romantic-looking alcove booth. She looked at us tenderly, as though we were newlyweds on our honeymoon.

"Oh, but we're not . . . ," I started to say, embarrassed.

But Phoenix interrupted me.

"That will be perfect, thank you."

The waitress left us shortly after with my order, disappointed that my "husband" wasn't hungry. As for me, it would be a miracle if my stomach didn't start banging out Beethoven's Ninth Symphony in major growls.

"These booths are quite intimate. It will make it easier to talk."

"But that waitress thinks we're a couple!"

"So what? If it makes her happy, we can play along."

I knew I immediately turned beet red with embarrassment. The waitress had taken the menu with her, so I couldn't even hide behind it.

My boss laughed.

"Stop blushing like that. I will not go that far. After five hundred years, I think I have learned my etiquette."

Point made. I blushed even more, but this time out of shame.

"You really have a knack for making me uncomfortable."

"Come now, you are embarrassed because a waitress thinks we are newlyweds when just a while ago, I do not know how, you took to task an entire group of unaccommodating leather-jacketed gang members! Let's not even mention the angry vampire. What an upside-down world."

"I've told you from the beginning that you shouldn't try to understand my logic."

"That is exactly what I am discovering."

He asked me to tell him how I'd managed to gain the respect of Bobby the Eel and his gang. As my tale unfolded, his face expressed more and more incredulity, with a hint of pride.

"You are full of resources, Samantha. I would have liked to see you at work."

"Bah! You were too busy with Bill . . . Actually, I'm not a specialist on behavior, even less so when it's about decoding vampires, but I think he lied. He knows something."

"Of course he knows something."

"So why did you let him go?"

"I want him to think that I do not suspect him. That way, he will lead me straight to the answers that I want. Not right away, though. He is going to be prudent until he feels confident again. Soon."

"Maybe he'll lead you to the Kentwood vampires, then. How did you come across them in the first place?"

"I had heard rumors that several disappearances took place in a short amount of time. I went to Kentwood to take a look around, and as I was leaving the apartment of one of the victims, I ran into one of the two men you encountered. Now you must understand that vampires passing through the area must make themselves known. That is the law.

Those who do not comply have something to hide. It was obvious to me that this was the case for those two because when they saw me, they recognized me and attacked me right away. I am not easy to kill, so they finally gave up and tried to run away, but I was able to trap them in the alley where we met. You know the rest."

I didn't have time to respond because the waitress brought my plate then. That evening had made me hungry, and I salivated at the sight of my calzone, which I promptly began to devour. At the first bite, I relaxed in my seat and said, "Yum, that's good."

My dining companion watched me.

"You surprise me, Samantha. You are eating heartily now, but barely an hour ago, you were staring death in the eye."

"Do forgive me, Phoenix, but I've learned that if I stop eating when something shocks me and I'm in front of you, I'll end up in the cemetery pretty quick."

He said nothing. I drank my glass of wine before asking the burning question that was on my mind.

"Who are Talanus and Ysis?"

He looked at me with exasperation. I knew they were important, so I burned with curiosity.

"They are my employers and the leaders of our community," he said in a solemn voice.

"You mean that they're the king and queen of the vampires?" I said, impressed.

"No. They lead a sector that includes the counties of Kerington, Springfield, and others. Each sector leader is assisted by an angel. Together, their mission is to ensure the strict application of vampire law. They are watched over by people even more important, and it is better that you know nothing about them. If sector leaders are ever deemed incompetent, they are replaced. Everything they do is to control our population and stop humans from discovering us. Normally, there is only one sector leader, but Talanus and Ysis have worked together for centuries without any problems."

"They must be exceptional. How old are they?"

"Talanus was a general in the age of Augustus. And Ysis was a companion of Cleopatra's. They met shortly before Cleopatra's death, incidentally."

I almost choked again, but this time on a piece of calzone. Those two vampires were more than two thousand years old! And this Ysis had rubbed elbows with Cleopatra! Surely historians would kill to talk with her.

"That's incredible! Why do they reign together? You told me that you all guard your independence jealously."

"Except when love comes into consideration." He made a face. "They have loved each other for two thousand years, and despite that weakness, their territory is one of the calmest. Strange."

That idea about love making people weak really got on my nerves.

"Oh, for pity's sake! Worrying about someone other than yourself is never a sign of weakness. Haven't you ever felt something for a woman in five hundred years of existing? Not even when you were human?"

"I say that even without being a vampire, I was never destined for love. I have had the pleasure of female company, both human and vampire, but I have never felt love. And I do not wish for it either."

I frowned. I didn't know that humans and vampires were compatible, especially considering how vampires saw us. It seemed I was mistaken. In any case, I doubted that human women would have consented when they learned about the true nature of their partner. That was troubling enough.

"I find your view of love absolutely ridiculous. It's a marvelous feeling that makes a person stronger."

Phoenix fixed me with his X-ray stare. I should have kept quiet.

"You're speaking from experience, I suppose."

There it was. I had fallen into my own trap, and I would only get out of it by exposing myself. I couldn't lie, because Phoenix would know immediately. I felt a wildfire ravaging my cheeks while I racked my brains for an answer.

"Uh, well, I'm speaking . . . generally . . . um, I . . ." Quick, find something to say before he figures out the truth!

"You're being quite indiscreet." I tried to look offended, but it was certainly only panic that my boss read on my face.

I was horrified as, slowly, his sardonic smile started to appear. He'd understood.

"You have never loved a man, in all senses of the word. So why should I listen to your lessons in sentimental education?"

That rebuke was quite the cold reality shower, and its coldness should be written down in annals. I had to answer him, if only just to have the last word.

"I may have never had the chance to know love, but at least, unlike you, I believe in it. I'm not one of those romantic dreamers who waits around for Prince Charming to appear, but it doesn't seem stupid to hope to *matter* to someone, at least as much as that someone matters for you. That's life after all."

His smile had disappeared. He didn't seem to be mocking me anymore.

"Except that, in my case, I am dead."

His bitterness was palpable, just like mine.

"And I'm still a virgin at almost thirty. We're both love's rejects. *You*, because you don't want love. *Me*, because love doesn't want me. What a great team we make!"

He gave me a displeased look but said nothing. The ambiance of our dinner had cooled off a bit, and thus it was in silence that I ate my dessert. When we left the pizzeria, Phoenix offered me his arm, a gesture of supreme gallantry that I accepted gladly.

We were walking toward the car when he asked, "Why do you think you are a reject of love?"

My employer was a specialist in abrupt and indiscreet questions.

"It's simple. Getting to this age and never being engaged is quite pathetic. Because I'm so boring-looking, I can say that I'll end up an old maid, no doubt, or, like Bridget Jones says, devoured by German shepherds. Or by a vampire."

"You are very severe with yourself."

"I'm just making an observation about my failures with men. They're not interested in me. I'm not to their liking."

"You are a beautiful woman. They do not notice you because you have no confidence."

Did he just say that I was beautiful?

"Your closed-off attitude makes you seem unremarkable and uninteresting. You should work on that."

I expected that the compliment would be followed by a criticism. After all, it was the first time a man other than my father had told me that I was beautiful. Even though it was Phoenix and he had no feelings for me, I was happy about it because it was an objective assessment.

"What can I do, in your opinion?"

"What you did with that gang before. You impressed them with your strength and charisma."

Hm . . . that remained to be seen. We reached the car. I was relieved, for now we could change the subject; discussing my love life with my boss was disconcerting, and I was exhausted.

"Would it bother you if I get in back? I'm so tired."

"As long as you are not sick, I am fine with it."

I slept all the way through our return trip and, as I realized when I woke up in my own bed, through Phoenix carrying me to my room.

This strange man, this bloodthirsty vampire capable of flaying one of his own kind without any qualms, could be attentive and behave like a true gentleman with me. My feelings toward him these past eight weeks had evolved. The terror that he inspired at the beginning had given way to curiosity and respect.

I was very grateful to him for the transformation he had inspired in me. I'd never felt so confident in the future and in my own abilities. Without knowing it, Phoenix was pushing me to become the woman I had secretly wished to be before: strong, determined, and appealing. He hadn't just provided me with pretty clothes and lessons in combat. He'd made me realize the person I could be and guided me to her every day.

He knew everything about me, and in return I truly hoped that one day, he would let his guard down and decide to actually trust me.

*** 

The next three weeks passed by so quickly that I didn't even notice. To start, I was making it a point of honor to train at least an hour per day in combat and especially shooting. I was also drafting reports about my nocturnal outings with my boss. We weren't wasting any time. Nearly every night, we trained after dinner and then left around eleven o'clock for Kerington or its environs.

For hours, we patrolled in the industrial zone, looking for abnormal activity. Phoenix was persuaded that what was happening there was connected to the kidnappings. The problem was that the place was enormous and the kidnappers could be anywhere. We thought if Thirsty Bill had warned them that the sector's angel was on their trail, they must be laying low, at least for now. Phoenix was incensed that they had escaped him.

During the day, I checked to see if there had been any new disappearances, and I made a note of them on my map. I erased the names of the ones who were later found alive. I was taking this whole business to heart, sincerely wanting to help stop these criminals. It helped that I'd been able to break into the police database . . . I was up to date on everything they knew too.

All this work demanded a fair bit of my time and energy.

I was starting to get used to my nocturnal routine, but beyond a certain hour, I still found it hard to stay awake. Thus on our return trips Phoenix let me sleep in the back of the car. Several times I would wake up the next day, still dressed, under my blankets. My boss, not wanting to wake me, always carried me to my room.

As it happens, I found that he was smiling more. He even laughed at some of my jokes, but more often, he maintained a mask of impenetrability, striking and mysterious.

Though once, after another of our *Stargate SG-1* marathons, we launched into a heated debate to determine which character in the show was the most charismatic.

"Jack is a man of action who knows how to make the right decision in difficult moments. He has the very soul of a leader," he argued.

"And he would have been imprisoned or worse dozens of times if the talents of the linguist and negotiator Daniel weren't so impressive. And he's incredibly sexy."

"You're mixing up charisma and sex appeal."

"Admit that it tips the balance in his favor."

We didn't come to an agreement, but it was a pleasant evening. I felt like I was talking with a friend.

It was in those moments that I told myself that Phoenix's opinion on how far he could trust humans, and me in particular, might evolve in the right direction. That was why I never told him that I knew where he kept his bags of A+ blood that he liked so much. I was waiting for him to tell me himself.

As if that would happen! I wasn't an idiot. Even if I hoped for it, I knew that he would never consider me a friend, just a replaceable employee at the most. Nevertheless, after recent events, I thought I had at least won his respect.

In sum, we were working hard, and I needed to put everything into perspective.

I often found myself in downtown Scarborough in the afternoon. Phoenix was right to say that the people there weren't very curious. After a week, my presence didn't make them do double takes anymore. I worried every time I saw Ginger Wood since I knew that in less than an hour or two, everyone would know that I was there, but the excitement about me quickly subsided. I seemed to have become one of their own.

I went to the bookshop frequently, stunned by the richness and beauty of the books that were sold there. Angela was thrilled to share her passion with someone, and it wasn't long before we became friends. I appreciated that she didn't pester me about my pseudo-grandfather.

I'd also developed relationships with Matthew and Danny Robertson. Every time he saw me, Danny asked when I was going to eat at his restaurant again. I always laughed, saying I would like to but that I got up way too late for lunch, which was strictly speaking the truth. With all the searches in Kerington's warehouses, I hadn't managed to get out of bed before two o'clock in the afternoon. And I couldn't have dinner at Danny's since Phoenix needed me at work in the evening.

Matthew had proposed a tour of some places around town that were worth seeing. I'd gladly accepted his invitation, but with my complicated schedule, we hadn't had enough time for it yet. During my quick trips to town, when I wasn't with Angela, I passed the time discussing everything and nothing with Matthew, that is, when he gave himself some time off, buried as he was in the accounts for his father's restaurant. Apparently, Danny was an excellent chef but too flighty to take care of the paperwork. That reminded me of Phoenix, of course.

Matthew and his adoptive father were true partners, despite their differences. Matthew was calm and discreet; Danny was a real whirlwind. I cringed when, one day while I was passing his restaurant, Danny came out with his apron slung over his shoulder, caught up with me, kneeled down in front of me, and began singing a serenade, the refrain of which was "Come back to eat at Danny's, beautiful lady!"

He only stopped when I promised to come in the following week. In any case, that night Phoenix was finally going to give me my first paycheck, and I was curious to know at what price he valued my monthly work.

As a librarian, no one could have said that I was rolling in money, but I got by rather well. Returning to the manor that evening, there's no question I was excited: I was finally going to have my own money to spend again, money I had earned.

Of course, at the beginning it amused me to make my boss pay for everything, but I wasn't raised like that. My parents had passed down a strict work ethic, and I didn't see myself as anything less than financially independent. Even if I were paid only as much as I had been as the high school librarian, I would be satisfied.

When Phoenix joined me in the kitchen, I couldn't stop myself from looking to see if he had an envelope in his hand. He didn't, and I didn't quite know how to broach the subject.

"Do you realize that we're already at the end of March? That means we've known each other for three months!" I exclaimed, all smiles.

Phoenix looked up from his newspaper.

"OK, what do you want?"

Caught unawares by such brusque perception, I could only stammer, "Uh, well . . . me? I . . . well . . ."

He returned to his reading. "When you know what it is, say it so I can understand you."

Humph. "I would like to be paid! Three months' pay!"

He slowly put down the paper. Gulp.

"We have already discussed your pay for the previous months. In most industries, people are only paid for real working time. Last I heard, students do not get paid. Therefore, you did not really start your job until you met Kiro."

That was too much. He had kidnapped me and imposed Green Beret–level combat training on me, and he compared that difficult time to classes that a student takes peacefully seated in a university lecture hall.

"What a con! I should've suspected that you would do something like this. Only you could insinuate that my first weeks here were a vacation at your expense!"

"I am not insinuating anything."

What arrogance! Not knowing what more to say, I got up from the table and went to soothe my nerves by washing my dishes.

With a sidelong glance, I watched as he finished with his reading, folded up his paper, and slipped it under his arm before heading toward the exit. While I was cursing him silently, I jerked in surprise when a hand holding an envelope appeared above my head. I turned around and saw my boss staring at me with his irritating sardonic smile.

I took the envelope he was holding out to me, or rather I grabbed it from him.

"What is this?" I said unpleasantly, opening the envelope.

There were two bank account statements. One was in the name of Samantha Stratford, the other Samantha Jones. I almost fainted when I saw the two account balances. I looked up, but Phoenix wasn't there. On each statement was double the amount of my librarian salary: I was making four times as much as before. Incredible.

I started jumping up and down in place, clapping my hands. Then I remembered my exclamations from earlier and my smile tensed up.

I had some apologies to make the next day.

*** 

A few days later, I was finally able to accept Matthew's offer for a tour. Phoenix had told me the evening before that he didn't need me, so I gave myself an entire day of relaxation.

I started by inviting Angela to eat at Danny's with me; he was delighted to see that his serenade had worked. Angela and I had so much in common, and we got along marvelously. Unlike Phoenix, she had loved the Twilight saga, and we talked about it a lot that day. Angela admitted that even if she was surrounded by the great classics of literature, all of which she had read, she also devoured any and all books that spoke of legends, especially vampires. She was even more fascinated by the different reactions people had to these mythical figures. She genuinely pitied those who, in the absence of historical context, venerated vampires. As for me, knowing the truth, I found them all completely crazy.

We were still on this topic when Matthew arrived. The three of us took up the conversation again, but after a while, Angela said she needed to go back to her bookshop. Before she left, she asked about Matthew's tour, and he gave her a list of the places he wanted to take me. I thought again about what Ginger had said about an inevitable romantic relationship between my two friends. I didn't want to stir up trouble between them, even if I was doing it unintentionally. But Angela's reaction calmed my fears. She added another place to my devoted admirer's list.

Shortly after she left, Matthew and I headed out. During our stroll, Matthew told me the town's history. It had been founded at the beginning of the twentieth century following the establishment of a sawmill that took advantage of the vast surrounding forests. The workers flooded in, and small businesses opened up, and Scarborough was born. Although I had already read Ellen McCoy's book, I listened to him attentively. However, despite his characteristic discretion, he wanted to know more about me.

"Tell me about your grandfather. You keep very quiet about him."

Oh boy. When anyone asked me questions about Peter Stratford, I always managed to dodge them or keep my answers perfunctory. I would have to do more than that to be believable to Matthew.

"What do you want to know?"

"Well, I don't know. Is he nice to you, for instance? Seeing as how you're his live-in nurse."

I didn't expect such concern. I was touched by Matthew's kindness and curiosity.

"Well, I think of him as a polar bear. He can be kind, but he can also be as glacial as an Antarctic breeze." That description was rather faithful, even if I was not going to go so far as to say Phoenix was a teddy bear. That would be a grievous error. "But he is endearing and always concerned for my well-being, even if he doesn't show it."

I realized that I'd perfectly summed up my boss. After all, if he wasn't concerned about me, he would have abandoned me on the backseat of his car in his unheated garage at least once.

"Do you miss your parents?" Matthew asked, very seriously.

It seemed that we'd started fifteen minutes of truth-telling. Why not?

"I think about them every day, but the pain has dulled some with time." I looked at him surreptitiously; he seemed lost in thought. "And your birth parents? Do you miss them?" I ventured.

"Danny never hid the fact that I'm adopted. When I was eighteen and I wanted to know more about my origins, he helped me look for my parents. But as had been the case when he looked for them right after he found me, we didn't discover anything. That was hard to accept at first, but I realized that I couldn't have asked for a better father than Danny Robertson. I have a good life now, but I must admit that sometimes I think about them. Maybe because you're an orphan too, I feel strangely close to you."

I wasn't expecting that at all. Close? To what point? How should I respond? Help! I had to find some way to wriggle out of this to clarify things.

"Wherever I go in this town, people tell me that the person you're closest to is Angela. That makes sense since you've known her forever . . . and me . . ."

I didn't even time to finish my sentence.

"It's not the same. I know that everyone sees Angela and I married one day, but she's only a friend. Listen, I don't want to make you uncomfortable, but I have different feelings for you than the ones I have for Angela."

I didn't know what to say. I'd never considered Matthew that way. I was sixteen the last time I'd been interested in a boy! Romantic relationships were a real mystery to me, and I admit that until then, my inconspicuousness had suited me just fine because it protected me from the pain of being rejected.

"You're not saying anything," he observed.

He came closer to me. Dangerously close.

"I wasn't expecting that. We hardly know each other," I answered, taking a step back. "You're going too fast."

I might have sounded harsh, but I was being sincere. He had succeeded in ruining my day. I only had one desire: to go back to the manor and not think about any of this.

"I'm sorry. I didn't mean to offend you. Even if I'm more discreet than my father, I always say what I feel. But in this case, I think I've completely blundered."

You could say that. I didn't doubt that Matthew was the type to occasionally put his foot in his mouth.

"I forgive you, but give us some time to get to know each other before bringing this up again," I said, my smile tense.

It wasn't very late, but I said I needed to get back to town, and we returned in an embarrassed silence. For the first time, I was happy to see the Audi. There was a moment of hesitation, and then Matthew sighed.

Before he said whatever he wanted to say, I launched in, "Well, until next time!" I gave him a little smile, which he returned.

"Later."

When I started the car and drove off in the direction of the manor, I exhaled at length. I was disturbed; my day, which had started off so well, had ended in a declaration unexpected in my sentimental desert, and no one could say that my reaction had been the best.

As I got within sight of the manor, I decided that I couldn't do anything about it except to give myself some time to see if I also felt something for Matthew Robertson. In any case, not for love or money would I let my evening be ruined too. I had some peace, quiet, and idleness on the horizon, and no one could take that away from me.

\*\*\*

Though I expected Phoenix to emerge at sunset, he didn't, so I figured he had left to take care of business as soon as he had woken up. I kept my cell phone on hand in case he needed me, but I doubted he'd call.

I wanted to cook, and I pampered myself with a fabulous meal: osso buco with tagliatelle, a glass of wine, and a slice of homemade lemon pie. Delicious.

After eating, I went into the parlor and channel surfed until I found a film that interested me. I settled comfortably into the big sofa; I pulled a plaid blanket over my legs, and it kept me agreeably warm. The film was good, but then I felt myself drifting off during the news.

A noise woke me up. I looked at the clock: two o'clock in the morning. I yawned widely as I got up to turn off the television. I couldn't wait to get into my soft bed.

Then I heard that noise again . . . it was strange, as if someone were scraping the wall. It was coming from the hallway, and I went to take a look.

Turning my head toward the entryway, I jumped back and let out a cry of fright. When my brain started working again, I realized that the dark mass collapsed against the wall, trying to move, was my employer.

"My God! Phoenix!" I exclaimed, noticing he was injured.

I rushed toward him and positioned myself so he could lean on me. Despite his weight, I succeeded in getting him to the parlor, where he slumped onto the sofa. I could then see the extent of his injuries. His handsome suit was shredded, his shirt was covered in blood (was it only his own?), and his face . . . He'd been beaten up, I was sure of it. He seemed so weak, hardly even conscious.

"Phoenix! Tell me what to do! How can I help you?"

I thought for a moment that he'd fainted, but he managed to say, weakly, "Bl . . . Blood."

I didn't wait for any other orders. I ran out of the parlor to the kitchen to find the bags of blood in the fridge. My heart was pounding harder than ever, and it wasn't because of my task. I was really worried about Phoenix. I'd never seen him show the least weakness, but here he was clearly in a very bad way. I had to help him.

After I activated the mechanism, I grabbed several bags at random and turned back without taking the time to heat them up. The whole operation hadn't taken me more than a minute, but it felt like I was moving in slow motion. Upon returning, I almost fell to the ground, slipping on the tiles. Finally, I sat down on the edge of the sofa. Phoenix wasn't moving anymore.

With my fingertips, I pushed him to wake him up, but nothing happened. I took him by the shoulders and shook him sharply.

"Wake up! I have blood! Wake up!" I shouted.

With no response from Phoenix, I decided to pour the contents of the pouch directly into his mouth, making sure he swallowed it. It was a success with the first one. I thought that the drink was taking effect, so I opened a second. When I tried to pour it into his mouth, the situation got out of control.

Vampires are predators that feed on human blood. Put a vampire in a situation of intense thirst, shake a pouch of his favorite blood under his nose, and you'll not be disappointed by the result. Especially if the hand holding the pouch is filled with blood of the same type . . .

When I saw my boss's eyelids open, I had a moment of joy that was too quickly deflated by the metallic, luminescent color of his eyes, announcing misfortune for the human being who stupidly found herself in the same room as the creature to whom those eyes belonged.

I'd barely realized the precariousness of my situation when things took a downturn. A steel grip closed over my right arm; at the same time, I heard a bestial growl, and I felt something like two knife blades sink into my flesh. I emitted a cry of pain and fell back in shock.

My attacker had followed the movement, and I found myself once again pressed against the floor, Phoenix above me, just like that horrible episode in the office but worse because this time, he had truly stuck his fangs in my forearm. The pain was dreadful, but I had to act before he drained me dry.

I tried to hit him, but without success. I tried to shake my arm free, but that only managed to make the pain worse, causing me to cry out again. His fangs were so firmly planted in my arm that moving would only tear up my already damaged flesh. What's more, fighting galvanized him. I didn't know what to do.

I had to think of something, for I knew that soon the hemorrhage he was subjecting me to would invariably lead to a loss of consciousness and, eventually, my death.

"Phoenix, please! It's me, Samantha! You're going to kill me, and you said you don't want to kill innocents anymore."

No reaction. Just an awful sucking sound that made me want to vomit.

"Phoenix! Stop! Please!"

Nothing. How many times had humans begged to be spared at the moment when Phoenix was sucking the life out of them? He must have heard this refrain thousands of times. What's the point . . . a few minutes passed . . .

What a strange sensation, feeling my strength leave, feeling death approach . . . I was light, nothing was important anymore. I was going to leave for good, and I welcomed my fate without any anger. One thing pained me: the guilt that my boss would feel once he realized what he'd done. Not having killed me—I wasn't naive—but letting himself be controlled by his thirst. I wasn't mad at him, and he had to know that.

Gently, I placed my other hand on his face and murmured his name.

"Phoenix."

He stopped drinking and looked at me. His eyes still shone, and his mouth, fangs out, was stained with my blood. As my last bit of strength was leaving me, I gave him a feeble smile with which I projected all the power of my forgiveness. And then there was a black hole . . .

*** 

I was slowly gaining consciousness, I felt it. The preceding events came back to the surface. I recognized Phoenix for the predator he was, attacking me: his eyes, his fangs, my blood in his mouth, that sickening sucking noise. I remembered the pain I'd felt. Next to this, being used as a cannonball was comparable to a mosquito bite. I remembered the feeling of powerlessness I had felt as my life escaped from me, then the calm that had taken over. Strange. To untangle all that, there was only one solution.

I opened my eyes.

I was indeed in my room, in my bed. There was a difference between this and the other times I'd woken up here, however. I had an IV in one arm, and on the other, the one that had provided Phoenix with his blue-plate special, was an enormous bandage. I was in a nightgown, and to my great relief, it covered me and wasn't transparent.

"I know that you are modest, but I was obliged to change your clothes."

I quickly lifted my head. Phoenix was seated in the same armchair he'd sat in when I first arrived here. His clothes were impeccable. The whole scene provoked a touch of déjà vu, but this time I wasn't afraid.

"Why are you so far away?" I asked.

He stared at me, his face impenetrable.

"After what happened, I did not want to scare you when you woke up."

I sighed. "Nonsense. Your reasoning is off. Waking up is a relief. It means that you didn't finish what you started. By the way, how are you?"

"You are asking me how I'm doing when I almost killed you to assure my own survival? Who is talking nonsense now?"

I wasn't in the mood for wordplay. "What do you want me to say? That I'm mad at you? That I hate you? Go ahead and think that if it makes you feel better, but I won't tell you something I'm not thinking or feeling. You weren't yourself. I get that you're a vampire. You're a predator and all that. But I know that what happened in the parlor is not something you wanted."

He stood up and started pacing. "You don't understand. I wanted you, Samantha. I wanted to drink your blood, and that desire totally overwhelmed me! When I bit you, I completely lost control. I could not stop."

What was bothering him more? That he bit me or that he'd lost control of himself?

"What stopped you?" I asked, curious.

He stopped pacing. "You."

"Me? But I couldn't do anything . . ."

He shook his head. "You stopped fighting and . . . what you said . . . finally . . ." It was his turn to stammer. "Why did you look at me like that?"

It seemed like he was angry with me.

"What are you talking about? I don't understand any of this."

"Your eyes. They were telling me something, something no one had ever granted me . . ."

"Forgiveness?"

"That completely unsettled me. Suddenly I could control myself again. When I realized what I had done . . . I infused you and I had to make you drink my blood to heal the wound on your arm."

I wouldn't know what he'd felt. Too bad. But what did he say? He'd made me drink his blood? I blanched.

"Don't act disgusted. Your arm was in a sorry state."

"If you say so. But I find it revolting."

We stared daggers at each other. Then I asked, "Um . . . is it morning now or evening?"

"Afternoon, actually."

It was my turn to be surprised. "But you should be sleeping."

"And who else could check to see that your condition was stable?" he said sarcastically.

With that information, I plucked up my courage and said, "You . . . you were worried about me?"

I asked the question, but I had no idea how I would react to his answer. Would I be disappointed if he told me he hadn't been?

I didn't need to put him to the test.

He came closer and removed the IV from my arm. "I think that will do. I must sleep. We shall talk about this later."

He left the room without another word.

***

Later that evening, Phoenix joined me in the kitchen as usual except this time he opened the fridge and retrieved a bag of A+ without hiding what he was doing. Seeing my reaction, he shrugged his shoulders.

"I do not see why I should hide this given that you have already discovered my pantry. Fortunately, of course, or else I would no longer be here."

"Is that your way of thanking me?"

"It is my way of saying don't forget to close the fridge door from now on."

Har-har.

"I'll think of that the next time you drag yourself in here after taking a beating," I said scornfully, my arms crossed.

He smiled while pouring the blood into a glass. He was going to have to say something by way of explanation.

"What happened to you?"

"I made a mistake."

I didn't know he was even capable of questioning his own judgment. Interesting.

"What mistake?"

"That vampire who wanted to kill you in Kentwood, I did not take his threats seriously. He told me to watch my back."

"But how did he find you? You travel all the time."

"He and his henchmen came across me near where my employers live. Their address is not so secret . . . In any case, I am surprised they waited so long."

"Maybe that's because we were on the right track, searching Kerington's industrial areas. They wanted to warn you off."

He looked at me as though I had just come out of a psych ward.

"One of them had a silver ax! It was more than a warning."

"Oh . . . at least they didn't kill you. How many were there?"

"Six, I think. But I didn't see the faces on the other five. They were wearing hoods."

"Six? Well, I'm glad I'm on your side."

"Thanks. Before everything got out of hand, how was your relaxing day off?"

Super. This was the perfect moment to want to make small talk, and on *that* particular subject. I must have made a funny face, because I was treated to a sardonic pout and a new sarcastic remark.

"Gauging from your expression, it would seem that the company of the living is not all that you wished for. You are not too disappointed, I hope."

"That's not it at all. The people in Scarborough are charming, and I've made friends."

"Very good. So what are you complaining about? This is what you wanted, isn't it?"

It was a delicate subject. I didn't want to talk about it with Phoenix, but the intensity of his expression made it clear he was expecting an answer from me. He should have been a detective. With him, there'd be no mistakes: seeing his eyes would make criminals hurry to confess to their crimes, and much more.

"I went to take a walk with someone. His name is Matthew. I met him at Danny Robertson's restaurant. He's Danny's son. We've known each other for a few weeks, and I was happy to develop friendships with him and his friend Angela. And then he told me that he's attracted to me. There! Happy?"

I was on the defensive because I could never know with Phoenix if he was going to be understanding or sarcastic. He raised an eyebrow—a bad sign.

"In the end, I think that your love stories are none of my business."

It was like the air had suddenly cooled at the sound of his voice.

"But you're the one asking me so many questions! You don't know what you want."

He turned around and came closer.

"And you, Samantha? Do you know what you want when it comes to this Matthew?"

"Of course I don't know what I want. My life has always been a romantic desert. But I'm not going to throw myself into the arms of the first person who comes along just because he finds me attractive. I have a bit more of a brain than that."

"Thrilled to hear you say it. Love is a distraction that risks making you lose focus in your work."

"I said that I was going to take time to get to know him, not that I'm going to be a nun. You're not going to forbid me from falling in love."

Dreadful. Even if I'd never been confronted by love, I still hoped to find it one day.

"Oh, humans and love," he growled, rolling his eyes to the ceiling.

He disappeared for a moment, then returned to the kitchen, dressed to go out.

"You didn't tell me we were going out tonight. Wait, I'll go get ready," I launched in, heading to the door.

He grabbed me by the arm and made me take a step back.

"I'm going, you're staying."

"Why?"

"An attack on an angel is not insignificant. I have to make my report in person to Talanus and Ysis."

"Why aren't you taking me with you?"

"Please understand. There's a rumor already circulating that a human woman is following me around in my travels. I prefer not pointing you out. You never know. And no human has ever been authorized to enter my employers' home."

"Even the plumber?" I said sarcastically.

"Humans are not allowed. Talanus and Ysis are the highest authorities in our region, and no one can approach them like that."

"OK, OK, but be careful."

"If I were not careful, I would have reached hell several centuries ago. And you—you must not do anything stupid while I am gone."

"Never fear. I'll lock the door."

He left, and I had the evening to recover from the previous night.

\*\*\*

Phoenix's meeting with Talanus and Ysis came to nothing, so my boss and I resumed our usual routine. I'd quickly recovered from my arm wound, and I asked Phoenix to start my combat training again. For some time he'd been teaching me to fight with knives and swords, but I was clearly less at ease with blades than with firearms.

One evening, Phoenix ordered me to practice avoidance and attack maneuvers. I had to avoid wooden knives he threw at me and send my own blades at the targets he pointed out. That exercise turned sour when instead of hitting my targets, my knives were planted in my employer's stomach. My blood froze in my veins.

"Oh my God!" I ran to him.

He rewarded me with a look of exasperation and a heavy sigh, and then he pulled the knives out as if they were nothing, even though they would have killed him if he'd been human.

"Luckily this is steel. How many times have I told you to aim before you throw."

"I'm sorry! Are you hurt?"

In lieu of response, he lifted his T-shirt a little. There, where he should have had an open, bloody wound, there was just perfect, uncut skin, lightly tanned, and well-defined abs.

"Wow, your healing speed is remarkable."

"It is an asset when you are facing someone with *two left hands*."

I deserved that, but I hadn't had centuries to train. We decided then to drop knife training for a bit.

We'd spaced out our sweeps of Kerington's industrial area. Phoenix thought that if the kidnappers felt safe again, they would pick up their activities and he could catch them red-handed.

I kept to a well-established routine. I trained and I ate. I did the paperwork before noon (I didn't let myself give in to the appeal of sleeping in). I took notes and did some research on the Internet.

I also went to town at least two times a week. My relationship with Matthew had become normal again, and Danny showed me a surly affection that warmed my heart. My friendship with Angela grew so close that she was starting to become the sister I'd never had.

But the disappearances continued without us finding a single clue, and Phoenix was starting to get truly irritated when he finally got a call from Kiro. The strange nocturnal activities in Kerington's industrial zone had started up again. My boss was ready to go there the following evening, and I was going too.

*** 

"In April, don't remove a single layer of clothing." This French saying about the unreliability of April weather was rather appropriate given the temperature outside. It was April, and it was bitterly cold.

I had anticipated the need for warm clothing: black corduroy pants, boots, a thick white sweater, and my big black coat. Phoenix was on edge. He was convinced that he would discover something that evening. I was rather skeptical; until then, we hadn't found anything in all those warehouses. Except this time, Kiro had given us information that helped us to reduce our search perimeter.

The trip was pretty unpleasant for me. My boss was so absorbed in his thoughts that he stayed as still as the grave. Additionally, I'd barely turned on the radio when he turned it off to concentrate. What about me? I could only sit in the silence and be bored.

We arrived at our destination around midnight. Kiro's contacts had discovered that that zone only started to show activity around that time of night.

Once in place, we started driving around the warehouses, bouncing from one to the next like a marble in a pinball machine. I was starting to yawn when suddenly Phoenix stopped short.

He signaled to the right with his head. There was a light on a bit farther down. I began to prepare myself to get out and investigate, but he put his hand on my arm to stop me.

"Not yet. Stay in the car and watch your phone. I'll call you if it is clear out there."

"Very well."

He got out of the car and walked in the direction of the light, his silhouette ghostly in that heavy darkness. I hoped he wouldn't take too long to call . . .

The wait was very stressful. I was wondering what he was up to when suddenly I noticed movement. Luckily, our car was well hidden and no one would see it. Shadowy figures headed toward one of the warehouses. Two vehicles that looked like refrigerated trucks were parked in front of it. Suspicious indeed.

What to do? I couldn't call Phoenix at the risk of having the ring signal his presence, but I also couldn't wait in the car and let the men get away. I plucked up my courage and got out.

It was very cold. As I was cursing the manufacturers for exacerbating climactic disturbances with their pollution, I moved forward as discreetly as possible.

The way was clear outside, and there were no guards. That wasn't very smart.

I noticed a trash pile that looked over one of the building's windows, and I headed toward it. Even for me it was a piece of cake to climb it. I'd had the great idea of putting on boots without heels and taking a cross-body bag to free my hands, so it was easy.

I finally arrived at the summit of that randomly assembled tower of trash, and I could see what was happening inside . . .

At my first glance, I had to hold back a wave of nausea. I turned away from the window to get my breath back and recover from the horrible scene I had just witnessed. It took me a few seconds to pull myself together. Finally I found the courage to turn back and observe again.

What a horror. It was something beyond imagination, but what was in front of me was the exact description of cruelty Phoenix had told me vampires were capable of.

You would have thought it was a medical center where the doctors were all psychopaths. There were hospital beds everywhere; on each were ashy-faced people. From my vantage point, I recognized one of their faces: she was one of the kidnapped people listed in the police database.

It was Kate Savage, a beautiful young blond woman, nineteen years old. Her parents had appeared on television to make an appeal to her kidnappers; her mother had been desperate. But that was nothing compared to the expression I read on the face of her daughter at this very moment: she had resigned herself to death. Then I looked at the other people long enough to see each of their faces. There was Samuel Hurt, thirty-five, rising business owner, and Milly Kent, twenty-seven, Miss Falk City 2000. I didn't know the others. They might have been homeless or from socially marginalized groups.

They were naked under bed sheets, which covered them but didn't protect them from the cold. The explanation of their weakened state was simple: numerous red tubes led from their bodies to plastic pouches, which were filling up with vital liquid—the blood that was being removed from them.

As soon as a pouch was full, a man came along and replaced it with an empty one; then he put the full pouch in a large-capacity refrigerated case. On each case were labels indicating the blood type. The cases that were full were brought outside to the refrigerated trucks.

I finally had confirmation that vampires were behind the kidnappings, and I learned that their motivation was blood trafficking. Vampire law was only enforced in rich countries; members of the vampire community got their supplies strictly from blood banks and authorized hospitals, which allowed them to maintain a certain control over the population. What I was seeing went against all the established laws. But for what reason?

My attention was drawn to a movement at the back of the building. Two armed Asian vampires were monitoring a group of ten bound and gagged people, surely the next group of "donors." They were well aware of what was awaiting them, because one had collapsed onto a neighbor, shoulders shaking with sobs. My heart sank. There was nothing I could do.

But when I looked again, my heart had a different reaction. It skipped a beat when I caught sight of the blond vampire I'd encountered in Kentwood. He was firmly gripping the arm of a young woman, eighteen or nineteen years old, very beautiful with porcelain skin, short brown hair in a bob, and long, slender legs. Naked, she was no less dignified amid the absurdity and cruelty of her situation. She wasn't fighting; she must have known it was futile.

However, when the big blond vampire pulled the woman to his chest, she found the courage to spit in his face. This seemingly inconsequential gesture was an act of supreme rebellion when confronting a vampire. I felt a great flash of admiration and at the same time a feeling of infinite pity. She had only hastened the hour of her death.

Indeed, my former attacker wouldn't tolerate a human challenging him. In a split second, he turned her around, pulled her head back by her hair, and swooped down on her neck, fangs out.

The woman uttered a dreadful shriek and pathetically kicked her legs before finishing her cry with a sickening gurgle. It took all my self-control to not vomit.

Once sated, the killer let his burden drop to the ground like garbage and turned his attention to another vampire. I could only see his back and his fair hair, but given the deference with which the others spoke to him, I identified him easily as the leader.

I couldn't stop myself from contemplating the cadaver of that courageous unknown woman. By spitting on him, she had chosen her death. She had manipulated the bloodthirsty vampire into carrying out the fate she'd chosen. He hadn't broken her spirit; she'd freed herself.

I realized that tears had started flowing down my face. The fate of that extraordinary young woman wrecked my heart as it simultaneously established a fierce and ruthless hatred for her killers. I only wanted one thing: to see them all dead, and soon. I had to warn Phoenix.

As I was dialing his number, the unthinkable happened: my phone rang. Good heavens. I'd forgotten to put it on silent! I jumped, turned it off quickly, and then, horrified, I looked through the window to see if my presence had been discovered.

The luminescent eyes of the big blond had turned in my direction. His predator smile was directed at me, making my hair stand on end.

Panicked, I didn't wait for him to react. I tumbled down my tower as fast as I could. As soon as I hit the ground, I started running like a maniac, terror seeming to lend me wings.

In the distance, I saw the warehouse that Phoenix had gone to check out, but I knew that I would never reach it.

There was only one thing to do.

"Aaaahhh!"

Still running, and despite the fire in my lungs, I yelled as loudly as I could, hoping that my boss would hear.

Then, as in a nightmare, I felt resistance on my right arm. In an instant, I was propelled backward by a Herculean force that sent me flying onto the concrete and then against the sheet-metal wall of one of the buildings.

The shock was violent, but I was still conscious. I had scratches on my hands and my pants were torn, making my bloody knees visible. The pain in my torso suggested a broken rib. And I won't even mention the headache.

I didn't have time to dwell on my wounds. I got up and leaned against the metal wall so I could look at my adversary while remaining upright. It was the big blond.

"Well, well, well . . . we meet again . . . my little snoop from Kentwood. So, Phoenix let you live. He's getting old, poor guy . . ." He burst out laughing at his own joke. A second later, he was fixing me with a stare, a lion ready to pounce on his prey. "Where is he?"

I thought about the stranger from earlier and decided to fight in tribute to her while performing just as bravely as she did. I straightened up and looked at him scornfully. "You can go fry in the sunlight! I won't tell you anything, you swine!" I spit out with all the hatred he inspired in me.

"Your courage is honorable, miserable human, but I'm not stupid. There are rumors that say our angel has engaged the services of a female of your species. I know our laws. He should have killed you in Kentwood. That means you are the dog he's been dragging around. So he must not be far, and you're going to tell me where he is."

I had to buy myself some time. Slowly, and as discreetly as possible, I tried to reach my gun hidden in my coat. I had to make him talk, if only just to learn more.

"You say that you know your laws, but you're breaking them without any qualms. I suspect that when Talanus and Ysis learn that you're not respecting the Great Change and you're threatening the Secret, they'll have an unenviable fate in store when they get their hands on you. And I hope I'm there to see it."

"Phoenix told you more than he should have. He really should take care around you, seeing how many secrets you know. Ripping your limbs from your body one by one while thinking about him will amuse me."

I managed to get out my gun. I didn't wait for the big blond to react, I just fired. I couldn't kill him, knowing that he held information likely to help our search, so I'd aimed at his shoulder. I didn't miss.

The silver bullet was having an effect. He fell to his knees. His vampire powers should have been blocked because of his wound. He only represented a small risk, so I crept forward, ready to shoot at him a second time.

That was a big mistake. He got up faster than I'd anticipated and crashed into me heavily. I fell backward, dropping my gun, while he, still standing, looked down at me from above.

"Bitch! You should have hit my heart, because even with that silver bullet, I'm capable of breaking your neck!"

Just as I started to tell myself that I was done for, a silhouette stopped in front of me at a surprising speed, pushing my attacker back. I breathed a sigh of relief when I saw my boss had heard my cry for help.

He helped me get to my feet, then turned to the big blond who had recovered his arrogance despite his shoulder wound.

"Who are you? You are not from this sector." Phoenix's voice cracked like a whip in the glacial night.

"My name will get you nowhere, so I'll give it to you. My name is Heath, and I must say, dear angel, that you have a rather disagreeable habit of mixing yourself up in things that don't concern you. Your little trips in this area have really been a nuisance to us."

"What kind of traffic are you running here?"

I answered for Heath. "Blood! They're trafficking human blood."

A heavy silence fell upon the three of us. The two vampires faced each other, their eyes luminescent.

"Your little bitch has shown too much curiosity. She will suffer and die horribly. As will you."

"You will not touch her! I'm stronger than you," said Phoenix, his tone glacial and menacing.

The small smile, confident and cruel, that my attacker was sporting put me ill at ease. He had something up his sleeve.

"Against me, sure . . . But against them, that's another story . . ." And he whistled.

Suddenly, fifteen or so hooded vampires surrounded us. Phoenix had defeated six foes only a few days ago, but against fifteen, I doubted that he would have the upper hand, and I wouldn't either.

The circle of vampires started to close in on us. I caught a glimpse of our death, which promised to be horrific.

Suddenly, Phoenix turned toward me, and before I could even imagine what would happen next, he lifted me up and took me in his arms. In the space of a single breath, we took off into the air at an unbelievable speed.

The vampires below could surely hear the echo of my scream as we charged at the clouds . . .

***

"Aaaahhh! Aaaahhh! Let me down! Let me down! Aaaahhh!" I screamed and gesticulated wildly, my eyes wide open in terror at the panorama that was spreading out below us.

One of the reasons I'd never strayed far from Kentwood (I'd even picked a university that, while not the best, was at least the closest to home) was a tenacious and powerful vertigo that prevented me from ever daring to hope to take a plane one day. So I'll let you imagine my reaction as I flew in the arms of a vampire above the highest buildings in Kerington.

I'd lost all sense of safety, and my living-dead vehicle didn't miss the opportunity to make me aware of it, particularly by tightening his grip, which cut off my breath. It was rather painful, with my broken rib.

"Are you going to stop moving? Do you want us to crash? Continue flailing like that and I *will* drop you!" he thundered.

His voice reached me distinctly despite the wind that whipped at my face.

His threat had the intended effect. I stopped fighting. To avoid the terrifying view, I burrowed my face into the crook of his neck, wrapped my arms around his neck, and gripped him tight.

We'd never been so close before.

I'd never noticed that he used cologne; he smelled nice and his skin, so cold, was nevertheless incredibly soft. Strangely, I felt comforted, and I started to regain control over my breathing, and then think about my new situation . . .

It took us less time to get back to Scarborough going as the crow flies than by car. Phoenix landed smoothly on the lawn of the property, and after that, I lost it.

I began by pushing him as hard as I could. Might as well push a mountain with my bare hands. However, he took a step back. My legs turned to jelly, making me lose my balance. My boss reached out an arm to help me, but I pushed it away violently, gathering all my strength to face him.

I was so furious that it took me a few seconds before I could speak.

"You . . . you said that vampires didn't have other powers than those I could see . . ."

I tried to get control over my quivering voice, as anger burned in my veins.

Phoenix's face had resumed that impenetrable mask that refused everyone entry to his thoughts.

"I told you we do not have powers of suggestion. I also told you our powers increase with time."

His tone didn't predict anything good.

"But you never told me that you could fly! You lied to me!" I screamed, tears in my eyes.

"I did not lie to you. It had not yet been the right time to tell you."

"And when would the right time be, hm? You never intended to tell me, because for you I'm nothing, just a replaceable slave only good for serving as an emergency blood bag! I was loyal to you, and what did I get in return? You lie to me and give me no choice in the matter!"

Since our first encounter, I'd never seen Phoenix display his anger toward me in any other way than his cold and threatening voice. But now he raised his voice.

"And what did you want me to do? Reveal all my secrets to a mortal I have only known for a few months? Pour my heart out on your sympathetic shoulder? Good grief, come back to earth, Samantha! I am a *vampire* and I do not have to answer to a pathetic human *whiner* like you! Why should I keep you alive if not to help me? If you are expecting a different attitude from me, you are stupider than I thought!"

I remained speechless for a second, time enough to absorb the horrors he'd just thrown in my face. Then I reacted.

Without realizing what I was about to do, I struck Phoenix with the most monumental slap imaginable.

I immediately felt an immense pain in my hand and its waves spreading throughout my arm. I was incapable of speech.

Before another word was uttered by the man whose betrayal had broken my heart, I turned away, swallowing my tears, and ran to my room.

I slammed the bedroom door and leaned against it, trying to catch the breath I'd lost, as much from my run as from the pain.

Phoenix's words tumbled around in my head, playing on a loop, making me understand how much I'd been deluding myself, how naive and stupid I'd been.

I had vainly hoped for something that couldn't happen. I'd thought that my boss's attitude toward Kiro was a sign of the possibility that he would open up to me, that he would become my friend. But like me, Kiro was just a human who Phoenix had allowed to live. Nothing more.

Why did I want to gain Phoenix's friendship so much? After all, I had Matthew and Angela, and Danny, and even Ginger.

Why did I feel so betrayed? I'd been warned. I knew that Phoenix didn't trust anyone, especially humans. However . . .

Despite the violent circumstances of our meeting, despite the fear that he'd inspired and could still inspire, despite his coldness and acerbic remarks, I'd slowly become attached to him. His attentiveness, his thoughtfulness, his advice, and the real Samantha that he had helped to reveal—all that led me to believe I was important to him. And it was because of all he had given me that I was so keen to be his friend—so I could return his kindness with friendship.

How ridiculous I could be . . .

Tears ran down my face, and I did nothing to stop them. Then there was a knock on the door. The red veil reappeared over my eyes. I felt my blood boil in my veins, and anger was overtaken by a state of uncontrollable fury.

I grabbed a decorative porcelain water pitcher that was on the dressing table and pitched it against the door.

"Go to hell!" I shouted.

Overwhelmed by a sudden desire to break everything, I scanned the room frenetically, looking for objects to destroy. Like a tornado, I made a tour of the room, picking up everything I could carry and positioning myself in front of the door.

"Samantha . . . open up. You need to be healed."

That reviled voice increased my fury.

"Go . . . !"

Smash! A bottle of perfume . . .

"Burn . . . !"

Bam! A bottle of water, now dripping everywhere . . .

"In hell!"

Bang! Bang! Books that Phoenix had recommended.

"That's where you'll end up anyway! You bastard!"

More porcelain breaking. Another lamp. With all the strength I'd put into that throw, it'd literally exploded.

Suddenly, I started crying without restraint, a weakness that exasperated me even more.

*"You're a monster and I hate you! You've ruined my life! I never want to see you again!"* I managed to scream between sobs.

To put a definitive end to the conversation, and to prove just how beside myself I was, I sent my brand-new DVD player crashing and scattering against the door.

I didn't hear anything more from him. Being careful to not cut myself on any pieces of broken glass, I opened the door and peered into the hallway. He was gone.

I threw myself on the bed and emptied my body of all my sobs and tears. I thought about my parents. Their love had been unconditional and exclusive, and it always comforted me when that almost constant feeling of being invisible and useless threatened to strangle me. Since their death, that feeling had only intensified until I met Phoenix and my friends in Scarborough. And while that scar was fading little by little, here, in one evening, with just a few excruciatingly hurtful words, all that fell apart. I'd reverted to a nobody, and a complete idiot as well.

I'd let myself embark on a dangerous path in which I was risking my life because Phoenix had opened my eyes to my potential. He may have revealed it to me, but deep down he couldn't care less. Just like he couldn't care less about me . . .

It was with that sad statement that I fell into a troubled sleep, riddled with nightmares.

***

The next day, I woke up early. I wasn't able to fall back asleep, and besides, I'd already made my decision, so just as well that I carry it out as quickly as possible.

After taking a shower and getting dressed, I took the biggest bag I had and stuffed it with some clothes, my papers, and some cash. I called a taxi, and when it arrived I asked the driver to take me to the Scarborough bus station, where I made myself as small as possible so no one would recognize me. It was easy.

During the trip, which was scheduled for two hours given all the stops, I closed my mind to all stray thoughts and only concentrated on the countryside passing by.

I'd nodded off by the time I heard, "Kentwood! Next stop!"

I yawned, then grabbed my bag and exited the bus.

I know the town like the back of my hand, but I felt like I didn't recognize anything. Three months' absence made me feel like a stranger in my own hometown. Despite that, I set off on foot to my destination.

Once in front of my house, I realized I didn't know what I was expecting. I wasn't in danger during the day. Even if after our encounter Heath still wanted to come after me, he would have to wait until nightfall. It was only a few minutes past two in the afternoon; sunset would be around seven thirty.

I encountered some resistance when trying to open the door. It was actually a pile of mail amassed on the other side that was blocking it, but between advertisements and bills, there was nothing there that suggested anyone had taken an interest in my fate.

I checked the answering machine, just in case. "Miss Watkins, Mr. Plummer here, your boss. We've received your message that you've quit. Consider your resignation accepted. Good-bye." Click. "End of new messages."

Heath was definitely talented at erasing traces of a person's life. As for the principal, upon hearing the ease with which he'd accepted my departure after all that I'd done for the school, I only felt disgust for him.

Heath's interventions meant that since I technically hadn't disappeared, the police certainly hadn't come here. That was now confirmed.

I stayed longer than anticipated. The nostalgia of that house and everything connected to it overwhelmed me and delayed my leaving. But it was getting late, and I needed to pack up and go.

I went up to my room, grabbed the big suitcase that took up most of the space in my closet; I'd never even used it before. I put everything I could in there, clothes, some of my mother's jewelry.

Once my packing was done, I got down and crawled under the bed. There was a floorboard under there that I could pry up; I used it to hide my savings. I always kept some money there because I didn't really trust banks, even if both my parents had worked for one. The financial crisis had proved that I'd been right. With what I had under the bed, I had enough to live off of for a while, which was good since I didn't think I'd be able to access any of the money Phoenix had paid me.

When I was ready, I toured the house, taking it all in. When I passed through the door of my childhood home for the last time, a tear ran down my cheek . . . a new chapter of my life had just begun . . .

I arrived at the Kentwood train station and looked over the schedule. I wanted to go far away, beyond Kerington County. The only train that went any distance that night was the one to Eden in North Carolina. It would arrive around six, in half an hour. I bought a one-way ticket.

I sat down on a bench and skimmed the newspaper that an old man was handing out at the entrance. My blood turned to ice when I turned the page to a photo of a young, smiling woman, about twenty years old. The photo was just below a missing persons appeal. Her name was Melanie Aubry, and she'd just moved to Kentwood to study nursing.

She was the woman Heath had killed before my very eyes. No one would ever see her again; no one other than me would ever know the truth about what happened to her.

Silently, I prayed for Melanie, that courageous young woman who had become an example for me to follow.

Reading that newspaper became unbearable, so I threw it into the garbage. I heard an announcement that my train had just been canceled and I would have to wait for the next one, expected at nine. I tried to forget about night falling soon, thinking only about my one-way trip. Phoenix wouldn't know where to find me, I supposed, so there wasn't anything I could do but sit and wait. I sighed.

It was a long wait, so I went to have something to eat. Around eight, I came out of the diner and sat back down on the same bench as before and waited. I watched the comings and goings of the travelers. Some seemed stressed and tired; others beamed; still others ran into the arms of people welcoming them. Those were the lucky ones . . .

"Train to Eden now entering the station. Platform four."

Just when I'd had more than my fill of waiting . . . That was good timing.

"Samantha . . ."

That voice . . . behind me . . . I froze. I'd of course recognized it. I would've recognized it anywhere. Phoenix walked around the bench and came to sit beside me. I kept looking straight ahead, at the platform, because I didn't want to see him.

"I have been looking for you everywhere. I finally ended up at your house. I saw that someone had emptied your closet. I also smelled your perfume so I knew I was on the right track. Nothing was keeping you in Kentwood, so I figured you would want to get far away from here. So here I am."

What did he want? A medal for finding me with his super sense of smell? That was a valuable quality for drug detection dogs on police task forces. I kept quiet.

Suddenly, he took my hand in his. This gesture, so unusual for him, made me turn my head in his direction and stare at him in amazement. It was the first time I could read the emotions on his face, and he didn't seem at all patronizing. Was that . . . remorse?

"Samantha . . . when I took you with me, I only planned on avoiding a task I hate and being able to confide in a fragile person, especially a mortal. You were nothing more than . . . you said it yourself . . . a replaceable slave."

Why was he talking about the past? Why did he seem so miserable?

"But I got caught up in it. I have been living alone for a long time, and I did not know what it was like to . . . to have someone to talk to. Please understand, I never expected to find your company . . . agreeable. Comforting. I lost the habit of worrying about anyone, but when I saw you confronting Heath, alone, I was afraid in a way I never have been since becoming a vampire. I was afraid of losing someone dear. You are important to me, Samantha. I started to realize that when I bit you. I should not have felt so guilty . . . but it's worse now, because I have hurt you more profoundly by telling you things that I do not even think. I am asking you to forgive me . . . my friend."

There was nothing sharp or cold about his voice in that moment. It was filled with vulnerability, the gauge of true sincerity. I'd held my breath during his speech, and now that it was over and he was searching my face for my reaction, I was finding it difficult to breathe. Unable to do anything else, I let the flood of tears I'd been holding back stream down my face.

His confession completely floored me. If he was telling me all this, it was because he was afraid of his attachment to me. He considered affection—emotional and physical affection—so weak that he refused to open up to me. However . . . he thought of me as a true friend. I realized it was the same for me. Even if I got along with Angela and Matthew, I knew that they would never know me as well as the vampire beside me, and he was waiting to hear if I forgave him or not.

I took a deep breath and looked him straight in the eye.

"You hurt me. Never do it again."

"I promise you."

He was surprised when I closed the distance between us and nestled against him. I found that his smell comforted me, and that sensation increased when he wrapped his arms around me and held me against him.

That simple promise was enough to purge me of all the heartache that was weighing me down. It meant that from now on, the vampire and his human were connected by an unfailing friendship, founded on trust and sincerity.

I was ready to go back with him, but at the station exit I gave him the conditions of my return.

"Now that everything is in order, you can call me Sam. And since friends do each other favors, you can call a taxi to get us back to Scarborough. I forgive you, but it's out of the question for me to find myself flying again like a bird riding a bat."

He stared, smiled, then whistled at the first taxi that approached the station.

# CHAPTER EIGHT

## *Encounters*

When we returned to the manor, it was almost eleven o'clock, but I wasn't tired at all. Phoenix settled into the sofa in the parlor while I got us both something to drink. Seated in an armchair, I sipped my lemonade before testing just how far Phoenix trusted me.

"Phoenix . . . that's not your real name, right?"

Silence. He must have been weighing the pros and cons of telling me. But then he spoke.

"I chose that name when I became a vampire. After all, I had risen from the dead."

"What is your name?" I asked, wanting to learn as much as possible about his life before.

"My family was Irish. I was Aydan MacKinley."

"Aydan . . . ," I murmured.

I liked the name.

"No one has called me that for centuries."

"Tell me about your family . . . please."

He sighed and stared fixedly at his glass of blood, as if recalling old memories revived emotions that had disappeared long ago.

"We were just peasants. We farmed the land of an English nobleman named Carson. He was a greedy brute without any regard for the woman he took to bed. My sister, Keira, was beautiful, and unfortunately for her, Lord Carson noticed her one day as he was passing by our farm . . ."

He gritted his teeth. I was afraid that I'd been too nosy and he would clam up again. I knew that his story didn't have a happy ending, and I didn't want to open old wounds just to satisfy my curiosity.

"I'm sorry . . . it's fine if you stop there."

"No. I think that you must hear this story in order to better understand me."

I nodded.

"I loved my sister, and I was very happy when my parents allowed her to marry the man she loved. As for me, despite being the eldest and thirty years old, I was still unmarried. It drove my father crazy, but I did not care much about that. My sister was sixteen, and I protected her fiercely. Her fiancé, Thomas, really had to prove himself before he could hope to even talk to her." Phoenix smiled at that.

"One night, when we'd organized a small party with the villagers to seal the union between our two families, two riders passing by came, attracted by our singing. The first was Lord Carson, the second, one of his guests, a man called Finn. When our lord asked my parents why we were celebrating, they spoke of Thomas and Keira's upcoming wedding and asked for his blessing. As soon as he saw my sister, I saw the lust in his eyes. I was the only one to notice it. Suddenly anxious about Keira's future, I had not noticed that I had also caught someone's eye . . . Finn's . . . but I shall return to that.

"What I had feared happened. Two days before the wedding, I was helping my father repair our roof when we saw several men on horseback heading in our direction. They ordered Keira to go with them for the honor of being deflowered by our lord. It had already happened to Shannon, another young woman in our village. Shannon was never the same afterward . . . and I could not stand for that . . ."

I was at once captivated and horrified by his words. I thought about the movie *Braveheart*, and I was sure that the outcome of Phoenix's story would be just as tragic.

"I asked Shannon's brothers to help me free Keira from these knights before they arrived at their castle and all would be lost. Our knowledge of the area gave us the advantage to catch up with them quickly, and we knew a shortcut that allowed us to set up an ambush. We only had stones, sticks, and the element of surprise. We managed to break Keira free, and I hid her in another village, with an elderly relative. I thought that in time our lord would forget everything, but I was wrong. He deployed all his forces to find us, and when he did, his vengeance knew no limits.

"Keira and Thomas were hanged together in the public square, and Lord Carson's men made us watch. When they hanged my parents and the parents of my accomplices, Carson had a front-row seat, and he savored every minute of each horrific spectacle. Then it was our turn.

"To make it more enjoyable, our judge chose to burn us alive at midnight. He made everyone in the village come to watch. Finn was there too.

"Before bringing us to the pyre, we were forced to stand in front of our lord to beg his forgiveness. Of course, we had been tortured prior to that. All my accomplices yielded to the whims of the man behind our misfortune, but not me. I wanted to spit on his face, but the executioner stopped me. I struggled so much they had to tie me up. All that made Lord Carson laugh. Finn, who was by his side, said nothing and was content to examine me strangely. I learned why later, after seeing my friends perish in the flames, smelling the stench of their burned flesh while I waited to follow them into that grisly death.

"Lord Carson and Finn came up to me then. The lord stared at me, his smile cruel.

"He said, 'I do not know if you can call yourself lucky, given what is waiting for you, but Finn has gotten you a reprieve. You have impressed him. You should know that one of his favorite activities is to break arrogant rebels like you. He told me what is in store for you. Believe me, you will be amused. Come on. You can thank me for putting you in the hands of such a lord. Ha-ha-ha! Bring him!' he ordered his guards.

"The following night, they chained me up and made me get on a horse, ready to follow my new master. We rode for a week, and he never said a single word. I did not understand why, but we only traveled at night. Sometimes he would tie me up in a stable while he went off on his own. When he came back, he always seemed healthier and more energetic than before.

"When we finally reached his estate, vast lands and a majestic manor, his plans for me became clear. That very evening, he summoned me before him and ordered that my chains be removed. I stared at him, confused, and he said, 'Those chains are of little use since you will not be going anywhere. I have big plans for you.'

"Then he announced point-blank that the courage I had shown at the death of my family had made an impression on him, and so he had chosen me to be his son."

Phoenix stared into his glass. I hung on his every word.

"His son, you said?"

"I was just as surprised as you. But the adoption he had in mind entailed taking a step I was not ready for. My death."

A light bulb went on in my head.

"So Finn is your creator? It's him. He's the one who gave you that scar on your back, isn't he?"

"You are perceptive as well as observant. But stop cutting me off. It is rude."

Oops.

"Well, I had not gone through all that suffering just for someone to kill me and then bring me back to life as a blood-drinking monster, and then to make me serve the one who did it. The next day, I escaped. I ran as far as I could, but once night fell, he found me. I tried to get away from him, but that is when he cut open my back with his knife. When I fell to the ground, bathed in my own blood, he told me that I would keep that mark forever, that it would always be a reminder that he could find me anywhere. He then picked me up and took flight. Now you know where I get that ability from.

"He did not come near me again until the wound on my back started to heal over. I had an infection and a fever, despite the attentions of the servants . . . but Finn would not let me die. As I hallucinated, he drained me of my blood. I can say that despite my delirium, I felt an indescribable pain that reached its height when he began the Blood Exchange to transform me from a human into a vampire. The transformation of a human into a vampire causes horrible suffering, which explains why in most cases the humans end up dying, for good. But I woke up . . .

"It was night, and I was starving. The only thing I wanted was blood and not just any blood—Lord Carson's. Finn used his authority as my creator to stop me from going to kill my former master. I was connected to Finn, and I could not disobey him no matter how much I hated him. So he trained me, for a long time. When he finally deemed me ready, he let me carry out the vengeance that would mark the definitive loss of my humanity . . . but I would prefer to not talk about that."

I understood why. Phoenix must have thought that I would look upon him with absolute horror if he ever described the hell he must have given Lord Carson before ending his life. Maybe that would have been my reaction . . .

He continued. "Finn and I went from continent to continent. He taught me everything he knew about life, humans, the vampire community, and weaponry. I learned to respect him over time, and in a way, he did act as a father to me. At least as much as a vampire could be a father. We stayed together for a hundred years, then he decided he had nothing more to teach me. He set me free, and here I am."

I looked at him wide-eyed. How could the story be over? I wanted to hear more.

"But . . . he set you free, and that's it? You never heard from him again? He can't force you to carry out his will anymore?"

"The reason why I learned to respect Finn, and why I still respect him, wherever he is, is that he taught me that I can be a vampire without necessarily being a monster, because he was not one. Well, at least compared to others. I told you before, it is rare for creators and their protégés to stay together for several centuries, because the need for independence always takes priority. Generally, when the young vampires are ready, their creators free them from their authority so they can be autonomous. Young vampires always demonstrate exceptional loyalty to their creators."

"You say you respect him. Does that mean you've forgiven him for giving you that scar? And for making you suffer so much as you became a vampire?"

"The transformation does not just change our body. Our moral codes are no longer the same. We do not see things the same way. We are not human anymore."

"That means you accept it . . ."

"But I'll never forget," he said.

Incredible. Phoenix had revealed his whole story to me, and except for the part about his sister, not a single emotion had registered on his face.

"Thank you, Phoenix . . . for opening up. I understand certain things better now."

"I am not used to talking about my life from before. You are the first person I have told that to. Even my friends don't know the details of my human life. Only Finn knows."

Very selfishly, I felt an immense burst of pride. After all, I'd finally gotten what I wanted, and more. However, I also felt compassion for Phoenix and his tragic life story.

"You can trust me."

"I know. I found that out when you confronted Heath. You did not tell him where I was," he said, looking at me closely.

"I told him to go fry in the sunlight!" I smiled.

"You showed great courage . . ."

I wasn't fishing for laurels, but the compliment pleased me.

"And you were hurt."

Ah. Yes. Damn, I'd almost forgotten. Walking around with a broken rib was not supposed to be easy, but strangely this was the case for me. I felt a throbbing pain of course, but nothing really bad. I must have been bizarrely constituted.

"I don't know what Heath likes about my arm, but he has an unpleasant tendency to pull on it and then send me flying across the pavement like a barrel at every one of our meetings. At least I got away with no more than a broken rib."

"You know you need to be treated . . . and you cannot really go to a hospital. Someone will ask how that happened."

I tensed up suddenly, understanding his meaning.

"Oh no! Not that!"

Phoenix sighed. "And what other option do we have?"

"Oh, there are people who live quite well with only one kidney, so I could live with a broken rib. You'll see, I won't complain about it at all," I said, full of hope.

"You were right. When you panic, you will say just about anything. Come on. It's not the end of the world, you will *not* become a vampire, I promise!"

After all that I'd read about his species, I dreaded the side effects that a small amount of his blood would have on me. The first time Phoenix made me drink his blood, I'd been unconscious, but now I was fully awake, and I balked at the thought of becoming some kind of junkie or nymphomaniac.

"But yuck! It's too gross! I don't want to become a raging madwoman after drinking it. I didn't make sure to avoid cults all my life only to suffer *delirium tremens* thanks to vampire blood."

"Don't be scared, nothing bad will happen. You will just feel a bit warmer."

"So hot that I'll take off my clothes!" Oops. I'd let my thought escape. I blushed. "Oh, fine, OK!"

He gestured for me to join him on the sofa, and I rolled my eyes before complying. I was not overly confident about this.

"Are you ready?"

As my answer, I looked at him like a beaten dog. He abruptly brought his wrist to his mouth and cut open his skin with his fangs. He showed his wrist to me, blood dripping from his lips.

"Drink," he ordered.

I gagged, but I couldn't back out now.

Carefully, I leaned forward, took his wrist in my hands, and took a taste. A tenth of a second later, I sat straight up, disgusted, and I heard Phoenix growl.

"Drink, Sam!"

It was not so much his insistence as the use of my nickname that affected me. Once again, I held his wrist, and this time, I drank in his blood, more intentionally. I found the first mouthful terrible. Then, my revulsion yielded to indifference, then curiosity. At the same time, a strange warmth invaded my body and brought warmth to my cheeks. The warmth wasn't burning me, though; it was keeping me in a kind of pleasurable state that got more and more pronounced. Reaching the height of that warmth, my eyes closed of their own accord, and I squirmed in my seat. At the very moment of an explosion of sensuality in my body, Phoenix pulled away . . .

"I think that's enough."

Immediately brought down to earth, I realized what had happened and nearly choked with shame and indignation.

"Good grief," I panted, ready to explode, but for a different reason.

"You do not need to be ashamed. Your reaction is perfectly normal. And before you drive a stake through my heart, remember that I told you to expect feeling a certain . . . heat."

"You definitely didn't define what you meant by heat!" I roared.

"Maybe, but I told you the truth. Are you still in pain?"

He wanted to distract me so I wouldn't jump down his throat, but that suited me well enough. I didn't want to elaborate on the tidal wave that had taken me by surprise. Just thinking about it again . . . Argh! It was too embarrassing! I focused my attention on my rib cage.

"No, I don't feel anything anymore. Did my bruises disappear too? Because I was starting to look like a raisin, there were so many."

"I cannot predict the effect my blood will have on you. Maybe it will heal more than your broken rib, maybe not. You will know tomorrow."

"I read somewhere that a connection is created between a vampire and a human who drinks the vampire's blood. Is that true?"

"No, not at all. My blood has no effect other than the one you just felt, but at the same time, I have never had anyone else drink from me."

At the mention of my response to his blood, I immediately blushed scarlet, so I rushed to turn the focus to his second point.

"You've never, um, what do you call that? Created someone? Since becoming a vampire?"

"No. I do not feel the need. And it's not like we can bring new vampires into the world as we please."

"Oh, yeah, population control."

"Exactly."

"It's strange . . . the words you use. 'Son.' 'Bring into the world.' It's as if transforming someone is just like childbirth."

"Since we are dead, and even though we can have physical relations with other vampires and humans, procreation is impossible for us. Therefore, transforming someone has symbolic value in our eyes, and we do not take it lightly. Most do it to have a companion after a long, solitary existence, and the tie that binds the two parties can take different forms. Parent and adopted child, master and pupil, a sexual relationship. Each vampire is responsible for his or her student. If it turns out that the master has flouted our laws by neglecting the student's training, both are equally punished."

"You're not joking, then. Who's in charge of making sure everyone respects these laws?"

"I am not allowed to talk to you about that. You are not supposed to know as much as you do about Talanus and Ysis either. But it will facilitate your meeting with them."

I was just about to take a swallow of lemonade when I realized the importance of what he just said.

"What? You want me to meet them? But you said that their home was forbidden to humans!"

"In these circumstances, they will understand the necessity of meeting you. I will call them as soon you go upstairs to bed."

I couldn't get over it. He wanted me to meet the ones he had such immense difficulty talking about! While the prospect of finding myself with the most powerful vampires in the region terrified me, the thought of having a face-to-face with two figures from history, ones who had known Augustus and Cleopatra personally, made me want to hurry to their house with a notepad and ask them a million questions. But still . . .

"Why do I have to go there with you? You just have to tell them what happened. You know as much as I do."

"I did not see the inside of the warehouse . . ."

Thinking about that gave me stomach pains. I kept quiet until they subsided.

"It was awful . . . all those people hooked up, being emptied . . . as if they were worthless bags of blood. And Melanie . . ." The memory of that brave girl made me go quiet.

Phoenix raised an eyebrow. "Melanie? Who is that?"

"She would have been lying down on one of the stretchers like the others, having her blood drawn and stored in refrigerated cases, but Heath was making her walk around naked like a dog on a leash, to demean and dehumanize her . . . She died a heroine . . . I know her name is Melanie because I saw a missing persons notice with her photo in the newspaper."

My boss waited a beat before responding.

"This situation is very serious. We have to use all the means we have to discover who is in charge of this blood trafficking. Your eyewitness account may be crucial. Ysis will be able to see your memories."

"What?"

I started to worry . . .

"She has the ability to read minds."

. . . and I clearly wasn't wrong to.

Imagining a quasi–vampire queen having access to my more-than-complicated mind gave me goose bumps. I stood up abruptly.

"I don't want anyone rummaging around in my head. What's this about all vampires having an extra superpower? Speed and Herculean strength aren't enough?"

Phoenix moved to reassure me.

"These extra superpowers, as you call them, are very rare. Do not worry, she can read minds, sure, but she can only see what you are focusing on. Just avoid thinking about Matthew, for instance, and it will all be fine . . ."

He was trying to be friendly, but his remark about Matthew was irritating. It was time to go to sleep. In two days, I'd had my fill of emotions, wounds, fatigue. I wasn't going to add more anxiety to that list.

"We'll see about that . . . Maybe they won't want to see me at all. On that note of scant hope, I wish you good night."

I left the parlor.

On the stairs leading to my room, I remembered the rage that I'd felt in my bedroom the last time I was in it, and all the things I'd sent flying to break against the door. My boss would have cleaned it all up.

However, when I pushed open my door, I encountered resistance, just like at my childhood home. Debris was scattered across the floor, though I could see that someone had made a path through the room. Phoenix.

He wouldn't have left this mess without a good reason, and he'd already given it to me: he'd left to look for me. Someone had paid enough attention to me to immediately go after me, and knowing that warmed my heart.

Perked up now, I cleaned the room and made note that I really only had to replace the DVD player. When I was done, I changed into my nightgown, and just as I was drawing back the covers to climb into bed, there was a knock at my door.

"Come in," I said, pulling on a bathrobe.

Phoenix came through the door.

"I brought up your suitcase, and I wanted to tell you that Talanus and Ysis have agreed to meet with us tomorrow evening at nine."

He rolled the suitcase over to the dressing table.

"Very well."

That wasn't exactly what I was thinking, but it was all I could manage to say at that moment. He gave me a soft smile and was about to leave when he stopped in the doorway, turning back to me.

"I'm happy you're back, Sam."

"Me too," I answered, sincerely.

"Good night," he said as he left.

"Good night."

I was delighted to reclaim my soft bed, and I slept incredibly well for someone about to face a rather challenging day.

\*\*\*

The first thing I did when I woke up was hurry to my big mirror for a complete diagnosis.

One, my rib was definitely back in place; two, the scrapes on my arms had disappeared, as well as the bump on the back of my head; three, I still looked like a raisin from all the purplish bruises that covered my body, even if my head had been spared; four, I felt perfectly healthy, as if all the accumulated tiredness of the past few weeks had miraculously gone away.

I suspected that this sudden alertness was also not random: Phoenix's blood had taken effect. But I would have liked it to have taken care of my bruises too. It would take days for them to go away. I could at least consider myself lucky to be in generally good condition.

With my inspection done, I returned to my usual morning routine. I exercised a little, and I wrote a report for Talanus and Ysis of the incident of two nights before, trying to give as much detail as possible.

When I finished my work, I headed to Angela's bookshop. I needed some girl time.

As usual, the little bell rang out to announce the arrival of a customer. My friend was busy helping two teenagers who were asking for books for their project on ancient Egypt. I kept myself from laughing at the irony: that very evening, I would be meeting with one of Egypt's former inhabitants . . .

Anyway, even for me, it wasn't very funny, so I changed my angle of attack.

"Hello, Angela. Hello, gentlemen. What a joy to see that there are still young people who take the time to look in books rather than surf the Internet. This bookshop is an information goldmine," I said with a beaming smile, winking at the two teenagers.

They both understood my meaning and that I knew they were using the pretext of a school project to come admire my friend. One of them looked like he was about to drool. Pathetic.

The two boys mumbled something about their parents waiting for them to go shopping and scurried away without further ado.

"What's gotten into them?"

"Angela! You didn't notice that those two teens were raging with hormones just from looking at you? If they're not using the Internet to do their research, it's just so they can come drool over your stunning figure."

"What? You think so?"

She blushed. She might have a good head on her shoulders, but she was also blond and curvy. When it came to her beauty, her modesty bordered on naiveté. Frankly, if I had her figure, I would certainly have more self-confidence; I could even imagine I might become narcissistic . . .

"Honestly, with all these men circling around you, I don't understand why you haven't found the love of your life yet."

I had that thought every time I saw Angela. The area wasn't bereft of handsome men, so she had every chance to come across her future husband. And no, she wasn't a lesbian.

"I know. Everyone says that to me all the time. But I can't do anything about it. That's just how it is."

"Anyway, it's better to take your time than end up with the wrong guy. But it must weigh on you, knowing that everyone wants you to marry Matthew."

"Don't talk about that! The minute anyone sees us together, we're asked when the wedding will be. It's really irritating. But it's eased up a bit, probably because everyone knows that Matthew is interested in you . . . ," she said, a smile playing at the corner of her mouth.

I sighed. I knew very well that at some point we would have that conversation, she and I. Being Matthew's best friend since kindergarten, he must have told her he had feelings for me . . . and that I had turned him down.

"I like Matthew . . . but for the moment, I don't see him as a potential boyfriend. We hardly know each other."

Angela stared at me intensely, then made a pronouncement. "You're with someone else."

I was caught off guard.

"No, I'm not. What are you even talking about?" I stammered pathetically.

"Matthew is the most attractive man for miles around. He's *gorgeous*! Your excuse for rejecting him is 'we hardly know each other'? Come on, give me a break."

Angela's relentless logic made me turn scarlet. But I'd told the truth!

"No, no, there's no one. I'm too complicated . . . and . . . and . . . that's all there is to it. What's your excuse, then, for not throwing yourself at him?"

Hooray! I could turn this right around.

"I think I know him too well. His habits would annoy me too much in the long run. I could never be his wife."

"That seems clear."

"Yes, but you, *you* left the door wide open for him. He won't give up easily. I can tell you this, he really likes you, and he hopes that as you get to know him better, your feelings for him will change."

What was wrong with me? No man had ever demonstrated the slightest interest in me, and the first time it happened—and it was someone charming to boot—I was irritated and embarrassed rather than pleased and flattered.

I'd taken time to think about my feelings for Matthew. I'd searched my inner heart and had only found respect and friendship. I didn't have any experience in romance, and someone could have told me that, unconsciously, my heart was beating for him. But despite the fact that I was a novice in matters of the heart, I knew how I felt. I just wasn't in love with Matthew, period.

As for knowing whether I would ever fall in love one day . . . given the combination of my usual lack of luck and my boss, whose vampire nature made me work at night and sleep part of the day, it was unlikely I would have any semblance of a social life that would allow me to meet someone. It was more likely that I would end up alone and wrinkly than married and satisfied—at least, if I lived long enough to see my first wrinkles appear.

"I think of Matthew as a friend. And for me, for now, that's enough," I said.

"I understand. But you should know he won't let it go easily. He'll wait, patiently. He's a real romantic."

I'd never wondered if the man of my dreams would be a romantic, especially since I certainly wasn't one.

Suddenly, Phoenix's face superimposed itself over that of Matthew in my head. A vampire with glowing eyes, fangs out, roaring like a raging lion, took the place of a handsome man with a gentle face. I shivered. Now there's a man for whom talk of love caused nausea. Imagining Phoenix with stars in his eyes for his lady love was almost comical, given how much it contrasted with his character.

"Why are you smiling?" Angela asked me.

Oops.

"Um, uh, nothing. I lost track of what you were saying. In fact, can we talk about something else? This topic is making me uncomfortable."

"As you wish."

We chatted about this and that for a couple of hours, with only occasional interruptions by customers asking for recommendations. Given my previous career as a librarian, I was able to offer Angela a bit of help.

When it was nearly sunset, I left under the pretext that it was time to make dinner for my dear grandfather. In fact, it was *my* meal that I had to whip up. I would need energy for the upcoming meeting, so I cooked my favorite: steak and homemade fries (frozen fries—ew!). The days were longer now that it was spring, and I had more time to savor my evening meal.

Nevertheless, I didn't wait for my boss to wake up before getting changed. I needed to look elegant and worthy of appearing before Talanus and Ysis. I didn't know the protocol, but I suspected the less disheveled the better in front of the area's vampire leaders.

I selected a red suit; the skirt was short but tasteful. A white top and black heels completed the look. The result, with a bit of makeup, a necklace, and earrings, astonished me. I looked sexy, which wasn't really the image I was going for.

But before I had time to consider changing, there was a knock on the door.

"Come in," I said softly.

There was no need to speak loudly with a vampire—he could hear you whistle from several hundred feet away.

When Phoenix entered my room, his classic elegance and charisma impressed me, as always. Clearly his black suit had been tailored to measure. Though I was no fashion expert, I could tell that the suit was made by a high-profile designer. Despite my effort to dress elegantly, next to my boss, I once again I felt like I was wearing a potato sack.

As for him, he'd stopped in his eagerness to talk to me and was instead staring at me.

"What? Do I have a stain somewhere?" I said, turning around and around looking for some flaw in my clothes.

"Hm . . . no, you're perfect," he said, turning away. "I will wait for you downstairs."

If I'd been perfectly dressed for the occasion, he certainly had a strange way of showing it. I cast one last glance at the mirror before leaving my room and joining him below.

I tried to be friendly, smiling as I said, "You look sharp."

He gave me my coat and instead of responding to the compliment he said, "We're expected. We can't be late."

He set off for the garage, where there was only the very hallmark of discretion: the Camaro.

Following him, I couldn't help whispering a comment under my breath, knowing full well he would hear it. "Translation, you're in a bad mood."

***

Though the beginning of the trip was made in silence, before long Phoenix did tell me about the kind of formality I should adopt with his employers. To start, others of his kind would certainly be there. I shouldn't look at them, at least not before speaking to Talanus and Ysis. Next, I wouldn't have to bow or curtsy or put on airs like humans do when meeting people of distinction. A simple nod would suffice. Finally, I had to do whatever they asked of me. I didn't like that last part at all, but Phoenix promised me that by responding appropriately, I could hope to leave their nest alive.

What do you want? There are arguments like that, things we didn't discuss, even if I wasn't at all comforted by it.

"You'll protect me?"

I must have seemed ridiculous asking that question, but knowing that Phoenix would watch over my safety gave me some comfort.

Silence.

Then finally, "I'll be there, for the whole interview."

"For my interrogation, you mean."

He nodded.

"Thanks," I said.

He had no reaction.

We arrived in Kerington at the appointed time. We were in Harper Hill, one of the posh areas of the city; Phoenix's Camaro looked like a cart in comparison to the sports cars and hot rods that were parked there. No one here worried about carjackers because the perimeter was secured and guarded by a security company run by former military.

Our hosts' property was in a somewhat remote location. And what a property it was. Phoenix had told me that several acres of woods and gardens blocked the street view of an enormous villa built in the style of Ancient Rome. Inside the gates, armed men stood guard. There was no need to wonder what their true nature was . . .

We gained entry at the gate after we identified ourselves via an intercom equipped with a camera.

The guards greeted my boss with a nod of the head before staring at me. I was already nervous, but the thought of being the first human to infiltrate this vampire nest petrified me. Phoenix had to walk around the car, open my door, and hold out his hand so that I could steel myself to get out. I was slightly dizzy, and my legs were like jelly, but my boss caught me and murmured, "You are strong, so show it."

I nodded and regained my courage. A vampire butler led us into a vast entryway that was soberly and simply decorated. He took our coats and motioned for us to enter the great hall.

With every step we took, we passed another vampire. It seemed like all the area vampires had appointments. They were all remarkably beautiful, so much so they depressed me.

Phoenix and the others greeted one another courteously, but once they realized who they were greeting, they showed deference and stepped out of his path.

I looked at them surreptitiously, noticing that their attitude toward him was partly one of respect but more so of fear. That was truly something.

When their gazes landed on me, their faces registered surprise, curiosity, even total disbelief. I felt them inspecting me from head to toe, watching every step we took, while I kept my eyes on my boss's back as he walked in front of me.

Finally, after we passed by a seemingly interminable parade of faces, we arrived in a large room. At the back of the room, two majestic figures waited for us, seated on . . . thrones? Oh, well, they certainly knew their status.

At the same time, anyone who met them wouldn't have denied that they had a royal aura about them. They were soberly dressed, which could have made them appear austere, but on the contrary it gave them a powerful magnetism, even more so than Phoenix. I felt very small compared to them.

Talanus had been a Roman general in the empire of Augustus. His face still had traces of the great battles he had led before his death. Far from making him ugly, they gave him a fierce and terrifying beauty that made me want to know him and flee him at the same time. With his short hair, his military bearing, and conqueror's posture, he had all the qualities of a ruthless leader of armies.

Ysis, holding Talanus's hand, took my breath away. A pure Egyptian beauty, her generous figure and her dark hair made my head spin. Her husband emanated power; she emanated wisdom. When I was close enough to see her eyes, I knew immediately that they possessed an intelligence of incomparable depth. When she looked at me, I lowered my eyes—not out of weakness but out of respect.

I was looking at the black-and-white flagstones that covered the floor when things began to get serious.

Talanus spoke first. "Angel Phoenix, our most loyal subject. You asked us to break our own laws so you could bring this human to us."

That didn't sound good. Talanus seemed really angry. In the midst of this spectacle, it would be better to keep still than to make a run for it.

"You know that by letting her live, you are now responsible for her ability to keep the Secret. Are you sure of her loyalty to you?"

Phoenix remained unshakeable, and with determination he said, "Yes, I am completely sure."

Talanus gave him a severe look and started speaking again, "Tell us now why you decided to bring her here tonight."

He already knew. Phoenix had told him everything over the phone. Thus this game of domination was just politics: it was a farce intended to remind everyone of the hierarchical order more than it was to get real information. I told myself that the real interrogation wouldn't happen in front of a curious audience. Talanus and Ysis would give them just enough to occupy them for transparency's sake before putting their cards on the table in private.

"I have new information about the strange disappearances happening in Kerington County. My assistant can attest to it."

I heard murmuring behind us. Obviously everyone was eager to get to the bottom of the whole business. Too bad for them.

"*Silence!*" In a mere fraction of a second, Talanus's outburst reduced the audience to total muteness. "Get out, all of you!"

When the doors were closed, the four of us found ourselves alone in that great hall. Despite my resolution to be courageous, I couldn't help but inch closer to Phoenix for comfort.

"Welcome, Samantha Watkins." For the first time, Ysis spoke. Her warm voice contrasted sharply with her husband's reception. "Phoenix has kept us informed from the beginning. I must say that I definitely prefer his reports since you have been writing them."

"Thank you," I said simply, nodding my head.

It seemed funny to me to hear my real name. I stiffened when she stood up and came close to me. I didn't even dare to breathe. She stopped several inches away and tilted her head to the side to examine me better.

"Your eyes . . . they are so black. I have only ever seen eyes like that once before in my life . . ."

Ysis was so close that if she could have breathed, I would've felt her breath on me. I also had a pretty good view of her fangs, very sharp, which shouldn't have come out. It wasn't very reassuring, especially because she dragged out her inspection.

I was expecting to hear the rest of the story about a black-eyed person, but clearly she was not disposed to elaborate further on that subject. She turned instead to my boss (to my great relief).

"This woman, she trusts you."

Phoenix cast me a sidelong glance before answering. "And I trust her."

Talanus, who had come closer too, seemed surprised and stared at me.

"You must be very special, Miss Watkins, for Phoenix to grant you, a human, what he hardly ever grants his own kind."

I didn't know what to say. Ysis answered for me, catching hold of my chin to study me again.

"She is special . . . the Night chose her."

I felt sharp relief when she finally consented to let go of me, and from that nebulous phrase, I understood that she meant Phoenix's choice to make me his assistant. If not, I didn't get what she was referring to at all. Even so, she was a little strange, as if she were . . . daydreaming.

Regardless, I didn't like this situation, being examined from every angle. Luckily, Phoenix came to my rescue.

"She saw what was happening in the warehouse. She brought you the report, but I thought that you could find out even more by probing her mind."

Ysis looked hard at me again.

"What do you think, Samantha?"

I thought it would be better to be honest.

"I don't like the idea of someone searching my mind, even if it's to find information that could save lives. The mind is supposed to be a last defense, somewhere to take refuge. If you pass through that barrier, what freedom remains for me?"

There was a slight movement and a look of warning (too late) from my boss, which made me think that I was about to be disemboweled . . .

But that wasn't the case.

"So many of those around us spend their time flattering us and lying to us that your sincerity is disarming and . . . forgivable," said Talanus.

"Yes, your words are wise," Ysis added.

"But that doesn't mean that I have a choice. It doesn't matter anyway. I want to help you catch that band of murderers, so let's finish this, please."

"You have courage," Ysis said, positioning herself directly in front of me. "You are going to tell us everything you remember, visualizing everything at the same time in your mind. Concentrate. Avoid all stray thoughts. I can only see what you show me. Ready?"

I took a deep breath and closed my eyes. "Ready."

Two cold hands touched my temples. I had to begin. The narration of my tale was straightforward, but it was less easy to call on my memories at the same time. This was real, a strenuous task of concentration.

"I climbed up a mountain of garbage to be able to see what was happening inside . . ."

I kept going with my recollection easily enough until I got to the part about Melanie. Seeing her horrific death again made me tremble all over, and my breathing became more and more irregular.

"He killed her in front of me . . . Her name was Melanie . . . he . . . he . . . oh, I don't feel well!"

I was overcome by nausea.

"Concentrate. Breathe. What happened then?"

I tried to focus on the one who seemed to be the leader of that atrocity, but I couldn't stop the image of Melanie dying in a violent gurgling, thrown to the ground like a bag of garbage. I felt tears on my face. The words that followed couldn't even get me out of my nightmare.

I heard Ysis say, "I am losing her. Phoenix, come here."

The warmth of her voice had disappeared, replaced by the pure and harsh authority of someone who wasn't used to being disobeyed.

"What can I do?" Phoenix asked.

"Reassure her!" Ysis snapped back, her order cracking like a whip.

Even though I was trapped within a horrible vision, I could feel a presence against my back, hands on my shoulders.

"Sam. Come back. You can do it."

Phoenix. He said he would be at my side. His hands were applying a gentle pressure on my shoulders, reminding me that my boss, my friend, was protecting me. He trusted me, just as I trusted him.

Suddenly, I was able to wrench myself away from the sight of Melanie's death and resume my account without leaving out anything.

"Heath tried to kill us to shut us up, but we were able to escape."

I lost control again.

Feeling Phoenix's hands made me remember how he had taken my hand during our conversation at the bus station. I tried to get back to my story, but I was thinking about how he had stepped between Heath and me, how he'd said Heath would never lay a hand on me, the moment when Phoenix had turned to me to get us to safety by flying away . . .

I opened my eyes.

Ysis fixed me with a look, then turned her riveted glance to my employer. Even the most talented of behavioral specialists wouldn't have been able to say what she was thinking at that moment. I even felt Phoenix quiver under the burden of her green eyes.

"I think I have seen enough," she concluded, abruptly heading toward her husband and leaving my boss and me flabbergasted, too dazed to move.

Well, at least that was my case. I couldn't speak for Phoenix.

"Did you recognize any of the vampires?" Talanus asked as he gently took Ysis's hand.

"Despite Samantha's efforts to see their leader, he remains a mystery, only visible from the back," Ysis answered. "It is maddening . . . As for the others, I do not know them. All I can say is that they are not from here. In her memories, they were speaking Chinese."

I'd been too far away to hear anything. Ysis must have been able to read lips and understand them. In two millennia, she'd had time to learn several languages.

"Did you discover anything that can put us on the right track?" Phoenix asked.

"No, except that two of them were making plans to meet in a Kerington club to discuss the sale of a large quantity of contraband. But they turned around before giving a name."

"It is a start. In my opinion, Heath called in strangers to avoid leaks. They must be under orders to stay discreet, but if these are mafiosi, they won't be able to stop themselves from taking advantage of this to make their own deals. If we find their favorite bar, we can find these vampires and have a chance to sort this all out."

"And don't forget Thirsty Bill. He lied to you, telling you he knew nothing. We need to keep an eye on him," I ventured.

Phoenix nodded his agreement. "Sam is right. But it will be difficult for me to be in two places at once. I can contact Karl and François to lend me a hand."

Talanus took a step toward Phoenix. "You will have to act fast. This has been going on for far too long. Ysis and I were obligated to inform the Elders. If this business is not settled quickly, we risk them coming in person. And you know what that means . . ."

My boss nodded his head gravely. Good for him that he'd understood; I was completely lost. Who were these Elders? Talanus seemed really concerned, so it couldn't mean anything good.

"We will need help," Talanus said. "Ichimi and Kaiko have already dealt with the local Japanese mafia. Their members do not like how their Chinese rivals have increased their power. They could maybe get information about bars and clubs that would attract our targets."

Phoenix unmistakably registered his disapproval at this, his fangs out, emitting an incensed growl.

"I know that you do not like them, Phoenix, and that the feeling is mutual, but if you are my right hand, Ichimi is my left. Out of loyalty, he will help you. As for Kaiko, she will do what Ichimi orders her to do."

My boss retreated into silence before finally sighing. "As you wish. But I will only tell them the bare minimum, and I ask you to not tell them about my assistant's role in all this."

Talanus threw him a look of exasperation. "Come on, Phoenix. They would not go so far as to touch her just to provoke you. They are well above all that."

Yeah, boss. They're above all that. My God, make sure that they are!

It would be best for my well-being if my employer reconsidered his ability to make enemies and provoke them.

"Maybe you are underestimating them," Phoenix added.

The small cry of surprise and terror that came from my mouth came too late: everything happened so fast. Talanus had grabbed Phoenix by the throat, lifted him from the ground, and then slammed him to the ground in the same movement. The force with which he'd brought Phoenix to the ground would have been enough to reduce any human in his place to a bloody pulp.

Talanus's eyes turned yellow and glowing, and his menacing growl set off new tremors in my legs. However, his victim made no move to defend himself.

"You dare question my judgment, you, whose recent existence is in no way comparable to my own?"

When he squeezed Phoenix's throat even harder, I couldn't stand it anymore. I tried to move forward so I could make him let go, even if that would have meant my death. I took two steps when a hand on my shoulder held me back. Ysis. Silently, she signaled to me that it would be best if I stopped right there.

"I beg your forgiveness, master. That was not my place."

Freed from the vise around his throat, Phoenix apologized with great humility.

Talanus stood up at once and held out his hand. My boss took it and got up. The vampire hierarchy was obviously as strict as could be, and unlike in human schools, physical punishment was an acceptable form of discipline.

Ysis approached them, smiling. "Phoenix, you truly have found a rare pearl. Your human was ready to face Talanus to free you."

Humph. Do vampires not have any tact at all? My cheeks were on fire, as quickly as a pine forest under a southerly wind, but I still decided to be proud of my courage, or my stupidity, so I lifted my cheek, defying anyone to make fun of me.

But my employer's glacial stare put an end to my defiance.

"I have forgotten how quickly humans blush. However, I must say that this one breaks all records in that regard . . . ," Talanus said. He didn't show any hostility, but rather amused curiosity. You would have thought that his altercation with Phoenix hadn't taken place just thirty seconds earlier.

He approached me and began inspecting me head to toe.

"Hm . . . your courage is not obvious at first, but you have true potential. I see why our angel respects you so much." He turned away, my presence already forgotten. "Before leaving, go see Ichimi and Kaiko and let them know. We shall see to Karl and François. Keep sending us your reports. Ysis is right . . . I like them more now . . ."

Without another word, he exited by a hidden door. Ysis made to follow him when she reconsidered and came back over to us. She looked each of us in the eye before saying something I wouldn't understand until much later.

"You are connected by the Night. The protector must guide the steps of the one the Night has chosen, at the cost of great sacrifice . . ."

She disappeared as well, leaving us in a total daze.

\*\*\*

"What did she mean?" I asked, stunned.

"Ysis has premonitions of a sort. But her words will not have any meaning for those who hear them, except for her. We will understand it one day. For now, we have more pressing concerns."

His tone made me think he was angry with me, which was irritating.

"What did I do now? Let's have it all out before we meet with our sworn enemies," I said, my hands on my hips, ready to attack.

My reaction seemed to surprise Phoenix, but he still jumped at the chance to argue.

"You should not have stepped in. I was not in any danger. But you, you almost got yourself killed. Have you forgotten everything I taught you about vampire ways, or are you just completely reckless?"

He was reprimanding me like a parent exasperated by his child's bad behavior.

"Oh, well, excuse me for worrying about you! Next time, I'll just let the first bloodsucker who comes along go ahead and decapitate you. I'll have you know that Ysis stopped me from getting too close. I know a bit about your kind's pride—I do live with the most *hotheaded* specimen that ever existed!" I shouted.

He really had a gift for making me fly off the handle.

His reaction stunned me. He didn't say a word, and then a smile appeared on his face as his anger subsided, giving way to amusement. When he started to snort with laughter, I wondered if he'd gone mad.

"Hotheaded?" he chuckled, looking at me.

I didn't know where I'd come up with that word. Calling a vampire of Phoenix's moral caliber a hothead was rather comical actually, so it wasn't long before I was smiling too.

"I know it's stupid."

Won over by this ridiculous situation, I followed my boss's example and let the hilarity overcome my anger.

We finally calmed down, but that interlude did us some good, preparing us to face the horde of dreadfully curious vampires waiting for us.

"Hey, your friends out there didn't hear us, did they?"

"Lead. In the walls and doors."

Oh yes. Useful.

"Ready?"

"I will try not to screw up this time."

"That would be best. Ichimi and Kaiko are far less tolerant than Talanus and Ysis."

"You hate them," I observed.

"You will shortly know why. Let's go."

After opening the doors, he moved forward by my side . . .

It was like facing a tsunami. A whole bunch of faces and arms jostled around us, asking us what was happening exactly in the county. Phoenix remained stone-faced. I tried to imitate him, but being the center of attention of human-blood lovers was truly frightening. I could at least testify to the fact that this was nothing compared to meeting Talanus's left-hand man.

Ichimi and Kaiko (my boss had indicated that she was Ichimi's lover) were standing near the exit, as if they were expecting Phoenix to report to them as well before leaving. That thought must have also crossed my boss's mind, for he seemed even colder than during our gauntlet through the vampire crowd.

Once we were standing right in front of them, he murmured only "not here" before leading the march to a quieter spot.

We entered a small room, a poker room by the looks of the table in the middle of the space. In our haste, I wasn't able to inspect our two Japanese vampires until the door had closed behind us.

There weren't any Japanese residents in Kentwood, and the first Japanese person I'd ever met was Kiro. He hadn't exactly left a lasting impression on me apart from his disgusting old-man lewdness. I only knew his country's culture from documentaries and reports that I'd seen on television, but it was enough to help me pinpoint what, or rather who, Ichimi reminded me of: a samurai. His whole body radiated the mastery of Bushido, giving him a calm and lethal aura. He was tall and thin, and he had an impressive scar on his face that ran from his right ear to the corner of his mouth. I could detect a strong animosity toward Phoenix in Ichimi's piercing brown eyes. However, it was nothing compared to the hatred that burned in the eyes of that war goddess incarnate next to him, Kaiko. I took a step back involuntarily. I shouldn't have.

"You are right to back away, miserable human. If Phoenix is weak enough to walk by your side as if you were an equal, that is his business, but I want you and your human stink at a distance that shows your inferiority properly."

Kaiko spit out these words with such disgust and with such cruelty that it left me speechless. Phoenix reacted for me, drawing back his lips to reveal his fangs.

"Be careful what you say, Kaiko, or I will make you swallow your insults and your fangs with them."

They faced each other in a concert of threatening growls—the effect was startling.

Ichimi spoke up. "How about you just say what you want from us so we can be done with you and your human plaything?" He seemed perfectly bored by what was happening right in front of him; he even stifled a yawn.

My boss outlined their mission without ever going further than absolutely necessary in the details; he never mentioned the role I'd taken either. He asked them if they were up to the task.

Kaiko lifted her chin defiantly. "Do you think we are incompetent?"

Phoenix's sardonic smile reappeared. "You can interpret it as you like."

Provoking her no longer seemed like a fun idea when she readied to attack him again. Fortunately, Ichimi grabbed her and quickly pulled her back.

"Shut up, woman. You are being ridiculous. As for you, angel, keep an eye on your phone."

He turned around, opened the door, and left with his lover trailing after him, but not without her giving us one last murderous look.

"I want to leave."

After what I'd just witnessed, I'd had my fill of vampires for the night.

"Come."

I followed my boss back to the car, hurrying to get in. I only felt better once we were out of the secured area.

"Breathe, Samantha."

"It's OK . . . I'm fine . . . It's just that . . ."

"Kaiko and Ichimi?"

"Yes."

"I told you that you would understand why I do not like them. Their arrogance and their disdain of others, humans most of all, disgusts me. Ichimi is slightly less expressive than his lover because of the samurai code, but that does not mean he thinks any differently than she does."

"Why does she hate you?"

The memory of the murderous desire shining in Kaiko's eyes made me shiver.

"I don't know."

"You never took the time to find out?"

"Kaiko is wild and maniacal. Talking to her serves no purpose . . . what's more, just looking at her makes me want to kill her, so I prefer to avoid long conversations."

"But Talanus and Ysis seem to appreciate the two of them. There must be a reason."

Phoenix sighed.

"They have known each other since the Middle Ages, since Ichimi saved Talanus in the Balkans more than six hundred years ago. After the discovery of the New World, when Talanus and Ysis were chosen by the Elders to run the new sector here, Ichimi was sent back to Japan, where his presence was required. It was then that he met Kaiko. I know they always stayed in contact with Talanus, and when Ichimi was free of his obligations after the death of his sector leader, he accepted his old friend's offer to come join him here. It was just after I had taken up the post of angel. Since then, they have been inseparable. Talanus thinks that Bushido made Ichimi an honorable man . . . People change . . . but I cannot call my master's choices into question."

He'd paid the price for that, as I'd seen.

"Pff. I think I've overdosed on vampires."

"Thanks a lot," Phoenix said, smiling.

He knew I wasn't including him with that group.

"It was a lot all at once. Did they organize a meeting before we got there or what?"

"The mood in town is tense with all these disappearances . . . The Secret is in ever more danger."

"Is that why the Elders are likely to come?"

"All this has not fallen on deaf ears as far as I can tell. The ones we call the Elders, or the Greats, are ten of the oldest and wisest vampires in our community. The youngest is a thousand years old. They live in the Balkans, and their mission is to ensure the preservation of the secret of our existence. They are surrounded by a substantial number of people in their service who are responsible for reading all the reports sent in from sector leaders the world over and for warning them of potential threats. No one would ever lie to them, because they have spy networks everywhere. Even if they had wanted to, Talanus and Ysis could not have hidden this blood trafficking for a long time. These people are the highest authority for our species, and it is impossible to flout our laws without them finding you and making you pay a steep price . . . If the Elders come here, it will be to clean up the region. They will begin by replacing Talanus, Ysis, and me before tackling the trafficking problem. They will find them, you can be sure of that. And their punishment will be dreadful."

"What will you do if they fire you?"

"Nothing. I will be dead."

"What?"

"When the Greats intervene somewhere, it is not good for the sector leader or the angel. They are executed if it turns out that incompetence of one or the other has endangered the Secret."

Finding out that Phoenix's life depended on the dismantling of a blood-trafficking ring heightened my need to resolve this whole affair.

"Why are we waiting to check out the clubs?" I declared forcefully.

Phoenix seemed surprised by my determination and raised his eyebrows.

"I thought I would bring you back to Scarborough. This evening has not been very easy for you."

"Are you joking? Turn around now and head to the Sexy Thong Show."

An idea came to me as I was talking, and I thought it was a good one. After all, we needed a hand.

"I do not think that going to Bill Miller's establishment is smart—unless we want to put him on alert."

"I don't want to go to Bill's. You'll park far away and let me handle it."

I wasn't ready to reveal my plan to him, for I was too focused on what I wanted to say.

"What do you have in mind?" he insisted.

"Shh. I'm thinking."

His response was a deep growl that made me realize I was truly exasperating my chauffeur. Too bad.

When we arrived in the east neighborhoods of Kerington, I knew what I had to do.

"The club is three blocks ahead. Should I keep going?"

"No, here's fine."

He parked the car, and I took my bag and stepped out. Before closing my door, I leaned back in. "Give me all the cash you have on you."

"Excuse me?"

"I know you always carry a substantial sum in case you need it. Hurry up! We don't have all night," I ordered, and he grudgingly obeyed. "Wait for me here. I won't be long . . . and don't follow me by flying."

"But . . ."

Wham! I slammed the door, too much in a hurry to hear his complaints. I headed to my destination at a swift pace, but I didn't run to avoid attracting attention. At Sexy Thong Show's street corner, I saw what I was looking for . . .

***

Luckily my coat had a hood. I didn't want the bouncer to recognize me. With my face nicely hidden, I headed for the gaggle of noisy and formidable Dark Angels, aiming particularly for their leader, Bobby the Eel, who was recognizable by his abundant curly hair.

These wannabe gangsters seemed dumbfounded by the sight of a woman walking alone toward them without the smallest sign of anxiety. Two of them—enormous, unshaven, and tattooed to the upper neck—blocked my path, doubtless to remind the innocent woman (that I wasn't) that I was supposed to cross to the other side of the street and keep my head down.

"I need to talk to your boss. Get out of my way, or I'll break your arms," I said loudly so Bobby could hear me.

The two watchdogs didn't take my threat seriously and, laughing, made to come closer. One of them had arms double the size of my thighs; tattoos of "Mom" and "I love you" spoiled the image of the thick brute.

As I prepared to get rid of them, I heard, "Hey, hey, hey! Careful, guys! If I was you, I'd let the lady pass before you end up on the ground with your arm ripped off, crying for your momma."

The Eel saved them from a tight spot; considering my foul mood, I wouldn't have given them any mercy. They scattered, letting me pass through without fully understanding how a woman with such a small build could have done them any harm.

"Bobby the Eel, I'm happy to see that you and your Dark Angels are faithfully at your post," I greeted him.

He seemed flattered that I remembered him and his gang. The bigwigs in general don't deal with small-time thugs who think of themselves as sheriffs.

"Miss I-Don't-Know-Your-Name, thrilled to see you again."

He hadn't forgotten to be polite around me. Gold star for him, but I didn't have time to waste.

"I have some work for you and your guys. Discretion and danger are givens. Can we talk elsewhere? I don't like the neighbors much . . ."

I tilted my head in the direction of the strip club and its bouncer, who was watching us, curious to know who was there and why, for once, no one was brawling.

"Follow me," said Bobby.

I trailed the Eel to an alley down the street. Only a few months before this, the idea of following a guy in a leather jacket into a dark alley wouldn't have crossed my mind unless it was in a nightmare. It was crazy how I'd changed since my arrival at the manor in Scarborough.

"I'm listening," he said.

Bobby had intuited the importance of my arrival, and he wasn't even strutting. He was completely serious.

"Have you been hearing about all these disappearances happening around here?" I asked.

"I know that it's worse than what they say on TV. I have a friend—she's a junkie—she vanished and no one did anything to find her."

"My boss and I are looking for the ones behind all that. I can't tell you everything, but we think that the mafiosi who came here recently from China are part of it. You know a lot of people in the poorer parts of town. I want you to open your eyes and ears wide so we can find out where the strangers are hiding."

"If it's the Chinese, they must do their business in the Chinatown clubs, where we won't be welcome."

"We've already looked there. But if they want to go unnoticed, they won't compete against their own on shared turf. There's no national solidarity in the mafia. They all have their own territories. I think they're aiming for an entirely different clientele, which is where you can help me. But be careful. Don't approach them under any circumstances. These men are murderers, and they will kill you all to preserve their anonymity. The only thing I ask is that you call me if you learn something useful."

Bobby considered my proposition while biting his nails. "You're offering us work, sure, OK, but we'll be the ones risking our necks out there. I'm not sure . . ."

He seemed almost afraid, and his expression set my nerves to boil. When I spoke again, it was with a glacial and contemptuous tone.

"I see I was mistaken about you. You want people to respect you as an enforcer, but when someone proposes a job in that regard, you hesitate, too terrified to act. I don't want to deal with idiots. I'm going to go find a gang that's worth the effort."

I turned and strode away briskly. My plan just collapsed, and the countdown to Phoenix's death continued.

"Wait!"

I stopped without turning around, hearing someone run toward me. Bobby the Eel caught up and blocked my path.

"It's a deal."

I raised an eyebrow to show that I found his sudden change of heart surprising.

"If we want people to respect us, we can't be afraid to get our hands dirty. I've acted like a coward, but I guarantee you it won't happen again. Give me your number, and I promise you we'll find your Chink—I mean, your Chinese mafiosi."

I glared at him, inspecting him to make sure I could count on him: his need to make his gang essential within the mafia was very strong. He would do what I asked.

"My name is Samantha Jones. Here's my number," I said, offering him my card, ignoring Bobby's smirk at the mention of my name, so well chosen by my boss who had never seen *Sex and the City*. "Memorize it, then destroy the card. You will be the *only* one I talk to. Your friends will only know the minimum, and they must do everything in their power to avoid being found out."

He nodded.

"Oh, I forgot something." I took from my bag the fat wad of cash I'd taken from my boss. "Here's an advance to give you another source of motivation. Nothing is free. You'll have double that if you help us catch these men."

Taking the money and realizing how much he had in his hands, I thought his eyeballs would bulge out of their sockets.

"Do we have a deal?" I asked to end the conversation.

"We have a deal," he replied, offering me his hand to shake on it.

"One last thing. When all this is over, you'll forget all about this. Our deal, my existence, and that of my boss. Got it?"

I didn't really want to sound too commanding in that moment, but my words smacked the air like an order that would suffer no response.

Bobby the Eel gawked at me a few seconds before nodding again to show he agreed.

Without another look, I turned back to rejoin the man who was going to give me the scolding of the century once he learned what I'd done.

***

"Took you long enough."

Phoenix's tone was aggressive, and his eyes were brighter than usual.

"It's nice of you to be worried about me," I mocked as I settled into the passenger side.

He groaned before answering. "I really do not like this."

"It's the same for everyone, don't worry."

He started the car and turned back to the manor. I was totally exhausted, but I couldn't sleep; I had to tell Phoenix about the agreement I'd made with the Dark Angels, and there were some questions I wanted to ask him. Unable to wait any longer, he beat me to it, getting the conversation rolling.

"Are you going to tell me now what you were doing? I thought I was going crazy waiting in this damn car for you to come back."

I smiled, taking an obvious pleasure in hearing him complain.

"Calm down. I went to see the bikers from the other night. I've given them their first real gangster work."

Phoenix gritted his teeth so hard I could hear them grinding against each other. Oops. I had serious reason to worry.

"Elaborate, please."

"You remember Bobby the Eel? He and his gang will be our eyes and ears in the bars and clubs of east Kerington in exchange for financial compensation."

"You told him why, I assume." His voice was just above a whisper . . . probably to avoid yelling at me.

"I didn't tell him anything important, and the disappearances aren't a secret. He only knows that he needs to call me if he hears anything about our Chinese men."

He exhaled, as though he were relieved that my initiative hadn't been the catastrophe he was expecting. *Thanks for your confidence, Phoenix.*

"I hope you know what you are doing."

"You said yourself that we need help, so might as well take it where we can get it. Besides, I don't think our vampires will take their business to Chinatown. That part will keep Kaiko and Ichimi busy, at least."

"Why did you not say anything about this earlier?"

"I thought that giving them a bone to chew on would get them out of our way without offending them."

Phoenix smiled. "When you put it like that, I think I should congratulate you instead of strangling you."

"Well, given the amount of money you'll have to pay our informants, I would prefer that, yes. And while I'm thinking about it, who are Karl and François?"

"My friends."

So I was finally going to know the ones who'd figured out how to soften up my boss. I was waiting for him to continue in order to satisfy my curiosity, but Phoenix still had some difficulty sustaining a conversation, the numbskull.

"And? Is there any more?" I grumbled.

"Oh. Karl and François are my closest friends, or rather my only friends. Hm, except for you, now."

Good save.

"I met Karl Sarlsberg in Northern France during the time of the sixth Italian war, from 1521 to 1526, which was between Charles V of the Holy Roman Empire and the French king François I. It was complete chaos at the time, and for a vampire, it was an ideal scenario for feeding without suspicion. Karl still considered himself a subject of the Holy Roman Empire, and so he was laying waste to the French garrisons. We met when he was being pursued by a group of soldiers who took him for a spy. The imbeciles . . ."

There again, Phoenix didn't want to shock me by putting into words what those soldiers suffered, but this time I wouldn't settle for omission.

"You helped him?"

I already knew his answer.

"Yes. I was still a young vampire, I was hungry, and despite the training of my master, Finn, who had left to get supplies in a nearby village, I could not resist. We massacred them."

Phoenix got quiet, letting me absorb his words.

"At the time, violence was wholly a part of me. I could not resist the urge. It was in my nature. It took a long time to be able to control myself. Believe me, a hundred years with Finn was not overlong."

What I was hearing was enough to make my hair stand on end, but sometimes things happened and it wasn't worth stewing over them. The vampire next to me surely no longer resembled the vampire he'd been just after his transformation. I knew he had killed; he'd told me that much. I also knew that since then, in a certain way, in his role as an angel, he was also saving hundreds of lives, just like he was protecting my own.

"What did Finn say when he returned?"

"He was not happy. He almost decapitated Karl when he learned what we had done. But he spared him on the condition that Karl stay with him to learn how to be a respectable vampire. Karl was transformed around the same time as me, but his creator had abandoned him."

"That's when you became friends."

"Yes. He stayed with us for fifty years, but his disagreements with Finn became intolerable for both of them. Finn reproached him for not taking his training seriously. Karl finally left and found another vampire to guide him. I never learned who it was. When I saw Karl again much later, he was much calmer. He told me his master, for whom he professed an eternal admiration, was dead. I was free and we reunited like two brothers. We see each other much less since I became Talanus and Ysis's angel, but I know I can always count on him."

My boss was almost smiling at the memory of his friendship with Karl. Their connection seemed strong despite the usual vampire predilection for emotional independence.

"What about François?"

"François Caron was one of Louis XIV's musketeers. When I met him in Paris in 1665, he was still human. I saw him at a tavern with some of his associates. He was the only one not drinking, the only one refusing the pleasant company of women. I overheard his friends ridiculing him for it. Apparently, they were reproaching him for his sense of virtue. Never drinking excessively, saving himself for the woman who would be his wife. I admit that it made me laugh too. Anyway, some time later, I came across two vampires who were hunting neighborhood thieves. One of them was François. I approached to introduce myself to that ex-musketeer, but he tried to attack me. His master, Jacques Chinon, did not let him, fortunately . . . As the years went by, François calmed down and we became the best of friends. Incredibly, his transformation did not prevent him from keeping his same moral values. He was cultivated and devout. It was still out of the question for him to lose his virtue before marriage, even if he would never find a priest who would marry him. He is an extraordinary person, but he speaks so little that it can be exasperating. He always tells me that words are useless unless absolutely necessary."

"You've certainly followed that advice to the letter, from what I can see," I laughed.

He snorted. "If you find that I do not talk much, wait until you meet François. You will not be disappointed. When he picks up the phone, he does not even acknowledge it. The silence is the only thing that indicates that he is there and listening."

"I feel like seeing you two talk together will be a treat for my eyes and my ears," I said, laughing.

I really wanted to meet this François. I didn't know why, but his first friend, Karl, whom Phoenix considered a brother, hadn't made a good impression on me. As for François, Phoenix recounted several other episodes from their lives, and that reinforced my desire to meet the king's musketeer. Their adventures were absolutely riveting.

I wasn't looking out the window, so I didn't realize we'd left Kerington until much later.

"Wait, we're going back to the manor?"

"I would prefer to. We will need some preparation so we will not be detected, and you, you will need some rest if you want to come with me. It is late, and you should sleep."

"What about you, do you ever feel tired?"

"Yes, during the day I sleep like a log."

The way he'd said that made me burst out laughing. With all the stress of that evening, my laughter became uncontrollable, and tears started streaming down my face. With Phoenix, I'd gotten used to the formal language of a distinguished man, so to hear him use an idiom was utterly funny and unexpected. Soon my boss, whose face moved from alarm to consternation to amusement, wound up laughing with me. When he laughed, he lost that mask of austerity and danger that he normally wore. He seemed . . . innocent, calm. I liked seeing him that way. I didn't know why.

"Where . . . where do you sleep?" I asked, slowly becoming serious again.

"I shall show you later."

If I had still doubted the trust that Phoenix was showing me, my doubts would have been swept away that very instant. Indeed, for a vampire, nothing was more important than security while asleep. Showing it to me was a sign of extraordinary trust. I was extremely touched.

"Have I said something wrong?" he said, worried, seeing me stare out the car window.

Why had he needed to say that to me while in a car, where I couldn't hide?

"Uh, no . . . I have something in my eye," I answered, frantically rubbing at the traitorous organ that had dared let a tear slip out.

Ouch. I'd rubbed a little too hard.

My boss didn't press me for more, and so we finished the trip in silence. He woke me up once we were in the garage. I yawned powerfully before getting out.

"I'm so tired I could fall asleep standing up."

"Go to bed. I have no more need of you tonight."

"No, before that, I want to see where you sleep. In case of emergency, I need to be able to find you anywhere."

The curiosity overrode my exhaustion, and I couldn't wait to discover my boss's lair.

He led me to his office on the first floor and headed to the philosophical section of his bookshelves.

"Who is your favorite philosopher, Samantha?"

"Voltaire! Who else is there?" I gushed.

I loved that man and his sense of irony. Phoenix smiled.

"I knew it."

On that enigmatic note, he pulled on the spine of one of the books. The entire bookcase moved forward silently before sliding open to give way to a hidden room. It made me think of the day when his sudden arrival had almost made me choke to death (murder by lollipop). As concentrated as I was on my work, I hadn't seen him come out of his hiding place.

"You really like sliding mechanisms, don't you? So which is it, the book key?"

"*Candide*. What else is there?"

He passed ahead of me, sporting his usual smile in the corner of his mouth.

It was clear that thanks to my boss, I'd discovered the world at a different angle. "Cultivate our garden," as Voltaire said. I'd unearthed the living dead, and I'd bound myself through friendship to someone who made me work for him. Voltaire would have laughed . . .

The light came on, and I had a moment of hesitation.

"What? Do not tell me you were expecting a coffin," sighed Phoenix, rolling his eyes.

I didn't know exactly what I was expecting, though the notion of a coffin had certainly crossed my mind. But this . . .

The room was spacious, with enough area to move between the bed, desk, closet, and armchair. The walls were a pale gray, and landscape paintings cheered them. A copy of *The Lord of the Rings* was on the night table. I noticed these details, but something else had caught my attention.

The bed . . . was . . . enormous. The ebony frame of this four-poster bed was finely sculpted; the white of the sheets stood out against the dark wood.

"Wow! You must move around a lot when you sleep!" I exclaimed.

What was I sticking my nose into? I could say the stupidest things. Best to find another topic of conversation, and quickly. I took up my inspection again. No alarm clock.

"Do you always know when the sun sets?"

"Yes. Another advantage of being what we are."

I turned around, but I hadn't noticed that he was right behind me. Being somewhat clumsy, I ran straight into him.

It felt like banging against a mountain of marble before I lost my balance and found myself seated and stupefied on his bed.

"Are you all right?" Phoenix asked, approaching to check.

"Ugh, you don't have skin on your bones, you're made of granite," I grumbled while holding my head in my hands.

He pulled my hands away to see if I was laying it on thick. His face was close to mine, and while he scrutinized me, looking for a wound he could heal, I stiffened. The situation reminded me of the episode with Matthew, and I was afraid of my reaction.

I stood up abruptly, almost knocking him on the head with my own in the process; it would have resulted in me cracking my skull wide open.

"I'm OK. I've seen worse, remember."

He didn't say anything, which added to my unease.

"Your room is very beautiful, in any case."

As a diversion, I could've done better.

"Thank you," he responded.

"Good, um, well . . . OK. I think I'll go to bed now. If I need you, I have your number and . . . I know where to find you. Uh . . . good night."

I skedaddled without further ado, troubled by the sensation that I'd felt when my boss had grabbed my hands and looked at me that way. He must have thought I was crazy.

It'd made me remember the moment when Matthew had been dangerously close to me. If I'd let him, he might have kissed me. That would have been my first kiss . . . and I'd pushed him away. Every time that memory came back to me, I felt embarrassed. Phoenix would have immediately noticed a change in the rhythm of my heartbeat, and if that was the case, he might get ideas about my feelings for him . . . Heaven help me if he thought that I was in love with him when that wasn't the case, and I'd already had so much trouble getting him to think of me as a friend!

On the other hand, fleeing like that hadn't been any smarter. Fine, whatever. I was too tired to rack my brains about my natural tactlessness. I ran to my room, flung off my clothes, and jumped into bed, grateful that it was so soft. Then, to use my boss's expression, I slept like a log.

***

I spent the next day doing nothing, which did me good because I needed to recuperate. My interview with Talanus and Ysis hadn't been the most relaxing; thinking about Kaiko's crazy eyes chilled me to the bone. I also wondered what Phoenix's employer could have meant by "the Night chose her" and "you are connected by the Night." Ysis had used the word *Night* with such reverence it must have some importance for her.

It hadn't worried my boss much. According to him, acting like an incomprehensible oracle happened to Ysis every now and then. In my opinion, she was more than bizarre, traveling between her planet and ours.

I followed my boss's advice and brushed that mystery out of my mind. If it had any meaning, we would understand it in due time.

I took advantage of the rest of the day to tackle my new favorite pastime: cooking. In my old house, I would prepare good meals, but the kitchen wasn't as big as the one in the manor, so it limited my possibilities. Here, though, everything was available and I had plenty of room, so I threw myself into it wholeheartedly. Sometimes, when I made too many muffins, I took some to Danny, who was crazy about them and despaired that he could never achieve the same result, even though I'd given him my recipe.

Once, even, Phoenix had tried the roast beef I'd taken out of the oven, all hot and bloody, with potatoes. He'd been enticed by the smell and couldn't resist trying human food. I thought I was going to die of laughter seeing him grimace and almost choke on the bite he'd forgotten to chew (because he was used to a liquid diet). He couldn't die because he was already dead, but seeing him fight with that little piece of meat caught in the back of his throat caused one of the biggest fits of laughter of my entire life. It must have been more than five hundred years since anyone had made fun of Phoenix, so I'll let you imagine how vexed he was at this. Of course, he was angrier with himself because he'd caused his own ridicule.

By the time Phoenix appeared, I'd already eaten dinner.

"I am going to Drake Hill to see Kiro. I have to ask him to use his connections to help us find our vampires."

"You can't just give him a call?"

"No, I prefer talking to him in person. Kiro cannot hear anything on the phone. It is a miracle that he understood we were coming the last time."

"But . . . he heard us pretty well."

"He wears a hearing aid. The phone sets off a ringing sound in his hearing aid, so he has to remove it, and then it is like talking to a wall," he informed me, rolling his eyes to the sky with a clear message: *Ah, old age!*

"I didn't notice. OK, I'll get my bag and I'll come."

"No, it will be faster if I fly. Besides, I will not be long."

The means of travel settled the matter. I didn't insist. It was out of the question to fly again, especially since I'd just eaten. He left, and I was alone in the big manor.

During his absence, I installed myself in the office and surfed the Internet, looking for new information about the disappearances. There had been three new kidnappings, in Drake Hill, Williamsburg, and Kerington. All three victims were pretty blond women around twenty-five; the police were frustrated by the insignificance of the evidence they collected. Thanks to my proficiency with computers, I was able to hack into the police database, so I knew exactly where the investigation was . . . Phoenix couldn't get over it the first time I'd shown him.

My eyes were starting to prickle from staring at the computer screen, so I decided to take a break in the parlor. I sat down on the sofa and closed my eyes, trying to figure out a geographical connection between all the disappearances that would help find the murderers' headquarters.

Suddenly, I felt something like a gust of wind behind me, and I turned around quickly.

"Phoenix?"

No one.

I must have been dreaming. When I resumed my research, I had the alarming feeling that someone had touched my neck.

All the windows were closed, so no breeze could have reached me, and last I checked, breezes didn't have fingers. Though I was tense, I forced myself to slow my heart rate and act normally, in the hope that the invisible presence would show itself. Still seated to fool the intruder into thinking I didn't know he was there, I closed my eyes again, but not entirely this time, and I slid my hand between the sofa cushions, where there was always a gun hidden, loaded with silver bullets.

This time, I was ready. When all the hairs on the back of my neck bristled to signal that someone was truly behind me that very moment, I stood up and turned around in one fluid movement, shooting without hesitation.

I'd put a hole in the wall, but I swore I'd only missed my target by a hair.

"Luckily I heard you click off the safety, or else I would already be a pile of dust on the proprietor's pretty carpet," said someone behind me.

I reacted instantly and faced the intruder, aiming at him again. He raised his hands so I wouldn't shoot.

"Calm down, gorgeous. I mean you no harm," he said, serious this time, his fangs visible.

"Lesson number one, never trust a vampire. Especially when you don't know him. You're going to tell me who you are and what you're doing here, or I swear the next time I shoot I will not miss," I answered, ready to shoot directly into his heart.

The smile that spread over his face that moment irritated me tremendously, just like his nonchalant attitude and the way he looked at me, like a gourmand letting himself be tempted by a small treat. He looked like he might lick his lips in anticipation. Gross.

"I see Phoenix has trained you well. He has very good taste in his choice of assistant. You are very sexy. I see myself taking your clothes off, piece by piece, and then we will have something to do to pass the time while we wait for him to come back. You will only have one desire . . . that he is delayed . . . and delayed . . ."

He looked as if he was about to step forward, but I kept him in line by gripping my gun more tightly.

"You're crazy! If you persist in not telling me who you are, you're dead! Is that clear?"

"I could disarm you in a second if I wanted," he growled, threatening.

"You could try! But my silver bullet will have time to do some damage!" I hissed, lifting my head to really show him he didn't intimidate me.

He suddenly abandoned his aggressive posture and scratched his chin.

"I see we're at an impasse, my goddess. What shall we do now?"

His coolness irritated me more than if he'd insulted me.

"Tell me who you are!" I ordered again.

If he didn't cooperate that time, I was really going to shoot him, and too bad about the carpet stains.

"Karl! When are you going to stop behaving like a fifty-year-old vampire?"

That velvet voice, recognizable out of a thousand, was coming from the parlor door. My boss had just returned, and he hadn't immediately killed the man that I was aiming at. Moreover, he'd called him Karl, the name of the man he considered almost a brother.

"Lower your weapon, Samantha. He will not do anything to you," Phoenix said, passing by me to welcome his friend. "Karl! How long has it been since you last stopped by here?" he asked warmly.

"Too long, my friend, far too long . . ."

I realized that I was still aiming my gun at the stranger, who was amiably shaking hands with my boss. It was an authentic gesture of affection given that vampire salutations were usually just simple nods at each other. I lowered my arm and stared at them.

Karl easily could be confused for a model, his face and his body were *that* perfect. His blond hair was short and silky, his nose aquiline, his eyes blue, and the rest . . . Despite his clothes (a black shirt and a pair of jeans), I could detect a torso with sublime abdominal muscles. A real Adonis.

However, I felt an immediate and genuine aversion to him. Karl's eyes sparkled, but they seemed to do so with malice and so came across as rather cold and calculating. His toothy grin, which must have thrilled his lady admirers, had something downright frightening about it. I recalled his voracious look when he was examining me like a piece of meat just a moment earlier. Despite the affection Phoenix was showing him, I knew then that I would only ever hate my boss's best friend.

Remembering that I was there, the two friends stopped reminiscing and turned toward me.

"Oh, Karl, I am neglecting my duties. I present Samantha—" Phoenix began.

"Jones. Samantha Jones," I interrupted, curtly nodding my head at our guest.

It was completely out of the question that my boss reveal my real name to this guy, and I knew he almost did—and this was the man who was always preaching prudence to me!

In return, I got a severe look from Phoenix, who must not understand why I was introducing myself under a false name when I'd not protested at all against the fact that Talanus and Ysis knew my true identity.

Karl directed his predatory smile at me before clapping Phoenix on the back.

"Congratulations, Little Brother. You are quite resourceful. I should maybe find myself a pretty assistant too, though I do not think I will be able to find one as attractive and with a name that hints at hidden talents . . . I have always dreamed of having a woman who could fulfill all my desires, professional and sexual. That *is* what's going on between you two, right? If not . . ."

He didn't finish his sentence and he didn't need to. What he was hinting at was perfectly clear: if Phoenix wasn't "tapping that" (me), he wanted to try. Rage unfurled in me like a tsunami, and I stepped toward him, forgetting all prudence as I bridged the gap between me and the two vampires.

"Who do you think you are? You show up here unannounced, you act like a perverted baby vampire, you talk to me like I'm nothing more than a sexual object, and what's more, you dare insult us both with your insinuations! You may be like a brother to Phoenix, but compared to him, you're just an uneducated barbarian! And—aaaahhh! Put me down! Put me down, for God's sake!"

Phoenix stopped my verbal outburst by suddenly grabbing me and tossing me over his shoulder. I had just enough time to see the anger blazing on Karl's face when I'd compared him negatively to his best friend.

"Forgive her, Karl. I think she is just getting emotional," Phoenix said apologetically, loudly enough to hear over my shouts of "put me down!"

While I was still struggling against him, Phoenix marched upstairs, kicked my bedroom door open, and, without the least bit of gentleness, threw me squarely onto my bed.

"Are you completely nuts? What's gotten into you?" I shrieked at him as I landed, my blood boiling at being treated like this.

Instead of leaving, my boss took a step back and slammed my door so hard that it almost splintered into a thousand pieces.

"I should ask you the same question! Your attitude toward Karl is shameful! Even if he surprised and scared you, you have no reason to treat him like that!" he shouted.

"He disrespected me! How did you not notice?" I yelled back.

"You do not know *anything*. Instead of being prejudiced against someone, you would do well to learn to get to know them."

"Are you sure that you know the guy in the parlor all that well?"

Phoenix immediately fixed me with a glare, his eyes full of a hardly contained cold anger. When he spoke again, it was with a contemptuous tone.

"Who are you to tell me to judge Karl, whom I have known for five hundred years, when you have only spent a few minutes with him!"

Touché.

Who was I, indeed? I was only his friend of a few months who'd decided to hate his friend of several centuries based only on a few vague first impressions. I wasn't proud of myself, and I looked down in shame.

"I will not need your services this evening. You should stay in here where you can be ignored."

With that curt order, he left. Lesson learned. I'd been deposited in my room like a little girl who had gotten into serious trouble.

However, I understood his reaction. I'd been really rude and aggressive toward Karl even if I'd only been reacting to his gross insinuations. Phoenix must not have heard them.

On the other hand, Karl maybe hadn't meant to be disrespectful and was actually just behaving like a vampire whose sense of honor and formality had evaporated at the same time as his humanity. I was used to how civilized my boss always was, so his friend's words had shocked me more than necessary . . .

No. He hadn't been so crude in front of Phoenix. He had paid attention . . . his predatory smile had only been addressed to me.

I decided it was best to keep my opinion about Karl secret, to keep a low profile until my boss forgave this evening's sudden outburst. I would take advantage of the time to study his friend more closely. After all, that's what my boss wanted, right? For me to get to know Karl?

With that solid resolution, I wanted to have a DVD marathon, but—what a wasted evening—I'd forgotten that I hadn't yet replaced the broken one.

Now in a murderous mood, I got into bed and grabbed my favorite book, Jane Austen's *Pride and Prejudice*, which I'd started to read again for at least the eight hundredth time. And to think that she described Darcy as too proud! Humph.

\*\*\*

I desperately needed fresh air when I woke up. Once ready, I called for a taxi to take me to Scarborough, where I'd decided to spend the day.

I went to see a movie before going to eat at Danny's. I'd also thought of going to the used-car dealership to invest in a simple means of transportation that would belong to me and me alone. I wasn't really car savvy, and Matthew had offered to help me choose.

The film was nothing extraordinary, but I enjoyed it. I wasn't much of a romantic, but I liked romantic comedies. When I got to the restaurant, I discussed the movie with Danny, who was a walking manual of seduction. He confessed that every time he brought a woman to see a romantic comedy, she would, without fail, fall into his arms, believing that he had just revealed the secret feminine side women swore was hidden in every man.

"Oh, women," he said, laughing, forgetting apparently that I was also in that category and that it was not a given that I would appreciate his methods of manipulating women through our so-called romantic stupidity.

"You know, Danny, if a man brought me to see a horror film, I wouldn't throw myself at him. I wait, to know a bit more."

Danny looked at me like I was crazy. "And miss out on a chance to have a good time?"

"Oh, men," I sighed.

We spent the rest of the meal squabbling over masculine and feminine characteristics. When Matthew came downstairs from the office, he found us in full debate mode.

"No matter what, we all live on the same planet and belong to the same species, but men and women have such radically different ways of thinking. You men, you don't understand anything about women."

I'd finally shut Danny up, to the sounds of applause from all the women in the restaurant.

Matthew said, "Well, I certainly hope to understand *you* one day. I see it's just mission impossible."

Matthew was joking, but he wasn't wrong. He didn't know the truth about me, so he could never understand. Of course, he didn't know that.

"OK, Matthew, enough of this. Ready to be my guide in all things automobile?"

"At your service, my lady."

I paid Danny, promising to return soon with more muffins, and led the march to the exit. The dealership wasn't far, so we decided to walk.

"It's just as well since I don't have a car today. I came by taxi."

"What happened to your grandfather's Audi?"

Hm . . . How was I supposed to answer that? We had to leave it in the warehouse district, where vampires adept at exsanguinations were hiding en masse, so we could escape by flying like Superman, and my 'grandfather' had found it burned up some time later. No, it was better to not say any of that.

"Uh, I had a little accident . . . it's scrap metal now."

I gave Matthew a sheepish look, and he took the bait.

"Women and big cars like that don't mix well, generally. I suppose your grandfather must be delighted," he said, laughing.

"Thanks for the sexist remark about women drivers. Basically, he was beside himself, and I thought he was going to go into cardiac arrest. He threatened to take it out of the small salary he pays me for the help I give him."

"He doesn't have another car?"

I sighed. "A Camaro, but I hate driving it. It's too conspicuous."

"If your grandfather doesn't use it anymore, why does he keep it? He should invest in something more practical."

"He's a collector. Even though he can't take them out for a ride, he likes looking at them. Well, looking at *it*, now, since I've smashed up the other one. You understand now why I must have my own car, at all costs."

"Of course I understand. Well, here we are. Gary Show is the best car dealer around, and he won't cheat you. He'll help us out."

Indeed, Gary welcomed us warmly and put us at ease. He was very patient while we inspected the cars he proposed, and as a car connoisseur and mechanic, he was able to answer all our questions.

I ended up buying a 1995 gray Buick Skylark with low mileage and comfortable seats. The price was right, and Matthew assured me that it was a good deal. I paid in cash, and Gary said he'd take care of the paperwork. He handed me the keys, and Matthew and I drove over to Angela's bookstore.

Matthew ran inside to tell Angela that there was a surprise outside. When she came out, I shouted, "Ta-da! What do you think?"

"I don't know anything about cars, but if Matthew said you could buy this one, it must be fine. Anyway, from the outside, it looks pretty good."

"Thanks. At least I won't be terrified that I'll scratch the rims and have to replace them."

"Is your grandfather still mad about the Audi?"

"He hasn't spoken to me in two days. He's really got a bad temper."

"Do you ever think about doing another job than the one you're doing now?" Matthew asked. "If you look for work here, you'll be able to find something easily. And Cory Gillis is a home health assistant, so he could take over with your grandfather."

Matthew's idea wouldn't have been bad if I really was taking care of my grandfather. "Thanks, but my grandfather won't deal with strangers, which is at least part of why I'm here now. And despite his bad temper, I actually like looking after him." I smiled, hoping to successfully convince Matthew and Angela that my current life suited me just fine.

That was the truth, my life did suit me fine, even when I had to deal with danger and Phoenix's moods. Karl's arrival didn't please me at all, but apart from that, I was doing well. If only . . .

"Oh! I have to go buy a DVD player."

I tend to think out loud, but changing the subject that abruptly startled my friends a bit. "Uh . . . sorry," I apologized.

"We're getting used to it, don't worry," Angela said. "Do you think that your grandfather would ever let us visit his manor, Matthew and me? I went there once when I was little, but I would love to go back. And when it comes to you, we're not strangers anymore."

Oh dear, what I'd been dreading was happening. It was impossible to satisfy their curiosity without compromising my cover story.

"I'm sorry, Angela . . . but my grandfather was very clear when I came to live with him. No one else is allowed in the manor. His phobia is too intense."

"Can he be treated?" Angela's compassionate tone couldn't mask her disappointment.

"He's seen a lot of doctors, but he only began to feel at peace once he'd cut himself off from the outside world. That's why he came here. He feels good here."

Matthew leaned against the Buick and put his hands in his pockets.

"Angela, we've learned more about Peter Stratford in this discussion than we have in the last five years."

"That's true. Well, too bad about the manor. I'll just have to be happy reading books about it," Angela said.

None of this made me happy, but I didn't have a choice. I had to lie to my friends to keep them safe. Phoenix protected me, but I doubted that Talanus and Ysis would allow Matthew and Angela to be spared if they ever discovered the existence of vampires. To protect the Secret, they would have to be killed, and it would fall to my boss to carry out that task.

The three of us chatted a bit more, but before long Angela had to run her shop and Matthew had to return to his bookkeeping. I still had a few hours to kill before having to confront the glacial stare of my boss and the foul presence of his perverted friend. Shoot. I couldn't be so unequivocal about Karl; I needed to give him a chance. It was what I normally did, but in this case it was really challenging.

After buying a new DVD player, I went to wander around the movie rental shop. The owner, Mike Newell, was starting to get to know me, especially since I'd begun to chat with him about one film or another. Since I didn't want to return to the manor any earlier than necessary, I stalled at Mike's until dusk, though I didn't end up renting anything.

Before going back to the manor, I wanted to restock my supply of candy and chocolates at Ginger's. She welcomed me with open arms and the latest gossip. I usually didn't pay much attention, but according to Ginger, rumors were flying about my supposed romance with Matthew. Everyone wanted to know if we were going to end up together.

"You can tell *me*, my little Samantha. It'll stay between us."

Did I really seem that naive? I had to put a stop to this.

"You can tell your friends that when a man and a woman spend time together, it doesn't necessarily mean they're a couple. You'll have to find something else to gossip about. Sorry," I said coolly.

I genuinely liked Ginger, but her meddling ways were more than irritating. Every time we saw each other, she pestered me with questions about Phoenix . . . well, about Peter Stratford. I always managed to politely deflect that conversation, but this prodding about Matthew was getting unbearable.

"Oh, come on. Everyone sees how Matthew looks at you. Don't you lie to me."

Accusing me of lying was the last straw. Suddenly I couldn't be polite anymore. I put my money on the counter to pay for my candy and took a deep breath.

"You want the truth? The truth is that you really should mind your own business and learn how to hold your tongue if you don't want all this to bite you in the butt. The whole town knows that your daughter is miserable because she has no desire to take over this shop, but she's terrified of disappointing you. So take a good look in the mirror before you meddle in the private lives of others."

From the shocked expression on Ginger's pale face, I knew that I'd crossed a line, but I also knew that I was right. I'd met Valerie briefly once, and it grieved me to see her make so much effort to share her mother's passion. Ginger was the only one blind to the issue. Unfortunately for her, the one who'd brought things to light was an insensitive stranger who was on edge about the evening that lay ahead of her . . . My temper was just begging to blow. And . . . too bad. I'd said the truth. I felt no remorse. Ginger would get over it.

The sun had been set for an hour already when I returned to the manor. I was late.

\*\*\*

I switched off the engine, stepped out of my Buick, and grabbed my purchases from the trunk. I didn't know if Phoenix would allow me to use his garage for what he would see as an old clunker, so I'd parked along the gravel driveway.

As I was leaning down to grab the DVD player box, which had slid to the back of the trunk, I heard a voice. "I thought you'd left again."

I jumped and banged my head hard.

"Owwww!" I screamed, massaging the crown of my head and turning toward Phoenix with my eyes narrowed.

Phoenix didn't seem at all angry with me, unlike like what I'd been fearing, as though what happened the night before was a distant memory.

"Why would you think that?" I asked, surprised.

"I . . . mistreated you yesterday. Even if I still think that you behaved badly toward my guest, I should not have acted toward you as I did. So . . . I thought that . . ."

"Even if I basically only reacted to a provocation, I do admit that my attitude was immature and idiotic. You're right, I have to get to know people before judging them, so I'll make an effort with Karl." I held out my hand to shake his. "Friends?"

He smiled. "Friends." He shook my hand before leaning to one side to admire my car. "What do we have here?"

I shut the trunk after handing him my DVD player. After all, he might as well help.

"It's a Buick," I declared enthusiastically.

Unlike my human friends, he made no effort whatsoever to hide his revulsion that my new car inspired.

"You could at least pretend to like it."

"Sorry. But this? I just can't," he said apologetically.

"You're hopeless. Not everyone likes those Hollywood hot rods. Come on, let's go in, nothing to see here."

Phoenix followed me inside, but he didn't get a chance to update me on what was happening in the parlor before I got there.

Another vampire was conversing with Karl. His long black hair was in a ponytail, and his very loose shirt, black jeans, and boots recalled the musketeer he used to be. With a little imagination, you could almost see the sword and baldric attached to his belt.

My mentor stood by my side and tried to make the introductions. "Samantha, here . . ."

"François," I blurted out with a big smile, thrilled at the idea of speaking with this tall man with a marble face but gentle green eyes.

You could almost believe that this wasn't a vampire at all, he inspired that much confidence. The man in question stared at me in amazement before giving me a formal and traditional salutation—that is, a deep, elegant bow.

"Mademoiselle."

I returned his gesture less formally but just as respectfully, and took a step closer.

"Phoenix told me about you. I'm so happy to meet you. After all, you don't meet a former royal musketeer every day."

I felt a hand on my shoulder.

"Samantha . . ." Phoenix was shaking his head in exasperation, and then he turned to his friend. "Please excuse her. She is a French history buff, particularly Louis XIV. She also finds it very difficult to stop herself from saying everything that crosses her mind."

He was still reprimanding me like a child. He could be so irritating.

"Only since I met you. Who else taught me to be confident?"

"Being confident does not necessarily mean rushing headlong into things."

He was frowning, so I must have been irritating him too.

"Oh, come on, you're one to talk."

While we were readying ourselves for our thousandth fight, François's deep laugh stopped us. Phoenix looked at him as though it were the first time that had happened since they had known each other.

"This is the first time I have ever seen you like this, Phoenix. You are funny, the two of you, bickering like an old couple."

I flushed scarlet, but Phoenix tried to recover his usual impenetrable mask (with some difficulty, by the way).

Karl chose that moment to intervene. "Do not say that, François. She was very welcoming with *you*," he spat out, "but she might jump down your throat if you do not watch what you say. That human woman knows how to be a real tigress."

I had to be careful with my reaction if I didn't want to offend my boss again.

"Only when I'm provoked. What happened last night was only the result of a misunderstanding, am I right?"

I made it easy for him; it was up to him to be smart enough to pick up on it.

"Actually, I was rude and your reaction was understandable. I promise you that in the future, I won't act like an uncivilized and uneducated barbarian, but as a perfect gentleman. Do you forgive me?"

He certainly had a good sense of formality. His apology almost seemed credible. In any case, Phoenix was smiling. All right, then.

"I forgive you. Let's start over. It's the best thing to do."

François hadn't understood the entirety of our exchange, but he also seemed satisfied with our truce.

Phoenix came forward and immediately sobered up the reunion.

"I'm happy that you're here, my friends. Dark times are ahead, and if we don't put a stop to the blood trafficking in this region, it means my death and the deaths of our leaders."

# CHAPTER NINE

## *Pursuit*

Our conversation was not lightened by the joy that friends feel after a long separation. Our faces were serious, the atmosphere heavy. We knew we only had a short amount of time before the Greats decided to take matters into their own hands and take the heads of Phoenix, Talanus, and Ysis along the way.

I couldn't accept that this man who'd offered me a second life would lose his own. I couldn't stand losing my best friend, the only person who accepted me for who I really was and who pushed me to become the person I should be. His death was unthinkable, and I would do anything to save him.

Phoenix had explained everything to François and Karl. He truly trusted them, which was troubling, given Phoenix's usual insistence on the untrustworthiness of vampires. But he said that friendship could be deep between them . . .

"Karl, do you remember Bill Miller?"

"You mean Thirsty Bill?"

"Yes. He runs a strip club in east Kerington, the Sexy Thong Show."

Karl raised his eyebrows at the name, trying not to laugh, which made my boss roll his eyes.

"If you know Bill, you also know that he has never been very clever."

"Indeed. What do you need me to do?"

"He is connected to the blood trafficking. Shadow him. He might lead us to their hideout. François, you will go with him."

François nodded in agreement.

"And you two?" Karl asked.

"Sam and I will do our part. We cannot afford to wait for news from Kaiko and Ichimi."

I knew what he was talking about: he wanted to put my idea into action that evening, and I wasn't dressed to hit the clubs yet. I was rather disheveled, I must say. Now that it was spring, the days were getting longer, and the weather was getting nicer, so I'd opened the window in the Buick and taken advantage of the fresh air. The result was some seriously wind-tousled hair. And François had called me his demoiselle. Would someone from the seventeenth century celebrate bad hair days the way that people today do? I doubted it.

"I'll go get ready," I said before rushing off to my room.

It would take some time to prepare for what I had in mind. I went directly to the armoire, which was filled with the clothes Phoenix had given me—the ones I'd sworn never to wear. I knew that to do what I was about to, I believed he must truly be in danger.

Some time later, I looked at my reflection in the mirror and smiled. Not bad. It was the result I was hoping for . . . My inspection came to an abrupt end when my phone rang.

"Hello?"

"Please accept my humblest apologies if I've disturbed you, but we're starting to get impatient."

Phoenix hung up before I could say anything. It didn't matter; I was going to join them anyway.

I thanked heaven that I hadn't tumbled down the stairs in my heels, and then I walked into the parlor.

***

Phoenix, Karl, and François turned toward me, and simultaneously, they froze in place, mouths agape, stupefied. I instantly transformed three centuries-old vampires into ridiculous, gawking statues. The worst of the three was my boss, who looked like he was choking on a piece of meat again. Seeing their expressions, I thought that maybe I'd gone overboard.

I'd put my hair into a complicated bun, a little like the ones sported by the starlets of the moment, with so many bobby pins I felt like a porcupine. To emphasize my eyes, I'd applied dark eye shadow and liner. Simple earrings, a necklace, and a bracelet completed the look and tempered my silver dress, which was so dazzling and so . . . short. Phoenix must have thought it was just a top, forgetting that today's styles were no longer those of five hundred years ago; now women were showing off a lot more than they once did, too much even. I'd managed to slip on black shiny pumps that I'd found in my armoire. Lastly, I put on my favorite perfume, Escada.

I thought I looked the part of a young, naive escort for a stylish and wealthy client, the kind of man allowed entry into any nightclub he wished. Alone, my boss could have seemed suspect, but with me dressed like this at his side, he could pass for a powerful man who wanted to show off and have a good time.

But seeing his face, I had it all wrong.

"Too much, is that it?" I guessed, fearing the answer.

Karl and Phoenix stayed silent as the grave. I felt immense relief when François came to my rescue.

"I think I see what you were going for. It is a good idea to want to play the ostentation card to avoid suspicion. Additionally, dressed like that, I doubt that the vampires you met at the warehouse will recognize you. Is she not magnificent?" he concluded, turning to his companions and emphasizing his question so they would finally react and decide to speak.

"Uh . . ." I don't know what Phoenix was going to say, because Karl interrupted him.

"Of course she is magnificent. Look at her, she is positively delectable. Yum . . ."

It took an incredible effort to not lose my cool, seeing his mocking smile and his barely disguised insinuation. He'd promised to behave like a gentleman and so had chosen his vocabulary carefully, but I still found him repugnant.

"Karl, François, good luck. We shall check in tomorrow at sunset."

My boss thus called everyone to action and, in doing so, brushed aside the issue of the length of my dress. It was time to get to work.

In the blink of an eye, his friends left, and we were alone. We got in the Camaro and headed in the direction of the bars and clubs in east Kerington; I'd made a list of them with the help of the Internet.

"You think we'll find anything?" I asked, suddenly doubtful of the merits of our plan.

"We must. I do not have a choice."

"*We* don't have a choice. We're in the same boat, you and me. I'd be annoyed if you died."

"Happy to hear it," he said, smiling slightly.

"Besides, if that happens, I doubt that the Greats will let me live, knowing all that I do."

I'd intended it as a joke, but I realized as I said it that it was entirely the truth. If Phoenix was executed, I would have to die with him to preserve the Secret. My mouth got suddenly dry, and I had trouble swallowing. The smile on my boss's face had completely disappeared, and what he said next terrified me completely.

"I know."

After a few minutes of mutual reflection, I decided it would be best to keep the conversation going rather than be depressed.

"I hope I didn't shock you too much earlier. You must have thought that this dress was just a T-shirt when you gave it to me."

He waited before answering. "Your era leaves little to the imagination. People praise transparency, they analyze everything with technology that gets more and more sophisticated, and no one ever even needs to imagine women without clothes, because they only ever wear a strip of fabric by way of a dress."

I bit the inside of my cheek to stop myself from laughing and annoying him.

"It's crazy how old-fashioned you are . . ."

A growl echoed through the car, but I wasn't intimidated.

"Say what you will, but as for me, I think you have to get with the times. Besides, showing their bodies allows women to have some self-confidence."

"I do not see any difference except that you are dressed in less than usual."

"I'm not different. But you know me, maybe better than anyone, by the way. This evening, it's important that people don't see me as a threat, just the plaything of some golden boy. That way they'll leave us alone."

"This from the same woman who made a scene with Karl because he took you for a sexual object," he said.

"It isn't the same thing," I said. "Honestly, do you think I overdid it? I wanted to seem sexy, not give the impression that I'm . . . uh . . . lacking in . . ."

Good grief. I hoped he wouldn't say that I looked like a prostitute. But he kept his eyes on the road.

"You are perfect."

I should have been relieved, but I felt strangely frustrated by his answer.

"How should we proceed tonight?" I asked.

"I have selected four nightclubs on the outskirts of the east Kerington. We shall stay about an hour in each one and see if that comes to anything."

"As easy as looking for a needle in a haystack."

"It was your idea, if you recall."

"Well, I'm starting to wonder if it was a bad one."

"It is either this or wait for Kaiko and Ichimi to call."

"I forgot to tell you something . . ."

"What?" he said, worried.

"I don't know how to dance."

***

We arrived at Pacific Dreams, a very selective club that could be of interest to the Chinese gang we were looking for, given the rich and powerful men who went there to have fun and do business, legal or not. The line to get in was at least a hundred people long, and as I headed to the end of the line to join them, Phoenix grabbed my arm and pulled me close to him as he walked to the entrance. My high heels had me so off balance that he almost sent me flying into the gutter, but he wasn't paying attention. He only wanted to skip the line and enter like a VIP. I was mortified by the looks of shock and outrage from those who saw us walk straight to the door. I preferred to not listen to what they were muttering behind us, knowing full well that my boss could hear them fine.

We reached the bouncer, who was built like a tank, six and a half feet tall with muscles the Incredible Hulk would envy. Phoenix looked at him with scorn and arrogance. The guy had a list of names, and I doubted that Peter Livingstone's was on there. He was going to throw us out, pure and simple, and in front of a curious audience who was expecting it.

Against all odds, the bouncer stepped aside and let us through.

"What did you do to him? You couldn't have hypnotized him, but I'm sure you did something," I asked Phoenix after handing over our coats to the coat check.

"I just signaled to him that he should check his coat pocket."

"Huh?"

"Your human eye did not have enough time to see me put a thick stack of bills into his pocket."

Of course. Nicely done.

The music was blasting so loud I couldn't even respond. The club's decor was immaculate, and you could tell from the magnums of champagne being paraded about what kind of clientele was served here. Looking at the dance floor, I couldn't help but laugh. I tapped on my boss's shoulder, and he came closer so I could shout in his ear.

"And you thought my dress was too short!"

Indeed, top model lookalikes were wriggling their hips to the rhythm of the music without any concern for the way their gold hot pants gave glimpses of half of their behinds or the necklines of their tops reached their navels. Some of their skirts were so short they just barely hid what women should never expose in public. The vision of these shimmying girls was worthy of the most cultish scenes of the *Fast and the Furious* movies: enough thin girls and fast cars to make men dream . . . Speaking of, one of the men in the audience was seated at the edge of the dance floor, holding a handkerchief and wiping away the drool from his gaping mouth as he stared at all that fresh flesh. Gross.

My boss led me to a table where we could keep an eye on the scene. Once we were settled next to each other, he called for a server and ordered champagne.

"Get closer and massage my shoulders."

"What? Absolutely not!"

"Need I remind you that I am supposed to be someone important and you are my groupie? Stop acting like a frightened virgin."

He must have realized the enormity of what he'd said just as he said it, and my look of outrage only emphasized it.

"Forgive me. That was rude and disrespectful of me. In short, it was despicable," he said right away, sincerely.

I stared at him severely. "You're starting to master the formalities of apologies. But don't make it a habit, or I might stop accepting your apologies."

"You are very hard on me. I find that I have made progress, though."

I burst out laughing at the chastised-dog look on his face.

"In another hundred years, you might be able to make a funny joke."

"If I live that long," he grumbled.

"Super. You really know how to kill the mood."

The server brought us our champagne, and for an hour we played at being a couple having a good time together. We were on alert every time someone entered. But it was always a disappointment.

Phoenix knew right away whether or not new arrivals were vampires. One vampire went to the dance floor. With his seductive charm, it wasn't hard for him to attract girls, who grinded up against him with an almost vulgar shamelessness. He murmured a few words to the prettiest of the bunch, who was thrilled by what he said. Unfortunately for him, he passed by our table, making eye contact with my boss, and catching a glimpse of fang.

Our mission didn't impede Phoenix from fulfilling his function as angel. Phoenix's growl of warning, low but loud enough for the other vampire to hear, was more than clear. The party vampire had no interest in hurting that girl if it meant losing his head, in the proper sense of the word, and he quickly rid himself of his companion and scampered off.

"Impressive," I murmured.

"Thank you, but that is my job. I have to be merciless to be credible."

He shrugged his shoulders.

"If only they knew . . . ," I said.

"Knew what?"

"That you're actually a good guy," I finished, swallowing the last drop from my champagne flute.

He shook his head. "Do not think of me like that. It would be a mistake. I am a vampire, and thus on the side of Evil, do you not remember?"

"That's all nonsense. You just saved that girl's life. So all this talk of vampires being on Evil's team, you can keep that to yourself. I don't claim to know you very well, but I do know one thing. You're a good guy. It doesn't matter what you say to convince me otherwise."

He looked serious and exasperated.

"You . . . ," he began, but I clapped my hand over his mouth.

"Shut up. The subject is closed. And unless you want to drag this out forever, seeing as there isn't even a shadow of a Chinese vampire here, I suggest we go elsewhere."

Without giving him a chance to object or agree, I stood up and headed for the coat check.

We went to another club, a bit less exclusive, called Miami Dance Floor, about fifteen minutes away. As we walked from the car, I shivered, wishing the temperature outside was the same as in Florida. Phoenix didn't bother to get in line here either, and another bribe gained us entry. Once again, we sat at a table with a strategic vantage point and ordered drinks. Nothing interesting was happening, so I passed the time sipping my champagne. Suddenly, though, I felt something was wrong.

"Phoenix, we're being watched."

"I know. Two people who come to a club together and yet sit apart without ever dancing, that is strange."

"We've been here an hour. We should leave now."

So we did.

In the car, I still had the sense something wasn't right. I wasn't sure what, just a feeling of being slightly disconnected from reality, of being too hot. But what was wrong with me? Finally, a light bulb shone in my befuddled head.

Good grief. It was because of the champagne, nothing more.

I hoped my boss hadn't taken notice. I needed to pull myself together. I opened the car window and let the air rush in to clear my head . . .

The Shining Rainbow was a classic club, contrasting with what you might think just from the sight of its bright rainbow sign. My deep breathing out the car window had its intended effect: my brain had unfogged. At least I thought it had.

In the red-and-gold alcove where we sat, Phoenix ordered champagne again, which I took care not to drink. We took up our surveillance of the clientele, but after a while, he stood up and held out his hand for me. I stared at him wide-eyed, not knowing what he wanted.

"We are going to end up attracting unwanted attention. I propose another means of observation."

"How?"

"By dancing."

I didn't know what to say; my jaw dropped. As though someone had just lobotomized me, my simple brain didn't understand anything anymore. He wanted me to dance with him? No. Way. Out of the question to ridicule me with my two left feet. I'd only ever danced with my father, who had challenged himself to teach me, but realizing just how clumsy I was, even he had abandoned the attempt.

Now my boss was suggesting he take me for a spin on the dance floor around a bunch of other, more sure-footed people. The idea made its way through my anesthetized mind, and I could at last answer the man who was patiently waiting for my neurons to reconnect.

"You're crazy. I'll make us both look ridiculous," I said, horrified.

Without waiting any longer, he leaned down and grabbed my hand. The little momentum he had put into his movement was enough to pull me out of my seat and propel me to his torso. Embarrassed, I raised my eyes to his.

"Do not be afraid. I will lead. Just let it happen," he said.

He led me to the dance floor.

The music had a good rhythm, and the people around us were dancing with abandon. Watching them, I felt my anxiety go up a notch. Phoenix lifted my chin and turned my face toward him.

"Look at me, only me. Listen to the music and forget everything else."

Easier said than done, but I had to try.

I cleared my head as if preparing for an attack and started to move along with Phoenix. He guided me with each step, and his smile was encouraging. It wasn't long before I was enjoying the dancing, and I surprised myself by laughing out loud. I'd completely forgotten to keep an eye out for our Chinese gang members.

But just as I was starting to gain confidence in my movements, the pop music was replaced with something more throbbing, more sensual.

I looked at Phoenix, expecting him to lead us back to our table, but instead he held me by my waist and pulled me closer. Gently, he placed one of his legs between mine and held me even tighter against his body. Trembling a little, I pressed my hands against his back and lifted my head. I was level with his neck, and despite the smoky smell of the nightclub, I could still make out his scent, so particular and reassuring. It was a mix of the cologne he wore and the smell of a pine forest at twilight. In the space of a single second, I closed my eyes to breathe it in and immerse myself in it. In the space of a single second, I found myself in a glade surrounded by pine trees, bathing in the light of a magnificent sunset. My boss must have sensed that I'd completely relaxed, for he moved slowly, his body leading mine in that sensual dance.

Suddenly, it was as though nothing else existed.

My senses were in overdrive, and I felt his right hand between my shoulder blades and his left hand on my hip with an intensity a thousand times stronger than usual. Since he had taken off his suit jacket, I felt the fabric of his shirt under my fingers and, even more so, the back muscles that his shirt covered. Drunk on his smell, I couldn't stop myself from moving my hands to his chest, and the sensation of that skin—so hard, but which I knew was also incredibly soft—fully intoxicated me.

I finally took the initiative, turning my back to him and following the slow rhythm by rolling my hips as sensually as possible, as I'd seen it done in movies. I felt his hands slide over my stomach, felt his whole body against mine. He molded his movements completely to mine, and I closed my eyes, the nape of my neck exposed to his mouth, which I couldn't feel but I knew was there. The pressure of his fingers through my dress made me feel something strange, and that feeling intensified when Phoenix turned me around, pulling me against him again, his fingers making their way slowly down from my neck to my waist.

I saw his face, and I realized that he'd also completely forgotten about the Chinese . . .

In the bluish light of the club, his eyes seemed more luminous, but without being frightening, as if they were two deep wells leading to an ocean of calm and wisdom. I'd never seen them like that before, and they were incredible, so overwhelming that I slid my hands around his neck and buried my face in his shoulder.

Then I was swept away by the return of that strange sensation that I'd felt at the touch of his fingers on my back. The song was ending, and the tempo was reaching its peak, forcing us to move even more sensually than before.

*\*\**

The song was reaching its final note, and I leaned backward into a dip like in the movies. I raised my right leg, and Phoenix seized my thigh, holding me steady. My dress had slipped even higher, and his hand on my bare skin should have shocked me back to reality. But in that position, I again experienced the strange feeling that had invaded and overwhelmed me. It was like an electric current was running through me, toes to head, and burning me in the places where his fingers touched my skin . . .

When he stood me up straight and we found ourselves face-to-face again, with only an inch or two between our noses, it felt like time had suddenly stopped. His indecipherable expression pierced through me, but I couldn't tear my eyes away from his. It was like I'd been hit with lightning. I didn't know where I was anymore, or what I was doing. I was floating . . .

That extended, intense moment ended abruptly when a horrible boom, boom assaulted our ears to announce a new song. The bubble that had cut us off from the world disintegrated, and the return to reality embarrassed me.

Desiring just one thing—to disappear into a deep hole—I used the first excuse I could to escape.

"Uh . . . I'll find you after . . . um . . . bathroom."

And I left him there in the crowd.

The restroom was filled to capacity by girls more interested in retouching their makeup than using the toilets, so I went into a stall and sat down to think.

Let's recap. I was on a mission to flush out murderous Chinese vampires, and I had drunk too much. I'd forgotten that the champagne would have no effect whatsoever on my boss, which gave him the upper hand.

And what of the rest! Good grief, what on earth had come over me?

I'd never danced with a man other than my father, and of course the first had to be my boss. It wasn't like we were waltzing either. I held my head in my hands, thinking again about our bodies undulating together to the rhythm of the music. There was no risk to him if he found me to his liking, but I feared that he would think I was a tease, or that I'd fallen in love with him and wanted to seduce him.

No. No! As a novice in all forms of close contact, I'd let myself get carried away by these new and exhilarating sensations and indulged in them, forgetting that I should have behaved better with my boss. That was all. He would understand. There!

This reasoning made me feel much better. I wasn't in love with Phoenix, and I hoped he would forget the momentary confusion of a nearly thirty-year-old virgin whose contacts with men had mostly included inadvertent brushing of hands as I was offered pamphlets on the sidewalk.

Anyway, to love him would only make my entire life miserable: he would never age, and he would never share those kinds of feelings with a human. It was already a miracle and a surprise for him that he considered me a friend.

No. Loving him would, without doubt, mean losing myself.

Luckily, I wasn't at that point. But I was going to have to leave the restroom and explain myself.

Without much conviction, I returned to our table and sat down next to Phoenix, who had taken up his surveillance of the club's clients again. A silence settled between us, and all I could do to try and calm myself was to shift in my seat from one side to another, shaking one leg up and down.

"Samantha, either break the tension and tell me what is making you so nervous, or I shall tie to your chair so you will stop fidgeting like that."

"I'm sorry."

He turned his head slowly toward me, and his stare was hardly warm.

"What are you apologizing for?"

"For behaving like a flirt because I'm drunk on the job," I said without daring to breathe and taking great care to look only at my shoes.

"We were both on the dance floor, I remind you. We were only following a song that has to be danced to the way we danced to it. This does not make us a couple if that is what is bothering you." Seeing my look of panic, he took a more amiable tone. "All that you did was let yourself be taken over by rhythm. That is what I asked you to do, is it not? You dance very well. It was an agreeable experience."

Well! He didn't seem to think that I'd fallen for him. Reassured by the state of our relationship, I relaxed and smiled at him, determined to change the subject.

"Anything happen while I was gone?"

"I saw our friend from Pacific Dreams again. He took off as soon as he saw me."

"Let's hope that this time he's learned his lesson."

"In my opinion, these two nightclubs will not have the pleasure of having him as a client for a while."

I yawned. It was very late, and I was exhausted.

During our return to Scarborough, I fell asleep in the backseat. When I woke up, I was in Phoenix's arms, and he was carrying me to my room.

"You can put me down. I'm awake."

He set me down gently and made sure I was steady enough to not fall down the stairs. He walked me to my door.

"Thanks . . . for never letting me sleep in the car."

He frowned. "That would not be very gentlemanly."

I smiled . . . "Good night."

Without thinking, I kissed him on the cheek. I didn't know why I did it, but I wasn't embarrassed.

With one last look at his indecipherable face, I closed my bedroom door. It was tempting to go to sleep fully clothed, but I took the time to wash off my makeup and slip on the first camisole I could find before climbing into bed. It was five thirty in the morning, and I needed to catch up on my rest.

\*\*\*

When I woke up, it seemed as if I'd only slept for five minutes. My eyes were still closed, and my bed was incredibly comfortable. I slowly stretched and yawned.

Then everything happened lightning quick.

With my eyes barely open and still adjusting to the dark, I realized that I wasn't alone in my room. Someone was sitting on my bed.

My heart skipped a beat, and though I couldn't clearly see who was in my room, I screamed as loud as I could, throwing my pillow—the only weapon at my disposal—at my attacker. I'd hidden a gun under my bed, but I couldn't get to it with the intruder sitting right there. What an idiot I was.

Before I could even blink, my bedroom door literally exploded in a million pieces when someone kicked it in. Immediately I knew it was Phoenix, and he grabbed the man on my bed and sent him flying against the opposite wall, where he landed on the dressing table, my things scattering all over the floor.

When the other man got up, I was trying to catch my breath and Phoenix was standing between us, ready to jump on his opponent. Except when the intruder turned to face us, we looked at him stupidly.

"What the . . . Karl? What are you doing in here?" Phoenix asked with complete surprise.

My heart was pounding as I watched my attacker stand up painfully.

"Karl . . . ," I whispered. I wanted to tear him to pieces.

"Yes, it's Karl! What has gotten into you two? Both get up on the wrong side of the bed? And you, Phoenix, didn't anyone ever teach you to think before attacking someone?"

"I heard Sam scream, so I came immediately. I never would have thought the man on her bed was you," Phoenix said.

"Of course I screamed! I almost died of fear when I woke up and someone was at the foot of my bed. I thought someone had come to kill me! Who told you that you could come into my room?" I asked Karl.

"François and I thought it was time to wake you up, seeing as you thought it was fine to go into a sleep coma during this critical time for Phoenix."

"You dirty—"

"*Stop!*" my boss interrupted, thus preventing a horrible fight between his two closest friends. "This is all a misunderstanding. The sun has set. He wanted to do you a favor, Samantha. As for you, Karl, I ask you to remember your manners when you are with my assistant. Now make peace, both of you."

I gave Karl a harsh look, but I wanted to avoid any more fighting. However . . . when I remembered that I was barely dressed in front of two centuries-old vampires, one of whom was even more debauched than Casanova, I saw red.

"Fine, we're fine, but get out of here, both of you, now!"

I didn't want to make a scene, certainly, but I still had my pride, and I couldn't stand one more minute with them and their peering eyes in my personal space.

Seeing my stance—on my knees, on my bed, pointing a vengeful finger at the door—my intruders understood it would be best to leave, and soon.

They both left, and before they disappeared down the hallway, I heard, "But really, why on earth would you go in her room?"

"I wanted to pull on a prank on her, that's all."

"Will you ever grow up?"

I had a hard time calming down. My usually very tidy room had become a dumping ground for the mixed-up remains of my door, dressing table, and everything found on it. Good-bye, Chanel No. 5. The bottle was broken, and its contents had spilled over the floor, filling the room with an expensive odor.

A glance at my alarm clock told me that it was already ten o'clock in the evening. What? How had I slept for so long? Well, it didn't matter. At least I would be ready to resume our tour of bars and clubs, and despite the fanfare of my waking up.

I took a shower and got dressed, opting for less flashy—and above all, more comfortable—clothes and shoes. The night before, my heels had killed my feet, and I had no desire to relive an attention-grabbing evening by wearing another dress barely long enough to cover my butt.

I was truly in a foul mood. I made no particular effort to play the part of a bimbo and slipped on dress pants, a red satin blouse, a blazer, and my ballerina flats. When I got downstairs, I found Phoenix and François playing chess and Karl watching a soccer match. They knew, of course, without seeing me, that I was there.

Karl deigned to look away from the television to look at me and roared with laughter.

"Well, someone is in less of a good mood than yesterday by the looks of her outfit. I guess that must not have been pretty to see on the dance floor."

I wished I had fangs too, so that the grimace I made would have been more impressive.

"There we go. Go ahead and make fun. In the meantime, you owe me a bottle of Chanel No. 5," I growled.

He laughed even more.

"No, you owe that bottle to Ysis," Phoenix corrected, still concentrated on his chess game.

"Ha-haaaa! And what is that bottle doing here in your house? Is Talanus aware of this?" Karl said ironically, his tone full of innuendos that exasperated me profoundly.

But my boss remained calm.

"Of course he is aware, it was he who ordered me to invite her here for a day. He had business to take care of alone, and he did not want to leave Ysis without protection. They showed up after one of their soirees.

Ysis left some of her things and her perfume behind. They were very useful to me when I brought Sam here."

So the evening gown that he'd had me wear when we first met belonged to Ysis, that powerful woman who could afford to forget her expensive things behind at her employee's house. I recalled our conversation from my first night here. Phoenix had told me the truth then, and I hadn't believed him, preferring to think that he was a psychopath about to skin me alive. I couldn't stop from smiling at the memory. Everything had changed since then.

"You are smiling, my dear. Is my charm finally working on you?" asked Karl as I took a seat on one of the armchairs near him.

"You're not my type," I snapped back.

He moved closer to me, seeming more seductive than ever. More than one girl must have been ensnared by that smoldering look.

"Are you sure of that?"

His languorous voice should have charmed me, but instead I raised my eyes to him and gave him a serious look.

"Very sure. Come on, aren't you going to drop this little game of yours? You're handsome, sure, I can admit that." His smile brightened up the room. "But without meaning to insult you, I have to say that you don't tempt me, that's all."

His toothy grin deflated with lightning speed, and his face looked like someone had just poured a bucket of ice water over his head.

"That is crazy. I just don't get it."

François spoke up then, mocking Karl and adding even more comedy to the scene. "What do you not understand? That for the first time in your life, a woman rejects you? You do not fit her criteria for seduction. You just have to accept this."

Ah, so that was why Karl seemed so irritated. In all his five hundred years, he'd never been snubbed before. Pretty good record. There had to be a first, and that was me. My look of satisfaction must have bothered him, for his counterattack was immediate.

"Her criteria must match our friend Phoenix, if you want my opinion," Karl said.

Now that was not smart. A heavy silence filled the room for a few seconds. It was up to me to break it by putting the indelicate Karl back in his place, so I took on the attitude of a school teacher to reprimand him.

"Jealousy makes people say stupid things. You may be five hundred years old, but you act like a spoiled-rotten teenager who can't stand it when someone tells him no. You could do with some growing up."

The minute I mentioned jealousy, I thought I could see a flash of cruelty in Karl's eyes. I hoped I had dreamed it.

"You almost sound like Finn," he growled.

"Maybe you should have listened more to your adoptive father's lessons."

Another silence, this one even more stifling. Suddenly, I knew that I'd made a mistake because his nostrils were flaring before he stared at Phoenix with barely contained rage. François seemed disconcerted, but he said nothing.

"You told her about Finn?" Karl asked Phoenix.

A storm was coming, a storm that my tactlessness—or rather my pride—had started.

"Yes. So what? Should I have asked him for permission?" Phoenix said, his voice devoid of emotion.

Karl stood up and pointed an accusatory finger at him. "You are the first one who has to keep our secrets, given your position as angel, and you shared our history with a pathetic human!" he spit out.

At a speed impossible for humans to follow, Phoenix crossed the distance that separated him from his friend to plant himself face-to-face with Karl. His eyes shone and his fangs were bared. I took a step backward, he was that frightening.

"Don't you dare insult her again in front of me! As my assistant, she represents me, and by attacking her, you are using her to target me.

So either you change your attitude about her, or get out of here . . . We can get by without your help."

The shock of his declaration overrode his friend's anger.

"You would set aside five hundred years of friendship for . . . her?" he said, designating me impolitely with his chin and with a disdain that was more than insulting.

Phoenix's silence was answer enough. Karl turned and headed for the exit. The unease in the parlor was intolerable. All this was my fault . . . and it made me feel ill.

"I—" I began to say.

My boss raised a hand to cut me off. "It's not your fault. Everything you said was true. Karl is not used to people standing up to him, and certainly not me. He will get over it."

"I feel bad about being the cause of the fight, though," I admitted.

To our surprise, François spoke again. He talked a lot for someone who was almost entirely mute! "Do not feel guilty, Sam. If Phoenix had not drawn the line with his best friend, what kind of credibility would he have with other vampires?"

My boss agreed, but I still felt horrible.

"Come, Sam. If you are ready, we shall go now."

I took a deep breath and followed him to the door.

Our trip to Kerington was somewhat annoying because my stomach wouldn't stop growling, and it didn't help my foul mood. Phoenix's mood wasn't any better, and our trip was silent until we reached east Kerington.

"We are going to The Palm," Phoenix said. "That way, you can eat something. They serve food at all hours."

The Palm was a restaurant and a club. Obviously, it wasn't reputed for its tropical cuisine, but rather for its nearly naked go-go dancers. I'd heard rumors about it, but I was still struck by the tacky decor: Antillean wood tables, statues of Jamaicans smoking huge joints, and tall columns shaped like coconut trees.

Later, as we were watching the clientele and I was voraciously eating my hamburger and fries, I couldn't help but revisit the altercation with Karl.

"Thank you for not letting him say that I'm only a pathetic human."

"It was nothing," he said, distracted.

"Is it nothing because it's me, or because you've changed your mind about humans?"

"Both."

"What?"

"Let's say for a reason that I do not know, you have made me change my opinion about your species. You humans can be . . . very surprising . . ."

There was a smile in the corner of his mouth.

"You mean to say strange, ridiculously laughable, hot tempered, and addicted to television," I added, returning his smile.

"And don't forget awkward, clumsy, blushing, and incredibly chatty."

I burst out laughing. "Touché."

Our evening passed just like the one before, except for the dancing, and we'd had no success when it came to finding the Chinese. When we returned to the manor, Karl was waiting for us on the lawn. When we reached him, I thought it preferable to leave the two friends to resolve their disagreement in private and wished them a good night. I hoped they would reconcile. I didn't want to be the cause of a long-lasting falling-out between them, so I resisted the urge to listen at the door and went to sleep.

My sleep was restless, and I woke the next day long before dusk. I took advantage of the extra time to catch up on my work and draft the reports of our evenings pursuing shadows for Talanus and Ysis. The weather had warmed up in the past few weeks, and now I could enjoy some of the May sunshine strolling in the gardens and sitting outside to clear my mind while reading a good novel.

At sunset, I was still outside relaxing on a blanket and eating my favorite sandwich: butter, ham, egg, tomato. I still had time to savor that soothing tranquility, but when I felt a breeze on my back, I knew my break was over.

"If you want to frighten me again, maybe you should have avoided overdoing it on the aftershave before coming at me from downwind," I said, thinking it was Karl.

"I will try to remember that for next time," answered a different voice.

I jumped and turned around.

"François! Oh, I'm sorry. I thought it was Karl who wanted to play another prank on me."

"You do not like him much, do you?"

He sat down next to me, his question more like a statement.

"It's not at all like with you."

He seemed surprised.

"Oh . . . oh! Don't be mistaken, I don't *like* you . . . I mean, yes, but no . . . oh crap . . ."

He laughed. My next one-woman show should be called "How to Make a Vampire Laugh in Ten Easy Lessons."

"Let me start again. From the moment I met you, I thought you were nice, maybe because of what Phoenix told me about you, I don't know. But Karl . . ."

"He is not always very gentlemanly."

"That's an understatement."

"Do not condemn him. He is not malicious, and he is very attached to Phoenix."

In certain circumstances, silence is golden, so I said nothing.

"Just like you," he concluded.

Oh, no, what was he going to think now?

"I'm not in love with him if that's what you're insinuating."

I was on the defensive and he knew it.

"Really?"

"I'm not an idiot. Loving him would be sentimental suicide, seeing how he looks at romanticism. No. I'm deeply connected to him, that's true, but that's not love."

Good grief, how on earth did I end up talking about this with François?

"Anyway, I am happy that you are at his side. He could certainly use an assistant, you know. He is the best angel in our community. All the sector chiefs envy Talanus and Ysis and dream of having Phoenix in their service. Until now, he hasn't been friends with anyone other than Karl and myself. I find that he has changed since you have been here. He seems . . . happy, to no longer be alone."

"He said he chose me so he wouldn't have to do paperwork anymore."

"If he said that, that is because it is true."

It was really strange talking to this man. Anyway, wasn't he supposed to be permanently walled up in silence?

"François? Excuse my forwardness, but Phoenix described you as someone . . . someone not very chatty. However, since I met, you've been quite talkative, and it surprised Phoenix."

He laughed. "That is how *Phoenix* presented me? That is truly the pot calling the kettle black. But it is true that I only talk when I think it is important. I do like talking with you."

"That's nice of you. Phoenix should follow your lead for conversation because sometimes he thinks his scary face is sufficient to make his deepest thoughts known. Except it's not that simple."

"Hm. All vampires tremble at the sight of the bluish flashes of his eyes when they become luminescent, and it takes a lot to make a vampire tremble."

"However, there's so much more in his eyes . . . ," I said without thinking, remembering the moment when I could see deep in his eyes during our dance.

François was polite enough to not notice my comment, and instead started another subject of conversation—one that was less charged and, so, more enjoyable.

"So, do you like science fiction?" he asked.

Thus we began a passionate debate on the best books and series in our field of expertise. Talking with François was a pure delight, and we were chatting like old friends when suddenly he froze . . .

"He is calling for us. It is time."

I hadn't heard anything, but my friend had a much more sensitive sense of hearing than I did. Walking back, I asked him how tailing Thirsty Bill was going.

"There is nothing to say about it. It is deadly boring. And you?"

"Same. Easier to find a needle in a haystack."

We both sighed at the same time. On that bitter note, we rejoined our partners in silence before resuming our tasks, the inefficiency and uselessness of which made us all crazy for several weeks.

***

The month of June brought us sun and warmth, yes, but also horrible news. Kaiko and Ichimi had equally failed to find a trace of our Chinese vampires, Bobby the Eel hadn't sent any word, and most important of all, the Greats were giving Talanus and Ysis until July 15 to take care of the situation, or they would come to take care of it themselves. That meant that Phoenix and his bosses would be among the first to be cleared out, and in barely a month. Of course, if they were gone, I would also be dismissed . . . at best.

Physically it was becoming difficult to sustain the rhythm of our work. I was more exhausted than ever and more and more nervous about the impending deadline. By contrast, my boss seemed serene at the idea. What was bothering him was not so much the perspective of his death, but rather the repeated failures of our attempts to put an end to the disappearances.

One evening when we were, as usual, at a club, exhaustion got the better of me, and I passed out, pure and simple. Phoenix had just enough time to catch me before I crashed to the ground, and through the fog of unconsciousness, I heard him grumble, "All this is useless, except for just passing time."

Then I saw the black hole again.

The next day, he ordered me to stay in Scarborough to rest.

"It was just a momentary weakness. I want to help you. I'm coming," I protested.

But Phoenix wouldn't give in and gently declined my offer.

"You cannot help me in the state you are in. Your concern is touching, but you are staying here, end of discussion."

Defeated, I was given two whole days to rest. Good grief, I truly needed it.

It was high time that I saw my friends again too. Angela and Matthew must have been wondering whether I'd vanished into thin air. I called Angela, who didn't take offense at my temporary disappearance; I explained that my grandfather had had a drop in blood pressure and I'd needed to stay at his bedside.

She told me that she and Matthew were going to a movie that night, and that she would let him know I'd be joining them.

I spent the day reading in my boss's library and looking forward to the evening with my friends. Though I thought about work, I knew Phoenix was right: in this state of exhaustion, I wouldn't have been of much use to him.

I was about to head to town when I saw François and Karl leaving their guest rooms. I had heard Phoenix leave a bit earlier.

"All this is leading nowhere. We are wasting our time. This guy can put on airs all he wants. He has nothing to do with this business."

Karl seemed furious.

"Phoenix seems to agree with you. As proof, he does not want us to follow Thirsty anymore. He told me before he left. Oh, good evening, Samantha."

Karl ignored my presence. "He is dropping it?"

"I am afraid that he is going to admit the outcome of this investigation, and he wants to get us out of the way so that the Greats will not be any more interested in us than necessary," François reasoned.

"To hell with those wannabe kings! Who do they think they are?"

I'd never heard Karl so incensed before. Apart from the future that they were reserving for his best friend, he must not hold the Elder vampires in great esteem. But suddenly, he remembered that I was only a few inches away from them, and he recovered his look of seduction.

"Good evening, Samantha."

Even if that annoyed me, I had to admit that I was happy Karl was staying, despite his oversized ego. The worry he felt for my boss was touching.

"Good evening, both of you. So we got nothing from Miller?"

"As well as being an idiot, that pig is a weakling and a megalomaniac."

Karl's description seemed a tiny bit exaggerated. When Thirsty had thrown Phoenix to the other side of his office, I hadn't thought he was weak at all . . .

"Phoenix was sure he was hiding something," I said.

"That's for sure. When his idiot of a creator transformed him, his intelligence must have gotten lost on the path to vampirism."

Karl was suggesting that Miller's intelligence had remained at the human stage, meaning the lowest level. I felt my temper rising, but François rolled his eyes to the sky to make me understand that taking offense at that kind of remark was a pure waste of time. He was right.

"Where are you going, Sam?" François asked to change the subject.

"Phoenix ordered me to rest, but I need a change of scenery. Some friends are waiting for me in Scarborough to go to the movies."

"Great. We also need a little time off. Let's go," Karl declared.

"What?" François and I exclaimed in unison.

Seeing our shocked faces, our German friend sighed. "Come on, let's go. It will do you good to loosen up from time to time, my friend. As for you, Sam, do not fear. We will not blow your cover. We will say we are distant cousins."

Very distant, in his case.

"Fine, very well. But I'm warning you, we're taking *my* car, *I* am driving the way I want, and I will tolerate *no commentary*."

"I am eager to see that," he teased.

The trip was punctuated by exasperated sighs related to the slowness of my driving. Even though François stayed quiet in the backseat, I could tell that Karl was impatient in the passenger seat.

"I said no commentary!"

"What now? Did you mean any unfortunate word that leaves my mouth?" Karl seemed offended.

"Pff . . ."

As we pulled up in front of the movie theater, Karl suddenly sat up straight.

"Good heavens! Who is that bombshell over there, next to the unsuccessful bodybuilder?"

I didn't appreciate his vocabulary, even less so since he was describing my friends.

"Those are my friends Angela Schumaker and Matthew Robertson, and I beg you to remember your manners."

Not at all impressed by my intervention, he contented himself with checking out his reflection in the rearview mirror, which he turned toward himself with no regard for safety.

"Hey! I already regret giving you permission to get in my car," I said through gritted teeth.

Karl laughed. "That's good, *Cousin*, you understand it all now. But car or not, I would have come, if only to meet that beauty over there."

I couldn't do anything other than hope Angela didn't fall for Karl or be hurt by his weapons of mass seduction.

As soon as I parked, Karl got out of the Buick like an emperor stepping out of his chariot of triumph, without an audience, and sported his biggest smile.

We walked over to Angela and Matthew, who were certainly wondering who my bodyguards were. I was afraid of the outcome of this meeting, but the situation took a turn so unexpected that even now, just thinking about it, I feel shocked all over again.

***

"Angela, Matthew, hi, this is—"

I didn't have the time to finish before Karl grabbed Angela's hand, kissed it, and introduced himself.

"Karl Sarlsberg, at your service. I am a distant cousin of Samantha's."

"From the family tree's *stupid* branch . . . ," I couldn't help muttering under my breath. Karl took advantage of the fact that I was next to him to give me a swift kick to the tibia. I held back a cry of pain and the slap he deserved. The idiot hadn't held back his strength, and I was going to have a bruise. What a brute.

"I must say that Samantha told me of your beauty, but this is beyond belief. You are out of this world."

Completely taken aback, Angela could only say, "Uh . . . pleasure."

Her not very enthusiastic reaction disappointed Casanova, who frowned and imperiously ignored Matthew's offered hand.

But nothing could have unnerved us more than what followed.

Karl finally deigned to move over to clear the way for François, whose patience would have deserved awards. Then it happened.

François and Angela had stepped closer to introduce themselves, stopped suddenly, and faced one another directly. They seemed perfectly happy to freeze in this moment of mutual contemplation. If it hadn't been reality, you could have believed that someone had pressed pause on the DVD remote.

Matthew, Karl, and I looked at each other, wondering what was happening to Angela and François. When they finally shook hands, I understood.

I had just witnessed love at first sight, like in Hollywood films. They couldn't tear their eyes away from each other, and their handshake looked like a soft caress that lasted longer than necessary. The electricity that seemed to be running between their fingers started to remind me of something . . .

But before the memory could fully surface, an indelicate and imperious throat clearing put an end to the scene in front of me. No need to clarify who made that disgraceful noise, which he followed by saying, "All this gushing is interesting, but we are going to miss the film."

The Karl I hated just reappeared in all his splendor, his oversized ego enormously injured, his verbal cruelty determined to enter the fray. Cooled and confused, François and Angela moved away from each other, red-faced with embarrassment—at least Angela was, and surely François would have been if he could have. A little disconcerted, my vampire friend greeted a beaming Matthew.

Apparently, the lightning strike of love hadn't escaped him either, and he seemed sincerely thrilled. It was at that moment that I knew with certainty that Matthew didn't feel any connection beyond a fraternal one for Angela or else he wouldn't have seemed so happy.

As for me, after the shock of the moment passed, I felt a certain unease realizing the implications that love between my two friends would entail.

Phoenix had explained to me that sexual relations between humans and vampires were quite common, but love stories were another matter. Knowing what he'd told me about the virtuous François, I doubted that his sudden attraction would only be a simple affair, and the same would go for Angela. If she had turned away all her suitors so far, it wasn't without reason. She was waiting for the right one . . .

And it seemed like the man of her dreams was a vampire, more open-minded than Phoenix, yes, but still a nest of problems, that was certain.

Love between two vampires was rare and unpopular. Now love between a human and a vampire! According to what my boss had said, it was impossible. Sexual attraction and one-night stands were common enough, but a serious relationship with real feelings . . . there was no precedent for that.

It seemed as though vampire creators only choose as their progeny selfish individuals incapable of feeling. That would explain their ridiculous vision of love. In short, we had enough problems on our hands without adding a dangerous and impossible liaison that would only attract the attention of the Greats. And I certainly didn't want to see my friends suffer. What kind of mess had I gotten us in now?

At the movie theater, I managed to separate the two lovebirds by arranging things so Angela was seated at the end of the row. Karl, Matthew, and I formed a barricade of bodies that kept Angela from being too close to François. Matthew sat next to me, which provoked a completely inappropriate question from Karl during the previews.

"So, Matthew, you are Sam's boyfriend? She talks a lot about you."

Turning beet red, I sat up straight in my chair and shot daggers at his impolite curiosity. Matthew must have thought that I was talking about him in these terms; he answered with a big smile full of hope.

"I'm flattered that she spoke of me to you."

I thought I'd better put things back in order without offending him.

"Of course I told them about you. After all, along with Angela, you're my best *friends*." I'd insisted on the word *friends* to make the situation clear, and seeing his face darken, I knew it had been successful. I thought I'd set things straight, but that was without taking into account

Karl's harsh verve; he was determined to take his vengeance on everyone for the insult he had suffered.

"Oh, yes, now that you mention it, she did say you were friends. It is true that before, she only ever spoke of her dear Phoenix, so that was a nice change of tune."

There was a silence, then a resounding thud of someone who just received an elbow to the ribs (François didn't hold back). I almost choked in horror, and the air seemed to have completely escaped from my lungs. How had he dared to speak of his friend, my boss, a vampire whose existence must absolutely remain a secret, just to annoy me? Was he just a hothead or congenital idiot? Phoenix was going to tear the skin off his back! And knowing him, that wasn't a metaphor.

Livid, I risked a glance over at Matthew, who was frowning deeply. "Who is this . . . Phoenix?"

"Uh . . . well, that's a . . . um . . . ," I stuttered pathetically. Quick, an idea! "He's my ex" was the only thing I could think of.

Matthew couldn't see him, but Karl was convulsing with laughter. It took an incredible effort for me to recover my composure and look Matthew straight in the eyes while offering him the lie of the century.

"Really, his name is . . . Aydan."

Good heavens, why had I used that name? Phoenix was going to kill me when he learned that I'd given his real name in this sordid conversation. Karl and François weren't reacting at all, since they didn't know Phoenix's real identity. I'd just betrayed him. Good grief. All that work to gain his confidence lost through my mistake and the incredible arrogance of his best friend. If I could, I would have cried, but I had to continue lying.

"We were together for . . . three years . . . but he was a workaholic. That was what ruined our relationship. It was really hard . . . I came here, and then . . . life goes on . . ."

I looked at Matthew's face for any sign of hate, but to my astonishment he said, "So if you don't want to go out with me, is it because you're afraid of being in a new relationship and suffering again?"

Luckily I was already sitting down because my knees were trembling with relief. I owed a thank you to pop psychology. Matthew thought he had seen right through me, and that suited me just fine. His compassion indicated to me that I'd gotten out of that quagmire without a scratch and with a reward: out of respect for my so-called romantic distress, he was going to leave me alone about going out with him, and for a good while.

"How did you guess?" I said, sniffling and adopting a tone of desperation, all while resting my head on his shoulder so he couldn't see me smile.

Even when he put his arm around my shoulders to comfort me, I didn't feel at all guilty. After all, it was Karl who'd forced me to make up something. However, my smile crumbled at the thought of my boss's reaction when his two friends, or at least one of them, hurried to recount this episode to him and mentioned the name I'd given. Suddenly, I wondered where I could hide for the nights to come.

I got out a tissue from my pocket and sat up to dab at my eyes and their false tears; that way, I could also escape the consoling embrace of my neighbor.

"Thanks for understanding. For me, love is out of the question since I can't forget Phoenix."

"I understand. But why that nickname? It's silly," Matthew asked.

Matthew had luckily turned his back to the two vampires, who didn't appreciate his remark and who, out of loyalty, started to have eyes that shone brighter than normal. Oh boy.

"Um . . . he was in a serious car accident and he almost died. He chose that name to remind himself that life is precious and its ephemeral nature entails exemplary behavior."

There it was. I'd remedied Matthew's question by giving the good role to my boss; that would have to be enough to calm my two maniacs.

"You're still in love with him, aren't you?"

Gulp.

"It's something I don't want to talk about."

Right on cue the lights went down and the film began. Angela whispered in my ear, "It is in your best interest to tell me more about your Phoenix. I want all the details."

Oh boy. I felt a headache starting. In an effort to escape the whole situation, I closed my eyes and fell asleep without compunction.

The final explosion of the enemy spaceship woke me with a start, and I wondered where I was. The light snoring on my right told me that Matthew hadn't found the film that interesting either. As for Angela . . .

"Do you think he likes me?" she murmured as I yawned noticeably.

*He could answer you himself because he heard you as if you were seated right next to him.* But I couldn't tell her that.

"Huh?" Playing dumb seemed a good idea to me . . .

"François! He's so gorgeous—the tall, dark, handsome type. I want him."

. . . Or not.

I caught a movement in the corner of my eye. François must have leaped up out of his seat when he heard that the woman he desired returned his desire, and ardently.

"Uh, shouldn't we talk about this later? I want to know how the film ends."

"Pff! Yeah, right, you've been sleeping since the opening credits. But you're right, it's not really the time. That way, when we see each other again, I can grill you about your ex."

"Hm . . ."

I hated Karl for making me lie through my teeth to my friends, especially since I was going to have to continue inventing an ex, who was Phoenix, no less. My temper was boiling, and the rest of the evening, I could barely contain it.

Walled up in silence, I was furious with every single one of my friends. At Karl for ruining my life, at François and Angela for complicating my life, and at Matthew for wanting to be a part of my life in a way I didn't want. My human friends blamed my bad mood on the memory of my breakup, but the others didn't need an explanation.

Before we left, Angela gave me a direct order to bring back "that angel who came down from heaven," and I had to put all my energy into channeling the volcano that threatened to erupt. Not even Karl dared provoke me.

It was after midnight by the time we returned to the manor. Furious, I slammed my car door and marched inside. In the entryway, I crossed paths with my boss. He seemed tired and . . . demoralized. Seeing him like that made me feel suddenly guilty about leaving him alone while I went to the movies and made mistake after mistake. My rage volcano quickly deflated, yielding to real distress and tears dangerously close to spilling over.

I tried to pass Phoenix without looking at him, and I fled toward my room.

From upstairs, I heard him growl, "Shit, Karl! What did you do to her now?"

It was the first time I'd ever heard him swear, but I didn't hear any more. I closed myself up in my room to cry in the dark.

***

A while later, someone knocked on my door. When I didn't answer, that someone came in, walked around the bed, and sat down next to me. His unique smell revealed his identity before he could even speak.

"Sam, turn on the light, please."

"You can see perfectly fine," I protested.

He leaned over, bumping into me a little to switch on the lamp on the nightstand. I would have liked to stay in the dark so he wouldn't see my red eyes and the pile of used tissues scattered across the floor and I wouldn't have to face his accusing stare. I kept my eyes down, but he gently lifted my chin and turned my head toward him. Once again his expression was completely inscrutable, and I couldn't stop shaking.

"You are entirely too emotional."

Only when it was about him. Why was that? I didn't feel as bad about having to lie to Matthew and Angela, but the very idea of losing Phoenix's friendship and trust because I'd given away his real name made me nauseous.

"I don't deserve your friendship . . ."

These few words were incredibly difficult to say, and without being able to do anything about it, I started to cry again, closing my eyes. I felt the caress of his fingers as he gently wiped away the uncontrollable flood of tears. At his touch, curiously, I relaxed and stopped crying. How did he do it?

"Nothing that Karl and François told me makes me think that. So why are you upset? The one at fault is that imbecile German."

"But he didn't tell everyone your real name, which is what I did. You trusted me, and I betrayed you."

There was an insufferable silence. Then finally he said, "You protected us all from Karl's foolishness. It does not matter what first name you used. You did not talk about my past to anyone, so you did not betray me."

I stared at him, incredulous at his leniency. "You forgive me?"

"There is nothing to forgive. You did nothing wrong," he said. "On the contrary, I should congratulate you. François says you are a wonderful actress."

The wave of relief overwhelmed me completely, and I immediately felt better. Maybe too much better.

Without either of us expecting it, I dove into his arms and snuggled up to him. His words reassured me, but a part of me wanted more. Gripping his shirt, my face nestled in the crook of his neck, I felt him put his arms around me . . .

He must have heard my heart pounding, but I didn't care. His embrace made me smile again, and soothed my conscience. Why did I feel so good now? His smell invaded me, and the contact with his cold, soft skin was as good as a caress. Only a few seconds must have passed, but even they made me wish that time would stop.

When he held me even closer to his chest, I slid my arms over his back and squeezed. In such a tight embrace, the coldness of his skin should have passed through our clothes and chilled me to the bone, but on the contrary, a veritable fire seemed to break out in every cell of my body. Like the evening when we danced, I lost control, and this time without a single drop of alcohol. My hands had a mind of their own, and they brushed up and down Phoenix's spine rather immodestly.

I felt one of his hands playing with a lock of my hair while the other radiated heat on my back where he'd placed it. His lips were dangerously close to my neck, and that idea, for whatever reason, was completely intoxicating. My heart went into a panic and pounded harder than ever in my chest. What on earth was coming over me?

I had to regain control over my noisy heart, and I tried to pull back a little. Then we were face-to-face, with very little distance between us, and our hands not yet sensibly pulled away as they should have been. Phoenix had once again that profound look that drew me in completely. My universe toppled over, and I wanted to fall into the ocean of Phoenix's blue eyes.

"Well, you are certainly taking your time to—Oh!"

The vision of paradise collapsed like the sound of glass breaking, yielding to reality. Noticing that we were really close to each other, our lips were less than an inch from touching, and, without knowing when it happened, our fingers were laced together, Phoenix and I broke away simultaneously, with an abruptness that reflected our total confusion.

In my doorway, Karl was doubled up with laughter, whereas François seemed embarrassed at having interrupted us.

"Ha-ha-ha! For someone so desperate, you seem completely blissful, Samantha. But this is not surprising. Ever since I have known him, Phoenix has been a champion at consoling damsels in distress. My apologies for interrupting."

The insinuation that my boss could have taken advantage of my weakness to seduce me, and that it wasn't the first time he might have done so, stabbed me right in the heart, more than the compromising situation in which Karl had found us. The portrait of Phoenix that Karl was painting seemed more like his own, a Don Juan without scruples—vain, selfish, and only concerned about adding another notch to his belt. That was the last straw.

My rage volcano woke up again and was determined more than ever to erupt. The red veil that only appeared in the most critical moments fell over my eyes again, and I got up slowly, staring at Karl like prey I wanted tear apart.

Phoenix tried to grab my hand to calm me down, but I pulled away from him unceremoniously.

"Karl, you had better leave the room," my boss warned him.

The German vampire laughed in response.

"No, I am having too much fun with you two."

"I hate you." My tone indicated that it was the pure truth. Despite all the respect I had for Phoenix, I couldn't pretend anymore. As if I were having an out-of-body experience, I saw myself moving around Phoenix and sliding my hand under my mattress and the bed frame.

"No, Sam."

"Shut up."

Taken aback by my aggressive answer, he didn't stop me from getting out the gun I'd hidden under the bed. Seeing it, Karl gave a dry chuckle that increased my murderous rage tenfold.

"It's high time that someone gave you the spanking your mother never gave you," I said, applying my boss's lessons in attack positions.

Karl immediately stopped laughing, and his eyes were blazing. "I would love to see that."

Before Phoenix or François, incredulous at the grotesque scene before them, could react, I jumped up.

Infinitely faster than I was, Karl dodged, mocking me, except I'd anticipated his move and I took my first shot. I wasn't playing at all. My conscious had fled my body and was watching my violent outburst from above. It was all very strange. In any case, Karl's horrible smile of satisfaction disappeared completely when he saw his arm was injured.

Rendered as powerless as a human because of the silver poison, he was weak enough that I could take him on. But I'd forgotten one thing: he had five hundred years of training behind him. Human or not, I figured he was a better fighter. I was certain of it when he hit me with a first punch that broke my jaw and a second that smashed two ribs before he violently slammed me to the ground.

Completely stunned, I still was able to see the incredible cruelty of his luminescent eyes as well as his mouth, which was twisted in a grimace filled with an indescribable hatred; he was about to club me in the face again, not to put me in my place, but to kill me. At the last instant, Phoenix sent him flying to the other side of the room with an authoritative uppercut. François knelt down next to me.

*"Nom de Dieu!"* I heard him mutter, horrified, propping my head up on his knees.

I couldn't have been a pretty sight. When François pulled his hands out from under my head, one of them was covered in blood. My blood.

Phoenix had been wrong to think that I'd be able to beat a vampire injured by a silver bullet. He'd said that such a vampire would have only a human strength, but not that it would be the strength of a heavy-weight boxing champ.

I started to slip into the fog of lost consciousness, but I heard fighting a few feet away. Then I saw a silhouette fly into the hallway and get up in evident pain.

Pointing an angry finger at his attacker, Karl howled, "Look at me, Phoenix! The way you treat me only proves what everyone is saying behind your back! You have gotten weak, and it is even worse now that you are with that human! Your love for her is sheer madness! Where is the friend who reduced those French soldiers to a pulp with me? I do not recognize you anymore, and I spit on the person you have become! You are dead to me until you get rid of that *thing* and remember what kind of vampire you *really* are!"

When Phoenix answered, his tone glacial, a friendship that had lasted several centuries shattered in an instant. "At any rate, not a vampire like you!"

I heard Karl's footsteps as he left the house and Phoenix, perhaps forever . . . But before I was completely taken over by unconsciousness, a single sentence came to mind: "The protector must guide the steps of the one the Night has chosen, at the cost of great sacrifice."

***

"Do you want me to give her my blood?"

"She belongs to me."

"I hope you know what you are doing."

"Do *not* lecture me. According to what Karl has said, you and I are in the same situation."

Huh? Was I still dreaming or were those the vague voices of Phoenix and François? I didn't understand any of what they were saying. What were they even talking about?

I slowly opened my eyes. Phoenix was leaning over me and rolling up the sleeve of his shirt.

"Sam, you need to drink my blood."

What? After what just happened? Out of the question! Since he'd surprised us in each other's arms, François must already be telling himself that there was more than friendship between us, so I didn't want to add fuel to the fire.

I shook my head.

"You are so stubborn! You have a broken jaw and several broken ribs. François also thinks that you have some sort of head injury. If you want a slow and painful recovery, fine. But if you want to speed up the process, you do not have a choice."

Busted jaw . . . I must look a mess. I really didn't want to suffer for a long time needlessly. Good grief.

Since I couldn't really talk, I nodded my assent. Phoenix cut into his wrist with his fangs. Blood dripping from the wound, he put his wrist up to my mouth.

Unfortunately, my jaw was so painful I couldn't open my mouth enough to drink the precious liquid.

"Phoenix, she cannot drink. You have to make your blood flow harder," said François.

"I know. The carotid?"

"Good idea."

I didn't understand how that would work, but I wasn't thinking straight. When Phoenix used my knife to cut his own throat, I caught on. I tried to pull away from him as a torrent of blood gushed from his neck wound, but my body refused to budge. And then he lay across me, imprisoning me with his weight without crushing me. I didn't dare even breathe.

"Sam, healing you will weaken me . . . We do not have a choice. We have to proceed with the exchange of blood. At the right moment, I shall have to bite you too."

Horrified, I tried again to pull away, but it was a wasted effort.

"It will be fine," said François, who had stepped aside.

*It will be fine?* Was that a joke? I was going to drink his blood, and he was going to drink mine? At the same time? I remembered all too well the terrible pain I'd felt when he'd bitten my arm! I didn't want to pick up where we left off.

But how could I help Phoenix investigate the disappearances if I was weak and hopped up on pain meds? I didn't have a choice. I'd truly had enough of *never* having a choice.

My nod gave him the signal to begin. He leaned over and offered me his neck. Disgusted, I placed my hands on his shoulders and started to drink the red liquid that flowed heavily from his neck. Like the last time, my body temperature heated up; like the last time, disgust gave way to contentment and then . . . the desire for more. I drank with abandon, pleasure taking hold of me and pushing the pain far, far from my consciousness. Satisfied, I took a break between two mouthfuls, sighing with well-being.

I shuddered when two canines sunk into my flesh and I felt my blood flowing out of me. It was surprising that it wasn't at all painful. On the contrary, something incredible was happening . . . or rather something incredibly embarrassing . . .

All the barriers and taboos connected to my upbringing were broken down in that instant. It was as though every fiber of my being was vibrating under the pleasure that was taking over. Eyes closed, I felt his lips like a passionate kiss pressing against my skin, drinking in my very life . . . and I wanted more.

Not able to stop myself, I grabbed a fistful of Phoenix's hair, pulled on it with one hand while with the other I dug my fingers into his back, all while arching my spine. I got a deep and satisfied growl in response, and I felt one of his hands slide under me to maintain his grip.

Electrified by his response, I gripped the fistful of hair harder, making him pull back and exposing his throat again. He let it happen, and before swooping down on his wound, I noticed that his eyes were literally ablaze, charged not with violence, but with desire . . .

When I started to drink his blood again, Phoenix let a small moan escape and buried his face in my hair, breathing in my scent.

To distribute his weight on top of me, I'd had to spread my legs; that position had the effect of an electric shock, and my hand wandered from his back . . . lower and lower . . .

Impatient, he changed positions and bit me on the other side, grabbing one of my thighs and raising it over his hip. A hurricane was brewing in my lower regions, reinforced by the sensation of his tongue licking my wound eagerly and that of our two bodies undulating so sensually against each other.

Suddenly, the explosion that washed over me made me arch my back violently, and I wrapped my legs around his waist as if to hold him prisoner there forever. I cried out in ecstasy, and he held my thighs firmly against his pelvis, joining me in incredible pleasure . . .

\*\*\*

I hadn't felt my bones knit back together, but I knew when we finished the exchange that everything was like before. More or less.

Falling quickly back to reality, I was paralyzed. Phoenix wasn't over-confident either; I felt him flinch before disengaging from my neck. Slowly he got up, the lower half of his face and his shirt covered in blood. I noticed too that his shirt was in tatters. Shame gripped me in an oppressive vise.

"Sam?" Phoenix kneeled beside me.

"Just a second."

Everything had gotten out of control so quickly. My evening should have proceeded simply: two friends, a movie, and a good night of sleep. But instead of that, I'd fought with Phoenix's best friend and ruptured their friendship; Karl had literally beaten me to a pulp; and to have any chance of healing, I'd surrendered myself to Phoenix. The blood exchange had led me to behave like a nymphomaniac in serious need of sex. It was all hard to digest . . .

A fraction of a second later, I sent my fist flying into my boss's face with the force of my bitterness. How dare he not warn me about the effect that a blood exchange would have on us? How could he have allowed me to behave like that, me who trembled at the thought of kissing a man for the first time? How . . . ?

Good heavens. Good *heavens*. What an idiot! I couldn't help shed a few tears even as I was clenching my teeth to not cry out in pain, that was how much the hand I'd used to hit him hurt. Why hadn't I learned from the last time? He'd again taken the hit without flinching or showing the least sign of pain, and that irritated me even more.

"I . . . you . . . I . . ." I was so angry that I couldn't even put my insults in order.

"Calm down, Samantha. Phoenix healed you. The blood exchange causes that kind of reaction. You should not feel ashamed," François said as he stepped closer.

I'd forgotten that he was still there.

François recoiled when I turned to him, as though he were afraid of me. I must have looked like a mad cannibal with all that blood spattered on my face and clothes.

Phoenix hadn't moved, simply waiting for my verdict. Slowly, I turned to him and stared at him without mercy.

"I know why you did it, but I'm angry that you didn't warn me . . . *again*. I'm going to take a shower and go to sleep. I don't want to hear another word about what happened here. And the next time I'm hurt, I'll go to the hospital."

I should have thanked him, but I did nothing of the sort. Anyway, I think he'd understood well enough. As for a discussion about Karl's departure, that would have to wait for the next day.

As I left the room, I heard Phoenix and François talking.

"What happened between you goes well beyond the blood exchange, and you know it. That is why you could not say anything to her."

"Be quiet, François."

A few steps more, and I was too far away to hear them. It was impossible that that conversation was real. Stifling a yawn, I decided that fatigue was playing tricks on me and it was better to go to sleep before hearing voices like Joan of Arc . . .

\*\*\*

While I slept, I dreamed of the blood exchange. The dreams, each more erotic than the one before, made me crazy, and I decided to get up. It was already four o'clock in the afternoon.

Having no desire whatsoever to go to Scarborough to hear Angela wax eloquent about her handsome François, or to see Matthew stare at me with a mixture of compassion and temptation, I preferred to stay near home and just took a short drive for a change of scenery. Before going back, I stopped at a food truck to buy a cheesy sandwich and fries to eat back at the manor. The vendor stared at me curiously, noticing that I was wearing a scarf even though it was hot out.

It bothered me too, but when I'd looked in the mirror, I'd been really annoyed by the two little red holes on both sides of my neck, so I'd decided to hide them. I hoped that the fact I couldn't see them anymore might even allow me to forget the unfortunate event that caused them.

When Phoenix and François turned up in the kitchen, they found me devouring my meal. Seeing my boss made the memory of feeling his body against mine come back in full force. I managed to control my embarrassment. After all, we'd decided to act as though it were nothing.

"Bon appétit," François said.

*"Merci, j'ai toujours aimé les sandwichs bien gras qui font dresser les cheveux sur la tête des nutritionnistes. Après tout, il n'y pas de mal à se faire du bien,"* I responded.

He seemed thrilled that I was fluent enough to describe how my sandwiches would make nutritionists cringe.

"You speak French?"

"No one ever came into my library, so I busied myself as best I could. I guess you could say I'm a bit of a Francophile," I said, stuffing a huge piece of bread into my mouth.

Phoenix chuckled. "You learned the language, but as for table manners, that remains to be seen."

Indeed, I'd just wiped the corner of my full mouth, where a bit of cheese had escaped. Not letting myself get flustered by my boss's comment, I said, "Maybe if you cooked me something to eat for once, I wouldn't have to go buy a sandwich."

Except that with all the bread I was still chewing, my answer was completely incomprehensible.

François changed the subject to something far less trivial.

"What are we doing this evening?"

Phoenix's face got dark. "Nothing. Because there is nothing to do. These men are too strong. Only the Greats can stop them."

A silence fell over the kitchen, each of us lost in our own dark thoughts.

"Because I didn't know how to control myself, I made you lose an asset, and a friend. I'm sorry."

We had to clear the air about Karl's departure at some point.

"You are not even thirty years old, and your reactions are led by your emotions and your humanity," Phoenix said. "Karl does not have that excuse. Furthermore, he never should have attacked you when I warned him that he should not disrespect you . . . In the end, I cannot forgive him for what he accused me of . . . or for hurting you."

His expression darkened even more. His relationship with Karl wasn't going to be fixed anytime soon. He thought of him like a brother, and I, not having brothers or sisters, I couldn't imagine the sense of loss Phoenix must be feeling. Since he was right next to me, I took his hand and squeezed. When he looked at me, surprised by my sudden change in attitude, I smiled gently.

Suddenly my phone rang, making me jump. Even though I didn't recognize the number, I answered all the same.

"Hello?"

"Miss Jones?"

"Who are you and where did you get this number?" I said defensively.

My two vampires stiffened and pricked up their ears.

"Bobby the Eel. You told me to contact you if we had news about the Chinese gang who's kidnapping people."

"I hope you called me for a reason."

"Yes. Important people have no time to waste. I've got some information that could help you, you and your boss, find those mafia guys. Come find me tonight at Sunnie's, midnight. I don't like phones."

"Very well, we'll be there. I hope that your information is worth it," I declared with a tone of warning that didn't escape Bobby the Eel.

"Don't you worry. We'll catch them. And if my guys and me can help you, so much the better."

"Later, then."

I hung up, and as I turned to Phoenix and François, I couldn't help smiling.

"Business is picking up again."

# CHAPTER TEN

## *Reunion*

"Who is this Bobby the Eel?" asked François.

"He is the leader of a small biker gang in Kerington that we met when visiting Thirsty. Sam won their respect and convinced them, for a fee, to do some digging on their end. I did not tell you or Karl about them because I did not really think that the arrangement would produce anything."

*Thanks for your vote of confidence, boss. That was a pleasure to hear.*

"I hope this doesn't surprise you," I said, selfishly forcing him to compliment me.

Phoenix rolled his eyes.

"I recognize that your devious mind and your bizarre ideas may be able to help us."

Such bad faith.

"Would it really kill you to thank me?" I grumbled.

"Let's hope that this information will lead us to the blood traffickers. Anyway, we do not have a choice but to listen to this gangster," François said, intervening before Phoenix and I started a quarrel.

"We still have time. I shall go prepare some things," he said as he left the kitchen.

I wanted to finish my sandwich. I was determined to fill up my stomach so I would have plenty of energy for the night ahead. François sat down next to me.

"Samantha, may I ask you a question?"

"Mm-hm." If I'd opened my mouth to answer, I would have risked spitting out my food and coming across as a cavewoman.

"Do you think that a vampire and a human . . . ?"

There was no need for him to finish his sentence for me to know that he was talking about Angela. I swallowed my food.

"The way you and Angela look at each other proves that true love between vampires and humans is possible, no matter what anyone says. But there are a number of obstacles that will crop up, and I'm afraid the situation has the risk of ending in broken hearts."

He looked discouraged, which saddened me. Maybe I'd been too honest, and I tried to take it back.

"But that's no reason not to try. You and Angela are a lot alike. You'll make a good couple."

François seemed relieved and looked at me with true affection.

"And you and Phoenix?"

I felt my cheeks burn red. "I already told you . . ."

"You are not in love with him, I know. But clinging to the illusion of your friendship is futile. Your connection is deeper than that."

"You sound just like Karl. What's gotten into you, all of you? You want us to be in love at all costs. I know perfectly well that that would lead nowhere, that it's impossible. Can't you be happy for us to just be friends? Phoenix is my friend and my boss and that's all."

"If you want to keep deluding yourself, please do, but let me say one thing. The blood exchange causes an increase in sexual desire between partners, but it is not powerful enough to set off a reaction as passionate as the one you two shared. I did not say this to you yesterday so you had a chance to calm down, but it is the truth."

I had trouble swallowing. He was suggesting that our unconscious minds had communicated during the blood exchange, revealing our true feelings. I pictured myself again, legs wrapped around Phoenix, moaning in ecstasy. For a single second, I'd thought I'd found paradise in his arms . . . I remembered the voices I'd heard in the hallway: François had been making the same comment to Phoenix, who had answered him curtly by telling him to shut up. However, that couldn't be true; my hearing wasn't that sensitive.

I shook my head, it was just a hallucination; François was mistaken. Phoenix was everything to me, but for all that, this wasn't love I was feeling for him. As for the blood exchange, given my reaction the first time he'd made me drink blood from his wrist, drinking it directly from a major artery, in his neck, must have . . . intoxicated me as if I'd had one drink too many, and that explained our behavior. There.

Perked up by this reasoning, I looked François right in the eyes and said coldly, "I don't mean to offend you, because of your virtuous principles, but I think that even you don't know the effect that a blood exchange can have. So stop inventing foolish romantic feelings for us and spend your time with the very real ones that are pushing you toward Angela! I'll see you in a bit." Then I left the kitchen.

He still had the last word.

"Do not say I did not warn you."

\*\*\*

The first half of the trip to Kerington was made in complete silence. I wanted to keep my distance from the two vampires, so I'd settled into the backseat and cut myself off from them by putting on headphones and listening to my MP3 player. Eventually Phoenix and François began a conversation, but not wanting to hear them, I just turned up the volume. Despite the singer's howling in my ears, I could hear the vampires with a clarity that annoyed me.

"Do you have to shout at each other to make yourselves heard? Can't I even listen to my music in peace?" I complained, exasperated.

They looked at each other, surprised, then François signaled to me to take off my headphones. The sound that was coming out of them was quite simply intolerable, that was how loud I'd set the volume. I turned the player off.

"You can hear us over the racket of that device of auditory torture?" Phoenix asked.

"Racket? You were talking so loudly I had to turn up the volume. It's your fault!" I exclaimed, outraged.

"We were talking very low precisely so we would not bother you. A normal human ear could not have heard us," François said, amazed.

"What?"

It was my turn to be surprised. François stared at me long and hard before turning back to Phoenix.

"Do you see? I told you. You have stamped her with your mark."

"For several days now, François, I have missed the times when you did not talk at all," Phoenix answered curtly.

I reacted right away.

"Hey! But you had this discussion yesterday."

They stayed quiet, waiting for me to finish.

"I was at the other end of the hallway after . . . uh . . . Phoenix healed me. You told François to shut up when he told you that our blood exchange had gotten out of control. I thought I'd dreamed it because I was too far away to reasonably hear you."

I was quiet for a moment, but then I cried out, "What did you do to me?"

I thought I was angry, but it was more likely fear that had made me react. Phoenix clenched his teeth so hard I could hear them grinding against each other. It was François who answered me.

"Phoenix told me he healed you recently, before this time."

"Yes. He bit me . . . by accident," I hurried to add. "Then there was my encounter with Heath."

"I see . . . You drank his blood again yesterday, and in a large quantity. The blood exchange can have unexpected consequences, especially when the two people in question have an attachment . . . like yours."

Phoenix gave a warning growl that triggered dreadful trembling throughout my body. François took the threat seriously. My boss didn't want to address the subject of our *attachment* either; he must find his friend's suppositions about the tie that bound us just as ridiculous as I did. I didn't know precisely why, but I was disappointed for a moment. I got a hold of myself, and François continued.

"Well . . . This sort of thing does not normally happen, but I think that Phoenix's blood left a mark in your body."

"But . . . that's absurd," I said in an effort to reassure myself.

"Of course it is absurd. Be quiet, François, or I promise that I will eject you from this car at the next curve," Phoenix said threateningly.

But François didn't back down.

"How else would you explain her sudden hearing acuteness if not from marking her?"

Phoenix was making a considerable *and* visible effort to contain the rage that was beginning to overwhelm him. The only thing I wanted to know at that moment was whether or not I would be turning into some sort of mutant monster.

"What's going to happen to me?"

"I heard that a human marked by a vampire only shares powers for a time, and to a lesser extent of course. But I would never have thought that a human who only drank blood from the same vampire three times could get the mark so quickly," said François, more wondering aloud than speaking to his audience. He seemed to find the whole thing fascinating. I found it horrifying.

I was going to share my boss's powers. I'd always dreamed of being a strong and intimidating woman, a bit like Xena the Warrior Princess, but now I was lost in a nightmare for which I wasn't at all prepared.

"But . . . I'll get better?"

Phoenix shuddered slightly, hearing my question, as though I was saying he'd infected me with a sexually transmitted disease. It wasn't nice, but too bad for him! It was his fault that we were in this mess. However, I also knew that if I hadn't jumped on Karl so intensely, this would never have happened. Bingo. My anger was gone.

"Of course," said François. "The mark's effects are temporary. But it could take some time before they disappear completely. Look on the bright side. You will be stronger against our enemies."

I'd never imagined . . . The beating I'd gotten from the fight with Karl had indeed been painful. This mark, even if it scared me, would allow me to be more effective when faced with danger. It was strange that other than my acute hearing, I didn't feel any different. I was going to have to do some experiments to see just how far my new abilities went.

"Well, in that case, it doesn't bother me as much."

Phoenix swerved so violently that I was thrown to the other side of the backseat. I should have put on my seat belt, so I quickly made to fix my mistake.

"What's gotten into you?"

My question set off one of my boss's violent tantrums. My knees were knocking at the very memory of it.

In a quarter of a second, he'd transformed into a god of wrath whose aura of absolute rage crushed me in an immobilizing fear.

"What has gotten into *me*? Are you crazy or just oblivious? François just told you that I have removed part of your humanity to replace it with . . . a stain! If that does not bother you, that's because you are completely deranged. Accepting that part of me is in you means rejecting your identity and your independence. How could you be so flippant?"

At the end of his tirade, his shoulders were heaving up and down as though he were trying to catch his breath.

He didn't understand how I could so easily accept having his mark in me. So he hadn't understood that I wanted to be stronger to help him?

Sobs threatened to force their way out of my mouth. I didn't realize that I'd bitten my lip, drawing blood, in my attempt to not cry, until I tasted blood. My trembling resumed with even greater intensity, a physical consequence of my struggle against crying and embarrassing myself in front of them.

Phoenix suddenly slammed on the brakes, and we went into a controlled skid that would have made auto racers green with jealousy. He parked on the side of the road.

Before opening his door, Phoenix looked at François with such anger that his friend shrank into his seat.

"You, don't you dare meddle in things that do not concern you ever again. If I see you get out of this car, I will tear your arms off."

I'd never seen him like this before. He slammed the car door so hard when he got out that it shook violently. He came around the car, and my heart skipped a beat when I realized he was heading toward me.

He opened my door abruptly and grabbed me by the arm. Luckily, I'd unbuckled my seat belt as soon as we'd stopped. It was dark, but he forged ahead without the slightest hesitation. He had a painfully tight grip on my wrist as he pulled me behind him, leading me to the woods. I was so shocked and so focused on trying not to trip that I didn't utter a single sound. Despite the darkness, the moonlight permitted me to see where I was stepping, and I heard the hoots of an owl, outraged at having been disturbed in her calm habitat.

Hidden under the trees, Phoenix pushed me brusquely ahead of him, and I collapsed on the ground, scraping my hands and knees. Too stunned to dwell on the pain, I settled for staring at him stupidly.

My look rekindled his anger, his eyes becoming so luminescent that their bluish and metallic flash was blinding.

"I free you from your obligations toward me," he said plainly.

That simple phrase knocked the wind right out of me. It was as though all my muscles instantly liquefied when the meaning of the words he'd used finally reached my brain. My mouth went dry, and I struggled to swallow.

"What?" was the only thing I was able to say.

"It's over. You are not my assistant anymore. You are fired."

*You are fired.* How could he say that to me after all the lengths to which he'd gone to keep me with him? After what he'd said to me at the train station?

"I . . . no."

The desperate emphasis of these monosyllables hadn't been overplayed: my world was collapsing. When he turned his back to me to leave, I almost fainted, except that I hadn't made such efforts to gain his trust to be treated like this.

I stood up, my legs like jelly.

*"Look at me!"* I shouted.

He could have continued walking and forgotten about me . . . but he stopped, though he didn't turn around.

"Nothing you can say will change my mind. Go back to your life and forget me."

Back to my life? Forget him?

"You . . . you told me I would die if I left . . . for the Secret."

I was prepared to do anything to gain time, to gather a little strength so I could follow him.

"I shall arrange things so that you will be left alone. Good-bye."

He took a few steps forward.

"You're going to leave me here?"

*Find something that will make him stay! Force him to stay with you!*

"There is a road that leads to a farmhouse over there. Ask them for shelter. From there, with your new identity, you can start over."

He took a couple more steps.

"I . . . *no!*" I screamed.

With all the force of despair, I started to run. I was afraid that he would use his powers to stop me from following him, but I caught up with him. Tripping on a branch, I stumbled and crashed into him with full force; the impact threw me backward and onto my ass. Refusing to admit defeat, I got up quickly and grabbed Phoenix by the arm.

He finally turned around; the look of disdain on his face pierced right through me and finally broke my heart. Closing my eyes, letting years flow down my cheeks, I threw myself against him and hammered his chest with my fists.

"How can you leave me when you came looking for me? How can you say these things to me when you said you were my friend? How can you abandon me when you're all I have in the world?"

With every word, I got closer and closer to hysteria. I hit him, again and again, and he didn't react.

Completely desperate, I knew that in a matter of seconds, I would lose him forever, and I let myself fall to my knees. My life had no meaning anymore without him guiding me. He was my anchor, my beacon, my only true friend. Seeing him leave would be like losing a part of myself, and I couldn't accept that. I'd never cried like this before, the pain that I had felt when Karl hit me was nothing compared to the suffering that was imprisoning me in that moment.

Even from my abyss of pain, I felt it when he kneeled in front of me and placed his trembling hands on my shoulders. I even heard his voice: "Sam . . . I . . . no . . . I must separate myself from you. I only bring you suffering. You do not deserve that."

His voice was utterly different. The disdain and anger had disappeared, and he sounded unsure, hesitant. I must have been dreaming.

Yes, I was dreaming, for his vampire notion about independence excluded the very possibility of sharing a part of himself with someone. And yet he had lost something to me, and for that reason he must hate me. That was it, he hated me, and that idea made me lose all control.

My torrent of suffering spilled forth in terrible sobs that made it hard to breathe normally. Points of light danced in front of my eyes, and a chasm threatened to swallow me up into the hell of his absence at any second.

After a moment that seemed infinite to me, while my consciousness decided to crouch down low and away from reality to save itself from my ocean of distress, a strange sensation came over me and forced me to wake up. I smelled a perfume . . . his scent. An embrace . . . again, his . . . the only one that could pull me out of my stupor.

Slowly, I came to. I was still on my knees on the ground . . . I was still having trouble breathing, but for another reason.

Phoenix was squeezing me against him so hard it hurt, and stroking my hair. It was his body against mine that had helped me regain consciousness. He hadn't abandoned me . . . not yet. Despite that horrible prospect, I wrapped my arms around his waist and breathed in, perhaps for the last time, his reassuring smell. In the middle of the night, in a humid and hostile wood, we remained intertwined and silent for a long time.

Phoenix spoke first. "I thought I was protecting you by letting you take your life back . . . I cannot bear to see you hurt because of me, it makes me sick . . . And that mark . . . that was the final straw. It made me crazy. I bring nothing good to your life, and yet you want to stay with me. Why?"

His words washed over me like a miraculous balm. He didn't hate me.

"Every day, you make me better. At your side, I feel like I'm the person I always wanted to be. You're the most important person in the world to me, my best friend."

"I promised to never hurt you . . . I have broken my promise."

Hope was starting to return to my heart, but I was too afraid of being wrong. Was he apologizing for wanting to send me away? Did he want me to come back?

"Sam . . . for five hundred years, I did not matter to anyone. There were François and Karl of course, but that is not the same . . . I did not think that you would react like that, I . . . I thought you would be happy to go back to your human life . . . without vampires. François was right . . . I feel connected to you, and the idea of something happening to you because of me is terrifying. I wish . . . no, I want you stay with me."

"Why?" I said in a whisper.

He held me a little closer. "Because I need you at my side to feel alive."

He'd said everything. The open wound in my chest closed up immediately, the chasm of despair disappeared, and my breathing became normal.

"I forbid you from abandoning me."

"I will never abandon you."

He resumed stroking my hair, and I finally relaxed.

"François thinks we are in love."

"The very idea," he said, laughing.

I smiled. "I'm relieved that there are no misunderstandings between us. Because when we get back to the car, he's going to believe it all the more."

"Let him believe what he wants. Will you be OK?"

"My legs are rubbery, but I think I can walk."

He helped me stand, then took my hands, staring me in the eyes.

"Can you forgive me?"

"You tried to protect me . . . it was badly done and very brutal. But I forgive you."

When we left the woods, I caught of glimpse François's face through the car window, and I saw his expression change from one of worry to immense relief. However, taking note of my boss's last warning, he didn't dare come to meet us and settled for watching us approach. Phoenix had put a protective right arm around my shoulders, and he was holding my right hand in his left. My knees were covered in mud, my hair had come undone, and my eyes were puffy and red from crying, but I was smiling.

Not a single word on the matter was exchanged inside the car for the rest of the trip to our destination.

Everything had been said, and now the secret of the strength of the bond that united us finally had been revealed. It would stay protected by the discretion of the fauna and flora of a little wood in Kerington County.

***

Sunnie's was frequented by all the biker gangs of east Kerington; any wars between them were buried in this sacrosanct bar, which was recognized for the quality of its beer. The proprietor, a giant bearded man as wide as he was tall, was capable of stopping the least dispute among the gang members. He never hesitated to knock troublemakers on their backsides with the butt of a rifle. He loved and collected guns—hence his nickname, Trigger-Finger Clyde.

In our field of vision, there were leather, beards, bandanas, and billiard cues, not to mention the pints of beer set on the tables. The room was filled with cigarette smoke and the looks . . . well, they were turned to the newcomers: Phoenix, François, and me.

"This is *my* playing field. Allow me," I said to the vampires as I stepped in front of them.

My first obstacle was two huge bikers whose arms had the same circumference as their thighs: instead of letting me pass, they barred my path. I wanted to take care of this like a professional to impress my boss and François.

"It's in your best interest to let me through."

When the two bodybuilders standing in front of me whistled with admiration after leering at me indiscreetly, the growl I identified as

Phoenix's, always so particular about manners, pushed me quickly into action.

Without a second thought, I seized the pint of beer from the hand of the one on the right, and while he looked at it stupidly, I planted a kick in the left one's junk, before doing the same to the other guy with my knee. Thanks to Phoenix's blood, I was much more accurate and powerful in my movements . . .

Since they were on the ground and rolling back and forth to try to soothe the pain in their nether regions, they no longer represented an immediate danger. However, I was going to have to deal with their friends.

Eyeing them with an infinitely superior air, I raised my enormous pint to them and drank it all down in great gulps before setting it down hard on the table to their looks of amazement.

"Where I'm from, that's how you deal with those who disrespect women! But you guys all seem to be much more polite, so next round's on me!" I shouted out to anyone who would listen, hoping that the ridiculous stereotypes about biker gangs and their insatiable thirst for drinking would be well-founded for once.

My offer was met with a thunder of applause, and a wave of large humans headed to the bar, but not without trampling the two idiots who had had the audacity to insult me.

As we fought our way through the beer-loving crowd with difficulty, Trigger-Finger Clyde stepped in front of us.

"Nice switcheroo there, little lady. You know how to talk to them. Except for me, I'm not happy with pretty words alone. I hope you have money to pay for that round."

Before I could answer, a thick wad of bills appeared in Clyde's hand.

"We have to see someone, and you are wasting our time. I hope that will be enough to cover our expenses . . . and the disruption," Phoenix said to cut the conversation short.

Not liking Phoenix's tone, Clyde tried to protest, but I managed to calm him.

"We won't be here long. I assure you that your establishment won't regret our presence, especially since we too will be consuming."

"Humph. Go ahead, but if you raise a stink again, I'll throw you out. Understood?"

"Don't worry about it," I reassured him with a big smile.

He left, and we began to look for Bobby the Eel. François whispered "I am very impressed by your combat technique, Samantha," which made me laugh. I couldn't help turning to my boss and throwing him a look full of meaning: *So you wanted to get rid of me, huh?*

He wasn't able to stop his smile before it appeared, and that delighted me.

Finally, I spotted our man.

"Over there."

Bobby the Eel was in a booth waiting for us, smile on his face.

"Truly, Miss Jones, every time we meet, you make me realize how better it is to be your friend than your enemy," he said as we sat down.

"You won't want to be the enemy of my friends here either."

His smile disappeared in seeing the hard and closed faces of my vampires. Their aura of power and danger must have made him want to run and hide. But this eel had some courage, for if he was afraid of my two friends, he didn't show it.

"We have something to discuss, I believe."

We might as well get to the heart of the matter. Finding me more comforting than my neighbors, Bobby thought it preferable to address me directly.

"Yeah. Who's that one?" he asked, tilting his chin toward François.

"Contract killer," I lied quickly to stop him from getting too curious. It seemed to work; Bobby shifted in his seat, uncomfortable.

"I see. Well, I have news about our matter."

"You found them?"

"The Chinese, no."

*So why make us come out?* He saw that his answer didn't satisfy us at all, so he hurried to add, "My guys came across a sleazy type who'd had too much to drink at The Underground. He was boasting about being a fence for Chinese mafia shot callers."

Our interest was piqued, so we leaned forward to hear more.

"Continue."

Thrilled at having gotten our attention, the Eel puffed up his chest like a peacock in a mating ritual.

"No one believed him because he was drunk as a skunk, but my guys buttered him up by buying him a few rounds. He told them that the Chinese yakuza had approached him to ask where they could find druggies and dropouts that no one would miss."

I decided not to correct him on the nationality of the yakuza. Other than that, the biker's information coincided with all the elements that we'd been able to glean from Kiro. But then, why had healthy and socially stable people been taken as well? Suddenly, the answer came to me in a flash, and I couldn't keep it from Phoenix. He felt my urgency and looked at me, confused, but I couldn't say anything because of Bobby the Eel.

"Does that mean something to you?" Phoenix ventured.

"What else?" I interrupted, directing my question at Bobby.

"This guy and his friends told them about squats, bridges, and other places where the homeless take shelter."

Phoenix spoke up. "Did he say if he had to meet with these men again?"

Bobby kept us in an intolerable suspense for several seconds.

"Yes."

The tension that was overwhelming me started to affect my colleagues, who, I could sense, were regaining hope.

"When?"

"Tomorrow night. He has to give them more places to look. They're meeting in the industrial zone, near the sugar storage warehouses at two in the morning. There's a squat not far from there."

Incredible. No one in Phoenix's entire information network, not even Kaiko and Ichimi, had been able to get the least sign of the traffickers. For weeks we'd failed in our own desperate attempts in the clubs in east Kerington. But here was Bobby the Eel, insignificant upstart gangster, and he'd made huge strides in our investigation.

I hoped that we would finally have enough information to shed some light on the trafficking and stop it so the Greats wouldn't intervene and Phoenix would be safe.

"My guys and me, we'll come with you to corner these bastards."

Bobby the Eel's voice jolted me out of my thoughts. He wanted to come with us and dance with danger, but all he would receive in return was getting disemboweled along with his friends. I didn't need to give my veto because Phoenix did it for me, and very convincingly.

"I admit that you have done your part of the work very efficiently, but for the rest of this matter, you are not at all up for confronting these people, so I advise you to not get involved. Your aid has been invaluable to us, and I will be sure to think of you if we need help again in the future . . ." My boss leaned slightly closer to the Eel and lowered his voice to a threatening murmur. "But if you disregard my recommendation and your presence tomorrow derails our plan of attack, I promise you that the fate I will reserve for you will make these junkie kidnappers look like choirboys. That is how much I will make you suffer before finishing you."

Bobby backed away, shrinking into his chair. He looked to me for help, or some indication that Phoenix was joking, but seeing my closed expression left him no doubt: if he dared to show his face the following night, he would regret ever being born.

"OK. I'll drop it. I hope you get those scumbags. If you need me, you know how to find me."

The exchange was over, and we stood up. Phoenix discreetly slid a thick envelope full of money toward Bobby the Eel, who shoved it into his black leather jacket. As I went to follow my friends, I reconsidered and turned back to Bobby.

"Thank you for your efficiency. We won't forget it," I said, extending my hand.

"It'll always be a pleasure to do business with you."

I was treated to a wink and a flirtatious smile before I rejoined my friends.

We breathed a lot better after we exited. The air outside was clear of smoke, and more importantly, we had a new lead, which gave us hope for our shared future.

***

"I know why they're not just taking drug addicts and homeless people," I blurted out, barely settled in the car.

"Please enlighten us," Phoenix responded, amused by my restlessness.

"When I saw your blood supply, I knew that you had preferences for certain types. Am I wrong?"

Silence. I could continue.

"When you drink someone's blood, do you taste particular flavors that make you like or hate it?"

"Well, not all blood types have the same texture, or the same quality," François said.

"If you drank the blood of an old homeless man, you would be satisfied, but wouldn't you have preferred to taste younger, purer blood of someone who didn't drink or take drugs?"

There was another silence, during which François and Phoenix must have grasped the full implications of my reasoning.

"A luxury range," said Phoenix.

"Bingo!" I exclaimed. "They sell the blood of marginalized people at a discount and get rich on selling the blood of healthy people."

"The ramifications of this kind of trafficking must extend to multiple countries, especially those where the population does not have the same health conditions as here. The blood must sell at high cost in foreign countries. That is why my informants did not know anything about it."

"We need to trace it back and root out of the brains of this operation," said François.

He and Phoenix launched into planning attacks, each one more ludicrous than the previous, during the entire return trip to Scarborough. As for me, I didn't take part in their debate, for an idea had started to take seed in my head, a very dangerous idea I had to think about, one that I would have to fight to convince my boss to go through with . . .

I waited until we got back to the manor and settled into the parlor, each of us with a refreshing beverage, to share my plan with my companions.

I plucked up courage and said, "I've found a solution . . . We need to infiltrate them."

Phoenix and François looked at me without understanding.

"They must certainly know my face, and as for François, they will never accept a stranger on their team. They will suspect something," my boss corrected.

I stared at them pointedly, not daring to speak, and what I was hoping would happen did: François raised his eyebrows as he realized what I was suggesting.

"I do not think she is talking about you or me."

"But then who are you . . ." Phoenix stopped in the middle of his sentence, the light finally going on in his head, and he stood up quickly. "Out of the question!" he said.

"Think about it. It's our best chance to discover the identity of their leaders. Besides, I won't be in any danger if you're there to look after me."

I didn't have a particular desire to risk my life by letting myself get voluntarily kidnapped, but I knew that this plan had a chance of working. In any case, it was better than if my friends rushed in. Besides, our lives were on hold until the Greats made their decision, so we shouldn't be standing around asking questions.

"I made you a promise."

He'd sworn to never hurt me again, not to stop me from risking any danger. I'd made my choice.

"And I ask that you honor that promise by respecting my wishes."

That was a low blow, but this wasn't the time to hesitate—he had to agree. Fenced in by my answer, Phoenix was angry. He didn't want me to serve as bait, but by rejecting my idea, he would betray his promise. Defeated, he sat down again and groaned.

"Very well, since you insist. But at the slightest sign of danger, I am coming to get you."

"No."

"What?" He almost choked with rage.

"I don't want you to turn up and ruin everything at the smallest sign of danger. Except in case of my imminent death, I forbid you from interfering. Discovering who is behind all this is more important than my safety."

Phoenix remained silent.

"Your logic is like a vampire's," François said, complimenting me.

"You are foolish," corrected my boss.

"I'm practical and determined, and at least I have a plan that has more chance of working than yours. I'm going to bed to be ready for tomorrow. Good night."

Thanks to my new abilities, I could hear Phoenix even as I was walking up the stairs.

"In all my five hundred years, I have never met a woman who drove me up the wall as much as that one does. I do not know how she does it, but she always manages to shut me up, and that is just insufferable."

François's low laugh resounded all the way to my ears even though I'd already arrived at my door. Before getting to bed, though, I lost some of my confidence thinking about the considerable risk I was taking, and I'd even asked for it. I'd come close to death several times, but this time, death could catch up with me for good. I had repeated nightmares while I slept, and I woke up each time in a cold sweat, more and more terrified by the madness I was about to mix myself up in.

The next day, before sunset, I started to seriously consider whether it had been a bad idea. To pass the time, I wandered up and down the hallways of the manor after doing my work. In the office on the ground floor, I found my survey of the dozens of disappearances throughout the county and came across the photo of Melanie Aubry.

The flashback to her death took me by surprise, and the horror of her fate crushed my heart. I didn't know why that young woman had touched me more than the other victims in the warehouse that day, but she had marked me irrevocably. Looking at her face in the photo and remembering her courage restored my determination. Whatever happened, I would not let her murder go unpunished. Heath and the other scumbags mixed up in this vile trafficking were going to pay . . .

I began prepping for my role as a homeless, miserable drug addict with no hope of ever being reintegrated into society. I put on an old T-shirt, a pair of jogging pants, and a jacket, all of which I'd brought from my parents' house. I used to wear these things when I was in high school, and they still fit. In fact, they were loose, since they were from my I'm-fat-and-I-refuse-to-look-in-a-mirror phase, and therefore practical for hiding something in my bra.

I went out into the garden and scrubbed them with dirt to look dirtier and shabbier, matching my character. For even more realism, I smudged my face and tangled up my hair; the result wasn't pretty. I couldn't help think about how some people lived every day in grime and poverty.

Evening arrived, and the knot that had formed in my stomach wouldn't let me eat anything. My nervousness reached its height when Phoenix and François showed up, but I managed to hide it. They stopped in their tracks when they saw how I was dressed.

"Very good," François said appreciatively.

Phoenix didn't say anything, but that didn't bother me; I knew he was worried about me.

"I hope they fall for it," I said.

"You do not have to do this."

No longer mute and still visibly against the whole idea, my boss was again trying to convince me to change my mind. I turned to François instead and asked, "Is he always in a foul mood when he wakes up? Or can he not understand these simple words?" I stared at Phoenix. "It's my choice!"

"What if they see you are a fraud? Have you considered Heath—he knows you."

"We're not even sure if the Chinese will lead us to him. But even if that's the case, dressed like this, how is he going to recognize me? Besides, thanks to your blood, I'm stronger than before."

"It will not be enough," he hissed.

"I know! Stop acting like a worried mama hen and have some confidence in me."

My outburst left him speechless. I thought that no one in five hundred years had ever called him, a bloodthirsty vampire, "a worried mama hen," but he deserved it. Anyway, it completely entertained François, who was trying to stifle a laugh by clasping his hand over his mouth.

"You are the most stubborn and aggravating human woman I have ever met," Phoenix yelled.

"That may be, but without me, you'll bore yourself to death. For a second time."

I'd silenced him once again, which triggered renewed mirth from our French friend. I'd only told the truth. I could at least be proud of that; between my idiotic remarks, my blushing cheeks, and my natural awkwardness, Phoenix must have laughed more during the past few months with me than the past fifty years. He'd said it himself. He grumbled between his teeth something intelligible, but I caught the last word, ". . . pigheaded!"

In response, I crossed my arms and stared at him with an air of superiority. War weary, he sighed and threw in the towel.

"Fine . . . I yield."

I suddenly felt much lighter. Or at least I had until he said, "We have to put together an extraction plan for Sam, before she is drained of blood, that is . . ."

Gulp.

We spent several hours working out the details: our arrival, the observation point, our weapons, and my extraction. We knew that the kidnappers would have to close to the sugar warehouses around two in the morning, and we had to get there ahead of them.

We arrived there around one. François had taken the wheel so Phoenix could scout ahead from above, checking to see if our enemies were in the neighborhood. We hid the car around a dark corner and waited for Phoenix to return.

I must say that when François muttered "here he is" while looking up at the sky and I followed his gaze, I was impressed by the silhouette flying in our direction. His suit jacket seemed to flap in the wind, and even at a distance, we could see the wind in his hair. His arms were alongside his body, not overhead like Superman's.

As he descended, I kept my eyes riveted on him, not able to tear myself away from this extraordinary spectacle. Even if he weren't a vampire, like in the books, the henchman of Evil, you could say he was an angel coming down from heaven . . .

When he landed, perfectly upright, in front of us, I had some difficulty recovering my breath and I tried to look elsewhere . . . François watched me with a smile.

Finally, my boss approached. "The way is clear. The squat is behind that warehouse."

"How did you find it?" I asked, curious.

"There is a strong concentration of beating hearts over there, even though the place should be deserted."

"How many?" François asked.

"A dozen or so, I would say."

"Because you can differentiate and count them?" I was stupefied by the sensitivity of vampire hearing. It was one thing to hear even a whisper from three hundred feet away, but to know the number of humans in one place by their heartbeats? That stunned me.

"Are you ready?"

Phoenix put on his usual impenetrable mask, thus barring my access to his thoughts.

I nodded.

"They are in a little run-down shed. With all the holes in the roof, we will not have any problem seeing what happens and getting you out of there if it goes badly."

"Fine, but don't forget, as long as they're not doing anything to me, don't intervene. With a little luck, they'll bring me straight to their leaders."

"Be careful."

After taking a deep breath, I turned in the direction Phoenix indicated, and went to the squat where murderers were readying for action.

***

When I entered the old warehouse and faced the spectacle in front of me, I had a moment in which I nearly changed my mind.

The place was dismal. A few candles flickering faintly were the only source of light. A couple was in the middle of . . . well, better say it . . . making out. The young man sitting on the remains of a floral sofa couldn't have been older than twenty-three, and his companion, who had to be one or two years younger than him, was straddling him in nothing but a very short leather skirt and a bra. They didn't give a damn about doing that in front of everyone. Gross.

Though it hardly mattered. Everyone else looked completely out of it, collapsed on old chairs or even the ground. On the low table in front of the two exhibitionists, there were razor blades coated in a white powder that I assumed was cocaine.

"Hey, you, grubby girl! Where you come from?"

In theory, those rude words, spoken hoarsely, had been directed at me. Their source was a tall black man, roughly forty years old, but he could have passed for eighty. He held a crack pipe in his hand.

"Carly gave me this address. I need a place to stay for the night."

Saying that I'd come here by word of mouth seemed like a good idea. This guy couldn't possibly know all the people who showed up here every now and then.

"Who's Carly?"

I needed a different angle. "You the police, asking so many questions?" I answered aggressively, chin raised in defiance. I hoped that would dissuade him from starting an interrogation that would surely end badly. Luckily it worked, and he shrugged his shoulders and turned away.

I'd made it through the first step.

I didn't want to sit down on a chair close to the two lovebirds, who were getting pretty heated up and handsy with each other, so I found a corner near a woman around sixty years old who seemed to be asleep.

I pulled out a bottle of whisky wrapped in a brown paper bag and swallowed a mouthful.

Ugh, I hated whisky, but I didn't have a choice. My breath needed to smell like alcohol for my performance to be believable, even if I spit the subsequent swallows back into the bottle.

"Do you have some for me?" The voice behind me made me jump.

The woman who seemed to be sleeping had suddenly woken up, maybe at the smell of whisky vapors. I hated to drink straight from the bottle after someone else, particularly a stranger who wasn't in the best of circumstances, but I had to keep up appearances. Reluctantly, I passed her the bottle.

"You're a saint. Bless you." She started to gulp down the contents of the bottle.

It didn't matter. What she said made me uncomfortable because I didn't think that God, whoever and wherever he was, would condone me leaving these people ignorant of what was in store for them. I didn't like it either. But for these murders to stop once and for all, we absolutely had to find the ones responsible, which meant not being able to save everyone. It wasn't easy.

I checked my watch: it was two thirty. What were they waiting for? I was going completely nuts, but it was the stress caused by the wait that was truly unbearable. I imagined it was worse for Phoenix and François, who were watching from above; my boss wasn't a model of patience.

The exhibitionist couple was rattling my nerves with their slobbery and noisy kissing, and the young man's high-pitched whining. The girl, visibly thrilled by the effect she was having on her partner, deliberately wriggled against his pelvis to excite him even more. For Pete's sake! The whole show was sickening.

When they started to tear their clothes off, I reached over to get my bottle back from the old woman to throw it at them. But I didn't get a chance.

Suddenly, six hooded men, dressed in black and armed with tranquilizer guns, burst into the room. As the only sober person there, I noticed them before anyone else, and I reacted by throwing myself to the ground.

The couple, still in full frolic, were the first hit. They collapsed quickly, tranquilized. In the chaos that followed, while the ones who weren't too drugged or drunk tried their best to escape, I managed to crawl toward a bureau behind the already tranquilized old woman. It was very important that I be the last to be found so I could see as much as possible, and this was a decent hiding place.

The vampires had put the ones who were too weak to move out of harm's way and set to work catching the last escapees, including the man who had coldly interrogated me earlier.

Suddenly everything was calm again. The shabbiness of the room when I first arrived was nothing compared to the mess now. Some of the people had fallen onto chairs that couldn't take their weight. From where I was hiding, I had a good view of the bodies lying motionless on the ground and the men who were approaching them.

One by one, the men removed their hoods, and I suppressed a sigh of relief when I saw Heath wasn't one of them. All six were Asian, and when I heard them speaking Chinese with each other, I knew that these were the men we were expecting.

The one who had to be their leader came forward then and started inspecting each person lying on the ground. I shivered when he looked in my direction, and I pressed myself against the bureau. I made a huge effort to stay calm, to keep my heart from racing so loudly that it would reveal my presence there as surely as sounding an alarm.

Holding my breath, I waited for him to finish looking at my whisky thief and move on to someone else. I didn't know what he was doing, because the bureau obscured my view of him, but then I heard a gun safety clicking off. A quarter of a second later, there was a shot, and my hiding place was spattered with blood.

Despite my training, a drum was beating in my chest, and there was nothing I could do about it. In a flash, the bureau flew from my field of vision and crashed some distance away from me. In its place was the leader of this pack of monsters, and he was staring at me with a predatory smile, his fangs out and his eyes bright yellow.

"Well, well . . . we almost forgot one. Is there a woman under all that grime?"

I didn't need to pretend to be afraid, because I truly was at the sight of the cruelty in his face. He grabbed me roughly by the arm and stood me up to face him. Getting my wits about me, I tried to look distraught.

"Please . . . don't kill me."

"A sweet little face like yours?"

His men laughed.

"I . . . I'll do whatever you want," I tried.

"Really?"

Before I even saw it coming, he swooped down and pulled me against him to kiss me fiercely. He held me in an iron grip that was impossible to escape. So this would be my first kiss? The magic moment all girls dream about had been ripped away from me by a sadist whose hand slid from my neck to my right breast, which he squeezed painfully.

No, I wouldn't let this happen to me. While he tried to force his way through the barricade of my lips with his tongue, I struggled against him like a she-devil, trying to hit him. Since that was pointless, I did the only sensible thing: I opened my mouth.

The second his tongue inserted itself there, I bit it with all my strength. Caught off guard, he pushed me away so forcefully that I flew backward and crashed into a big wooden table, destroying it in the process. I got up coughing. The impact with the table had cut off my breath, and I had to spit out the blood of that vermin who had attacked me. I had a horrible cut on my arm, and I saw points of light dancing in front of my eyes. I knew that I'd completely failed and Phoenix was going to come interfere because the guy, whose blood was running from his mouth abundantly, was going to want to take his vengeance and kill me immediately . . .

However, none of that happened. Instead, he said, "Ha-ha-ha! It's even better when they resist. The blood makes it better. The boss will be pleased," he shouted, laughing, wiping away the blood with his sleeve. "You know exactly what you want, my lovely, but that's not enough to stay alive. Tie her up!"

Two of his friends quickly pulled me from the debris and tied up my feet and hands and gagged me for good measure. Lying on the ground like that, I couldn't move. One of the men said something, informing me of their leader's name: Huan. The leader looked at me and offered a big smile from his bruised mouth.

"Just you wait and see what I'm going to do to get back at you for your stupidity, gorgeous. If you and your friends all shoot up, it's to go to a dream world, right? Welcome to the world of vampires!"

At an unbelievable speed, the leader seized the young woman on the sofa and sunk his fangs into her throat. He drained her in front of me, his eyes on me the whole time, as if to say, *I'm killing her because of you.*

This guy was a monster, and I swore that, like Heath who was at the top of my list, I would kill him myself.

Full at last, he threw his victim aside as if she were light as a feather and shouted new orders in Chinese. He tossed his gun to one of his men who took over the process the leader had started: disposing of the bodies whose blood had no market value. Within the next minute, three shots were fired, spattering more blood against the walls of this tomb.

Phoenix's training may have toughened me up, but seeing those corpses, including that of the whisky thief who was lying there, a bullet in her head, not far from me, I felt dreadful. I was sweating, blood was rushing back to my pale face, and it took a supreme effort to not vomit. Disgusted, I turned my head to the ceiling, and my eyes widened when I saw Phoenix looking at me from the gaping hole of the roof.

Finding comfort in seeing him there, I stared back to escape from the carnage that surrounded me.

"Bring them, and then burn everything," the leader said.

Before those pigs could take me away, I shook my head almost imperceptibly so that my boss wouldn't come to my rescue. When powerful arms grabbed hold of me, I still felt the burn of his look of disapproval.

Without any regard for the poor people they were condemning to die, Huan's men tossed their unconscious victims into the back of an ordinary white van. By chance, I was the last to be thrown in, and my fall was cushioned by the other bodies. While I was waiting for my turn, the vampires took care to burn everything so there wouldn't be a single trace of their activities. Five cadavers were left inside. Five anonymous bodies whose gruesome fate no one would ever know . . .

I couldn't see anything at all inside the van, but considering the fact that I was risking another confrontation with Heath, it would be better if I weren't the first to get out. I managed to drag myself to the back to hide among the victims, deciding to feign unconsciousness to go unnoticed, a performance that my arm wound made credible.

The bumps in the road were unbearable, and the air quickly became stifling in the vehicular prison. Rather frightened by the idea of dying of asphyxiation, I was desperate to arrive at our destination.

Finally, the van slowed down, and the jolting became much more pronounced; I took it as a sign that we'd turned onto a dirt road. When the van stopped and the engine was turned off, I let myself sigh in relief before lying down again and pretending to be unconscious.

The doors creaked open, and I came close to a heart attack when I heard someone say in English, "This isn't the number I was hoping for."

Heath. He must be looking in my direction . . . Luckily I'd hidden in the back and turned my face away.

"I know, but our informant guaranteed there would be more."

"I hope you enforced all our security measures."

"We took take care of him."

So they'd killed their informant, the Chinese gang fence. That imbecile should have been suspicious when they proposed a meeting in a deserted area.

"Good. Put him with the others. We're taking care of a batch now. These will have to wait their turn."

"Whatever you say. Will the boss be here tonight?"

"He's already here. He's supervising the first batch."

By the silence that followed, I realized that Heath had gone off to take care of more important business, and I could breathe again. If I wasn't discovered or killed before I met his boss, we would still have a good chance of discovering his identity. Reenergized at the prospect despite the danger I was in, I didn't flinch when someone threw me over his shoulder like a slab of meat. I risked half opening my eyes for a quick glance at where I was being taken.

***

From the little I could see, I knew that we weren't in a warehouse at all: we were in a country manor house. That seemed logical: since Kerington's industrial zone was being watched, the blood traffickers weren't taking the risk of draining their victims there anymore.

Once inside, I could make out the great hall, blocked off from the outside by closed shutters, and I saw the same exsanguination setup as at the Kerington warehouse. Once again, people were lying down on stretchers, their blood being drained.

I was brought into the wine cellar, a very large room with several spacious alcoves that were used to store barrels of wine before metal gates had been added that divided the cellar into prison cells.

No one was shouting or begging to be freed. All I could see were faces, all terrified by the vampires who were hurling people into the last cell, which was nearly full.

My porter was checking his grip on my hips, and I could tell that he was about to throw me like a sack of potatoes. Prepared for the shock, I managed to not cry out in pain when I crashed to the ground and continued to feign unconsciousness.

"How much more time up there?"

"Another fifteen minutes, I would say. Then we have these to take care of."

"They need to get a move on. I'd like to go have some fun for a chance. Tired of having to hide like rats because of that damn angel."

"From what I've been told, it's better to not cross paths with him."

"Anyway, won't be long before he's not a problem, believe me."

I heard them laughing as they went back upstairs and locked the door. Their conversation puzzled me. Were they aware of the Elder vampires' imminent arrival and what that meant for Phoenix? How?

I didn't have any answers, and I needed to stay focused on my situation. It didn't look like any vampires were watching us, and there were no security cameras. At the same time, there was no way to escape. Even if I got past the metal gate, twenty or so vampires were waiting upstairs; anyone who managed to escape wouldn't get very far. I looked at the other cells and counted about thirty people waiting in the cold, moist, and horrible death corridor. I was amazed by their calm. Of course, they all seemed driven to despair and some of them were crying, but none were panicking or crying for their mothers.

I took note of some of them in particular, recognizing the ones mentioned by journalists on the news only several days ago, before looking around my own cell again. Apart from my unconscious fellow prisoners, there were three men and five women. One of the women, a blond, was lying down on the other side, and I couldn't see her face. But something made me look at her more closely, because her silhouette seemed oddly familiar . . .

"You're not unconscious like the others?"

I didn't answer the question, asked by a man who, judging by his clothes, must have been taken while he was out jogging at night, and headed for the blond woman.

A strong sense of foreboding took hold of me as I approached her; it was telling me I was about to discover something truly horrific.

Slowly, I kneeled down beside the sleeping woman and reached out a trembling hand to turn her toward me. When I finally saw her face, my blood froze in my very veins.

Angela.

Panicked, I took her by the shoulders and shook her violently to wake her.

"Angela!" I whispered.

I knew that I was attracting attention from the other prisoners, but seeing my friend in that hell was unbearable. I had to save her. Shaking her wasn't helping, so I slapped her hard, which got me several disapproving looks and one "You're crazy!" from the man who had just spoken to me.

"Shut up!" was what he got in return for his attempt at playing the Good Samaritan.

Angela opened her eyes and woke up with a start. Still groggy, she didn't seem to be reconnecting with reality, and she wobbled as she sat up. I held her firmly and stopped her from slumping over. Then she stared at me and frowned, searching her memory to figure out who this dirty woman trying to help her was.

"Sam?"

I nodded my head solemnly. Angela looked at our prison and started to shake.

"Where are we? What are you doing here? And why are you dressed like that?"

She was utterly terrified, and I feared she wouldn't pay attention. I clapped my hand over her mouth and signaled that she should stay quiet, making her understand that we had an audience whose indiscreet ears were making me uneasy.

The other prisoners finally turned away and lost interest in us, refocusing on their own despair.

"Who brought you here?" I murmured to Angela.

Understanding that I didn't want us overheard, she answered in the same tone.

"I don't know . . . all I remember is that I went home after eating at Danny's and the door was open. All the lights were off . . . before I could find the switch, I felt someone sticking a needle into my neck, and I woke up here . . . What about you? Who brought you?"

I couldn't lie to her, not after what she'd been through . . . not with what was awaiting her . . . Anyway, there wasn't time for explanations.

"It's complicated, but you'll have to trust me . . . Listen. Roughly, I got myself taken on purpose and made sure that, in the very likely possibility that I'd be searched, my cell phone was in a place they wouldn't think to check."

I was really lucky that Huan had grabbed my right breast, because I'd hidden my phone in my bra, on the left, taking advantage of my loose clothing to cover it. Three cheers for modern technology and smaller devices!

"Are you going to call the police?" she said, full of hope.

"You must understand, the police can't do anything for us, and they must not interfere if we want to avoid a bloodbath. I have to call my boss."

The look of betrayal that passed over Angela's face chilled me to the bone.

"Good heavens, who are you?"

I had trouble meeting her gaze.

"Even if I'm not quite who you think I am, I'm still your friend. Hide me."

Knowing that I was her only chance of getting of there, she complied. I pulled out the phone and called Phoenix, who, I hoped, would get us out of there alive. He picked up on the first ring.

"Sam. What is going on?"

There was worry in his voice, but I couldn't really reassure him.

"Phoenix, we have a problem," I whispered, knowing that he would hear me as though I were right next to him.

"What kind of problem?"

"Angela. She's here."

Silence. Angela had jumped when she heard me use the name of ex to address my boss.

"That changes nothing."

Oh, really? For me, that added a whole new dimension to the situation. It was out of the question that I would sacrifice my friend.

"And what does François think?"

The tone of my voice was distinctly cool.

Another silence. I knew that François had truly felt something for Angela, and she jumped again at hearing the name of the man she was cherishing in secret. He would want to protect her.

"We cannot interfere for now. Our enemies are too numerous. We are looking for a way in without being noticed."

"There are about thirty of us crammed into a smelly old wine cellar, waiting to be drained of our blood any minute now by a bunch of psychopathic vampires. Their boss is supervising the first exsanguinations this very moment. So I suggest that you find a solution fast."

"He is there? Did you see him?"

"No, not yet, but Heath is here, and he *knows* me."

"I will not let him hurt you."

"All that I ask is that you let me kill him. Him and Huan," I said angrily.

"No. Huan is mine."

Phoenix hung up.

Meanwhile, I risked a glance over Angela's shoulder to see if anyone had heard my conversation. Evidently, only my friend had been close enough. As it happened, she turned and stared at me hard.

"Phoenix? François? Vampires and exsanguinations? What is going on?"

I sighed. I had to explain everything. I sat down beside her, sliding an arm over her shoulders so we would be against the wall where no one could see us talking; anyone looking would just think we were consoling each other.

"Up until a few months ago, my name was Samantha Watkins, I lived in Kentwood, where I was a librarian. I didn't believe that vampires exist, but I discovered I was wrong, and my discovery wouldn't let me go back to my normal life. Since then, I've been working for one of them, as his assistant. I had a hard time accepting it at first, but believe it or not, by doing this I'm protecting human lives. The vampires are peculiar, but not necessarily bad . . . and the one I work for is a good man who wants these disappearances perpetrated by criminal vampires to come to an end. We live in Scarborough undercover, and Phoenix's best friend François came to help us in our efforts. They followed me and they'll do all that they can to get out us out of here."

Angela seemed not to believe what I was saying. It was true that I'd given her an abridged version of my story, and that telling her about the existence of vampires in this point-blank way was enough to make me sound crazy. She shook her head.

"So . . . mysterious Peter and your Phoenix are the same person? He's your boss, not your fiancé, *or* your grandfather? A vampire?"

"Yes."

"So François . . ." She couldn't finish her thought out loud.

"Yes. He's a vampire too."

Seeing her look of alarm, I feared that she would reject him because of his nature. I could understand that since it would certainly complicate things between them, but that would have been a mistake. I took her by the hands and forced her to look at me.

"Angela, don't judge him too quickly, please. François is a vampire, that's undeniable, but he's a good and generous man—more so than many humans. He'll do everything he can to protect you. Don't reject him before you know him better."

My friend seemed shocked by my declaration. Maybe I'd said too much, but it had to be done, for François's sake.

Then we heard the door that separated us from the ground floor being unlocked. Our fifteen minutes were up.

\*\*\*

I hoped that Phoenix and François had succeeded in getting into the building. I turned quickly to Angela.

"They're coming. Listen to me. You don't know me, do you understand?"

"What?"

"Do what I say. Whatever happens, do not under any circumstances show that we have a connection. They'll likely lash out at you. Is that clear?"

She nodded her head, and I moved away and found a spot near the gate to put some distance between us. Five vampires, including Huan, opened the gates and ordered us to get up, not hesitating to dole out kicks to the ones who were having trouble regaining consciousness.

"What if we don't want to?" spit out the jogger, his defiant attitude hardly credible, because of his trembling legs.

Huan was behind him instantly. He broke the man's neck.

"You'll die immediately . . . Any other volunteers?" he asked, surveying the prisoners' faces.

Horrified, the people still in the cells came out without any more orders. I used Huan's momentary inattention to slip among everyone else. As we walked up the stairs, everyone was sobbing; I tried to not think about Angela, who was five people behind me. She must be completely panicking . . . as I was, knowing what awaited us above.

Once we were upstairs, we were marched into the great hall. There weren't enough stretchers for everyone, so Huan divided our group in two. My group, including Angela, was pushed into a corner and forced to sit down under the surveillance of two colossal men. Utterly powerless, we could only watch the spectacle of victims being made to undress, then being connected to tubes, which drained their life force from them. There were shrieks, then . . . nothing. They must have been given a strong dose of sedatives to calm them so they wouldn't move around too much during the procedure.

There was total silence in our corner. I thought that the cruelty and absurdity of the scene had taken away all sense of reality. My companions in misery were in a state of shock; I doubted they were even picturing that in a few minutes, it would be their turn. As for me, I was desperately impatient. I couldn't do anything until the leader showed himself, and in the interim, innocent people were dying; it was atrocious.

Suddenly Heath entered the room. There was someone behind him, but I couldn't risk revealing myself by trying too hard to see his face.

"We're almost done with this bunch, and she's one of them. You'll be happy."

The small smile of satisfaction of the tall blond vampire that I hated so profoundly made me want to drive a stake through his heart.

"I certainly hope so."

I recognized that voice at the same moment that Heath moved enough for me to finally see the man who was organizing all these murders. I felt as if I'd just had the wind knocked out of me. Luckily I knew how to compose myself and avoid attracting the attention of the murderer who was heading straight for Angela, a horrible and oh-so-familiar smile on his face.

"So, we've finally woken up, I see."

Using my hair to hide my face, I saw my friend utterly unsettled by the sight of a vampire she'd already met . . .

"Karl?"

His smile widened, becoming even crueler. I shuddered. What was he going to do? What were we going to do? Where was Phoenix? While I was panicking, the vampire went to detach the corpses from the stretchers and stack them like garbage in an adjacent room.

"But of course, my dear. So you're a great friend of a Samantha's . . . she is going to be so sad when I kill you. But you know what? That is the point. Don't worry, it's nothing personal against you, although I will take immense pleasure in seeing you die."

Without warning, he grabbed Angela by the arm and pulled her to him. She tried to struggle, crying, but Karl had her in a steel grip.

"Hook up the others," he ordered without worrying about his prisoner's attempt to free herself.

I didn't know what to do. Phoenix hadn't shown up, and Karl was getting ready to kill Angela. I had to do something.

As the vampires who had brought us here approached us menacingly, I positioned myself at the back of the group. I quickly charged forward and pushed aside the people ahead of me with all my strength, as I shouted, "We won't let you!"

Like dominos, the prisoners pushed against each other, and in the panic, they tried to scatter. Thinking it a mutiny, the vampires starting grabbing the fleeing people, without doing them any harm.

Taking advantage of the surrounding confusion, I managed to seize a pair of scissors left on one of the refrigerated cases. I rushed at Karl, who, without any interest in what was happening around him, was about to sink his fangs into my friend's neck.

With a roar of rage, I drove the scissors into his neck before jumping on his back, hammering him with punches. It was doubtless not the pain but rather the surprise that made him let go, but Angela was liberated from his vise grip.

"Run!" I shouted at her from my perch.

I had just enough time to see her try before someone grabbed me and sent me flying against the facing wall, then crashing to the floor. This time, I couldn't find the strength to get up.

Heath was now coming straight for me, and he wasn't messing around. Karl was right behind him.

Karl stopped Heath. "Heath. Catch the blond." Karl was looking in my direction suspiciously.

Heath took off, and Karl came slowly toward me, but he turned around when he heard Angela's cries from the main hall. Heath had already grabbed her and brought her back. That was fast.

"Hook her up."

Heath didn't want to get his hands dirty, so he gave Angela to one of the other vampires.

The German traitor returned his attention to me and bridged the gap between us. My hair had fallen over my face, and to finally see who he was dealing with, he reached out his hand to brush my hair aside . . . As soon as he did it, he took a step back, his pupils now bright and his fangs out.

"You!" he said furiously.

But instead of attacking me and tearing me into pieces, he stood up and screamed at his men. "It's a trap! Kill them all, we have to get out of here!" He turned back to me. "But not before you and I settle our score."

His men were about to comply when a velvet voice, dangerous and terrifying, rose above the din.

"It seems like you are about to leave, like your friends who are waiting outside . . . They are no longer with us."

Phoenix and François were standing in the doorway, armed and ready for a fight, their eyes bright and their clothes already stained with blood.

Silence fell over the room, each of the vampires having recognized their angel of death. In a flash, Karl had lifted me and was using me as a shield, a silver knife pressed against my throat. Phoenix stared at us intensely, but he had to act according to the priorities of the moment.

Huan was holding Angela; abandoning his hostage, he was the first to attack Phoenix, but in vain. Taken over by a murderous rage, my boss had no difficulty stopping him before slamming him to the ground and ripping out his tongue. François prevented anyone from getting close to Phoenix, though he didn't need to do much since everyone was petrified by my boss.

"*That* is for daring to kiss her!" Phoenix shouted, holding up his enemy's bloody tongue. "*This* is for daring to touch her!" He tore off Huan's left arm. Huan's shrieks filled the room, and the entire audience was hypnotized by that scene worthy of the most gruesome horror films . . .

"And *this* is for making her watch you kill that girl." He finished by pulling out Huan's fangs, which earned a new series of dreadful screams, and three of the hostages vomited at the sickening sight. Even Karl couldn't suppress a brief shudder. As for me, I didn't feel anything: not pleasure, not horror, not compassion . . . My conscience had become silent as the grave, estimating that after all Huan had done to me and to other people, he fully deserved his punishment.

Phoenix straightened his chest and stared at Heath and Karl with his steel gaze. "The others will not have your luck, Huan . . . Their deaths will be far from painless." In a rapid movement, he put an end to Huan's suffering by decapitating him with his bare hands. When he stood up, the tension was extreme; Karl's knife was pressing so hard that a stream of blood was escaping from my neck.

There were only six Chinese vampires, Heath, and Karl left. I saw Phoenix signal to François to take care of the six, who moved to face their opponent, totally forgetting the presence of their human victims. My boss looked at the humans.

"Leave this place and forget what happened here. No one will believe you anyway."

As my fellow prisoners moved to follow his orders, Phoenix spoke again. "One more thing. I know your faces. If any of you are stupid enough to talk to the press, I will find you wherever you are. You will not be safe anywhere, and you will only have to await my arrival to enjoy the same treatment as the carcass lying at my feet!"

As a group, fifteen people ran to safety without a single look back. All but one, that is. Angela stayed behind François, and she stared at me, afraid. I blinked at her to make her understand that she should leave too, and in tears, she obeyed, but not before sharing one last look with her heart's desire.

When she was gone, Phoenix said, "So, what are we waiting for?"

In an instant, the great hall became an apocalyptic battlefield.

***

As Phoenix carved a path toward Karl and me by violently pushing aside stretchers and full refrigerated cases that crashed against the walls, splattering blood everywhere, François killed every man who came too close to him. Knowing that he would be fine, I turned my attention back to my boss.

Phoenix was radiating so much anger and disgust that it looked like he was surrounded by a fiery aura. I'd never seen him like that before . . . Every part of him said Death, whose messenger he was.

He should have frightened me, as was surely the case for Heath and Karl, but on the contrary, I couldn't look away from him. Even if a large part of his anger had been provoked by the betrayal of the man he considered his brother, he'd been cruel toward Huan as a punishment for touching me. Even now, as he made his way forward, it was not his friend he was staring down . . . but me. He would not allow me to be hurt . . .

My fatigue dissipated quickly, and an enormous wave of energy from my innermost reserves gave me courage. With a subtle tilt of his head, Phoenix conveyed that he'd seen the change in me, and reassured, he now could turn his attention to the one who had claimed to be his friend.

"Let her go and I promise you when the hour of your execution comes, it will be quickly and without pain."

Karl stared at him with scorn.

"You must be dreaming, Brother . . . You are going to let me leave because I know how fond you are of this bitch who sticks her dirty human nose everywhere. You will not do anything to me, because she is too important to you to risk me killing her."

Phoenix got out a knife from his jacket and played with it. "Your flaw has always been arrogance. You think you know everything, but you know nothing. You think I am attached to her enough to run the risk of failing the mission Talanus and Ysis assigned me? It is not surprising that they never thought of making you their angel . . . You are entirely too naive."

Choking with rage, Karl held me even harder, almost crushing my bones; I couldn't stifle a cry of pain.

"And your flaw is too much confidence! The great Phoenix, hero to all vampires who sing your praises to the deepest corners of the Amazon. It all started with Finn, who only ever listened to you and who spent all his time belittling me. Everywhere I went I was Phoenix's friend, and the amazed and admiring sighs were unbearable because I know you, and I know that you are not even a *third* of what they imagine you to be! Playing your friend all this time when I hate you more than anyone was torture, but the one who ordered me to do it merits this sacrifice—he knows who you really are, and that I am worth more than you. You'll swallow your pride when the Greats come here, and we await that moment with impatience."

Nauseated by these horrible revelations, I looked for a reaction on my boss's face. I would have missed it if I hadn't noticed how Phoenix was grinding his teeth. Karl had meant a lot to him, and he'd defended him many times over, including against me. After forcibly throwing him out of his manor for what he did to me, Phoenix hadn't gotten over their quarrel.

I couldn't imagine the pain and betrayal he must have been feeling, faced with this man who had been lying to him for so long, who in fact wanted him to die quickly. By playing with Karl's supersized ego, Phoenix had made Karl admit that someone else was pulling the strings. But his admissions had revealed a hatred so well hidden that my boss could never have imagined it.

It was my turn to feel rage boiling in my veins. "You are just a piece of garbage who was never as talented as Phoenix and who was jealous of him because he's better than you! You're so blinded by your need for recognition that you just told us there's someone above you, you idiot. You've let yourself be manipulated, you, the great Karl. How about that?" I sniggered, my tone like acid.

"Shut up!" he screamed in my ear, tightening his grip.

It cut off my breath, but I wanted to push him more so that he'd make a mistake. Looking at Phoenix, I continued.

"I pity you. All this for that? Because the ugly duckling wasn't hugged enough as a kid? I tell you, I knew right away who you really are. Even me, a dirty human who sticks her nose everywhere like you say, it didn't escape me. You were nothing, you are nothing, and you will always be nothing!"

"*Shut up! Shut up!*" he screamed again, but this time shaking me so hard that I thought he would dislocate something.

I continued to stare at my savior, whose worry was becoming more pronounced.

"You know what? I'm not afraid of you, because you're just an insignificant insect. Phoenix is important to the Greats in this region and to all those who want to have him in their service. Phoenix is important to François, who didn't hesitate a single second to choose his side when he saw that you were behind all this. And he's important to me, and all I feel for you is disgust."

That was one comment too much.

*"I'm going to kill you, you bitch!"* roared Karl, pushing me brutally away from him so he could look at me when he stabbed his knife into my chest.

That was the mistake Phoenix and I were waiting for. Blinded by rage, Karl had let his guard down, giving my boss the opportunity to send his own knife flying into his Karl's chest. However, it didn't happen as expected . . .

Heath, understanding our little game, threw himself on Phoenix at the last minute to prevent him from getting to Karl. But the knife had already been thrown, and it landed in Karl's right lung.

In unbearable pain, my executioner pushed me away with a Herculean force, and I landed on a stretcher that was on the ground. The shock made me see stars, and I had some difficulty getting back to my feet to try and help Phoenix, who was grappling with Heath in a fight to the death. Their super speed prevented me from discerning their movements well, but the struggle was relentless.

Meanwhile, Karl managed to break a window in an effort to escape. I sped in his direction to hold him back with whatever was on hand (which was not much).

As Phoenix finally got the upper hand over Heath and I heard the characteristic sound of bones crushing in a bare-handed decapitation, I saw Karl pull the knife out of his chest wound and brandish it with the intent to throw it at my boss while his back was turned.

Without thinking, I threw myself into its path.

*"Phoenix!"* I screamed, facing Karl and opening my arms to protect my boss.

As he turned around, alarmed by my shout, I felt the terrible pain of the blade piercing my stomach. I cried in horror before falling to the ground. In the same moment, I heard the howl of the man I'd protected and who hadn't had the time to do anything to help me.

*"No!"*

He raced over to me and tried to press his hands to the bloody stain that was already spreading over my clothes, but I stopped him.

"Get him!" I shouted, pointing at the open window where Karl had fled.

François hadn't finished with the Chinese. Everything had happened so fast . . .

"I will not leave you," he said, coming closer again. I tried to push him away again. "François is busy. You're the only one who can catch up and make him say who is really behind all this! It's the only way to save you! Leave me!" I ended by shouting despite my suffering, because most of all, I wanted him to survive this. I felt tears streaming down my face. I couldn't stand another second of his blue eyes staring so hard at me.

"No."

Surprised, I lifted my head toward him. There was no severity in his eyes . . . just tenderness and worry. I was floored by it.

"He can go to hell. I would rather see him leave than see you die."

Gently, he passed one arm around my shoulders and the other under my thigh.

"What are you doing?" I said, astonished.

"I have not forgotten what you said. Your wound can be healed if we hurry to a hospital."

His answer stunned me so much that I forgot the pain I was in and my bloody clothes. Taking advantage of my silent stupor, he lifted me in his arms and looked at François who was just finishing up with the last kidnapper.

"Burn it all and come find me at the Scarborough manor."

Without waiting for him to agree, Phoenix and I took off into the skies to get me treated at one of the Kerington hospitals. Closing my eyes so I wouldn't faint from fright, I realized that we'd made a huge leap in our investigation. We'd managed to find the kidnappers' base and save some of their victims, including Angela. Our plan had worked since we'd discovered the identity of their leader . . . but also because the truth often hurt. Phoenix and Karl's reunion had been memorable, and I knew that if they saw each other again, one of them would die. But which one?

# CHAPTER ELEVEN
## *Danger Settles In*

I was getting colder and colder. I'd finally opened my eyes and looked down at the city lights. Phoenix was holding me tight against him, but you couldn't say that he was a good source of heat. I was frozen because of the loss of blood but also because of the glacial wind that was stinging me as we flew. I found the whole situation completely ridiculous, especially because sunrise was fast approaching. Unable to stand it anymore, I cried out, "Turn around!"

I retched when we stopped between two clouds after having flown at full speed for a long time.

"Do you feel sick?"

Yes, I was a bit under the weather, that was for sure.

"I want you to bring me back to Scarborough. I don't want to go to a hospital."

He didn't understand, obviously. I was going to have to be clearer.

"It's going to be day soon, and I don't want to be alone in a cold and dismal hospital, with a bunch of doctors and police officers coming to harass me until I tell them who stabbed me. I want to go *home*."

It was the first time I'd ever used that word to talk about the manor. But it was indisputable that it was indeed my home.

"I will drink."

He saw the determination in my eyes, and in his I saw pride. He nodded.

"As you wish. Hold on."

He sped up again, but this time at a pace that wouldn't make me feel ill . . .

***

I must have lost consciousness en route, for when I woke up, François was opening the doors for us.

"She is starting to regain consciousness."

Indeed, I could see the world around me again, but I felt strangely disconnected, as though I didn't even have enough strength to keep me tethered to the present.

"Time is of the essence," he continued.

Time? What did he have planned? What was of the essence? The fog threatened to seize me again, and I didn't understand anything anymore.

Phoenix placed me gently on the sofa, grabbing a pillow to put under my head. He'd hardly finished when he turned around and readied himself to defend me, a bestial roar coming from his throat. I only jumped, but the feminine shriek that I heard made me realize that another person was among the guests.

"What is she doing here?"

Phoenix growled dangerously, and I found the strength to turn my head to look at the intruder.

"Angela?" I laughed. "You met Phoenix? When was that? Your apartment has really changed, by the way."

Everything got muddled up in my mind, and I was spouting nonsense. My interruption got everyone's attention, and then François intervened: "She was waiting outside. She did not want to abandon Sam and now that she knows the truth, I thought that—"

"It does not matter!" My boss cut him off curtly, feverishly rolling up his shirt sleeve.

When I saw what he was doing, I smiled stupidly and exclaimed, "You have the softest skin in the world!" before bursting into giggles.

"What's wrong with her?" Angela worried.

"She is delirious. It means she will die soon," Phoenix answered, rendered aggressive by impatience.

I reacted the moment he bit his wrist.

"The most extraordinary man in the world . . . is also the worst at human relations."

I tried to laugh, but instead I was taken over by uncontrollable convulsions that would lead me into a coma and then to the gates of death. In the shadows of consciousness, I felt his hands holding me, and his voice calling out to me, "Resist, Sam. It's not your time. I forbid you from dying. Do you hear me? Good grief! You are the most stubborn woman in the world, so respond! Drink!"

As if by a miracle, one last flash of light shone in the darkness in which I was swimming, and I headed for it. I used it as a springboard to return to the voice of the man guiding me back to the light, and when I managed it, I felt the contact of his skin on my mouth and the blood flowing into it. I opened my lips, started to swallow the precious liquid, and heard three sighs of relief around me. I felt cold on my stomach and realized that they'd opened up my sweatshirt and lifted up my T-shirt to check to see if the wound was closing up.

"Incredible! It's healing her!" Angela exclaimed.

With each swallow, I felt better, but suddenly my return to the present was stopped.

Taken over once more by the whirlwind of sensations that was triggered by Phoenix's blood, I opened my eyes wide and sat up. He was next to me on the sofa, and I found myself only a few inches from his face, still holding his wrist right between my lips.

There was a huge silence when I looked at my savior—I learned the next day from Angela that my eyes had changed color. They had kept their normal black tint, but their gleam was irrefutably red, red like the blood I was greedily drinking. Phoenix shuddered and tried to pull back his arm . . . without being able to. A kind of animal growl rose from my throat in warning.

Angela told me later that from the moment I'd sat up, I wasn't at all myself and my strength had increased to the point of surpassing that of my boss. I had trouble believing it, but I had to rely on her retelling since I had no memory of any of it.

According to her, I'd just allowed him to pull away from my mouth a little before giving him a look of burning desire, before licking his wound with a very controlled indecency and slowness. I admit that I cringed when I learned of this, especially when Angela insisted that Phoenix had flipped out. After licking his wrist, I'd lain back down but not without first rewarding my generous donor with a cheeky wink.

This time when I opened my eyes, I was myself again . . . and I didn't understand anything about the conversation they were having.

"Her eyes are normal again." François brightened up.

"That damn mark," railed my boss, who had a strange timbre in his voice.

I sat up painfully and frowned at the faces that were staring at me like a circus freak.

"Hey! I'm fine now. Stop looking at me like that."

Realizing how strangely they were behaving, they regained composure.

"Angela?" I said, surprised, catching on that she should not have been there.

She smiled. "I couldn't stay home after François dropped me off without knowing if you were OK."

"You're not going home now. Stay the night here," I said, consulting Phoenix with a look. He stood up.

"Very well. François will show you to your room. Besides, we shall have to have a conversation tomorrow night, so it will be best if you do not try to slip away during the day to go back to your house."

"Don't worry. I owe you my life, so I can certainly wait here a little longer."

Phoenix nodded and signaled to François to take her away.

When they left, I tried to get up so I could go to my room for a well-deserved rest.

A small cry of surprise escaped me when Phoenix lifted me into his arms.

"What the . . . ?"

"Shh. You are still weak and you need to sleep. I shall take you to your room, and I forbid you from protesting. Tomorrow, you and I will also have a long conversation, one-on-one."

My heart was racing for reasons I was too exhausted to discern. I nestled against Phoenix as he carried me upstairs. He put me in the bathroom and ordered me to take a relaxing shower while he gathered my things for bedtime. That did me a world of good after all I'd gone through, and stepping out of the shower, I slipped on the pajamas he'd set on the sink. Back in my room, I was lifted by him again, into bed. By then I was feeling much better.

As he moved to leave, I held him by the arm and kneeled on the bed to come to his height.

"Thanks for saving my life . . . again," I murmured.

A bit hesitant, I leaned toward him and kissed him on the cheek before smiling warmly. Not expecting any return gesture, I was going to get under the blankets when his hand grabbed my arm and urged me to straighten up again. His impenetrable face wouldn't let me guess his intentions, but I held his gaze. Then it was his turn to hesitate, though he ended up leaning down and giving me a soft kiss on my cheek.

He wished me good night and left me alone and confused, my hand on the place where his lips had burned me.

***

"I did *what?*"

I was mortified by Angela's tale of my behavior from the night before. She chuckled, which intensified my feeling of shame.

We'd met in the garden that afternoon so we could talk about everything. We were settled on a blanket, a pitcher of lemonade and a selection of Ginger's candy for snacks. I was happy to have found such a friend, for she understood the reasons that had pushed me to lie to her. She was still in shock about what she'd gone through the night before, but she was a strong woman and would recover. She understood the extreme importance of keeping the secret of the existence of vampires. For a long time she'd loved stories people told about them, even if she wouldn't have ever thought that they were true, so she was taking this all rather well. She also spoke quite a bit with François.

What had they talked about? She preferred to keep it to herself . . . but seeing her smile, I suspected that it had touched her heart . . . She was brimming with joy, which was made clear to me that very moment as she laughed at my stunned expression.

"You're not yourself. François told me that it must be because of the mark. Phoenix's blood went straight to your head and you were drunk."

I'd already heard that part . . . I shuddered. "What were you all talking about, about my eyes? Why were you all looking at me like I was some sort of freak phenomenon?"

She stopped laughing. "Now that, that was really weird. The worst part is that Phoenix and François weren't expecting it at all, and that really freaked them out. That's why Phoenix tried to pull his wrist away . . . You should have seen his face when you stopped him with your strength . . ."

"The mark must be more significant than they thought," I tried to reassure myself.

But a small voice in my head was desperately trying to tell me that none of it had anything to do with the mark.

"Well, that was nothing compared to when you licked his wrist while looking at him as though you were going to rip his clothes off . . ."

She burst out laughing at my horrified expression. I put my head between my hands.

"Good grief! What on earth is he going to think of me?"

"You weren't yourself, Sam. He knows that."

I was biting my nails so voraciously that she started patting my back in an attempt to alleviate my anxiety.

"But seriously, Sam, is there something going on between you?"

In a flash, I saw him lean down and felt my cheek redden at the memory of the contact it made with his lips.

"You're blushing. Have I put my finger on something?"

I threw a murderous look in her direction.

"No, but you and François . . . same thing, right? How many times am I going to have to tell you? I'm not going to carry around a sign with 'I'm not in love with my long-toothed boss' written in fiery letters. Pay attention to your own love story with your French vampire and leave me alone, both of you!"

I caught my breath, already regretting getting so annoyed . . .

"If you're reacting like this, it's because I'm not wrong."

. . . and I was right to be annoyed.

"Everything is clear between us. When I told him about François's suspicions, which are the same as yours, he found the idea utterly absurd, just like me. So go ahead and live in your fantasy world, but don't meddle in all this."

This discussion had turned sour, and I didn't want to be disagreeable with my friend anymore.

"I'm tired again. I'm going to go rest."

I went back inside and up to my room, and I fell into a restful sleep not a second after my head hit my pillow.

***

*I am behind the bars of a prison cell . . . I am wondering what is going to happen to me when someone enters. Karl. He looks at me with such hatred that I back up against the wall, trembling.*

*"This time, he is not here to save you," Karl says.*

*His horrible smile appears, and a second later, he is on me. Despite my attempts to escape, I can only scream as I feel his fangs in my throat and my life flowing away from me . . .*

"Sam! Wake up! It is just a dream!"

I was barely opening my eyes and still struggling when I realized that I was safe in my room with Phoenix, who was holding my hand. My heart was threatening to beat right out of the chest in its panic, so I had some difficulty catching my breath.

"I thought that . . . I thought he . . . was killing me . . . ," I managed to say.

"Everything is fine. It was only a nightmare. I heard you shouting."

I sat up, rubbing my eyes to get rid of the last mists of sleep.

"What time is it? Where is Angela? I left her by herself."

"It is ten o'clock. François drove her home. She said that you got into a fight, and she felt bad about making you uncomfortable."

I stiffened. Did he know why?

"Let's just say I was tired and I got worked up needlessly."

"It does not matter. I would like to talk to you, now that we are alone."

I got immediately worried . . . Phoenix took my hand again, and I felt a curious electric charge at his touch. It was getting weird, how this happened when he touched me—did I have some kind of problem or what?

"I do not want you on the front lines again like last night. Until this whole matter is over and until further notice, you will stay here."

"What? You're crazy. I can't be shut up here while you and François take all the risks," I protested, shocked to be put on the sidelines.

"François will stay here too."

I stared openmouthed. What was he thinking? Then, I understood. "Karl. You're afraid that he'll come after me."

"He knows this place. It is a certainty. He will try to kill you first . . . to make me suffer."

We looked at each other for a moment, as if time were suspended on our lips.

"Would you really suffer . . . if that happened?"

My voice reached my ears in a whisper. Would he miss me if I disappeared? To what extent? And why was I even asking myself that question?

His eyes got a little brighter, and he slowly leaned toward me. Unsettled by his attitude, I tensed up and leaned away to keep my distance . . . but it didn't stop him. I found myself once again lying down, my head back on my pillow, not knowing how to react to the face that hovered mere inches above my own.

Phoenix was looking at me strangely, his fangs out.

"Samantha Watkins, former librarian of Griffith High School in Kentwood, so human, and yet so extraordinary . . ."

He was close . . . too close. My brain stubbornly refused to function, and I was hypnotized by his gaze.

"You are different from all the other women I have ever met."

As I abandoned my self-control, my heart began beating madly. I needed to catch my breath before I fainted, and when I inhaled, I caught a whiff of Phoenix's scent and closed my eyes. That heady perfume transported me again to the comfort of oblivion.

"You are something special. I saw it right away when we met in that alley, without knowing what it was. Yesterday, your eyes confirmed it . . . *Tell me your secret.*"

Pssssshht. My balloon of well-being deflated in a single second. I opened my eyes.

"That's what you wanted to talk about? My sudden fit of erotic sleepwalking? You don't think that I've been humiliated enough? You have to add another layer to it?" I hissed scathingly. "That's all? Because if that's it, I don't see why we have to play this game. This discussion could have been over in three seconds. I am perfectly ordinary, I have no secrets, and your mark is seriously starting to get on my nerves. Incidentally, would you kindly disengage . . . I'm hungry, and I'm tired of talking to you."

Bewildered by what I was saying, Phoenix complied slowly. I was completely beside myself with annoyance, and it would be better to put some distance between us. I sat up again, put my undone hair back in a ponytail without giving him a second glance, and then I got out of bed and left the room like a tornado.

In the kitchen, I picked out several boxes of cookies and grabbed a bottle of water. As I headed out to the garden, I saw François parking the car in the lane. I didn't even look at him.

I settled at the end of the garden, near a shrub of pink flowers, whose name I didn't know but which smelled really good, and began aggressively devouring the cookies. I only got a single minute of tranquility before François joined me, to my great despair.

"You two fought again," he noted.

Despite my irritation, I needed to get some things off my chest.

"I don't understand him. He says he wants to get better at relationships and try to be my friend, but at the first sign of conflict, he acts like a damn angel on a mission with me."

"He questioned you about yesterday."

"He's not interested in how I'm doing. All he wants to know is if what I did last night can be useful to him," I said bitterly.

"Do not be so harsh with him. He was truly worried about you."

"I know. But not enough, apparently."

François looked hard at me, as though weighing the pros and cons of what he wanted to tell me.

"This is the first time since I have known him that he has worried so much about someone. I know that it is hard to understand—even for me, I still do not understand it—but I can assure you that you mean a lot to him."

I thought again about our conversation in the woods.

"I know. But he acts so strangely with me that I lose sight of that."

"Listen. He almost ruined everything when he learned that Huan violated you in the abandoned warehouse."

I stared at François, surprised.

"You saw how he killed him . . . Phoenix does not usually take pleasure in killing, that is not his way. If he did that, it is because that man dared touch you . . . It made him crazy. I had to hold him back with my strength to keep him from attacking Huan that very moment. Then he chose not to pursue Karl because it meant leaving you. Before meeting you, he would never have made that choice."

I didn't dare fully assess the implication behind what François was saying, so I changed the subject.

"He doesn't want me to go with him anymore."

"It is only temporary."

"You think he'll be able to kill him?"

"He and Karl were very close. Despite the depth of Karl's betrayal, I am afraid that it will not be so simple."

"I think so too . . . So I'll do it for him," I declared fiercely.

"That would maybe be better, yes . . ."

After a long silence of mutual reflection, we returned to the manor and discovered that Phoenix had already left—to protect us, and maybe also to protect himself from us.

\*\*\*

A week passed, and Phoenix hadn't found a single trace of Karl. My boss had made his report directly to Talanus and Ysis, who were relieved to know that the blood traffickers had been massacred. However, our success wouldn't be enough to hold off the Elders, whose arrival was confirmed. They wouldn't tolerate the Secret being threatened again, and they would only consider the matter closed when the vampires who were behind the blood trafficking were presented to them for execution and would serve as an example to others. It wasn't promising . . .

We only had five days left. Phoenix got a call from Kiro, who shouted into the phone something about rumors circulating that one of the warehouses in Kerington's industrial area was starting to be the center of shady activity again. It could have been the mafia trafficking humans, but Kiro explained that a large, bald, tattooed man had been seen in the vicinity. Bingo. That was the very description of Thirsty Bill.

After hanging up without saying a word since Kiro wouldn't have been able to hear him anyway, Phoenix pulled on his coat. I planted myself in front of him.

"I'm coming."

He stepped around me and headed for the door. Determined, I caught up and blocked his path.

"Bring me with you."

At that, Phoenix looked up and stared hard into my eyes. "That is not up for discussion."

He tried to push me aside, but I held on to his arm.

"Karl was your friend. Let *me* kill him."

Phoenix mellowed when he realized I only wanted to spare him from executing the man he thought of as a brother. He slowly pulled his arm away from my hand and looked at me kindly.

"Thank you. But this is a task I have to carry out alone."

Defeated and terribly worried, I let him leave, hoping he would return safe and sound. I returned to the parlor and sat near François, who looked as gloomy as I felt.

"Sorry you have to babysit," I said sincerely.

"It is better to not leave you alone. Karl could return to have his revenge."

"Hm . . . I admit that I'm not sleeping well at the moment. When I think about what he said . . . he's hated Phoenix all this time . . . Phoenix doesn't show it, but I know he's in pain, despite all that you vampires say about your emotional independence."

"He was my friend too . . . he fooled me as well."

His bitterness was almost palpable.

"I'm sorry."

He offered me a contrite smile and suggested changing the subject.

"Angela told me that her return home went well," I began.

"Yes. No one noticed her disappearance except Matthew. She told him that an elderly aunt needed her urgently. I think she was able to convince him."

"Poor Matthew. Now two of us are lying to him."

"Sometimes it is better to remain ignorant about the reality of the world."

"Well, I don't regret no longer being ignorant. My life may be more dangerous now, but it's also much more interesting. Besides, now . . . I have friends."

François smiled sincerely that time and tapped me gently on my knee with his hand. Then we embarked on our thousandth conversation about science fiction. During one of our many talks, we'd discovered a mutual love for *Battlestar Galactica*.

We'd moved on to a debate about Hellboy's personality when we heard a noise coming from the entryway. We stopped talking at once and listened carefully. François stood up, but I held him back.

"What are you doing?" I whispered.

"Stay here, I will go look."

Had he never seen any horror films? When someone went to look for the source of a strange noise, that was when the character got stabbed, or cut into pieces, or eaten, or all that at once. It wasn't a good idea to split up, but François must have been thinking that even the psychopath from *The Texas Chain Saw Massacre* couldn't do much to him. He left my line of sight.

Mere seconds passed, but they felt like hours. I was starting to be truly afraid.

"François?" I ventured, rising from the sofa and staring hard at the door to the dining room without daring to go in.

"Sorry, but François is . . . as one might say . . . dead. For good this time."

As if I'd been thrown into a lake in the middle of winter, my blood froze in my veins hearing that reviled voice from the other side of the door. My hair would have stood straight on end if it could have, as well as every hair on my body, to warn me that Death had finally decided to come looking for me in the form of the hateful and horribly smug Karl.

He entered the room and smiled at me in a way that revealed all that he had planned for me.

"I know where you keep your weapon. Don't try to reach under the sofa, or I will rip your arm off."

The threat was simple and efficient, his goal very clear. He was going to kill me, and I wasn't armed. Well, I didn't have a gun. After our return to the manor, Phoenix had made me wear two silver knives on my belt . . . except that I was still no good at throwing them. To have a chance at getting out of this alive, I would have to fight Karl in close combat, and I didn't want that at all. I didn't know when my boss would return, so I could only count on myself.

"So you finally decided to show up," I hissed.

"As you can see. I have missed you since the other night. I should finish what I started."

"You're just too afraid to fight Phoenix directly."

His horrible smile widened, increasing my fear.

"I have a score to settle with you first."

"And you killed François while you were at it."

He was still moving forward, closing the distance between us. I was going to have to act. If Karl was lying and François wasn't dead, François would have already come to help me, so I knew I only had myself to rely on.

"He was in my way. You are alone now, and you are mine. This time, Phoenix is not here to save you."

His promise, an echo of my nightmare, was the trigger. I ran to the hallway, throwing everything I could get my hands on at Karl's head. The last thing I sent flying at him, before he caught up, was a vase filled with flowers that I'd picked the evening before. He lifted me up from the ground as if I were a feather and threw me against the wall with incredible power.

Lying on the ground, surrounded by the shards of mirror that had come with me in my fall, I didn't have enough time to react when he grabbed me and threw me against the wall again. Then he grabbed me by my hair and sent me crashing into a table, which shattered into pieces as well.

The pain was so intense I couldn't even think. My vision was blurred, and I only just had time to move before Karl jumped on me again. I was near Phoenix's office.

When my attacker grabbed my arm again, he didn't send me flying this time. Instead he pulled me from the debris and dragged me along the floor to the middle of the hallway. His eyes were shining, and his fangs seemed to be begging to sink into my flesh as soon as possible. However, he didn't swoop in on my neck. He did something worse.

Sitting down on top of me, he tore my shirt open and licked his lips greedily, staring at my bra. Having perfectly understood his intentions, I shrieked and struggled like a whirlwind . . . which earned me a magisterial slap that almost made me lose consciousness. He responded by shaking me.

"Hey, stay with me, Sam. I want you to be fully awake when I fuck you. I want you to enjoy the show and take pleasure from me just as I will from you."

Shaken by the shock and the crude description of what he was about to do, I let him rip open my bra; however, his laughter and his hands on me brought me to reality in all its horror. I tried to defend myself again and fight him off with my legs, but my efforts were in vain. When he tore my skirt and his hand traveled up my thigh, panic overwhelmed me and I screamed in despair.

My fist slammed into his temple, and he backed off, stunned. He stared at me, not understanding how I could have shown such force, but I knew. The mark was acting on my body again, and despite his absence, Phoenix was lending me his strength to encourage me to keep fighting. After all, I still had two assets on my belt . . .

The very moment Karl jumped back toward me, I grabbed my knives and planted them in the first place that presented itself: his eyes.

A torrent of blood spilled over me, and my enemy uttered an atrocious howl, testament to the indescribable suffering he must have been feeling. Despite being blind, he tried to grab at me again.

"I'm going to break your neck! You won't get out of here alive!" he shouted.

As I was trying to escape him, sliding on the ground because of the viscous liquid that covered the hallway floor, his words reverberated in my ears and led me toward safety: I couldn't get out, but I could hide. I heard Karl behind me, tripping, falling, and swearing, but I was faster.

With all the adrenaline of desperation, I ran to the bookshelf where *Candide* was shelved and pulled on the book. I thought all was lost when my attacker arrived as the door of the hidden room was still closing. Luckily, his blindness prevented him from finding me even as he turned in my direction and shouted, *"I'll kill you!"*

Phoenix had explained that the door and the walls of his room contained lead, so in theory, I was protected from Karl's destructive fury since he couldn't find me using his supernatural hearing. I had no trouble whatsoever imagining the torrent of swearing and cursing flowing from his cruel mouth because of his frustration at not being able to find me, and I remained paralyzed, half naked, covered in blood, and staring at the door in absolute terror, awaiting Death.

***

A noise brought me out of my stupor: the door mechanism had been activated. In a second, Karl would enter and finish what he'd started . . . My state of shock made it impossible to move. All I seemed able to do was wait, stuck in that room that would soon become my tomb.

The door opened completely, allowing me to see the face of the man now in front of me.

Phoenix.

Understanding that I was now safe liberated me from the tension that had overwhelmed me, and I started to fall to my knees. My boss caught me at the last moment and held me to him. I'd hardly wrapped my arms around his body when I was taken over by violent and incontrollable sobs—a release of the stress, fear, and pain that had piled up during my encounter with Karl.

The whole time I was crying and clinging to him, Phoenix stroked my hair and murmured soothing words. When I finally calmed down enough to speak, he gently pulled away from me. His gaze on my naked skin and my shredded clothes didn't reveal anything, but I knew from his clenched jaw that he was ready to erupt with anger. Without a word, he took off his jacket and put it around my shoulders to protect my modesty.

Feeling tears starting again, I gave him the news.

"Karl. He killed François."

Phoenix's eyes were shining brightly, and I couldn't imagine the rage that was boiling behind them. He buttoned up the jacket for me.

"No. He is alive and recovering slowly in the parlor. Karl stabbed him with a silver knife close to the heart. If he had moved at all, it would have killed him. I pulled it out when I arrived."

"Why did he spare him?" I asked, astonished.

"He told François to tell me, in detail, everything he was going to do to you. You did not see him in the entryway but François was there. He ended up losing consciousness when . . . did he . . . ?"

I had some difficulty swallowing at the memory of what I'd gone through.

"He tried," I whispered, holding back the sobs that threatened again.

Phoenix pulled me to him.

"I am going to kill him," he murmured.

His tone left no room for doubt. Phoenix wouldn't hesitate a second to kill Karl . . . and neither would I.

For the time being, I abandoned myself completely to his protective arms, where I was recovering little by little. I'd just had a brush with death and . . . rape. Even if the memory of my powerlessness and his hands on me would follow me for some time, I would get over it, I knew it . . . because I'd escaped him . . . thanks to Phoenix . . .

I raised my eyes to my boss and looked at him with gratitude.

"Thank you."

Still in thrall to his anger, he didn't catch on to the meaning of my words until a few seconds later.

"I was not here. I could not protect you."

"If you hadn't shown me your hiding place or given me your mark, I wouldn't be here to tell you about it."

Silence. I thought I should explain.

"Something strange happened, like the other night. When Karl was trying to"—I swallowed hard—"when he was on top of me, I hit him . . . he felt it, which let me stab his eyes with my knives."

"You were heroic whereas I fell for a trap, hook, line, and sinker," Phoenix said miserably.

"It was a trap?"

"Yes. When I got to the warehouses, I found Bill's trace. There were hospital stretchers and refrigerated cases, but no victims. I should have known. Thirsty attacked me, and we fought. When I finally got the upper hand, he laughed, telling me he was just a diversion and that a surprise was waiting for me at home . . . I decapitated him and rushed back. When I came across François and saw all that blood and debris, I thought I had a real heart again, that it was going to stop once more. François told me what happened while I pulled out the knife. I must say that it was your corpse I was looking for. I did not have any shred of hope until I saw the disorder in the office. I do not know what I would have done if you were not behind this door, safe and sound."

On those last words, his voice shook, quickening my heartbeat. He shook his head and smiled at me. "Who else would I fight with?"

I laughed, then remembered something.

"Maybe we should get out of here. François must be worried."

Phoenix nodded and lifted me in his arms to carry me into the parlor. After a few steps, he frowned while looking at me. "It looks like you only have superficial wounds."

I checked myself over. Setting aside the cuts, bruises, and the lingering state of shock, I was fine, which was very surprising given how many times I'd been thrown around and crashed into things, and especially given the amount of blood that had spattered all over the hallway walls.

"I'm OK. This time, I think some antiseptic and bandages will do the trick."

He smiled and started for the parlor again.

When we appeared in the doorway, François, who was still lying on the sofa, gave a very audible sigh of relief. He immediately got up despite his weakness and ordered Phoenix to place me on the couch instead. Phoenix complied and stood next to me for a moment.

"I am going to get you some clothes. I will be back in a minute."

Turning my attention to my French friend, I was stunned by the look of remorse on his face.

"It's not your fault, François. He set a trap for us both."

"He almost killed you because of my incompetence. I am nothing but a fool."

I didn't know what to say to ease his anguish.

"I am an idiotic, weak man who could not even stay conscious long enough to stop him from . . ."

His voice broke, and his distress filled me with compassion. I had to reassure him. Despite my pain, I got up and clasped his hands, forcing him to look at me.

"François, he didn't rape me."

A glimmer of hope appeared in his eyes.

"He tried . . . but Phoenix's mark saved me. I found the strength to escape."

"And for all our security, it would be better if this business about the mark and its effects on you stayed between us," Phoenix said. My boss had just rejoined us and was carrying a T-shirt, a pair of shorts, a bowl of water, and a first-aid kit. Judging from the way he was ignoring François, I knew that it would take some time before Phoenix forgave him for failing his assignment. I couldn't say anything about it. They had to settle that between themselves.

My two friends turned away so I could change my clothes. I was sore all over, and I was happy to sit back down again. As soon as I did,

Phoenix carefully took stock of my wounds. I had a huge bump on the back of my head, as well as a cut that had left a hideous crust of dried blood above my right ear. Talking made my jaw hurt even more, and numerous bruises and cuts covered my arms and legs.

Despite my protestations, my boss took charge of treating my wounds. He didn't lose patience, even when I whined in pain as he poured antiseptic over my wounds.

François must have felt uncomfortable and thought it would be best to leave us alone. My boss acted like he didn't even exist. A few minutes later, I snatched away the cotton gauze that was torturing me with electric shocks with each swipe.

"That's enough, stop, I can't take anymore!"

"After all that you have been through the past few months, I did not think that you would still be so delicate."

"Humph," I said, offended.

"I have never known you to be so subdued when it comes to insults."

"Don't worry, I'll be inspired soon enough," I grumbled as he put a bandage on my left thigh.

"That would be perfectly entertaining."

"Ow!"

I jumped in pain when he pulled the bandage tight to make it hold.

"I think the rest will be fine. It is the psychological scars that worry me."

I got serious again, and said, "I'll be OK."

"When I chose you, I admit I never would have thought that there would be such strength in you. I am impressed."

"I have a good teacher."

I put my hand on his and smiled. "Forgive François. He did what he could."

Phoenix's face clouded over, but he wasn't annoyed.

"You just cannot help yourself . . ."

"I'm asking as a favor to me. We have to be united if we're going to have any chance."

"Fine, since you wish it. But do not count on me to tell him myself."

"I knew that deep down you had a great heart."

Exasperated, he sighed, rolled his eyes, and then got up to put the first-aid kit away.

Unfortunately, a few days later, I had to bow before the inevitable. The Greats were coming.

# CHAPTER TWELVE

## *"Great" Changes*

It was July 15. Good grief, it was *July 15*!

The time accorded by the Greats to take care of the blood trafficking had passed, they were due to arrive at sunset. It was an utter catastrophe.

Their arrival signaled the condemning of the master vampires in the region as well as their angel, my best friend and mentor. I neglected to think about how his end also meant my own, a poor, insignificant human woman getting in the way of the safekeeping of the Secret.

I was in a state of stress that bordered on madness. Since Karl's escape, we found ourselves once again at a standstill, waiting for judgment day. Far from panicking, Phoenix welcomed the date of his execution with a calm that I envied. Having noticed my panic and the bad mood that accompanied it, my boss decided to distract me with interminable and exhausting training sessions.

Under no circumstances would I get angry at him for it, because I well understood that his goal was to take my mind off things. He'd also forbidden me from wasting time on "pointless activities" like doing research during the day, and in fact, he'd ordered me to go relax with my friends.

As if I could. I was bursting with energy. Matthew seemed completely befuddled by my attitude and didn't know where he stood. I was so on edge that the least provocation could make fly me off the handle. The poor guy was paying the price of wanting to tease me about the fact that a stressed-out nurse could hardly take care of a sick old man effectively. He didn't mean to be hurtful, but I'd literally exploded with anger because, without intending to, he'd reminded me that I was powerless to save Phoenix. Blowing off steam, I gave him the dressing-down of the century in the middle of Danny's restaurant, in front of an audience of petrified patrons and Danny—all of whom were silenced in shock. I hadn't spoken to him since.

Angela knew very well what was happening and shared my anxiety. Even though Phoenix had told her he'd do everything in his power to prevent the Elders from punishing François and me, she was worried.

Moreover, my French friend and Angela were seeing each other every night. After each visit, she couldn't suppress her need to share with me everything they discussed and the extent to which her feelings for him were growing. I was happy for them, unlike my boss who, clearly, didn't have a high opinion of the matter. I had other concerns.

As we found out from taking up my training again, the influence of Phoenix's mark was strong in my body. I was faster and stronger, and my senses were sharper. For all that, it was very temporary. The first time, believing the effects would be permanent, my boss hadn't held back. That worked until my strength suddenly dissipated, and the kick that I should have avoided knocked me down and sent me flying, my lungs on fire.

When he pulled me to my feet, I was completely winded and incapable of walking on my own. Thereafter, having learned our lesson, we took up a pace slightly less than that for vampires. It did me good because I absolutely had to alleviate stress.

The evening before the arrival of the Elders, Phoenix wasn't going easy on me, and I was so bogged down with worry about the next day that I took hit after hit.

"Good grief, Samantha. Where is your head? I could have killed you at least fifty times."

Shock and the thought of the next day were monopolizing too much of my brainpower to be able to defend myself correctly; his disappointment was the final straw. I burst into tears and turned away.

"Nothing will happen to you," he said, coming up behind me and putting his hands on my shoulders.

"I'm not worried about *me*."

In the ensuing silence, we only heard the ticking of the clock following its rhythm. I took a deep breath, then turned to meet his eyes.

"Is there no way that they'll spare you?"

"Our laws are very strict but necessary. I accept my fate, for I know that it will force our replacements to be more vigilant and to save human lives more effectively."

I bit my lip before answering. "But I don't accept it. What will I do without you?"

Looking at me solemnly, he caressed my cheek gently.

"I have confidence in your strength. You will be able to follow your own path . . . and François will look after you."

Tears ran down my cheeks again. Unable to stand the weight of his stare, a look that was telling me good-bye, I fell into his arms. Holding me, Phoenix said, "Your friendship has helped me make peace with my existence. I will leave happy, knowing that I met you."

His declaration broke my heart. When I looked up at him again, he was smiling tenderly. Like an out-of-body experience, I felt myself shudder and put my hands on his chest. I saw the distance between us close in slowly . . .

My hair was undone, I was disheveled and sweating; he was perfect. He'd removed his shirt while we were training, so he was bare chested.

The contact with my skin during our embrace had once again sparked an electric charge in my whole being, but with an intensity a thousand times more powerful than all the times before. Feeling his muscles flex under my fingers had amplified the charge, and his particular scent pierced through me like never before.

As I was held captive by his metallic, bluish gaze, some invisible and incomprehensible force pushing us toward each other, my senses that normally encouraged me to keep my distance had shut up for once . . .

"What do you want, François?"

It took me a second to realize that Phoenix, who had spoken so closely to me, hadn't been talking to me.

My boss had already turned to look at François, and red-faced, I followed suit.

Judging by his stance, François had tried to leave before Phoenix realized he was there. His sheepish look was so funny that I couldn't suppress a nervous laugh.

"I just wanted to tell you that Talanus called me. You seem to have forgotten to turn your phone on . . . ," he said, looking at me and then staring at my boss's naked torso.

Probably prompted by an expression of warning on Phoenix's face that I couldn't see, François rushed to continue.

"Well, they want to see us now . . . about tomorrow."

Phoenix nodded before turning back to me.

"You should rest. I shall see you when I wake up."

As I was about to wish him good luck, François cleared his throat loudly. Exasperated, my boss turned to look at him.

"Sorry . . . ," François apologized. "But she has to come too. Ysis's orders."

In response to our surprised expressions, our French friend found the appropriate reaction . . . He shrugged his shoulders.

***

Our arrival at Talanus and Ysis's property was far less theatrical than the first time. In fact, we were led into their private rooms via a route sheltered from curious eyes and watched over by vampires armed to the teeth.

When Phoenix pushed open the doors leading to the rooms exclusively reserved for his masters, I marveled at the opulent decor. We were far from the somber colors of the manor in Scarborough. Here, red and gold gave the space an almost surreal ambiance.

Everywhere shelves were filled with souvenirs . . . souvenirs from *two thousand years'* worth of existence.

Dazed by this incredible sight, I slowed my pace to better contemplate all these marvels . . . and then returned to a more appropriate pace when François walked right into me.

Talanus and Ysis welcomed us into a small room equipped with sofas and cigars. We were only missing brandy to complete the picture of being in a first-class parlor on the *Titanic*.

Just as intimidating as before, the master of the place gave me an irrepressible desire to run away screaming. Hidden behind the tall silhouette of my boss, I managed to regain control over my emotions. Ysis stared at me with an intensity that would have made the most courageous Navy SEAL shiver in fear.

She signaled for us to sit down in front of them, and immediately a vampire appeared to serve us two glasses of blood and a glass of lemonade. A microsecond later, he disappeared.

"Here we are again." Talanus's deep voice made me jump. "Phoenix, we had you come tonight to update you on our situation. According to what you have told us, you have not been able to locate Karl."

"I looked everywhere he might hide . . . without success."

"The question is no longer whether we will escape our fate, but rather what arrangements we can make for those will stay behind."

A silence followed, during which the only sound the vampires could have heard was my heart, fluttering like a butterfly in my chest, as it had been since we'd arrived. Phoenix broke the silence.

"I would like your help convincing the Greats to leave François and my assistant alone."

Talanus stared hard at me. "For François, that will not be a problem. But it could be difficult as far as your assistant is concerned."

"She has proven her loyalty."

"That—"

Ysis interrupted her husband by putting her hand on his knee. "We will take care of it."

Frowning, Talanus continued, "The Greats are going to ask us who would be likely to succeed us. You must know already."

"Ichimi and Kaiko," sighed my boss.

"Despite your differences of opinion, you must admit that Ichimi is the most qualified to take my place. He will figure out how to find these traffickers. I expect you to tell the Greats the same."

"Even if I dislike Ichimi and Kaiko, they have always been effective in the missions that you have given them. I shall tell the truth."

Satisfied at that, Talanus settled back into his chair and put an arm around his wife's shoulders.

"Well, here we are. After an existence like ours, I think I can say that Death does not scare me anymore. It has been a pleasure, Phoenix."

He raised his glass in Phoenix's direction. I realized that this was a great mark of respect and recognition when my boss bowed his head and replied, "For me as well."

This casual conversation about their impending deaths made me nauseous. How could they be so calm and resigned? I couldn't even drink my lemonade. I glanced quickly at François, who seemed to be contemplating his glass of blood without really seeing it.

"Your friends show you a very rare loyalty."

When Ysis spoke, everyone stared at her, not knowing if her next remark would make any sense or not. Phoenix clenched his teeth before answering her.

"It seems that one of them makes an exception." Of course, he was talking about Karl, whose betrayal was still fresh for all of us.

"Loyalty . . . is what will save us all."

Ysis closed her eyes after making that declaration, so we took the opportunity to glance at each other, trying to see if any of us had understood the meaning behind it. I was wondering if our hostess hadn't smoked something other than cigars before our arrival.

Suddenly, she opened her eyes and pointed at me.

"You. Stand up."

Disturbed by the biting tone of her voice, I gave my boss a questioning look; he signaled me to obey. Slowly, I complied.

"Come here."

Once in front of her, I shifted from one foot to the other out of anxiety. When she leaned forward to inspect my eyes, I couldn't help taking a step backward . . . and was brought back again by her hand grabbing the front of my shirt. I heard a strange noise behind me, like someone jumping out of a chair.

"Stay seated. She has nothing to fear."

Phoenix must have risen to protect me, but he had been immediately put in his place by Talanus. Anyway, I had a more urgent problem than what was happening behind me. I didn't know what Ysis was looking for in my pupils, but whatever it was, I greatly hoped that she would find it and let me flee from her unbearable examination.

"You belong to him," she said roughly.

Without warning, she imprisoned my head in the vise grip of her hands and focused all her attention on me, ignoring my cries of pain. The sounds of struggle that followed reached my ears but distantly, because Ysis's words had propelled me into my memories. I saw myself with Phoenix during our blood exchange, then images from my infiltration of the blood traffickers and my fight with Karl. I felt the pain of the knife in my stomach again from stepping between my attacker and my boss, then saw the wound disappear as I drank from my boss's wrist. Finally, in a flash, my subconscious remembered what had happened and made me recall my unbelievable behavior, both at that moment with Phoenix and during my fight with Karl at the manor. Then the vision faded . . .

The return to reality was brutal and shocking. I'd fallen to my knees. And I had trouble getting my bearings.

Something strange had happened: Ysis was trying painfully to stand up, trying to recover her breath, something she hadn't had to do for thousands of years. Behind me, an appalling scene was playing out. François was standing between Talanus and Phoenix to keep them from going at each other. Not a few minutes before, they had shown each other respect, but now they were ready to fight.

"Stop! You're crazy!" I shouted.

We were on the same side! Well, sure, Ysis had taken me by surprise . . . but that wasn't reason enough to kill each other. Or almost . . .

"The Night chose her and you . . ." Ysis pointed her finger at my boss, her fangs out. "*You* marked her!"

Our hostess's anger was so immense that the walls around us were starting to shake. Ysis grabbed me by the throat and forced me to stand, dragging me unceremoniously to Phoenix.

"How dare you? You were supposed to protect her!"

If such accusations bewildered him, my boss didn't let it show.

"That is what I did, giving her my blood. That is nothing out of the ordinary. Who could have predicted that the mark would appear? I am not at fault here."

Ysis's nostrils flared. "Your human is special. I thought you had understood that, but I underestimated your ignorance. You never should have given her your blood. Now it is impossible to know what effect it will have on her."

Like a fury, she abandoned me to his arms and started pacing the room, muttering incomprehensibly. My throat hurt, and I'd had enough of her little game. Without my boss being able to stop me, I blocked the Egyptian's path and met her anger with my own.

"Now that's enough! If you have information about my so-called specialness, spit it out so we can end this charade! If you had directly told us what was wrong with me instead of confusing us with your nonsensical metaphors about the Night, Phoenix would certainly have done differently, so calm down and find someone else to be your scapegoat! We have enough problems without adding the ranting of a crazy vampire!"

In the ensuing silence, during which Phoenix and François simultaneously lowered their eyes, the Egyptian looked down at me with scorn from her full height, her eyes luminous and her fangs a chilling sight.

"I have killed for less than that," she said sharply.

I stood up straight and stared right back at her. "I suppose that was also because your victims thought to give you a piece of their mind? Phoenix has nothing to do with this, so leave him alone, or you'll have to deal with me."

I was sincere, ready to fight if necessary.

Ysis, who was surely tougher than Karl, reacted the exact opposite from how I expected.

She smiled. "Perhaps all is not lost, then."

In a blur, she grabbed me by the shoulders, turned me around, and threw me again at my boss. Tripping on the carpet, I fell forward, but he caught me at the last moment, all while keeping Ysis and Talanus in sight. Talanus, however, seemed just as dumbfounded as we did, and stared at his wife with total disbelief. She spoke again, addressing Phoenix.

"Until the Elders officially dismiss us, I am still your leader. As such, I order you to not hide her. It is vital that she remain in Scarborough."

"Why?"

"Do not ask questions, just do it. In return, I shall forgive her disrespect."

I was floored by this exchange. Ysis would forgive me only if I stayed at the manor? Phoenix must have arranged for François to take me to a safe place and thus avoid an unfortunate encounter with the overseers of vampire law. He hadn't spoken to me of it because he suspected I would refuse, I'm sure of it. In a way, that suited me fine, but in another, I didn't understand why it would be so important for me to stay in Scarborough. Ysis must still be in some state of delirium . . . anyway, it was better I keep that opinion to myself.

Talanus intervened. "Believe me. If you trust her visions just once in your life, now is the time."

Visibly skeptical, Phoenix seemed to weigh the pros and cons. "At any rate, if the Greats really want to, they will find her," he sighed. "Agreed . . . But I want your word that you will not tell them about that mark."

Ysis rolled her eyes. "We are not foolish enough to tell them that. They will likely make us all pay. Now go."

The matter was closed; we were ordered to leave. Without waiting, we walked out in a deathly silence.

I didn't allow myself to relax one bit until we had put some distance between us and Kerington. Not a word had been exchanged since our departure.

"Is what she said true? You wanted to make me leave?" I ventured, knowing the answer in advance.

"I do not know if they will send their men to the manor, or what they will do if they find you there. I would prefer to put you somewhere safe."

"You said it yourself—safety is illusory, they'll find me wherever I go. I'd prefer to stay at the manor . . . it's my home too . . . You believe what she said about me?"

"Ysis is strange but also very powerful. I do not know what she has in mind, but I also cannot take her words lightly. You should not have insulted her."

I saw his accusing stare in the rearview mirror.

"She was unfair and insulting first. One of the qualities of a great leader is moderation."

"It's more than moderation for her. Any vampire of her rank would have cut your throat for saying what you said."

"I think it has been centuries since anyone put her in her place. It was definitely discourteous but also justified," François pleaded.

"It is useless to dwell on the matter too much. It is a miracle that she forgave you, and frankly, I do not understand it . . . but we will follow her orders. Tomorrow, you will stay in Scarborough. I do not know if I will be able to return in person, so François will act as intermediary between us."

"How much time will there be, between their arrival and your execution?"

"Two, maybe three days. At most."

A chill passed through my spine as I realized our new and terrible deadline.

***

It was July 15. Good grief, it was *July 15*!

The time accorded by the Greats to take care of the blood trafficking had passed, and their arrival was set for sunset. It was an utter catastrophe.

That's enough of that. There was no more time to dwell on the past few days.

These were my somber thoughts when I woke from my brief and oh-so-agitated sleep. I'd tossed and turned so much that my blankets and sheets were completely undone and twisted.

Barely awake, and my stress levels were already at the maximum. It was almost noon, and I needed to find a way to kill time while waiting for nightfall. I got dressed and went downstairs to the kitchen.

I launched into prep for beef bourguignon. I had to keep my mind busy, and my passion for French cuisine would help me with that. Between peeling the carrots, onions, and potatoes and chopping the meat, the complexity of the dish kept me occupied. But it had barely begun to simmer when I felt the need to concoct something else.

The heat from the oven and July's high temperatures transformed my workspace into a veritable furnace. Completely immersed in my task, I started one recipe after another—all before the previous one was finished—to leave no downtime. I threw myself into the cooking, body and soul, and as incredible it sounds, it worked, and I was calming down.

When I raised my eyes to the door that just opened, I felt a momentarily wave of hesitation before understanding what was happening.

My two vampires had woken up and no doubt wanted to say good-bye before going to see the ones who held their fates in their hands. Usually they would find me with my nose in a book or . . . in a tissue, like the crybaby I'd become.

From their faces, I could tell that the state they'd found me in didn't correspond at all with their expectations. Phoenix was staring at me as if I'd completely lost it. Suddenly self-conscious, I turned and looked at my reflection in the window.

"Ah!" I shrieked, startled.

It was enough to frighten, that's for sure. My hair, frizzed and full from the steam and heat, was dancing about my skull like a bad halo. My cheeks were on fire, I was sweating buckets, and I was covered in stains and flour.

The kitchen was in a state too. There were pans everywhere, full and empty; heaps of crepes, waffles, and muffins covered the table; the sink was brimming with dirty dishes; and all the burners were still hard at work cooking sauces.

François glanced around with astonishment and admiration, but Phoenix gave me a severe look that made me want to flee.

"I did not know that humans could eat so much!" exclaimed François.

Miserable, I decided to look down at my shoes.

"François, would you leave us? I shall join you in a minute."

Phoenix's serious and harsh tone didn't signal anything good.

"I will wait outside by the car. Sam, I will return later, no matter what happens."

Appreciating his concern, I gave him a weak smile.

"*Merci*, François."

After François left, Phoenix crossed his arms over his chest and seemed to be waiting for me to speak first. Intent on not obliging him, I turned the water on in the sink and poured in some dish soap. A fraction of a second later, the water was no longer running, and I was facing my boss.

Gulping painfully, I declared, "Don't expect me to say good-bye to you!"

He grabbed my chin to force me to look him in the eye.

"Do not expect me to leave without saying good-bye to you."

He caressed my cheek softly, setting off completely irregular heart palpitations.

"Before leaving, I would like you to help me . . ."

"Anything you need," I said without knowing what to expect.

"For the first time in five hundred years, I would like to remember what it is like to be human . . . Please, say my name . . . my real name."

Surprised, I tried to figure out his emotions . . . but his eyes were unreadable. I wondered if hearing his name would really help him remember his former existence, and I truly hoped that it would.

"Aydan . . ."

He smiled before touching his forehead to mine.

"Thank you, Sam."

He gave me a chaste kiss on the top of my head, and at that contact, I shivered. He pulled away quickly, but before he left, he turned and offered up his sardonic smile.

"By the way, clean this mess up."

Far from being annoyed or amused, his response—our last exchange before his execution—made me sink into despair.

***

Putting the food into plastic containers destined for the freezer and for Danny's restaurant, washing the dishes, cleaning the kitchen . . . all that took quite some time and calmed me down. However, afterward, I had nothing else to do except wait for François's return, so I went to the parlor to distract myself by watching some TV shows.

Talanus seemed confident about the decision the Elders would make regarding François. Our French friend had never been officially assigned to our mission; he was only helping out. Consequently, they couldn't legally punish him for incompetence. I wasn't terribly worried about him, but my mind was busy with thoughts of Phoenix. I started to wonder about the depths of despair Phoenix's absence might take me to.

Phoenix had an exceptional place in my life, but my attachment to him didn't seem normal. I had no point of comparison, though, since I'd never really had friends before. Now I had Angela and Matthew too, and I loved them, truly. Angela and I were so similar we'd become like sisters; I appreciated Matthew's spirit and his infectious energy. But despite my very strong feelings for my two friends, they just didn't compare to my feelings for Phoenix.

My boss had become my best friend, sure, but also my guide. Could that explain the deep attachment I felt toward him? No, there was something else.

Suddenly, something buried deep in my mind seemed to come to the surface, something that would give me the explanation I was looking for . . . I was ready to understand everything in all its truth when . . .

. . . I seized the weapon hidden in the sofa and stood up as fast as I could.

I'd felt a presence behind me, and the memory of recent events reminded me that it couldn't be amicable. My first encounter with Karl served as a lesson, and I needed to defend my own life. I waited until I was completely turned around before clicking off the safety. But I wasn't fast enough . . .

Disarmed, I tried to hit and grab at the powerful arm and hand that had lifted me by the neck. My throat was being held in a firm grip, and the lack of air was making me suffocate and see stars dance in front of my eyes. My legs were flailing in the air, but I couldn't reach far enough to kick my attacker. I was going to die, crushed by this strange man whose steely eyes were probing mine.

"Where is he?"

Getting only silence in return, he shook me and tightened his grip.

"Where is my son?"

On the edge of blacking out, the meaning of his question still came to me clearly, like a light in the night. In a short time, I would asphyxiate, and I had to gather my strength to make him let go.

"F . . . F . . . Finn," I managed to whisper with incredible effort, hoping that hearing his own name would be enough to let me live.

I crashed down to the ground, freed from the pressure of his fingers. My throat in throbbing pain, I coughed to breathe normally again; little by little my vision returned, along with the ability to speak.

"Are you Finn?" I asked him, massaging my throat and finding the courage to look at him.

He was a tall man, with wide shoulders and clearly outlined muscles. He emitted incredible charisma, and it blended well with an aura of wisdom acquired from time. In short, he was a blend of Talanus and Ysis in one person, with something else that made the two others look like amateurs . . . and that was saying something. I knew that this vampire facing me was extremely old. However, just as Phoenix had described, he looked more like he was about forty. His hair was somewhere between blond and strawberry blond, and he must have had origins in northern Europe, maybe Norway or Sweden. His blue eyes could have made me think that he and my boss had real family ties, if I ignored the radical way of creating vampires. He had a cleft chin à la Kirk Douglas that gave him an austere and severe look, without actually making him more frightening. He was impressive, in the noblest sense of the term, and he demanded immediate respect with his presence. I had trouble meeting his gaze.

"Who are you and what are you doing here, human?"

Still in shock, I stood up painfully and pointed at the armchair to signal to him that I wasn't trying to escape, or have this discussion while on all fours. With unusual elegance, he imitated me and sat across from me, taking care to set his suit jacket on the armrest; this was a practice that Phoenix had adopted.

"Um . . . I'm Samantha Watkins."

In front of my boss's creator, there was no use for secret identities.

"Your son, Aydan . . . um, Phoenix, hired me as an assistant, and I live here, with him."

If that surprised him, he didn't show it. This man was a master in the art of dissimulation; that much was obvious.

"You are his mistress," he said, staring me straight in the eyes.

I immediately burned scarlet.

"What? No! I work for him . . . he's my friend," I stuttered.

"Well then . . . people change," he murmured, mostly for himself. "Where is he?"

"He was summoned to Talanus and Ysis's house. The Elders are going to decide his fate, but it's likely that Phoenix and his leaders will be sentenced to execution. Since the real head of the blood-trafficking operation has escaped them, Phoenix's mission is considered a failure, and he and his leaders will pay the price for it."

Finn clenched his teeth. "I was in Siberia when I heard he was having problems. Communication is not easy in that part of the world."

"I understand."

There was a silence, then he looked at me.

"It does not matter how long it takes, I want you to explain everything to me, from the beginning, including your intercession and your role in all this. Do not omit a single detail. You will also tell me how you know his true identity."

Over several hours, I revisited all the incredible events that had punctuated and changed my life since January: how we had tracked the Chinese vampires and witnessed them harvesting blood from missing humans, how those vampires had led us to Heath and Karl . . . Finn repeatedly insisted that I be as specific as possible, so the smallest anecdotes evolved into epic tales. Though my mouth was dry from talking, I didn't dare get up for something to drink, nor did I offer anything to my guest. When I told him about how Karl, his deceptive adoptive son, had escaped us, I sensed from the way he stiffened that I'd piqued his interest, but he never interrupted.

I ended with Ysis's strange prediction about the Night, intentionally omitting the part about the mark, a subject that was too intimate and embarrassing for my taste.

"That Ysis is only good for spouting gibberish in the guise of visions. However, the person who ignores them is indeed very foolish. The future will tell us what she saw for you."

This was a subject without any importance in comparison with the reasons for his visit. I was completely in agreement with him: time would tell.

"We tried everything to find Karl and the one or ones who were giving him his orders, but we failed. Even Ichimi Ritsuye and Kaiko Ikeda, who hate him, tried everything to get at the leader. I don't know what else to do . . ."

"I am surprised by the attitude of those two. Honestly, they have made some progress."

"What do you mean?"

"I was with the Elders when Talanus and Ysis presented themselves as candidates for sector leaders in this New World," he said, gesturing vaguely at the surroundings. "Talanus made a strong impression, but the counsel was preparing to give the post to Ichimi. I convinced them not to do it, because his strong ambition put me ill at ease. Only sector leaders can aspire to be Elders one day, and I do not know why, but imagining that samurai in the counsel gave me chills. As for Kaiko, I do not know her well. What I know of her is just echoes of what I have heard . . . and it is not flattering."

"Talanus doesn't have the same concerns as you. According to Phoenix, they put a lot of effort into the investigation."

"Perhaps I judged them too harshly. Only the future can say."

"The future . . . that's why I'm worried about Phoenix."

"Why do you care so much about saving the man who stole your life from you?"

His question echoed my own thoughts. For a moment it felt as if the revelation Finn's appearance had prevented me from having earlier was about to make itself known. But just then, a bestial growl came from the dining room. I jumped from my seat and cried out in surprise.

François was standing on the table, crouched and ready to jump on his prey. Finn hardly deigned to glance over at the intruder. After quickly measuring him up, he shrugged his shoulders and relaxed back into his chair, his evident disdain insulting poor François, who didn't know if he should be amazed or enraged.

To avoid another bloodbath and more damage to the parlor, I rose and walked over to my musketeer friend.

"Calm down, François. Finn doesn't want to hurt us . . . at least, I don't think he does. He's Phoenix's creator."

François's anger disappeared quickly after absorbing that information. He greeted Finn very respectfully and approached him.

"I never thought I would get the chance to meet you. You are a legend among vampires."

What? François was looking at Finn with a veneration that resembled the mass hysteria of boy-band groupies. He may as well have asked for an autograph. What was with all this absurdity? Phoenix had told me that his master was powerful, but he hadn't mentioned that Finn was also as famous and adulated as the Beatles. At the same time, seeing the man himself, I could hardly imagine him singing "Hey Jude" in front of an ecstatic audience.

François's next statement made me tumble back immediately to earth.

"The Greats have decided."

I knew the verdict already, but it felt like an enormous rock had dropped into my stomach.

"The date of the execution is set for July 17 at midnight."

That wasn't even two whole nights! Luckily I was already sitting down, for my legs refused to hold me upright after hearing that information.

"You are *green*, Samantha," François said.

"I think I need air," I whispered.

I mostly needed to be alone.

Respecting my wish, Finn and François left me alone as I went outside.

I sat down on the steps to the manor and began a breathing exercise to chase away the sobs that threatened to escape. It was really late, or really early according to your line of thinking, and I could see the first light of dawn. The two vampires who were waiting for me inside couldn't delay sheltering themselves from the light, and I would have to give Finn a room.

Back in the parlor, I found François shaking. I looked at Finn severely.

"What did you do to him?"

As cool as could be, he said something that made me collapse to the ground, it was that unexpected: "I did not *do* anything, apart from saying that I am in a position to find Karl."

\*\*\*

"Let's go now!" my musketeer friend shouted.

I was distressed by my friend's heroism mixed with recklessness. "Go where? The sun is already rising. You'll be burned up before getting even ten miles."

Discouraged, François accepted my logic. There was nothing to be done for the time being.

"At last, I do not think it was so stupid on Phoenix's part to hire you," said Finn.

Finn's insult was rather a compliment, but it didn't give me much pleasure. All the vampires who knew about our partnership must have thought that I was a half-witted human in the service of a boss gone nuts due to overwork. Even if they changed their minds after meeting me, that didn't make it any more agreeable.

"You're too kind. Explain what you're going to do to find Karl."

"The oldest vampires who already have a power receive a second one after a certain period of existence. Mine is to find any and all members of my species, no matter where they are. That interested the Elders at one time, but I had no desire to associate with them. As a result, not knowing any other vampire with my ability, I could live discreetly."

François and I had the same expression of amazement on our faces, and our jaws dropped. This Finn was a gift from heaven!

I remembered then Ysis's words.

"Ysis! She knew you were coming. That's why she forbade me from leaving the manor. She knew you would be the key to finding Karl, and to saving them all."

I couldn't get over it—so that Egyptian wasn't just a crazy escapee from an asylum in antiquity. She really had the gift of foresight, and she had used it to help us save them. *Loyalty is what will save us all.* If we'd left despite her orders . . .

"Finn, tell me if I can do something while you sleep."

"Prepare two guns for us, knives, and silver chains . . . in short, everything we shall need to capture this traitor . . . and arrange the basement so that when we bring him back here, he cannot escape."

I nodded my head, heart swelling with a sense of hope that I thought I'd never feel again. Mentally taking note of the objects to ready, I let Finn and François figure out their parts in this mission.

When everything was organized, Finn spoke again: "I am going to need time to concentrate and find him. I shall get started as soon as the sun sets. Until then, we have to rest."

"Follow me," I said.

I gestured to him and walked ahead in the hallway after François disappeared into his own hiding place, and I led Finn down the hall to the office. There I went to the bookcase, pulled on *Candide*, and showed Finn the hidden room.

"I think Phoenix would have wanted you to use his room. After all he's told me, the connection between you two is very strong. So I think it's the best thing to do."

After glancing around the room and flipping through the copy of *The Lord of the Rings* that was still on the nightstand (it was even on the same page as my last visit), Finn honored me with a gesture of respect.

"I am happy that my progeny has found a friend such as you. Do not despair. We shall see each other tomorrow."

Then he activated the mechanism to close the door.

I made my way back to my room in a fog of exhaustion. To my great relief, my exhaustion won out over my anxiety; for the first time in a long time, I slept deeply and soundly.

The next day, I set to work as soon as I woke up. I went down to the basement and filled two bags with weapons that would be necessary to capture a vampire as powerful and wily as Karl without killing him. When I was sure I hadn't forgotten anything, I tackled the preparation of a room that would be properly suited to our guest.

To put it bluntly, I was assembling a torture chamber.

Oh, that didn't give me any pleasure at all, despite what Karl had tried to do to me . . . but we didn't have a choice. Karl was the only one who knew who was really behind the blood trafficking, and ironically, the only one who could save Phoenix. Thus despite my disgust at the thought of what would happen in the room, with the hooks and silver knives that I'd set out on a little table, my conscience kept quiet.

Finn and François appeared in the parlor and checked that their bags were ready. All that remained was finding our man . . . I didn't know how Finn's gift worked, but I'd laid out a map of the region just in case. Maybe it would be enough for him to close his eyes and he would be able to point to Karl's hiding place.

"Everything is ready. Is there anything you need to use your gift?"

"Maintain absolute silence until I tell you otherwise," he said, stretching out on the sofa as though he were about to take a nap.

Sure . . . I would have thought it would be something more impressive, a bit like the Halliwell sisters on *Charmed*; his manner of telling me to shut up was a tad on the annoying side . . . I sat down on one of the armchairs, crossing my arms to wait for Finn to find enlightenment, or his give his first snore . . .

To tell the truth, I still had trouble believing that luck was finally smiling on us. It was a true miracle that such a powerful vampire had arrived just when we needed him most, with a gift we needed to save Phoenix. Moreover, all this business about gifts bothered me a little . . .

Indeed, even if the official position was without a doubt to hide from human curiosity, there was a lot to fear if these super-vampires ever decided to come out and make us their slaves. Who would stop them? For the moment, it wasn't even a question, but one day maybe . . . I hoped that I wouldn't be here to see it.

Finn wanted to work alone, especially to make sure he wouldn't be used by the Greats for his gift. But after an hour, I wondered if he was leading us on. I couldn't stand to wait anymore for him to open his eyes. Besides, what even guaranteed that Karl would still be where Finn saw him by the time he and François reached the location?

What was Phoenix thinking about in his prison cell? Knowing him, he didn't fear his end, but I worried incessantly about him and I wished I knew how he was doing. I would have liked to share his mental tranquility, but I was *too* human and, as he liked to say, too emotional. It was true that since we'd met I'd had my fill of fear, pain, and despair. But friendship and the feeling of finally doing something with my life won out more or less over the rest. Friendship . . .

Since the other day, I'd felt bitterness over my friendly connection with my boss. Strange . . . did it have anything to do with the revelation that stubbornly refused to reveal itself to me when I knew it was so close?

"I know where he is, 21 Luis Pereza Avenue, in a villa in Drake Hill. Let's go."

Finn's sudden declaration brought me out of my reverie. He'd abruptly opened his eyes and stood up at the same time. François didn't utter a single comment; he leaped to his feet, ready to take action.

"Are you sure he will be there?" I asked, following them to the garage. All this time Karl had been nearby without even Kiro, however well-informed he was, knowing anything about it. For once, Karl had figured out how to be discreet.

"I never use this gift, but I do know one thing. It is infallible."

François got into the driver's seat, and the two of them squealed off at high speed toward our last chance to save Talanus, Ysis, and Phoenix.

\*\*\*

Drake Hill was an hour away from Scarborough. My companions had left around ten o'clock; accounting for the possible difficulty that capturing Karl would entail, they wouldn't be returning before one in the morning. Then I would have to help them get our hostage downstairs, where torture awaited him.

I wasn't completely, totally OK with that. While looking through my boss's weapons, I'd come across a several that seemed particularly suited to making recalcitrant vampires talk. Placing them near the table where Karl would be chained up with silver to immobilize him, I couldn't help but feel deep disgust for what would happen in that room. In any case, I didn't want to be present for it.

Yes, I wanted Karl Sarlsberg to die. Yes, I wanted it truly and deeply . . . but I wasn't cruel enough to want him suffer as much as I was sure he would. In fact, I hoped that he would crack and reveal his boss's identity as fast as possible to avoid torture, even if a little voice in my head whispered that that wasn't his way. The entire time I waited for Finn and François's return, I ruminated on dark thoughts and prayed that one day we'd be forgiven for the horrible act that we were about to commit. Well . . .

I watched out for my friends' arrival, and my heart skipped a beat when the entrance gate opened wide and three figures entered, struggling against each other like superpowered gladiators. I was stunned by Karl's strength as he fought against the two other vampires.

Suddenly, Karl smashed his fist into François's face, and François went flying, landing near me. Karl didn't have time to escape, for Finn had gotten out his gun and in a flash shot two bullets—one into each of Karl's thighs. Karl fell to the ground as the silver bullets rendered his legs useless.

Recovering my wits as I saw my companions begin to drag their burden in the direction of the basement, I walked ahead of them to open the door. Of course, the entire trip was punctuated by the most abominable cursing and insults ever . . .

Karl was tied up such that he couldn't even move a finger, and despite his anger, the fright in his eyes was clear as he looked at the instruments that were laid out near him.

"You can torture me all you want, I'll never tell you anything!" he shrieked.

Finn approached and leaned over him, smiling like a benevolent father would when wishing his son good night.

"I am also very happy to see you again, my dear son. Have you forgotten the fifty years you spent with me? It seems that is the case, or else you would never dare to claim that you can resist the treatment I am reserving for you. Do remind yourself how effective I am in that regard . . . ," Finn whispered.

Our hostage's terror attested to his executioner's words and made me even more nauseous about the prospect of what was to follow . . . Finn didn't want me to leave and ordered me to stay there along with François. I'd protested at first, but the look he'd thrown in my direction dissuaded me from continuing. As for my musketeer friend, he didn't seem bothered in the least, and it was then that his vampire nature truly showed.

Since we met, I'd found François to be more human than all his fellow vampires. He liked chatting with me and was interested in many things. Besides, his increasing love for Angela and our friendship had almost made me forget who he really was . . . But seeing his steady hand when he handed Finn instruments of torture, his impassibility when he heard the screams of our enemy, his old friend, and saw his blood spattering all over us as well as the walls . . . I had to face facts. There was nothing human about him . . . and I didn't have a place with them in that hell.

I had just enough time to run to a bucket before vomiting, unable to hold it in with that atrocious spectacle before my eyes.

"I won't stay another minute in this room! Strangle me if you must, I can't watch this!" I yelled at Finn. He looked at me with exasperation, clearly forgetting that humans still had a conscience.

Once I got upstairs and slammed the basement door closed behind me, I breathed in great gulps of air as if to wash out my lungs from the waves of absolute suffering emanating from Karl alongside his cries of agony. Cries that still reached my ears despite the distance . . .

Nausea overcame me, so I ran to the bathroom to purge myself again of this nightmare. Lifting my head from the toilet bowl, I saw traces of red on it: I was so covered in blood from head to toe that I'd left marks on the seat.

I frantically took off my clothes in a rush to get rid of my stained garments and take a shower. I wouldn't care one bit if either of the vampires came upstairs and saw me half naked; I put my things in a plastic bag, which I threw in the trash, before heading upstairs to shower.

I must have stayed in the bathroom for an hour, sobbing and trembling despite the hot water running over me. I hoped that my tears would wash away those ignoble images of torture forever. I took a sponge and rubbed at my skin so hard to remove all traces of Karl's blood that my skin became red and painful. It took me a long time to resolve to leave the bathroom, but I managed eventually. I didn't want to return downstairs, where the echoes of Karl's screams would continue to assail my ears, so I stayed in my room, on the sofa, waiting for news.

I waited a long time . . . a very long time . . .

I'd fallen asleep when François finally showed up. He woke up me gently, which didn't prevent me from jumping, and I appreciated the fact that he'd had the decency to change his clothes before coming to speak to me. He seemed tired.

"I came to give you the news before going to rest," he said, letting himself fall onto the sofa next to me.

"Did he talk?"

"No, and that is what worries us. No one has ever resisted Finn before during a torture session."

"What does that mean?"

"Finn thinks there is only one explanation. Karl is protecting his creator."

"I thought his creator abandoned him. At least, unless you mean the vampire who adopted him after he left Finn, but Karl said he was dead."

"No, not his adoptive father. The connection could not be as strong in that case. The only answer is that Karl has reconnected with his long-lost creator."

"That's completely crazy. I thought that the obedience connection had to go away after a hundred years because of the risks of the progeny rebelling."

"Not necessarily. If the creator never took the step to set the progeny free, the younger vampire can stay connected to the creator for an indefinite amount of time. The limit of a hundred years was adopted to avoid a master-slave relationship between the two, or to avoid jealousy in the case of multiple progenies."

"So the person we're looking for is the man who transformed Karl into a vampire . . ."

"And if he was ordered not to talk, even under the worst torture, it will be extremely difficult to get his creator's identity from Karl before Phoenix's execution."

"That's horrible," I murmured, almost sympathizing with the man who was undergoing great torments downstairs, to the utter indifference of the man who had never intended to act like a respectable father to his undesired progeny, who had abandoned him and left the duty of educating him to Finn and someone else, two complete strangers . . . only to reconnect with Karl now and force him to protect his identity at any cost.

We were silent for a few moments, united in our horror about the situation and the despair that despite everything we were trying, Phoenix's execution was inevitable.

"What time is it?" I asked.

"It is already day."

"Oh?"

"We have closed all the shutters to protect us against the sun, and we are taking turns with the, um, festivities downstairs. I will continue to torture the man I thought was my friend for more than three hundred years while Finn rests."

I placed my hand on his knee in a gesture of support, drawing from him a meager smile.

"I do not think that will be enough to save him. All that we are gaining from this is a butcher status."

At the very least, I knew that even if François was perpetrating some of the torture and tolerating the sight of Karl's blood on the walls, he wasn't any less disgusted by it. That was reassuring. I couldn't stand to be shut up in the manor anymore, just waiting for Karl to finally give us what we needed, so I made a decision.

"I'm going to go search that villa."

"What?"

"Knowing you, you were expedient enough when you went to retrieve him that the police or the neighbors wouldn't notice and come sniffing around. I'll go. I'm in no danger during the day, and maybe I'll find something that will help us find his creator. I can't stay here just twiddling my thumbs. I'll ask Angela to help me."

François considered my proposition for a second, then nodded.

"You are right, we have to put all the odds in our favor. Especially when we have a lot going against us."

He went to rest while I called Angela and explained to her roughly what I had planned. She was eager to help out. I prepped for my mission. Though Kiro was in Drake Hill, we needed more information than even he could provide at this point. With vampires of this caliber, we needed a miracle, and Finn had shown up . . . but I still wasn't sure about my chances.

We arrived at Drake Hill around noon, armed with the keys from the villa that François had taken. Angela noticed my nervousness and my pale face, but she didn't dare question me about it until we were at the gate to the villa.

"Something horrible happened, didn't it?"

Swallowing hard, I was actually relieved to be able to confide in a human friend who could understand what I was feeling.

"You have no idea," I said, getting out of the car.

It was hard to find the right key, but I managed to trigger the gate's opening mechanism and get us inside without attracting attention. Driving up the lane, I knew that Angela wasn't expecting me to continue.

"Sorry . . . what I saw . . ."

"You don't have to tell me, you know."

"No, you're the only one who can understand. All these vampires have hearts of stone and can bear the unbearable. But I have limits. I hate Karl, but I almost pity him, knowing what he's going through right now. I'm disgusted that I'm involved, even indirectly."

"I understand, but you shouldn't feel guilty. From what I understand, these things are usual in the vampire world. It existed before you, and it will exist after you. You can't do anything about it. Karl chose this, and you, you chose to save the vampires who for decades have been saving human lives in this area. I'm proud of you."

Her declaration left me speechless, and a wave of relief washed over me. I'd been right to confide in her . . . I pulled her toward me and hugged her tight.

"You're suffocating me," she cried out, laughing and returning my hug.

"I'm so happy you're here. A little estrogen in my world of vampire testosterone is good for me."

We laughed together before getting to the heart of the matter . . .

The villa wasn't very big, but the refined decor gave it an impression of spaciousness and relaxing Zen-ness. A large Buddha statue smiled in the direction of anyone who entered, and a long staircase led to the upper floor.

"What are we looking for?" Angela asked.

"This house definitely doesn't belong to Karl. Search upstairs, I'll take care of the ground floor. Look for anything that could tell us about the owners. We need to find out who they are."

"OK."

We split up for what seemed like a short time, but when she joined me in the office, which I'd made a mess of, it was already six o'clock. Angela had lost all her sex appeal: her eyes were red, her skin was pale, her blond hair (usually so carefully brushed and radiant) was all tangled like a lion's mane, and she was covered in dust.

"What happened to you?" I asked, startled.

"There was a hatch in the bedroom, leading to the attic. I searched it from top to bottom and then my allergies . . . Aaa . . . Aaatchoo! All that fuss for nothing."

She blew her nose noisily and sat down next to me.

"Did you find something?"

"No, this office is full of papers, but there are no names on the letterheads. It's crazy," I answered, frustrated.

"Are there any other rooms to look through?"

"I combed through the ground floor and the basement. Nothing." I put my head between my hands. "We don't have enough time. We have to find something."

Tick, tock, tick, tock, the clock continued its incessant ticking to remind me that Phoenix's end was near. Angela put her hand on my shoulder.

"We just hit a roadblock. We'll start again, and you'll see, this time we'll find something."

For two hours, we took up our search again, revisiting every last square inch that could have escaped our attention the first time. I was seriously starting to despair, knowing that July's summer sun would set in an hour at the most. I went to massage my neck a little, but as I did, my earring fell to the ground and rolled between the desk and the wall. Already in a bad mood, that didn't help matters, so I shoved the desk aside roughly to recover my earring. In the little space that opened up, luck finally smiled at me.

A document had fallen between the desk and the wall and must have been forgotten there by the owners. I grabbed it quickly, suddenly hopeful.

"Angela, I found something."

She came over, and we sat down on the floor together to read what seemed like official correspondence. The addressee's name wasn't mentioned, but at the top was the name of the sender.

"George Stanson," I read. "It's a copy of a notarized agreement concerning the new residential neighborhood being built at the city's periphery."

"His address is in Kerington's business quarter."

I got out my phone.

"What are you doing?"

"Making good use of my smartphone."

I typed in the name we'd found and let Google do its magic.

"He's an inheritance attorney. His clients aren't just anybody. They are celebrities and businessmen, so they must go to him for discretion. We'll have to go to Kerington and question him."

"He'll be at home by now, given the time."

"Not necessarily. These kinds of lawyers are always at the disposal of their clients. If they need him at night, he has to be able to see them."

I was greeted by George Stanson's secretary after dialing his office number.

"Mr. Stanson's office, Stella speaking."

"Hello, I'm Peter Livingstone's assistant, and I absolutely must see your boss within the next hour."

"I'm sorry, but Mr. Stanson has left for the evening. You must make an appointment."

I was expecting that answer, but I had other tricks up my sleeve.

"Very well, I think Mr. Stanson will be thrilled to learn that thanks to your diligence and efficacy, you've deprived him of the business of a man worth half a billion dollars. I'll call another inheritance specialist. I doubt that he will make the mistake of refusing a meeting with me. Have a good evening."

I'd played my last hand, but the biggest lies were often the most useful.

"Uh, wait!" The secretary's voice had lost all its arrogance, and she seemed much tenser than before. "One moment please."

She came back on the line less than a minute later.

"The offices will be closed in an hour, but we'll inform security. Mr. Stanson will be waiting for you, Miss . . . ?"

"Jones, Samantha Jones. All right, I'll be there in an hour with my secretary."

Without further ado, I hung up on her. Rich people didn't bother with niceties. I looked at my watch and then up at Angela.

"Let's go."

We rushed to the car, toward Kerington, toward George Stanson.

\*\*\*

Stanson's offices were situated in the business quarter downtown, on Marc Orsa Avenue, the richest and most valuable property in Kerington. Being well established here meant guaranteed success.

Despite my dangerous (and well over the speed limit) driving, during which Angela somehow managed to clean herself up, we didn't arrive until about nine thirty. I asked Angela to call François to tell him not to worry, but unfortunately Finn picked up the phone. I couldn't hear what he was saying, but given the way her face fell, it couldn't have been nice. Indignant, I held out my hand.

"Give me the phone."

She complied, visibly relieved.

"Finn, it's Samantha. I . . . No, we're not being imprudent . . . No, I haven't forgotten Phoenix, why would you think that . . . *Oh, shut up!*"

Creator or not, it wasn't polite to keep cutting me off like that, and I had to update him. In any case, he didn't say anything more after I shouted at him.

"Stay close to your phone and try to grill Karl on a George Stanson. He may know something. No vampire is going to let us humans into Talanus and Ysis's house, so we'll continue our search right to the end," I said.

He hung up on me. Well, I hadn't received any cursing or insults, so I concluded that I had carte blanche.

"Are you ready?" I asked my friend one last time as we left the parking garage.

"I'm the secretary to the assistant of Mr. Livingstone, multimillionaire, who wants to put his estate in the hands of a finance guru like Mr. Stanson."

"Perfect. Ah, just so you know, I wear a gun and several knives, don't be afraid if you see me get them out. If this guy knows more than he lets on, I won't hesitate to frighten him."

"Don't worry about me. If there's need, I'm prepared to give him a good beating myself . . . I hate lawyers."

The elevator brought us to the thirty-fifth floor, after the security guard checked my identification. Smartly, I'd dissuaded him from asking to see Angela's as well, because we couldn't give him her real name. Before the elevator doors opened, we both exhaled to give us courage. George Stanson was waiting for us.

I'd hardly taken a good look at him when I felt an immediate and firm aversion to him. His small stature and portliness would have given him a friendly demeanor without his smarmy smirk.

"Miss Jones, I'm pleased to make the acquaintance of the assistant to such an important and . . . discreet . . . man. I must admit I've never heard of him."

I looked at him with a disdain that surprised even me.

"Perhaps you don't have the right connections. Anyway, my boss is not the kind of man who holds meeting in public. He employs a number of people to ensure his activities and interests are handled discreetly."

The message couldn't have been clearer: stop asking stupid questions or we'll send our hired guns. Well, perhaps not *that* clear, but from the look on Stanson's face, he'd understood that he'd been put in his place.

"Uh . . . Follow me to my office. We'll be more comfortable there."

He opened the door and invited us to sit down. Of course his eyes followed the gracious movements of Angela's hips, and when he lifted his eyes and realized that I'd caught him, he blushed.

I intentionally imposed silence between us and gave Stanson a very severe look; he shifted from side to side in his seat, uncomfortable. My strategy was working: he was taking us seriously. I had to discover the identity of the villa's owner, for my instinct was screaming at me that that's who we'd been looking for from the beginning. My plan was nothing more than a bluff. I had to frighten him enough to get him to talk, without going so far as hurting him . . . I wasn't a monster.

"I only have a little time, so I'll cut to the chase. Mr. Livingstone is an important man whose wealth amounts to nearly a half a billion dollars, and he wants to pour some of that into real estate. It's obvious that discretion is of the utmost. We don't wish to attract attention."

"Are you proposing that I launder your money?" he said, offended.

I smiled at him, shrugging my shoulders.

"Come on. If I'm here, it's because I know all about you, so don't pretend to be offended."

He looked at me suspiciously. He must be wondering if I was a police informant.

"Fine. We're not going to spend the night here. I'm not police, if that's what you think," I said.

He seemed calmed by that, and he relaxed into his chair, ready to do business.

"Tell me what you want to invest in and what type of buildings, and I'll see what I can do for you."

"Mr. Livingstone likes Drake Hill and that whole posh neighborhood. Are there any properties there of interest to us?"

I didn't fail to notice the shudder that came over Stanson at the mention of Drake Hill, but I had to be sure he really knew something before revealing anything more.

"Hm . . . of course, an entire residential neighborhood is being constructed right now, and the city means to put more land on sale two months from now. It's ideal for investing."

"The clients you've already given this information to, what do they think?"

"Why do you want to know that?"

He seemed worried, but I had to keep pushing.

"It's normal that I would want to know if your clients are happy with your services."

"You've already investigated me, so that question is superfluous," he said, dabbing his forehead with a handkerchief.

"Come on, don't work yourself up. You could be working for vampires for all I care."

That time, his look of fear betrayed him. In a flash, I got out my gun from my bag, and Angela went to block the door to make sure he couldn't escape. Undeterred, Stanson jumped on his desk and tried to use his momentum to push my friend out of his way. What he hadn't considered was how well trained I was: he collapsed when I delivered a blow to the back of his neck.

Angela looked at me with a mixture of protest and astonishment. "You killed him!"

I sighed. "Of course not, but in two minutes, he's going to wake up with a severe headache. I'll take care of him. You go through his drawers and see if you can find any reference to the Drake Hill villa."

She quickly complied, which allowed me to turn my attention to our shady lawyer. To tell the truth, I was impressed by the leap he'd made despite his corpulence. He must have been scared out of his mind to be able to fly like that, trying to escape in spite of the gun aimed at him.

I managed to get him back in his chair and positioned myself in front of him, knives out. As expected, he woke up shortly after. Noticing that the woman he took for a secretary was emptying his drawers and the other woman was playing with silver knives under his very nose, Stanson trembled with fear, his face white as a sheet.

"Who . . . who are you? Are you vampires?"

"So, you do know about vampires . . . which means that in exchange for your life, you helped one of them," I said, moving closer and showing off the gleam of my blades.

"You . . . you're human? What do you want from me?"

"I want to know what vampire you're working for and what he or she looks like. If I don't get the information I want, I'll be happy to bleed you out like the stuck pig you are," I growled, imitating to perfection my boss's own threatening and velvet-wrapped voice.

I didn't know that human skin could turn so pale. Stanson became so white you would have thought he was a corpse.

"You won't find anything here. If I tell you anything, they'll kill me anyway."

I gave him the cruelest smile, taking Karl as my model.

"That's not the issue. Everything depends on the way you'll be killed. Vampires aren't the only ones who know deadly, slow, *meticulous* techniques, you know," I murmured, signaling him to follow the trajectory of my blade.

He jumped in horror, seeing my hand mime the cutting up of his masculine anatomy, located below the belt.

"It's time to choose, George. If you help us, we'll eliminate your boss, and then we'll be in a position to let you live."

He stared, searching my face for a sign that I was bluffing. Luckily for me, he didn't find any.

"So, George, freedom . . . or slow and painful death?"

Angela had joined me, and together we held our breath, waiting for him to decide . . .

He finally cracked and told us the identity of the vampire who was holding him hostage, as well as the extent of that vampire's investments in this region and beyond, and he showed us to a well-hidden safe where there was proof of his accusations. I had to pinch myself to stay in character. The whirlwind of emotions threatened to make me lose all self-control.

I didn't know how, but I played my part until the last moment, not forgetting to threaten George Stanson with the worst torture if he ever dared talk to anyone about our meeting and the existence of vampires. I must have been extremely convincing, for the poor man wet his pants.

Once we'd left the building, taking precautions that there weren't any curious ears around us, we jumped into the car as if the devil himself were in hot pursuit. After I peeled out of the parking garage, Angela dialed the phone and handed it to me. Finn was on the other end, and in the background I heard Karl's screams; he hadn't had a moment of respite between yesterday and today.

"Stop everything. You must meet me. Fly as fast as you can to Talanus and Ysis's house. François can take the car. Make sure he brings Karl, and tell him to step on it. I know who's behind all this!"

Once again, Finn hung up on me. But I wasn't angry at all, quite the contrary. There was an hour and a half drive between Scarborough and Kerington, and it was almost eleven o'clock. In an hour, by hierarchical order, Phoenix would be the first to die . . . and I hoped that his flying creator would arrive in time to stop all this.

# CHAPTER THIRTEEN

## *Revelations*

I was speeding so fast to get to Talanus and Ysis's house that I couldn't believe I hadn't been pursued by the police. I parked a block away from the master vampires' house and cut the engine.

"Angela, I'm going to get out and wait for Finn to arrive. Only he can get me inside. As for you, I want you to drive back to Scarborough."

"What?" she exclaimed, outraged. "I'm staying with you whether you like it or not!"

I shook my head and grabbed her by the shoulders.

"Listen to me. Finn can't get us both in. Besides, they know me. Don't forget that the mission of the Greats is to silence anyone who threatens to reveal the secret of their existence, so I have no guarantee where you're concerned. François would be inconsolable if something bad happened to you."

My implacable logic made its way to my friend's mind, but she wouldn't admit defeat.

"I don't want to abandon you."

"You aren't. And I didn't do all this just to die now. Believe me, I'll get out of this."

"I feel like I'm leaving you to enter the lion's den all alone."

"The only way for you to help me is to get yourself safe. If I'm worrying about you, I risk ruining everything."

Luckily Angela knew that I didn't think she was a nuisance and that I just wanted to protect her life and her freedom. She sighed.

"Fine. But I won't go to sleep until I hear from you. If I don't have any news by the time the sun rises, I promise you that I'll come back with the police, and we'll put stakes through all their hearts as they sleep."

"Later, then," I said, getting out of the car without truly believing that I'd see her again.

I watched her leave before I walked the block to the house. I found a bush across the street where I could hide from the guard vampires, a security detail that seemed to have doubled for the occasion. Since this was a residential neighborhood and there had to have been hundreds of people in the area, I wasn't afraid that my heartbeat would betray me. Forcing myself to calm down, I sat behind the bush and looked up at the sky, watching the moon and stars, to try to occupy myself during the most dreadful wait of my life.

*** 

I never read horoscopes, and I knew nothing about tides since I didn't live near the ocean. Because of that, I was surprised to note that the moon was full. It was a bit of a cliché for the Elders, as though by coincidence, to have picked this particular and supernaturally reputed night for the execution. If they believed in some sort of lunar power, they should spare Ysis, who vacationed there in her head most of the time.

That was mean of me. I had to recognize that if she hadn't anticipated Finn's arrival, we wouldn't be there trying to save all three of their lives. I didn't know what we would have done . . . Drinking a glass of champagne or blood to pay our last respects would have been a bit uncalled for. Then . . . what would I have done after, if they'd allowed me to live?

I actually hadn't thought about it. Would I stay in Scarborough with François, the two of us continuing the charade of old man Stratford and his granddaughter the nurse? Or start over in a new city? The second solution revolted me, and as for the first . . . I'd managed to put down roots in Scarborough and I felt at home there. But none of it made any sense without the man who had brought me there six months before. That seemed so long ago . . . and to think, I'd hated Phoenix at first whereas now . . .

I snapped out of my reverie when a dark shadow emerged from behind the clouds, bathed in that phantasmal lunar light. I looked at my watch; it was five minutes before midnight.

Without losing time, I ran to the tall iron gate that separated the estate from the street. I wasn't at all concerned about the vampires aiming their machine guns at me.

I screamed skyward, *"Finn!"*

The flying silhouette turned for the ground and, faster than a falcon, charged the guards who hadn't noticed his presence. Using the element of surprise and his incredible strength, Finn pushed aside the twenty vampires who were trying to keep him from entering. I was astounded. Even Phoenix, who was very powerful, couldn't have grappled with this many vampires, and his master had literally crushed Talanus and Ysis's entire guard.

Finn turned to me and approached the gate. His eyes were bright and his fangs so long and sharp that they gave me goose bumps. In one swift kick, the gate flew apart effortlessly, almost flattening me in passing. Finn seized me and lifted me into his arms before taking off again at full speed to the villa entryway.

The door, closed shut, seemed like an obstacle that my porter wouldn't take the time midflight to open correctly, and I feared being used as a battering ram to force it down. In a fraction of a second, we'd covered the distance between the street and that wooden door; with full force, we pierced through the door, which splintered into a thousand pieces.

When we stood up, scattered all over the floor were debris and unconscious vampires who had come to witness the death of their angel and their sector leaders. Those who had been far enough away to be spared by the violence of the impact were staring at us, amazed, before recognizing the man who accompanied me. All of them had the same expression: unlimited, blissful admiration.

Far from relishing that attention, Finn grabbed me again and held me against him. I had just enough time to check that I still had my bag of weapons and all Stanson's evidence before he raised us up a few inches from the ground, verifying the distance that separated him from the great hall entrance where the executioner's silver ax would be doing its job in mere seconds.

The first time I had come here, the walk had seemed very long. All those staring vampires had made me uncomfortable, and I preferred keeping my eyes on my boss's back. Seeing it this time, I knew that I hadn't been mistaken: the corridor was very long, not very wide, and crammed with curious vampires. How were we going to get through?

"What do we do?"

Finn crushed the jaw of a guard who, unnoticed by me, had come up behind us.

"We charge! I will take care of the Elders, and you go after the executioner! Hold on!"

Gulp.

If Finn had gone down in the history of his species as one of its heroes, it was definitely not this way. To clear a path in the crowd, there was only one thing to do: rush in.

Seeing all those men and women, usually so powerful and frightening, flying into the air like old trash, with expressions of fear or pure incomprehension, could have been funny in other circumstances. But this was completely out of control. Even if Finn had put his arms around me to lessen the impact, I still felt the other vampires, and it was true torture.

Finally my porter set me down abruptly, and he pushed aside the guards blocking our way. These guards seemed meaner and more dangerous than the ones outside; these guards were in the service of the Greats.

"Come on!" Finn yelled, showing me a little hole between our assailants, through which I could pass.

Without a second thought, I threw myself to the ground, crawling on my stomach to the small space, profiting from the shouts and ambient confusion to sneak in. Still crawling, I saw with horror that one of the Greats was signaling to the executioner to lift his ax, resuming the action that had been interrupted by our arrival—the decapitation of my boss, whose attention was turned toward his creator, an affectionate smile on his lips, and a good-bye in his eyes. Phoenix's neck rested on a kind of golden pedestal, and his hands were tied behind his back by a silver chain. He was awaiting his death peacefully.

Tangled up in the legs of the remaining spectators too taken aback to react, I couldn't close the distance of the last few inches separating me from the first row. Desperate, I ended up biting down with all my strength on the ankle of a fat vampire who was enjoying the show, a cup of blood in his hand. Even if he didn't feel any pain, the surprise made him drop his cup, spattering blood all over me.

"Hey!"

Surely because he didn't want to stain his nice suit, he finally moved over and gave me room to stand up, get out my gun, and feel my blood flow back into my face at the sight of the ax that, as though in bad slow motion, was unrelentingly falling toward my boss's neck.

*"Nooooo!"* I shrieked, taking aim.

The bullet had barely been fired when I saw the executioner, who was staring at me, stunned, miss his original target by only a hair, driving his ax into the floor. I didn't wait for anyone around me to react, much less the Greats, and I charged at the official murderer who was leaning down to collect his ax, planted in the floor, to finish the job. Phoenix hadn't moved.

I'd put all my remaining strength that remained into that purposeful collision, and propelled by fury, I drove my first silver knife into the executioner's stomach. My momentum and his sudden weakness made us both fly to the ground, and we landed at the feet of a man who looked about sixty but who must have been around two thousand years old or more—one of the Elders! With no time to think, I backed away, placing myself to the left of my boss, who had stood up, and aiming my weapon at the assembly, ready to shoot at anyone who dared approach. In the same instant, I was joined by Finn, who had gotten rid of his attackers and came to stand on Phoenix's right, taking away his chains with a single hand.

A deathly silence fell over the villa. Everything was going to happen—now.

***

Facing the most powerful and respected vampires in the world, I wasn't overconfident about our prospects, but I still held my gun steadily and resolutely. Finn stepped in front of us, signaling me to lower my weapon; I complied, not wanting to provoke the whole audience, seemingly ready to jump on us.

On our right, I could see Talanus and Ysis, chained and flanked by two of the Elders' bodyguards, as well as Ichimi and Kaiko, who already had replaced Talanus and Ysis in their duties and were expressing support and sympathy toward their former leaders. Once more, the murderous look on that Japanese female fury's face made me shudder.

"We're not here to fight you, my *sister*, my *brothers*." Finn emphasized his last words, raising his arms wide to a sign of peace. The executioner and the white-haired man in front of whom I'd landed approached and faced Finn.

"You say that you are not here to fight, yet you create chaos, all in the hopes of saving your progeny. Phoenix has been judged by our tribunal, a tribunal you have refused to join, I will remind you. You may well be the oldest vampire in the world, but you are still subject to our laws."

I wasn't expecting that! That was why everyone bowed at his feet and venerated him like a demigod. If he wasn't the first vampire, he was at least the very oldest. That explained his powerful presence and his ageless appearance. Shocked at not being informed of this, I shot a dark look at Phoenix, who simply shrugged his shoulders.

"I know our laws. I helped write them, after all, if you remember, Egire."

"And you are breaking them right now by coming here with a human woman and attacking your own kind!" thundered Egire.

What a strange name that was.

The other Elders nodded their approval. They all had to be more than a thousand years old . . . There were ten of them . . . these men (and one woman) ran the vampire world with an iron fist and were considered the protectors of their species. None of them looked like each other physically, but they shared an aura of incredible power. I didn't dare imagine what secret powers they possessed or how they would use them to achieve their ends. It was better to be on their side, that was for sure. I stopped my reflections of the circle of Elders that faced me when I saw that I'd attracted the attention of the only woman among them. Well, that wasn't quite the right word for her, for it would have been easy to mistake her for a seventeen-year-old girl. Her hair was bright red, and her youthful face would have given her a look of innocence if it weren't for the flash of hardness in her magnificent green eyes, the result of a very long life marked by hardship and the lessons learned from it. Her curiosity made me immediately backpedal and turn my attention to the man who, out of a sense of independence, had refused to preside over this close-minded vampiric group of Ten.

Finn straightened and looked scornfully at his younger siblings.

"I am only here to stop you from making a mistake by executing the wrong people."

Murmurs of indignation and admiration were creating a disagreeable din.

"*Silence!*" another Elder belted out, a grizzled and potbellied fifty-year-old with a cruel voice that contradicted the friendliness of his appearance.

Not a single person dared to make a single sound after that, which allowed Finn to continue, doing something that didn't please me at all: he pointed at me.

"Along with the assistant chosen by my progeny, we continued the search for the real minds behind this blood trafficking, and we were able to get our hands on their lieutenant."

More murmurs from the audience, but this time we could also make out voices shouting. You would have thought there was a fight breaking out behind us.

"Let me through, you congenital idiots!"

I didn't know what surprised me more: seeing François show up with Karl in tow, bloody and incapable of the least movement under three layers of silver chains, or his insult, so shocking for someone so refined. Anyway, he'd come at exactly the right time. I even could have believed that his arrival had been planned that way, it was so timely. The guards moved aside so François could deposit his burden at the feet of the Elders, who were wondering what was going on.

"Who is this?" asked Egire.

Finn pointed at the wounded and doubled-over body.

"My adopted son, Karl Sarlsberg. Let's say that he preferred to follow other teachings rather than my own, and here he is in front of you because he made bad choices. In short, he is an idiot, yes, but a fiendishly tough idiot. He has not said a word about the one who is protecting him. I think he found his creator again, who ordered Karl to stay silent even under torture. Karl was always stubborn, but he is a formidable enemy. Therefore between his impossible personality and the theory that he was never liberated from his creator, he managed to keep his creator's identity secret."

Egire considered the bloody mess on the ground, then returned his attention to Finn. "I know your methods, and even among us, no one holds a candle to you when it comes to getting information out of one of our own. If you failed, I do not see how we could get it out of him. We are at an impasse."

Adopting the posture of a conquering hero ready for victory, our ally stuck out his chest again and pointed at me once more. How rude.

"This human is the key. Let her speak, and you will see that she has important things to say."

What? Oh, no, not that. I had no desire whatsoever to prance around in front of an audience of vampires ready for a massacre. He only had to explain it to them!

Well, it was true that when I'd called him, he'd hung up without waiting to hear the names of the blood-trafficking bosses. Gulp. I couldn't escape this.

Avoiding Phoenix's gaze, which would have distracted me somewhat, I stepped forward to Finn's side and forced myself to look directly at Egire, the leader of the most powerful vampires in the world, who would listen to his advice if I didn't manage to convince him of my theory.

"Today, as Finn and François tried in their own way to get information out of Karl, I returned to the villa where they captured him. I had a hunch that we should look there, and I wasn't wrong. Searching the house from top to bottom, I came across a letter that allowed me to find the source of the trafficking."

I deliberately omitted Angela's participation in this excursion since I'd promised to keep her away from all this.

I resumed my tale after hearing the clamors of surprise from the audience finally fade.

"The truth surprised me, but upon reflection, it was logical. I will only ask you one question. Who had the most to gain from the fall of two of the most powerful and efficient sector leaders of your species?"

A deathly hush weighed heavy on the room. Since it didn't look like anyone was going to answer, I continued. "The ones who would have gotten their positions, but who had been set aside due to Finn's influence. Kaiko Ikeda and Ichimi Ritsuye."

Immediately, shrieks of rage, surprise, indignation, and incredulity filled my ears. The great hall—so silent just a moment before—became a veritable chaos, where supporters of this party or that seemed on the verge of ripping out each other's throats; the rest of the participants of this reunion were either loudly vocalizing their displeasure or silently watching the scene, utter disbelief in their eyes. I saw the Elders' guards stop the accused from leaping to kill me, and Phoenix moved close to protect me. The spectators had reached a boiling point. Talanus was looking at Ichimi as if he'd never seen him before, and Ysis was looking at me with a smile of open satisfaction. It was her smile, I think, that encouraged me to continue.

"You realize that your accusations are extremely serious, and they must be proved," Egire warned.

A terrible roar sounded out to my right: "We have known Talanus and Ysis since the Middle Ages when your ancestors were still pushing their plows and squealing like pigs! No one is more loyal to them than us!" screamed Ichimi, who had lost all self-control, staring at me with a murderous glint in his eye even more frightening than Kaiko's permanent furious glare.

Three guards were sitting on Kaiko to keep her from attacking; they were trying to silence her, horrified by the insults that were coming out of her cruel mouth in a furious torrent.

"Ichimi, for now, we have heard nothing that incriminates you, but continue acting like that, and you will raise suspicion. As for you Kaiko, it would be best to remain calm, or else I shall personally take care of ripping out your tongue and fangs to not hear you anymore," Egire said.

Seeing the effect of his words on them, Egire turned to me again.

"We are listening, miss."

I was overwhelmed by anger and the need to serve justice to this deceitful murderer. "If you're as loyal as you say, how do you explain the fact that the man I saw organize the methodic and industrial assassination of dozens of people was found, by chance, hidden in a villa that belongs to you?"

"Lies!" Ichimi cried out.

Luckily for me, I'd kept in my shoulder bag all the papers I'd taken from Stanson's office. I waved them in every direction, including almost under the nose of Egire, who took a step back as I began to shout, wild with rage about being called a liar.

"I have here a pile of documents that prove it. You sent all the money you earned from the blood trafficking through a shady lawyer to be laundered by investing in real estate, and all very discreetly. I met that man, and he described you so precisely that it's impossible to be mistaken. He recognized you, you and Kaiko!"

I turned to address the Elders.

"If you question them, you'll see I'm telling the truth. These documents are damning evidence. Their investments go well beyond the wealthy neighborhood of Drake Hill and even beyond the county of Kerington. They slowly wove their web for when they would become the most powerful vampires in the country, with Talanus and Ysis's colossal fortune at their disposal. They took full advantage of the fact that their best friend trusted them enough to name them his successors."

Turning back to Ichimi, I continued my indictment.

"Karl was the one who made me realize it. He said that he and his master were waiting impatiently for the Elders to come, to see Phoenix, Talanus, and Ysis fall."

As I was saying that, an idea came to me. It was pure speculation, but after all, I'd started in and I had to, at all costs, push him to making a mistake and admitting his crime, as Karl had done.

"The blood trafficking is only a pretext. All you wanted was their rank, for you know full well that to become an Elder, you have to have filled a leader role. And what's better than being at the head of their territory, which, after what I've heard, is the most powerful in this country and, incidentally, in the most powerful country in the world! You are Karl Sarlsberg's creator, and you ordered him to get close to Phoenix so you would know where we were in our investigation, so you could continue digging a pit for him to fall in, him and his masters! But it's over! Your desire to rule over the world ends now, because you know perfectly well that I'm telling the truth!"

The incredible silence my tirade commanded was broken by a stifled howl followed by several more. Before anyone could stop her, Kaiko sent the guards surrounding her flying into the air and shrieked, "All our work? Our dream reduced to nothing! *Die, dirty human!*"

As she prepared to run toward us, Phoenix tried to protect me by pushing me away so he could take care of her himself, but the red veil fell over my eyes, and anger washed over me. At the same time, as quick as lightning and with all my strength, I pushed Phoenix away and got out my last knife. Taken by surprise by the force of my push, my boss found himself on the ground as I readied myself . . .

Stopped midflight by the blade I'd thrown at her heart, Kaiko made an utterly grotesque grimace as she realized the seriousness of her wound. She looked at me, bewildered, and said words I would never forget, before she collapsed for the last time.

"By a human . . ."

I'd killed my first vampire.

\*\*\*

As his lover's body decomposed into dust in front of our very eyes, Ichimi finally lost control of his emotions and completely unmasked himself. A veritable incarnation of cruelty and violence, he turned to Talanus and spat in his direction. The guards holding him had real difficulty keeping him back, and the ones who had been wounded by Kaiko (but had recovered enough to fight again) came forward as reinforcements.

Still struggling, he stared at Talanus with his murderous gaze.

"You are not worthy of the honor bestowed upon you. I should have been in your place! You got this position because you are the oldest and that bitch Ysis has the gift of foresight! You knew that I wanted more than anything to have my place among the Greats one day and that did not stop you from strutting around me with all your characteristic arrogance and vanity! I managed to put up with it until I discovered that it was in fact Finn who had used his influence to make you the one the Elders chose."

He spat at Talanus again before turning to Finn with absolute rage. At that moment, one could have wondered if he'd really learned the values of Bushido and the code of conduct of true samurais. For the time being, anyway, they were far from his mind.

Finn betrayed no emotion when he answered. "I knew about your ambitions and your thirst for power. The circle of the Elders acts in the best interests of our species, not to satisfy personal glory. Unlike you, Talanus was worthy of becoming one of them one day."

Overwhelmed by the violence of frustration accumulated over centuries, Ichimi's true madness broke out.

"You are so pathetic, Finn! You think you are the wisest of us all, but you always act in your best interests, moving your pawns around as you like. Don't think you can make me believe otherwise. If you have refused to become one of the Greats, it is because you only want to follow your own rules and ambitions. What really motivates you is the desire to rule the world! You cannot reproach me for wanting to follow your example!"

The whole hall was paying careful attention to the criminal's revelations; he didn't seem to feel any remorse, lost in the madness that had completely put him over the edge.

"I swore to do everything to destroy you. I waited patiently for the right time, using my progeny to see my plan through, all while keeping an eye on your angel's investigations. But I did not anticipate your human sticking her nose in our business despite our attempts to eliminate her."

In the deathly stillness that followed, Egire walked to the center of the room and prepared to announce his verdict, after turning to his companions whose nods of approval answered his silent question.

"All of you here are witness to the confessions of Ichimi Ritsuye about his involvement in the blood trafficking that almost revealed our existence to the human world. As for his accusations against one of the oldest of our kind, Finn Jorgenson, whose loyalty to our laws goes without saying, those are just the ravings of a man whose depths of madness know no equal except the thirst for power that has motivated him for centuries. Consequently, we, the Elders, by our authority to render justice and pronounce sentences, declare that only the true guilty parties in this business will be punished in proportion with the seriousness of the charges laid against them. We dismiss the charges weighed against Talanus, Ysis, and their angel, Phoenix, given that the matter at hand has been resolved without calling into question their duties or competencies. Ichimi Ritsuye and Karl Sarlsberg, you will be detained and questioned by us before your execution through decapitation. I therefore declare this trial over."

A thunder of applause welcomed his verdict, and even the most skeptical joined in the general jubilation and relief brought about by the end of this somber story: the vampire community was safe, but numerous innocent humans had lost their lives. Justice had finally been served, and the criminals were going to pay a high price . . .

The nightmare of the last few months of inquiry and anxiety was finally over. An enormous weight lifted from my shoulders, and I was tempted to sit down on the ground to recover from this eventful night. I'd played the part of a wannabe lawyer, and my strategy of destabilizing the accused had worked beyond my wildest dreams. Kaiko had died at my hand; Ichimi was going to have a very hard time of it before being judged and executed by the tribunal of the Elders along with Karl.

Talanus, Ysis, and Phoenix were not only safe, but also returned to their respective duties. It was understood that since they'd been set up, no one could consider them incompetent, just demonstrating a naive friendship for people who didn't deserve it. In short, they'd been saved, and that was all that mattered.

There was only one little problem to take care of.

***

Egire had ordered Karl and Ichimi to be taken to a dungeon until the torture chamber was ready. Night wasn't over yet, so there was still time to make them regret ever having been born. However, I doubted that Phoenix's former best friend, in the state he was in, would be able to articulate the smallest sound. But fine . . . I had other worries on my mind.

All the Elders had formed a circle and were consulting each other to make the second crucial decision of the evening: the decision about my survival.

My boss had stepped close to me and didn't miss a single word from this spectacle, even though he couldn't hear words exchanged at an inhumanly low level of sound. Thus I was flanked by Phoenix on my right and François on my left, both supporting me with their soothing presence.

Too human and too emotional, however, that wasn't enough to stop my every limb from trembling, and I had to seize their hands and squeeze them hard to reassure myself a little. They returned the gesture, taking care to not break my bones, which touched me greatly. Tears in my eyes, and despite the indiscreet ears all around us, I said, "I've never been as happy as I've been since I met you. If this goes badly, have no regrets, because I have none. I love you, both of you."

I neither heard François's response nor felt the pressure of Phoenix's hand on mine, for among the Elders, one was turned in our direction . . . the woman-child, and she stared at me unrelentingly.

I had nothing left to lose. I returned her scrutinizing gaze for what seemed like an infinite amount of time before she turned away to murmur something in Egire's ear. When the circle of Elders dispersed and its members left the hall, Egire came toward us with all the majesty that his age and rank conferred upon him. Finn, meanwhile, had joined our group and was waiting for his "little brother" with barely concealed impatience.

"The tribunal of the Elders has made its decision concerning you," Egire declared.

Between that sentence and the next, I thought my heart had stopped beating.

"You came here uninvited, you attacked several members of our species, and killed one of them," he said icily.

Good grief. I was going to die. Me, who wanted to stay courageous. I felt the ground give way beneath my feet. My two friends fortunately caught me just in time and helped me to stand up and keep my dignity before my gruesome fate. Shaking my head to recover, I once again looked at Egire's ageless face, and I noticed that he was examining me with undisguised curiosity. Without hesitation, my cheeks burned red.

"That again? I've never seen a human blush so quickly. Your circulatory system must be of an exceptional fluidity," he said rapturously, forgetting that my blood flow wouldn't be extraordinary at all if he killed me.

"Egire! Will you please get to the point. I see Talanus and Ysis waiting for us. Perhaps you could cut it short so we can all go relax and have a drink?" Finn grumbled.

Finn's offhandedness about my upcoming execution pained me. He didn't care one jot. Nice . . .

"Oh, certainly . . . Where was I? Oh yes. Upon reflection, your actions were guided only by your loyalty to Phoenix, the very man who imposed this servile existence on you. By acting in this way, you have contributed to reestablishing the balance that preserves our Secret and preventing a war between our two peoples. Rather than a warning or a sanction, we offer you all our thanks. You are free," he concluded, smiling warmly.

Once the shock of that statement had passed, the joy of being alive washed over me, and I couldn't help crying in François's arms as he held me tight against him and laughed. Then he whispered in my ear that he had to join Talanus and Ysis and thus abandon me, as Phoenix and Finn already had. The vampires were all talking to each other. Well.

"Nice . . . ," I muttered.

"You do not make a sector leader wait, especially when it is Talanus."

Egire had stayed behind, and that explained why all the curious vampires—who were congregating and staring at me like a bone to chew on—hadn't yet gotten their hooks in me to make me tell them the whole story.

"This is the first time I have seen a human show such courage. You did not hesitate to confront a hundred of my fellows to set the record straight. I must say that I am impressed."

Getting only my modest silence in return, he continued.

"You could be useful to us, you know. The other Elders would agree to bring into their service people as devoted and competent as you. Your humanity would bring a fresh perspective to our work and permit us to imagine our actions under all possible angles."

I had the presence of mind to close my mouth quickly to not come across as a half-wit, but his proposal was enough to surprise anyone.

Discreetly, I cast a glance at my boss and noticed that he was staring at me intensely; he'd heard everything.

"I'm flattered by your offer, but I must decline it. Phoenix would be lost without me," I said, smiling, as much for Egire as for the main interested party.

After all, with everything I'd gone through, I felt honor-bound to be honest.

"There's one other thing. I know that you're protecting your species, and I admire your determination to make everyone obey the Great Change. But I think that I would have difficulty being good at the position you're offering me, knowing that a number of humans don't have the benefit of living in places where the change is applicable. At least, here with Phoenix, I have the opportunity to serve vampires, and to help save lives."

Egire stared at me for a moment, as if to size me up. He must not have been expecting me to be so direct with him. "I understand. You are a brave woman . . . You would make a very good vampire."

With those final words, he rewarded me with a nod, small but very respectful, that set off more commentary from our curious observers, before leaving me alone to face vultures worse than the paparazzi.

When Egire stepped away, a whirlwind of faces surrounded me. Every one of them wanted to have all the details about the matter and my role in it; however, their questions were incomprehensible because they were all talking over each other. Overwhelmed by the sudden tide of vampires, I didn't know how to respond. I was starting to get disheartened when Phoenix cleared a path to me and grabbed me by the arm to pull me away from my delirious fans.

With a protective and threatening attitude that dissuaded anyone from pursuing the interrogation, Phoenix brought me before Talanus and Ysis and greeted them respectfully.

"If you no longer have need of us tonight, we shall leave with Finn and François."

The Roman general seemed still in shock from his closest friend's betrayal, and it was actually his wife who answered us.

"Go rest. You have earned it."

Ysis approached me and took my hands.

"Your loyalty and courage during all this have been admirable, and that is why we all owe our lives to Samantha Jones. For a vampire, this is extremely important, and we shall not forget it. Go in peace. The Night protects you."

As if in a dream, she pulled Talanus away and disappeared from my field of vision. Finn yawned pointedly. "Well, I don't know about you, but I would like to leave here and relax with a nice glass of blood and a soft couch. Shall we?"

The idea of lingering any longer was far from our minds, so we left, all four of us, without worrying about the vampires following us and asking us one stupid question after another. Phoenix never let go of my arm.

When we reached the car, François wanted us to give him a minute to put a blanket down over the back seat, which had been stained by Karl's blood. Finn, though, didn't care, and climbed into the front passenger seat. It was time for me to brave looking at my boss.

I didn't even know where to begin, so I just offered Phoenix an embarrassed smile.

"I—"

But he interrupted, pressing his index finger over my lips.

"Not now," he said simply.

He pulled me toward him, stroking my hair. This simple gesture permitted me to completely let go of all my tension, closing my eyes and abandoning myself to his protecting arms.

"Thank you, Sam. You are right . . . I would be lost without you."

Nestling against him, I murmured, "I couldn't stay behind, doing nothing. I would be lost without you too."

In that intimate moment, I felt much lighter, and confident about the new future that was taking shape before us.

"If you can finally decide to get in this horrible Camaro, maybe we can hope to get home at some point." Finn had opened his car door and was muttering exasperatedly.

Once I was comfortably settled in the car and Kerington was far behind us, exhaustion suddenly weighed heavily on me; my eyelids didn't want to stay open anymore. I tried in vain to fight sleep, but it wanted to take me away and I sank into it little by little. In the fog that was enveloping me, I felt Phoenix pull me toward him so I could lie down, my head on his knees. I fell asleep to his fingers slowly caressing my hair. I was freed from my anxiety and all dark thoughts for the first time in days.

\*\*\*

After our return to the manor, I must say that my days passed much more peacefully. I wasn't stressed, I was even happy to resume my unique nocturnal life with my boss. Finn, thinking he'd fulfilled his fatherly duties by flying to Phoenix's rescue, had left to go to the Amazon, which was hostile territory for a vampire and a challenge for him to explore. His departure saddened me, for as strange as seemed, I also felt great admiration for him—not for his powers, but for the concern he'd shown Phoenix. His attitude throughout his brief stay in Scarborough had been that of a father . . . a surly one, but a father nonetheless, and I couldn't help but smile at the affection plainly visible on my boss's face in the presence of his creator. And to think it had begun badly between them.

François had thought to call and reassure Angela when we returned, for I was too exhausted to remember anything, and I didn't emerge from my sleep until very late in the afternoon the following day. As I opened my eyes, I thanked heaven for having such good friends, for I woke up comfortably settled into my own soft bed, a note on my nightstand telling me not to worry about Angela. While waiting for sunset, I called my friend at the bookshop, and we chatted for two hours about our adventures from the previous night, finding it hard to believe that all had ended so well. François was going to see her that evening, and by her own admission, the wait was killing her. I didn't dare ask her how far their relationship had gone. I doubted that since it was so new it had already become sexual in nature, but it was possible, and they knew how to be careful.

Anyway, I wasn't the most hesitant, far from it. Phoenix didn't understand what was happening to François, and several times I'd distracted him when he began to lecture François. However, my French friend quickly had enough and dug in his heels.

"That is all well and good for you to say when you yourself are too blind to understand what is happening to you."

That outburst had quickly turned sour: Phoenix's fangs were out, and he adopted an attack position to face François, ready to let rip. I'd had my fill of vampire battles, and this time, I left the room, passing in front of them like a fury.

"Oh, I've had it up to here of always being the idiot who smooths things over! If you want to disembowel each other, go right ahead! And good riddance!"

I left to get some fresh air in Scarborough, meeting Angela and Matthew for pizza at Danny's; he was happy to see us reconciled.

In fact, two days after our return to the manor safe and sound, I'd gone to see Matthew to apologize for the horrible way I'd treated him. I'd unleashed upon him all the anxiety and frustration I'd accumulated for days about the precarious health of my beloved grandfather (at least that was what I told Matthew), and I would understand if he was angry. Luckily, that wasn't the case, thanks to Angela and her support, and we found ourselves just as close as before.

After I returned home post-pizza, there were no traces of fighting, and each vampire seemed to be sulking in his own corner. My speech must have had an effect because, since then, Phoenix no longer lectured François about his liaison with a human woman, and François was keeping all his comments about us to himself. So even vampires could act like children.

As for Ichimi and Karl, we learned three days after the events of that night, just before Finn left, that they had admitted everything. The Greats had forced Ichimi to free Karl from his obligation, and Karl, unable to bear any further torture, had spilled everything he knew.

In theory, I'd hit the bull's-eye with my accusations. Ichimi had saved Talanus's life and had truly become friends with the Roman general who resembled him, but the connection that united them was nothing compared to the thirst for power that always burned in him, and that was revived by his lover, who pushed him further down that path. Ichimi finally admitted that the reason Kaiko hated my boss so much was simply because he was the progeny of Finn, the vampire who had killed her master. Unable to kill Finn because no one ever knew where to find him, she had turned all her anger on Phoenix. That anger hadn't stopped growing, and it became limitless when Phoenix had been named angel by the very people who had taken the post they'd dreamed of right from under their noses. They then recruited henchmen in China, where the laws of the Great Change were not applicable yet, a veritable El Dorado for vampires like Heath and Huan, who liked to indulge in luxuries and fresh blood. Ichimi and Kaiko promised them a part of the spoils that they would get from blood trafficking on such a scale: branches of the business extended to South Africa, and all the intermediaries implicated had serious reasons to worry for they would all be hunted down without mercy by the Greats for having disrespected their authority and broken their laws.

Karl's role in this matter hadn't been more than that of a pawn, so in the end, no one worried. He'd essentially been created in Europe by Ichimi to do business, but according to his creator, it had been accidental, and unaware that he had a son, Ichimi had returned to Japan. His friends were then nominated to take over the New World in his place, leading him slowly to a destructive madness. When, by an unfortunate coincidence, Karl found him again, Ichimi, Kaiko, and Karl were united by the same wounded pride, and they had dragged each other into bitterness against the entire world and especially against Talanus, Ysis, and Phoenix.

Ichimi's obligations kept him his own country, so he sent Karl to monitor Talanus and Ysis after teaching him the art of lying and self-control. In Karl's case, it wasn't enough to eliminate his arrogance and vanity; consumed by resentment, he had betrayed himself as well as his masters. There was a lesson to be learned: hatred only leads to misfortune, and those three hadn't learned how to overcome it . . . I knew that I wasn't like them and that even if I didn't feel any compassion about their fate, I wasn't angry anymore.

Justice had been done. It was time for me to discover the calmer side of my work . . .

\*\*\*

Weeks and then months passed. Most of Phoenix's contacts had accepted me and went through me to set meetings or to ask him for information. My boss finally had the tranquility he'd been dreaming of: carrying out his missions even if it put his life in danger, without having to bother with the paperwork he abhorred. As for me, I didn't have much to complain about either. Most of his missions were simple, meaning financial or real estate transactions that didn't require weapons or bloody hand-to-hand combat. I was only armed with my notepad and my smartphone, and that suited me perfectly.

Apart from that, Phoenix continued to train me, and I continued to progress in the mastery of all the combat techniques he knew. I was even learning to handle a sword!

We finally found the time for me to keep my promises, and I was giving him lessons in computer science. At first, he was an undisciplined and impatient student who, at any sign of difficulty, was ready to pulverize the computer. I had to exert all my influence to get him to spare the machine and learn to master it. In the end, he got by fine, and I was proud of being a good teacher. I had to compliment myself because if I'd had to wait for his gratitude, five hundred years wouldn't have been long enough. There was no question about it: he could really get irritating.

We'd resumed watching *Stargate SG-1*, and Phoenix never stopped commenting, which drove me crazy enough that at one point, I bashed him over the head with a pillow, threatening to gag him and tie him up with silver chains. I hadn't anticipated he would grab a second pillow to do the same to me. When François returned from his date with Angela and heard shouts and sounds of furniture being flipped over in the parlor, he appeared in the doorway, ready to attack. We hadn't even seen him staring at us, dazed, too busy running after each other and trying to knock each other out with pillows and laughing like children. Phoenix was the first to notice our French friend and stopped so short that I didn't have time to avoid him. Imagine slamming into a brick wall at full speed!

Seeing our faces—embarrassment for Phoenix, dizzy shock for me—François was content to give us a small mocking smile before disappearing from our sight. Disheveled and rumpled, we were still laughing when we resumed watching our show.

I was really happy, and things were going well. Before we knew it, it was the end of December, and the people of Scarborough were readying to celebrate Christmas like millions of people throughout the world. I loved that time of year, when people forgot their selfishness a little. Plus, I was an expert at decorating.

Phoenix hadn't celebrated Christmas since his entrance into the world of vampires, and I found that a shame because it was a moment of sharing and love between family and friends. Since my boss was both family and friend, I knew I wanted to celebrate. With François's help, I'd decorated the whole room in the spirit of Christmas, using my boss's brief trip to Talanus and Ysis's house as an opportunity to prepare it all, including the meal. Thanks to my new salary, I'd been able to go on a shopping spree and give free rein to my holiday fantasies. The result was red and green decorations throughout the room and a tree glittering with hundreds of lights. The turkey was cooking slowly in the oven, and the odor was mouthwatering. Even for the vampires. François was giving it the final touches on a platter when Phoenix arrived home and stood frozen in the doorway.

For a second, I was afraid that he would react badly. The last time he'd celebrated Christmas, his sister Keira had still been alive . . . I held my breath . . . and exhaled in relief when a smile spread over his face. Even better, the sudden gaiety transformed him and gave him a calm and innocent air.

Touched, I walked toward him and took his hand to show him our work.

"Merry Christmas, Phoenix."

Making the most of his silence, I stood on tiptoe to give him a peck on the cheek.

"Oh, no, not like that! We have to follow tradition all the way. Look up, you two," our musketeer interrupted from his stepladder.

We did, and there was a sprig of mistletoe hanging just above our heads. The implication behind François's insistence hit me immediately. My heart leaped in my chest, and I even wondered if Phoenix would almost just ignore it. Paralyzed, I risked a glance at my boss.

His face was still raised to the mistletoe; I had no idea what he was thinking. Finally, slowly, he lowered his head and fixed his eyes on mine. I thought I could see a bluish flash across his irises, but it was so fast that I wondered if I'd just dreamed it. Embarrassed by the closeness and that situation born out of a ridiculous tradition made up by people in need of affection, I tried to step away.

He put his hands against my back and held me to him. In the subdued light from the fireplace and the strings of lights on the tree, Phoenix's whole body was bathed in an unreal aura. His suit gave him an elegance that he already had naturally, his smooth and crepuscular scent enveloped me in a sensual warmth, while his face, so perfect despite a few rebellious locks of hair that fell across it, leaned gently toward mine.

"*O time, suspend your flight! And you, fortunate hours, stay your journey . . .*" I wasn't at a lake like Alphonse de Lamartine's companion in his poem, but I thought that this wish had been granted. I wondered if what was to come was really a good idea.

"Merry Christmas, Samantha."

His murmur was like a caress.

However, nothing could compare to the sensation of his lips on mine. Vampire bodies are cold because they've risen from the dead, but every time I touched Phoenix's skin, I only felt silken smoothness. I'd never wondered if his lips would have this same power, but I had to say that they surpassed by far the little I'd experienced before. It was like a foretaste of paradise.

Lost and ready to fall into a void of absolute bliss, I was floating away from reality and the flow of time. My whole body was nothing short of a red-hot and relentless inferno, obeying the whims of the man whose lips on mine in a first real, and pure, kiss were burning me with exquisite pleasure. I couldn't feel my body anymore, and my closed eyes kept me in a heavenly obscurity. All that was preventing me from believing it wasn't just a dream was the endless sensation of his body and his mouth, with which I was entirely one . . . Then . . .

Boom. That magic moment was torn from me at the same time as his lips, while he was straightening up, pushing me gently away so he could see my face. My return to the present was so brutal that I couldn't get my bearings or understand what had happened to me.

Baffled and shocked from the kiss but also by the reaction it had produced in me, I was tempted to flee and disappear. But I didn't want to ruin the joy that was still visible on my boss's face; he seemed to have already forgotten me, looking now with nostalgia at the Christmas tree that François and I had decorated.

François gave me an apologetic look. I knew that my confusion hadn't escaped him, and he regretted having put me in that situation. Unable to take any more, I muttered something about needing to check on the turkey. Once in the safety of the kitchen, I tried to calm down and get myself together, but I had a hard time putting my thoughts in order. François had set us up in an effort to check what feelings were really coming alive in us. Phoenix had hands down passed the test, but I'd utterly lost my footing. What had happened?

"Sam?" Phoenix called from the parlor. I checked the time on the oven clock and realized he must be wondering what I was doing.

Come on, I couldn't take a minute to focus in peace?

Adopting a festive attitude, I returned pushing a service cart upon which I'd placed the turkey and all the side dishes: potatoes, vegetables, fresh blood. Of course, the blood wasn't for me. That evening unfolded in good humor, my two friends telling funny and personal anecdotes from their long lives. This allowed me to push the kiss and my reaction to a corner of my mind, swearing to do like Scarlett O'Hara . . . and think about it tomorrow. At least, that's what I would have liked.

***

Taken over by a maelstrom of invitations (including one from Ginger, who, because of my clumsy intervention, had been able to reconcile with her daughter) during the day and by the heap of work that Talanus and Ysis were giving us at night, I'd almost completely forgotten that whole kiss thing . . . and that suited me just fine.

We arrived at New Year's Eve following what had become our routine. Phoenix had ordered me to rest that evening and enjoy being with my friends while he attended to some business in Pembroke, about twenty minutes away.

"Will you be home late?" I asked.

"Probably not before two or three in the morning, why?"

"I'll wait up for you."

He raised his eyebrows, a questioning look on his face. I smiled, embarrassed.

"I just want to wish you a Happy New Year. After all, it'll be almost a year since we met. That's not nothing."

My boss returned my smile. "I shall not dawdle, then."

And he left.

I hadn't thought to spend that evening with anyone other than Phoenix, so I'd declined invitations from Matthew, Angela, and François. To kill time, I stuffed my face with popcorn while watching television, flipping from documentaries to films, even watching some scenes from the daily life of the Kardashians. I really wasn't paying attention to the quality of what I was watching. Suddenly I heard my boss's cell phone ring and sat up straight. The sound was coming from the table in the dining room, where I'd left my own phone next to his.

Looking more closely, I realized that my boss must have grabbed the wrong one by mistake. Knowing how vital this means of communication was for him, I decided I shouldn't wait for his return, so I went looking for him.

The process didn't take me long, because I'd equipped our computer with GPS software and linked it to our phones so we could know each other's location. Phoenix was definitely still in Pembroke, and I had to hurry to not miss him. I memorized the route there and took off toward my destination, hoping to arrive in time to give my absentminded boss his phone.

I pulled up to 59 Cromwell Avenue, which was a luxury hotel. I walked toward reception, wondering what kind of business Phoenix would have in such a place.

"Good evening, how may I help you?" the concierge asked politely.

"Good evening, has a Mr. Livingstone come here? I'm his assistant, and he forgot his phone, which I need to give to him."

"Oh, yes. Mr. Livingstone is one of our best clients. He comes regularly to do business. Would you like me to call him to say you've arrived?"

"No, that's very kind, but he knows I'm coming. However, if you could give me his room number . . ."

"It's five seventeen. Take the elevator to the fifth floor, and it will be on your left."

"Thank you. Have a good evening."

At least I'd had the luck of getting in easily, since the concierge wasn't at all suspicious and hadn't even checked my identification. In any case, I hoped that Phoenix wouldn't be angry that I was interrupting a meeting, even if it was just to help him out. Not really worried, I whistled along to the elevator music. (The dentist I'd seen in Scarborough should have played the same station in his waiting room . . . He had a penchant for heavy metal, which all his patients loathed, especially since it was anything but relaxing). Finally, a bell rang, indicating I'd arrived at my floor. Following the concierge's directions, I found the room easily.

I took a deep breath and knocked on the door with one hand, holding the phone in the other, and heard muffled sounds coming from the other side. Fearing for my boss's safety, I didn't wait, but opened the unlocked door and entered . . .

"Phoe—"

The second syllable of his name got lost as my voice broke at the scene before my eyes. I stopped cold, thunderstruck and profoundly shocked by what I was seeing.

The man I'd come to help, who I thought was in the middle of negotiations with a reticent vampire, was standing in front of me, completely naked. My gaze was horribly aimed at the part of his body I'd never seen before. I dropped the phone, which fell and broke into several pieces. Someone was behind him . . .

A magnificent young woman, with brown hair like mine but a stunning figure and long legs, cried out indignantly and tried to hide—she was only wearing a lace thong—behind my boss's tall frame. He hadn't said a word, and I felt his metallic stare pierce through me. Realizing what I'd interrupted, something came over me.

At first, I felt my cheeks flame red, and I retreated, stuttering excuses and pointing at the broken phone on the floor. Avoiding Phoenix's eyes, I was trying to apologize as I backed up and pulled the door close, but only senseless syllables made their way out of my mouth. When I finally felt the door of that wretched room at my back, I turned quickly, left, and slammed it behind me.

I was feeling horrible, winded as though I'd just run a marathon, and I had to lean against a wall and close my eyes to get back to breathing normally. Once my lungs were filled with air again, I started to walk to the elevator to put as much distance as I could between that love nest and me.

At that thought, I realized that something else wasn't right. The shock I'd felt had sort of dulled my reaction as I arrived in that room, but now I was feeling it all too keenly . . . It was as though someone had sunk a white-hot blade right into my heart, trying to press down more to intensify the effects. Never before had I ever felt such pain, even when vampires had injured me.

But I didn't have time to question any of that, because my boss was catching up to me with superhuman speed, fortunately after taking the time to slip on a bathrobe. The effect of this garment was comical, but the situation . . . no.

"Sam," he said, blocking my path.

Too embarrassed to face him, I went around him. He grabbed my arm.

"Sam, I have to explain."

The blade seemed to sink even further into my heart, the pain so intense that I collapsed forward, grabbing my chest and crying out. Phoenix rushed to hold me up, but I pushed him away decisively. The effect must have been convincing, because he backed off.

My voice lowered to a threatening growl.

"There's nothing to explain. What an idiot I am! I really thought that you were here for business and that you wanted me to have fun tonight. When I saw that we'd switched phones, I didn't hesitate a second, and I did everything to find you. In fact, I never thought you'd have other needs, and certainly not for me."

The pain was unbearable, and I felt tears coming to my eyes; it was out of the question that I sob in front of Phoenix, so I turned my back to him.

"Sam, I am sorry."

Without looking at him, I answered. "And I'm sorry that once again you don't trust me enough to tell the truth. I'll see you tomorrow. Have fun conducting your *business*."

With those final bitter words, I pressed the elevator button. Thankfully, the doors opened right away, and I left.

\*\*\*

I managed to get myself out of Pembroke by focusing on the route back to the highway and the rules of the road. But once I'd reached the tranquility of the highway, my mind replayed the nightmare over and over. That was when the explosion happened.

Unable to hold it in anymore, I burst into tears from the pain crushing my heart. I couldn't stop crying, as if my suffering absolutely had to spill forth in torrents over my wet cheeks. It became more and more difficult to see the road through my tears, and I thanked heaven that I was alone on the highway at that hour.

I thought about how so many people were ringing in the new year. Predictably enough, the clock in my Buick was telling me it was midnight. Happy New Year! For sure, I would remember this one for a while. And to think I'd turned down invitations from Matthew, Angela, and François! All that for what? To celebrate this special moment with my boss, who in the end preferred to snuggle up in the arms of a tantalizing brunette in a thong!

The memory triggered more sobs, and I cursed that evening, Phoenix, the brunette, and the whole world. Most of all, I cursed myself for being so naive. How could I have thought he had set aside his sexual appetite since we'd met, just because I'd never seen him with a woman? Actually, he was satisfying his desires, just without telling me . . . Given my reaction, that was understandable . . .

For that matter, why *was* I reacting this way? After all, Phoenix didn't belong to me. He could see whomever he wanted. So why would I feel such hatred toward that woman? Hatred. That wasn't it . . . This fire burning in me . . . you'd almost think . . . jealousy?

Furiously wiping tears from my eyes, I tried to understand the emotions overwhelming me, and slowly, that strange feeling of an oncoming revelation crept in.

Phoenix . . . it all came back to him. He was at the center of everything, at the heart of my life. My daily life, so empty and dull just a year ago, had changed entirely, and I'd never before felt so happy and appreciated since the day he entered it. He'd revealed myself to me, he was my anchor, my guide . . . but that wasn't all of it.

The last levees of my unconscious mind abruptly broke open, and I had to face a flood of feelings, my true feelings, as they washed over me like a tsunami. Images flashed before my eyes one after another, obscuring the rest.

It began with the first time I ever saw Phoenix, and I remembered the fear I'd felt then. I saw us gradually get to know each other, me slowly learning to like him. Then I saw more intimate moments: our dance in the nightclub, the blood exchange, the good-byes in the kitchen . . . I remembered our conversation in the woods where he finally admitted that I was important to him . . . and then our kiss that haunted me once more.

That kiss . . . it had completely turned me upside down with its spontaneity and perfection. I'd never before felt as good as during that brief moment, feeling like I was flying to paradise. I'd also never been so embarrassed . . .

Technically, I had been more perturbed by the pig Huan, but that wasn't really what I'd been expecting. I didn't really know what I'd expected, actually, but the idea I'd had about my first kiss was that it would be a simple moment of shared tenderness. I hadn't been prepared to be transported like that.

That could only mean one thing . . . that something from the very beginning, from the first second I'd ever laid eyes on Phoenix, had been there, in me, and that I'd misinterpreted . . . something that had increased with time to the point of taking possession of my whole being . . . something I'd naively thought of as friendship . . .

When the revelation finally burst before my very eyes and I understood its implications, my wretched heart twitched in my chest. I took out my irritation on the steering wheel and cried out.

"Oh my God!"

A second later, my next shout had nothing more to do with the discovery of my true feelings.

*"Oh my God!"*

Racing at top speed and lost in my thoughts, I didn't see until it was too late the deer who had stopped on the road and was watching me come straight for her . . . My reflexes kicked in just in time, but sometimes in an emergency our reactions aren't always the best. I veered violently to the right to avoid the deer and thus charged right toward the guardrail . . .

How did I manage it? No idea. Maybe the guardrail yielded to the violence of shock or speed, but I flew right over it. The fact remains that I'd lost all control of my Buick, bouncing over bumps and holes; I remained paralyzed and powerless as the trees gave way. I saw, in the shaking glow of my headlights, the gigantic tree that I was about to crash into . . .

I didn't even have time to close my eyes. Death had finally caught up to me . . .

# ACKNOWLEDGMENTS

To my friends, and guinea pigs, who believed in Samantha's potential.

*Samantha Watkins: Chronicles of an Extraordinary Ordinary Life*

*Book 2: Origins*

When I woke up, it was around noon. As I endured a battery of tests, Angela and Matthew called Danny to give him the news. He wouldn't fail to inform all of Scarborough, starting with Ginger, who worried herself sick and harassed him constantly for more information on my condition.

My friends then spent the entire afternoon at my side, chatting with me even though I was incapable of saying a single word. They told me that I'd been in a deep coma for four days and they had despaired of ever seeing me come out of it. The accident had been so brutal . . .

At dawn, another driver had seen the wreckage of the guardrail and had stopped to investigate. He'd followed the path made by my Buick before finding us: the Buick smashed against the gigantic tree trunk and me smashed up as well but still alive and unconscious a few yards away.

I wasn't far from death to tell the truth, and in the ambulance, my heart stopped twice. I had a broken leg and several broken ribs, plus bruises all over. It had really been a close call . . . but I hung on. I was still alive.

In fact, I was a complete miracle as far as the fire and rescue workers were concerned; they didn't understand what I'd done to not end up crushed and broken against that tree. The doctors too had been rather pessimistic about my survival. Of course, they couldn't have known that Phoenix's mark in my body had strange and timely effects, notably that of making me stronger. However, I remembered perfectly that feeling of floating in another world, and a voice telling me my time hadn't yet come . . . Was that really just a dream? Better to not think about it.

I was there, and that was the most important thing. The firefighters had searched my bag and tried to call Phoenix's number. Unfortunately, Peter Stratford/Livingstone's phone was in pieces on the floor of a hotel room and didn't work anymore. But they couldn't have known that either. They made do with a photo of Angela, whose name I'd written on the back, and they'd been able to inform her instead.

Angela told me the rest when Matthew excused himself to go to the restroom. She'd waited impatiently for the sun to set, then called François. He and Phoenix had been about to go looking for me when she told them what had happened. Phoenix heard her perfectly, even though he hadn't been holding the phone, and François told Angela that she'd barely finished her sentence when Phoenix shot off toward the hospital in full flight. François had added that it would be preferable for Matthew and my boss not to find themselves in the same room to avoid unnecessary questions, and since then, Angela always arranged things so that they wouldn't cross paths during their visits. That Phoenix could only visit at night made this easier.

"He hasn't left you for a moment . . . except to hide from the sun," Angela confided, all smiles, ignoring the fact that this information did me more harm than good.

He must simply be feeling guilty . . .

We didn't get much farther on that subject because Matthew returned. Even if I couldn't talk, my friends stayed at my side for several more hours, which helped me not fret over the confrontation that wouldn't wait much longer. The sun was already setting . . .

Angela made several attempts to get Matthew to accompany her to the exit, but he lingered, clasping my hand in his own. His reassurance warmed my heart, and it would have been rude to pull away from him. However, I didn't anticipate that my boss would find us like that.

When I lifted my eyes to the doorway and my attention, until then occupied by Matthew's jokes, promptly identified the person standing there, my heart malfunctioned completely, and its disordered beats triggered all the alarms of my monitors. I must have blanched out of fear of meeting Phoenix's gaze and blushed with shame at setting off all that racket; actually, I must have looked ridiculous.

A heavy silence fell in the room when the alarms quieted and the doctors left after checking that I hadn't had a heart attack. No one dared speak. Matthew was staring at the newcomer suspiciously, not realizing that Phoenix was staring at Matthew's hand holding mine with a murderous gleam in his blue eyes.

"Who are you?" my devoted knight asked curtly, knowing instinctually that my visitor was his rival.

François judged it prudent to take the initiative to avoid a massacre and jumped in before Phoenix could answer. "That's Aydan. I called him."

Last year, François and Karl had posed as my cousins when my human friends and I had gone to the movies, and that German pig (who later proved to be a murderer) tried to put me in an awkward position by making Matthew believe that I was in love with a man called Phoenix. To sort it out, I'd lied by saying Phoenix's real name was Aydan and our recent breakup had traumatized me. Matthew must not have expected to find himself face-to-face with my "ex," and he frowned, seemingly measuring up his adversary to determine what I could have seen in him.

"You shouldn't be here," Matthew said aggressively. "You're not a part of her life anymore."

That time, François wasn't able to stop my boss.

"Who are you to say who should be at her bedside and who shouldn't? You're nobody, so run along."

Phoenix's glacial and contemptuous tone made me fear the worst, especially when Matthew stood up suddenly to face him. Forgetting all sense of prudence, I swiftly sat up to grab his arm and stop him from making one more step toward Phoenix; in so doing, my battered body sent its regards, wresting from me a moan of pain deep from my chest and forcing me to lie back down just as quickly.

Immediately, angry nurses rushed in and threatened to send us all out if my visitors didn't take better care. Angela took this as a sign to put her foot down and threaten Matthew with leaving without him since she'd driven them both there. He surrendered. However, instead of squeezing my hand good-bye as Angela did, he leaned over me and gave me a long, soft kiss on the forehead. He smiled at me and walked to the door; I don't know what he did to Phoenix in passing, but François grabbed Phoenix's arm to stop him from disemboweling my human friend. I was wondering what had gotten into him and felt my temper flaring. He had to go and defend his pride rather than check in on my health. The nerve, honestly.

However, my irritation was swept aside by the bluish flash of his eyes as he looked at me again. I didn't know how to react.

"I'll leave you alone. If you need me, I won't be far away," François said as he left the room too, closing the door behind him.

We were alone now, and I couldn't hide. What was he going to say to me?

"You must hate me."

I frowned as he stared down at me, awaiting my verdict. How could I answer him? *I couldn't possibly hate you, because my heart, my mind, my whole being is filled with you and . . . and I love you . . . I love you more than anything else in the world.* No. For the sake of our relationship, I had to—and I knew I should—suppress my feelings, even if that meant daily torture because it was inconceivable for me to leave him. Phoenix would never love me, and I didn't want to make him uncomfortable with this, so I had to keep quiet.

I lowered my eyes in resignation to gain some time, but my determination was at risk the moment Phoenix sat on the bed, leaned over me, and brushed aside a lock of hair that had fallen over my face. Defeated, I let him do it, and then he lifted my chin to make me face him.

"Sam, I . . ."

He didn't finish. Instead, he took my hand in his and caressed it before lifting it to his mouth. I held my breath to not lose control as he kissed it softly; at the touch of his lips, I experienced a powerful electric charge, the usual result of our close proximity. It took all my self-control not to throw myself into his arms despite all the pain I would feel. My internal conflict was so intense that I couldn't stop tears from flowing down my cheeks, nor could I stop Phoenix from seeing them. I thought I caught sight of chagrin in his eyes, but trying to figure out his emotions was always an impossible mission.

"I only seem to hurt you . . . I am not worthy of your friendship."

Indeed, the memory of the hotel room in Pembroke still stung painfully. Even if I knew that my boss didn't love me, and therefore didn't belong to me, I couldn't help feeling intense jealousy toward the young woman he'd been about to embrace in his perfect nakedness, as well as anger toward the man who chose to lie rather than admit that I wasn't sufficiently to his tastes to satisfy his carnal appetite. Besides, thinking about that kind of relationship with Phoenix quickly made my cheeks redden. If things had gone differently between us, would I have taken that step with him? A vampire? Knowing that it was possible and trying it were two different things. However, I was assessing my feelings for him, and the answer to that question was clear. With that thought, I felt fire taking over my cheeks for real, extending over my whole face; out of shame, and also to hide my discomfort, I hid my face in my hands.

"I should not have come . . . I should leave so you can rest . . ."

That statement, coming from his velvet voice, hurt and, with him already heading for the door, horrified me so much that I tried to scream at him not to abandon me. But no sound was able to break the barrier of my lips, and Phoenix passed through the door without seeing that from my bed I was trying in vain to keep him with me.

Suddenly, a force coming from the depths of my being came over me and permitted me to come out of my powerlessness. Like a fury, I tore the electrodes from my chest, and I pulled the IV from my arm. I only had a few moments before the doctors would come running to see if I'd died yet, so I jumped from my bed as fast as I could.

The pain in my chest seized me and struck me down to the floor, reinforced by the pain in my broken leg, which, despite the protection of the cast, hadn't appreciated the fall. My vision blurred, but something within me summoned enough strength for me to keep going. With a superhuman effort, I managed to stand up and open the door, ignoring the shocked faces of the nurses who froze at the sight of me. Panicking at the absence of my boss in my field of vision, there was only one solution left.

*"Phoenix!"* I yelled, holding on to the doorframe to not fall.

I was so afraid that he wouldn't hear me that I'd put all the strength I had left in that desperate cry; the result was a shrill shriek that transfixed everyone nearby. I was starting to wobble, looking crazily in every direction, when suddenly he appeared, after almost tearing the stairwell door off its hinges. I didn't wait for the audience to recover from this grotesque show; forgetting my wounds, I launched myself as well as I could toward the man already running to meet me . . .

A nurse cried out when my legs betrayed me and gave way, but Phoenix stopped me from crashing to the ground by catching me in his strong arms. Relief, and a flood of other feelings, washed over me as he carried me back to my room. It was only with a saintly amount of patience and comfort from Phoenix that I was finally able to let go of my madwoman grip on his shirt and give the doctors a chance to check my injuries.

# ABOUT THE AUTHOR

*Photo © 2015*

Aurélie Venem counts a diverse list of writers among her influences: from epic poets Homer and Virgil to bestselling contemporary young adult novelist Stephenie Meyer. Aurélie is a voracious reader and currently works as a teacher of history. *Samantha Watkins* is her first novel.

# ABOUT THE TRANSLATOR

S. E. Battis is a teacher and translator. She holds several degrees in French studies, which she earned through blood, sweat, tears, and an avid love for French culture and literature. Like Samantha Watkins, the only reason she would ever want to meet a vampire would be to talk about history.